PICKING UP THE PIECES

Wendy Dewar Hughes

PICKING UP
THE PIECES

Wendy Dewar Hughes

*Life is an
adventure !*

Wendy Dewar Hughes

SUMMER BAY PRESS

SUMMER BAY PRESS

PICKING UP THE PIECES

Copyright © 2011 by Wendy Dewar Hughes

Published by Summer Bay Press
#14 – 1884 Heath Road, Agassiz, B.C. Canada V0M 1A2

www.summerbaypress.com

Printed in Canada

ISBN: 978-0-9868775-0-6
Digital ISBN: 978-0-9810240-5-9

Cover design by Wendy Dewar Hughes

All scripture quotations are from King James Bible.

This book is dedicated to my parents,
Gordon and Inez Dewar,
for their unwavering love and support.

ACKNOWLEDGEMENTS

Writing a book is a big undertaking requiring hours and hours of work, concentration, research, revision, re-writing, editing, and mental mulling. It is also a whole lot of fun not only to live other people's lives during the writing, but to make up those people and their lives as you go along.

Needless to say, there are many people involved in the creation of a book. I could not have written this book without the support and enthusiasm of my husband, Gordon Hughes.

Another person without whose help I could not have finished this book is Dale Sigurdson. I had not gone very far before I realized that *Picking up the Pieces* would require a lot of research in order for me to get facts straight and historical events in order. At my bleat for help, Dale graciously stepped up to the plate and offered to act as my research assistant for as long as it took. We had a lot of fun creating this book, talking over plot twists, and discussing ancient history. My appreciation knows no bounds.

Many, many thanks and hugs go to my brilliant editor, Julene Hodges Schroeder. I am eternally grateful for her ongoing assistance and wisdom with words, her story insights, and her Biblical knowledge. Julene's faithful support throughout the entire writing process has been invaluable.

To my readers, I say thank-you for entertaining a different view of history, archaeology, and biblical truths. I hope you enjoy reading *Picking up the Pieces* as much as I enjoyed writing it and will communicate that with me.

Most of all, I thank God for giving me the story, the desire to write it, and the love of working with words. There is no story of my life without Jesus. For that, I am so thankful.

PROLOGUE

An ancient ceiling fan, grimy with neglect, spun slowly in the still afternoon air, emitting a rhythmic squeal with each revolution. Dust motes hung in the green-gold light and a heat-drunk bluebottle fly buzzed against the pane of a single gritty window that looked out on the platform. More than an hour before, the ticket agent had taken himself off on an extended lunch break or afternoon nap, probably both, snapping the sliding door down over a cavity in the glass under a faded sign that read *Billets*. A heat haze shimmered off the tracks and dusty leaves dangled from the trees lining the verge while villagers dozed away the warmth of the day, digesting midday meals, the edges of their minds rounded by rough red wine.

I glanced again at the clock on the wall over the door. The next train was not scheduled to arrive until two forty-five but this was France so timetables meant little. Reaching up, I twisted my thick, dark hair into a knot, fastening it away from my sweaty neck with a spring clip. Such a hot day for early May. Alone in the station, I sat on a hard wooden bench behind the room's only pillar, almost shielded from view from both the door to the street and the beaten-up, swinging doors that led out onto the platform. I drew in a long breath and exhaled slowly, purposefully relaxing the stiffness along the top of my shoulders and kneading the knotted muscles. I leaned my head against the back of the bench then thought better of it and sat up straight again.

The old book lay open on my lap, the gold edges of the thin paper fuzzy with age and wear. My finger traced the words underlined in red and I studied them again, searching for a clue, a hidden meaning, anything. There had to be something I was missing.

Outside on the cobblestone street, a vehicle roared to a grating stop. A car door slammed shut. Running footsteps rapped on the cobblestones and up the steps to the station door.

"*Duck*," the familiar voice spoke into my thoughts. Instantly, I dropped sideways behind the high backrest of the bench, tucking my feet up and pressing my cheek against the cool wood of the seat. The door of the station flew open, banging against the wall, and heavy footsteps thudded on the hard-tiled floor then skidded to a stop. I opened my mouth and drew silent, shallow breaths, not daring to move even my eyelids. With a muffled curse, the intruder stomped through the waiting room to the platform, flinging the doors aside.

"*Look now*," the voice again spoke into my thoughts. I peered over the arm of the bench. I could see a lone figure standing with his back toward me, hands on hips, head swinging from side to side in the white-hot light as he glared up the tracks first one way then the other. Dark glasses roosted on his beak of a nose and sunlight ricocheted off ink-black hair. My heartbeat thrummed in my ears.

I lay absolutely still, concealed by the back of the old-fashioned bench. Then I saw the man turn and run down the platform. A moment later the car door slammed again. The engine roared and tires squealed as the car sped away.

I let out a long slow breath and sat up. Tugging my damp shirt away from my back, I opened the book again. As the minutes slid by, my heartbeat slowed. The ceiling fan squealed on.

CHAPTER 1

"Jill Moss?" It was a man's voice on the telephone.

"Yes."

"My name is Scott Marchand. I am a colleague of your uncle, Neil Bryant. I have something for you that Neil wants me to deliver right away."

"What is it?"

"I would prefer not to talk about it over the phone," he answered. "Could we meet this afternoon?" I glanced at the clock over my table. It was twenty minutes past one.

"I suppose so."

"Meet me at the café on the corner of Yale Road and Number 9 at two o'clock, alright?"

"That's rather soon," I said.

"It's rather urgent."

I hung up the telephone and rinsed my paintbrush. Finishing this painting would have to wait.

Twenty-five minutes later, I pulled into the parking lot of Chaco's Grill. The restaurant stood away from the main road at the end of a steep, unpaved driveway. Dark green patio umbrellas dotted its wide terrace. I parked near the front door and got out. The lot was deserted except for a silver van under some trees at the rear and the white SUV next to my car.

A man stood on the stone steps to the terrace, one hand in a trouser pocket. He waved and removed the aviator sunglasses from his sunburned nose.

"You must be Scott," I said, shaking his hand.

"Thanks for coming at such short notice," he said, leading me to a table on the far corner of the terrace. "I have a tight schedule today."

"You said it was important. What is this about?"

A teenaged waitress appeared and we ordered coffee.

"I'll get straight to the point," he said, "though to be honest, I'm not entirely sure what it is."

I leaned into the shade of the umbrella. "What is my Uncle Neil up to now?"

Scott pulled a parcel from a bag at his feet and set it on the table with a thump. "He wanted me to see that you get this."

I tore away the brown paper wrapping. "It's his Bible. Why would he want me to have this?" The gold lettering on the leather cover had almost worn away and the corners curled from long years of use. I ran my fingertips over the pebbly surface.

"It came this morning by courier. Shortly after that Neil phoned. I could hardly hear him, even though he was shouting. There was a lot of noise going on in the background. I tried to find out where he was and why he was calling but all I could get was, 'Take the package to my niece, Jill. Call her.' He gave me your number. 'She'll know what to do,' he said. 'Go immediately and don't let anyone follow you.'" He spread his hands. "Presumably, you know what to do."

I frowned. "Why didn't he send it directly to me?"

"I don't know."

"Is Neil in some kind of trouble?"

"Like I said, I couldn't get much information out of him."

I looked at Scott. "What's your connection to my uncle?"

"We have a long history," he said, grinning. "I was his student a long time ago and we've worked together on several projects over the years. I'm surprised you haven't heard of me. Hasn't Neil ever mentioned the work we did on the Incas?"

"Were you involved in that fiasco with the helicopter crash in Ecuador?"

"That and a few of his other fiascos," he replied. "He is quite a character."

"I'm aware of that," I said, picking up the Bible. Turning the book over in my hands, I opened the front cover. A dry, pale green leaf fluttered to the stone terrace. I leaned down and gently picked it up. Holding it into the sunlight, I could see tiny, cramped handwriting on it which read, "Job 20:8".

"Look at this," I said, handing it to Scott.

"Funny that he wrote on a leaf," he said. "Neil must have run out of paper, or have been off on one of his solo jaunts. He does that sometimes, you know. He gets an idea and tears off on his own or with a single guide into the jungle and disappears for days. Scares the daylights out of the crew when he doesn't tell anyone where he's going. Any idea what this means?"

I flipped the pages of the old Bible until I found the verse. "Listen to this," I said. "'He shall fly away as a dream, and shall not be found: yea, he shall be chased away as a vision of the night.'" I glanced up from the text. "Does that mean anything to you?"

"Not a thing. Do you think it's a clue of some kind? You must know how Neil loves puzzles."

I nodded. Neil was notorious for his love of puzzles, which was partly what made him a great archaeologist. I moistened my fingertip and turned the fragile pages of the Bible. Many passages had been underlined. On most, the ink had blurred with age and notes scribbled in the margins had long since bled into blue-black smears, the cramped words barely distinguishable. But this verse was different. It had been underlined in fresh red ink.

"I don't know what I'm expected to do with this," I said. "Do you have any ideas?"

"The last time I saw Neil was about four months ago," Scott told me. "We both attended a conference in Montreal on the most recent archaeological discoveries in ancient Mayan civilizations. Neil was one of the speakers. He had just come back from Guatemala and Mexico. Since then I've spoken with him only once. He called me about six weeks ago to say that he was off on another jaunt into the jungles somewhere in Mexico and wanted to know if I would like to come along, but I couldn't get away from the university. Then today he called out of the blue to ask me to get this to you."

"Did it cross your mind to try to trace his call?"

"I did try, but all I could find out was that it came from Mexico. Telecommunications systems in some parts of the world aren't always up to our standards. I gathered he was in a rural area." He leaned back in his chair and took a swallow of coffee. "I'd be surprised if all this doesn't involve you having to tear off into some wild blue yonder."

"What makes you say that?"

"I just know Neil, that's all," Scott said, glancing at his watch. "But right now I have to get going myself. I've got a tutorial to lead in a half hour." He stood up and picked up his bag. "Let me know if you figure out Neil's puzzle. And if you need any archaeological information, give me a shout. I'll see if I can dig anything up for you." He grinned at his own joke and pulled a business card from a pocket of his shirt and handed it to me.

"Thanks," I said, squinting up at him. "I may do that."

I took another sip of coffee. It was cold. Neil feared nothing and that fearlessness had landed him in lots of trouble over the years. I scanned the rest of the page in the book before me. I noticed that a tiny reference in the centre margin had also been underlined, though it did not refer to the verse I had been reading. I made a mental note of it and flipped through the chapters until I found Psalm 102:5.

"That's odd," I murmured. This actual verse had not been marked; rather a passage further up in the chapter had been underlined, also in fresh red ink. "Hide not thy face from me in the day when I am in trouble: incline thine ear unto me: in the day when I call answer me speedily." I swallowed.

If Neil really was in peril, he would have to get in touch somehow. I placed the leaf between the pages of the book, gathered up the brown wrapping paper and walked back to my car. The silver van was still parked on the other side of the lot and I could see someone at the wheel. I had the distinct impression that he was watching me.

Getting into my car, I turned the key in the ignition. There was no way Neil could call his son Dennis for help. Dennis was a missionary in northern Mexico and almost impossible to reach. He only went to town every few weeks and the rest of the time he roamed around in the mountains. Dennis's sister, Sandra, worked as an emergency room doctor in the city. Not only did she have a busy career with crazy hours, but she had three teenagers at home.

A ripple of apprehension trickled down my spine. Clearly, Neil was in trouble and he needed me to help. The question was, what kind of trouble?

CHAPTER 2

When I heard the clock in the living room tone midnight, I rinsed my paintbrush in the water pot, turned off the light, and went down the stairs. A few minutes later, I stood in front of the bathroom mirror. I mopped eye make-up off and washed my face. After smoothing on cream that promised to give my forty-three year-old face the skin of a baby, I slipped a cotton nightgown over my head and flicked off the bathroom light.

In my bedroom, I folded back my puffy duvet. The pink-floral bedspread signalled final acknowledgement that Roger was never coming back. I crawled into bed and switched off the light.

"Lord," I said into the darkness, "I'm going to need more information if I'm to help Neil. Please show me what to do."

Earlier that afternoon, as soon as I had returned from my meeting with Scott Marchand, the front doorbell rang. A courier stood outside.

"Please sign," he said, in an accent I did not recognize. He had nearly black hair that curled softly, and he wore dark glasses and a plain grey uniform.

"Where is your van?"

He hesitated. "Around the corner," he said, handing me a small, padded envelope and walking away.

The end of the envelope gave way easily when I pulled on it. I squeezed the sides, shook it, and a small brass key with a white string tag attached fell into the palm of my hand. Written on the tag was simply, Box 12.

The key could only be for a mailbox. I poked the little brass key into my pocket and headed for the post office down the street. Slipping it into the lock of Box 12, I turned it and gave the little door a tug. Inside the box lay a single white envelope. On a slip of paper inside, a scribbled message read: "Call your mother from a pay phone now." There was nothing else. Since the nearest pay phone was right next to the post office, I went straight out and dialled my parents' home number.

"Oh, Jill, it's you," my mother shouted when she heard my voice. I held the receiver away from my ear. "Your Uncle Neil phoned and wanted me to give you a message but he said that under no circumstances was I to call you. I had to wait for you to call me. What is this about, Jill?"

"I don't know," I replied. "Apparently, Neil is having some kind of problem. What did he tell you?"

"Well, hardly anything," she replied. "He gave me an email address and said that I'm supposed to tell you that you are to go to an internet café and check this address. Don't use your computer at home, he said. Go where no one knows you. Do you have a pen? You'll need to write this down."

"Hold on a minute," I said. I dug a pen and the business card from a hair salon out of my purse, hastily copied the address, hung up the phone and went back into the post office.

"Hey, Jill," Phyllis Kidman said, grunting as she heaved a large cardboard box onto the counter. "There was someone here earlier asking about you." A pair of green-framed reading glasses hung on the end of Phyllis's nose. "He wouldn't tell me his name, and I wouldn't tell him what he wanted to know."

"Which was?"

"He asked me if I knew where he could find you. He was driving a brand new silver van. He was a looker, too. Tall, dark and handsome. It was weird, though. He mailed a letter to a mailbox here and asked if I would put it in there right away."

"And?"

"I told him I might know you and I might not. There is a Privacy Act, you know."

"Phyllis, you are a saint," I said, reaching across the counter and squeezing her wrist.

"Listen, Jill," she said, grabbing my hand. "I know you've had it kind of hard the last couple of years but you're not in any kind of trouble, are you?" She leaned forward and dropped her voice. "If you need help, if there's anything I can do, you just have to ask."

"It's okay, Phyllis," I replied. "I'm all right. I'm not in any trouble." *Not yet anyway*, I thought as I turned to leave.

Forty-five minutes later, I sat in a grubby orange chair in the back of a dingy internet café staring at a computer monitor. Video arcade machines pinged and whirred as boys in drooping jeans, their bodies moving in tandem with fantasy battles, fed change into them. A worn linoleum floor, splotched by a seedy past, grabbed at shoe soles passing by. With tattoos covering both of the massive, hairy arms protruding from a black leather vest, an aging biker sat watching television behind a long bar. A few bags of potato chips clung to a rack against the wall and next to it stood a glass-fronted drink cooler. Every few minutes another male sauntered in and called out, "Hey, Nate," before sloshing coffee into a stoneware mug next to the drip coffee pot, or grabbing a soft drink. I had driven a good half-hour from home to find this so-called internet café.

With the arrival of each new customer, I pressed myself deeper into the corner behind the computer. With clientele like these, I wanted Nate to be my best friend. I pulled the card out of my purse and found the website address I had scribbled on the back, logging on with the user ID and password my mother had given me, and read Neil's message.

Dear Jill,
I don't have much time so must make this brief. I have made an important discovery, probably the most important of my career, maybe

10

even my life. It could change the course of history. Certain factions want to get their hands on this relic, but that must not be allowed to happen under any circumstances. The artifact consists of sixteen pieces which I have sent separately to selected people I know and trust. Since my life is in jeopardy I have to ask you to go and collect them for me.

I realize this is a monumental request, but I am desperate. If you want to see me alive again, you must follow exactly the instructions that will be delivered to you. I can't tell you where I am. Please believe me when I say that this is a life or death situation. I have to warn you that this mission is extremely dangerous and you may be followed. Utmost secrecy is crucial. I will contact you as soon as I can.

Delete this email as soon as you have read it. The address will be cancelled by midnight.

God bless you.

Neil

I stared at the monitor and read the email four more times. Where was Neil? What had he found? And how could I possibly do what he asked? My own life had only just stopped teetering and righted itself into some semblance of stability. I had a painting commission on deadline to finish; my galleries wanted new work. I dragged my eyes away from the computer screen, stared out the dirty window and watched as the condensation trail from a jet streaked a double white line across the sky.

How could I refuse? I had no choice but to do as Neil asked. No choice at all. I deleted the email.

Across the street I saw a silver van pull to the curb and stop. I could have sworn that it was the same van I had seen at the restaurant earlier. The driver looked like the same courier who had been at my house not an hour before. I squinted at him, unsure. Then I picked up my handbag, paid Nate and hurried back to my car.

When I got home, I parked behind my house and let myself in through the kitchen door. My canary, Pianissimo, was twittering to himself when I came in but when he saw me he flapped his wings and let out a long, trilling note.

"Hello to you, too, Sunshine," I said. Sunbeams splashed dazzling patches on the black and white floor tiles and reflected on the pale yellow walls. I cranked the top off my espresso maker and filled the tank with enough water for one cup of coffee then tucked a china mug under the spout and picked up Neil's Bible from the counter where I had left it earlier. Dousing my coffee with cream, I sat down at the table and opened the book.

Sipping my coffee, I flipped the pages, watching for more smatterings of fresh red ink. I had just turned to Leviticus when the doorbell rang. A plump woman with curly, red hair stood on the veranda with a leather folder under her left arm.

"I'm looking for Jill Moss," she said. "Would that be you?"

Before I could answer, she continued. "I'm Deborah James from Unity Travel. I was asked to deliver some documents to you. May I come in?"

"Of course." I stood aside to allow her to enter then closed the door behind her. "Please come into the kitchen," I said. "I've just made a coffee. Would you like one?"

"Oh, no thanks, I'm fine," Deborah replied, waving away the offer. She pulled out a chair next to the table and sat down. Placing her portfolio on the table, she reached over and flicked the curtain closed then she unzipped her case and withdrew a folder. "Neil Bryant is a client of mine and he contacted me this morning about some travel arrangements for you. I have everything you need – your flights, hotels, maps, and other documents. You have a passport, don't you?"

"Yes," I replied, "I just got a new one." A few months previously, I had felt the urging of the Holy Spirit to renew my passport even though it was not due to expire until November. At the time I had thought it odd since I had no travel plans, but did it anyway.

"Good," said Deborah. "Okay, here is your itinerary." She pulled a pack of papers out of the folder and opened them to face me. "This is the confirmation for your flights. Obviously, these are e-tickets. You will be leaving tomorrow from

Vancouver at 13:30, which is twenty-four hour clock for 1:30 in the afternoon, on Air Canada Flight number 102 to Toronto, then connecting to Air Canada 882 at 22:25, or 10:25 in the evening."

I reached for the papers. "Where am I going?"

"Didn't Mr. Bryant tell you? You're going to Paris. You will be arriving at Charles De Gaulle airport at 12:00 noon the following day."

She nattered on about the check-in times and how much baggage I was allowed, details about boarding passes, and connection times. My head felt light as I stared at the flight documents. Paris! I thought Neil was in Mexico.

"How long am I supposed to be there?" I asked as calmly as I could, examining the documents.

"Afraid I can't answer that," Deborah replied. "It's only a one-way ticket."

"One-way?"

"Yes. One-way." We were both silent for a moment and then she started again. "Here is your reservation for the hotel. It's called the Grand Hotel Doré at 201 Avenue Daumesnil." She stumbled over the pronunciation. "It's near the Gare de Lyon and one of the Metro stations. That's the Paris underground. Have you been to Paris before?" I nodded. Roger and I had spent several months travelling in Europe during the first year of our marriage, backpacking from place to place and sleeping in hostels, one-star hotels, and on overnight trains. We had spent almost three weeks in Paris. Now it seemed like a long-ago dream. "I included a map in here for you," Deborah said as she pulled a folded paper out of the packet. The location of the hotel was marked with a neon green highlighter, as was Gare de Lyon. "It looks like the hotel is only a few blocks from the station."

"How many nights am I to be at this hotel?"

"Just one. Then you go to London." She pulled another sheaf of papers out of the ticket jacket and explained the departure time, stations, and other pertinent information for the channel tunnel train.

"And why am I going to London?"

Deborah shrugged. "I'm just the messenger," she said. "When you get to London, you have a reservation at a Bed and Breakfast near Waterloo Station. In fact, it's listed as one hundred yards from the station where the Channel Tunnel train stops." She rambled on about the reservation in London: small family-style establishment, nice and clean, run by Colin and Jo-anna Something-or-other, no pets allowed, check-in, check-out times, meals available. I was only half-listening.

"That's about it," said Deborah, refolding the papers and stuffing them back into the folder. "I've got to run," she said zipping her leather portfolio and picking up her purse. "Do you have any questions before I go?"

"Yes," I said, dragging my attention back to her. "I have several."

She set her back purse down.

"You say Mr. Bryant called this morning?"

"Yes," Deborah replied. "He insisted that we put a rush on the arrangements. I was lucky to get space on the flights so soon and to find places for you to stay."

"How did he sound to you?"

"He sounded ordinary, I guess, only in kind of a hurry. I don't actually know him that well. We have only met a few times. But there was something else. He said the whole trip was highly confidential, that our office was not to divulge this file to anyone. Of course, you know that your travel information is always confidential."

"Yes, yes," I said. "But you haven't mentioned a return flight from London."

"He didn't book one," said Deborah. "Maybe he's planning to let you know about that once you get there."

"I see." I said, standing up. Deborah James took the cue and stood, too. At the front door she fished a business card out of her handbag and handed it to me. "If you have any trouble, give me a shout." I watched her go down the walk and get in her car.

Before I could get back to the kitchen, the telephone rang again. It was my daughter, Julia, on the line.

"Hi Mom," she said. "I was wondering if you want to go to the ballet with me next week. I've got an extra ticket. It's Wednesday night. Are you free?"

"I'm sorry, Julia. I won't be able to go."

"But Mom" she moaned, "why not?" I remembered Neil's admonitions for secrecy and had no explanation ready.

"I had a meeting this afternoon with a man named Scott Marchand, from your great-uncle Neil's office."

"Nothing has happened to Uncle Neil, has it?" she asked.

"As far as I know, he's fine," I replied. "I'm not sure where he is right now, and I gather that's the way he wants it." I went on to tell her what had transpired since receiving the call from Scott, leaving out as much detail as possible.

"So you mean to tell me that you're going to drop everything and fly to Paris tomorrow without even knowing how you'll get back?"

"Presumably, I'll fly back," I answered. "I'm just not sure when or from where. That's why I need you to come by the house and pick up Pianissimo. I don't want to leave him home alone since I may be gone several days. If I knew I would only be gone a day or two, he'd be fine but you'd better look after him this time, just in case it turns into a longer trip than I anticipate."

She agreed.

"Julia," I said, "you do realize that secrecy in this matter is of utmost importance? I want you to know that it might be dangerous."

"Really?"

"Please don't worry, though," I said. "I'm sure God will look after me."

"Yeah, of course," she replied blandly. "I'll come right now and get the bird. I've got a dance class in an hour."

CHAPTER 3

At Charles de Gaulle airport I had flagged a taxi and now it squealed to a stop outside my hotel, a plain, brick building with tall, narrow windows. Dragging my tote bag across the seat behind me, I stepped into the bright afternoon sunshine. The driver, a squat man with thick glasses and a two-day beard, hauled my single suitcase from the trunk and set it on the sidewalk beside me, then removed his flat hat and scratched the dome of his skull. I paid him with Euros drawn from a machine at the airport and he waddled back to the driver's seat and sped off. Overhead the sky was a clear, pale blue. I yanked my suitcase handle up and pulled open the glass door of the hotel.

"Madame Moss," the desk clerk repeated after I settled my bags on the marble floor next to the chest-high counter. "*Ah, oui. Nous avons un message pour vous,*" he said. Turning, he reached into a cubicle on the wall behind him and pulled out a single white envelope and held it out to me with both hands. "*Si vous voulez...*"

"*Monsieur, s'il vous plaît,*" I said. "Do you speak English?" He nodded. "I have just spent the night on a long flight, and I am too tired to think in French just now. Perhaps tomorrow..." He nodded without smiling.

I tore open the sealed envelope. It contained a single card, and while the clerk checked me into the hotel I read the words. It had been hand-written with a fountain pen and it was in

16

French. "Gare de Lyon, 4:30, Voie 5," was all said. I slipped it into my jacket pocket.

The hotel's single elevator was out of order so I trudged up the winding staircase to the second floor and unlocked my room door. Inside, I dropped my luggage on the floor and looked around. Recent modernization had rendered the small room ugly and featureless. I rolled onto the hideous orange and red bed cover, let out a long groan, and closed my eyes.

A whining mo-ped engine outside my window woke me and I sat up, blinking and gasping for air in the stifling room. I drew the crumpled note from my pocket and smoothed it out to re-read while I twisted my watch around my wrist. It was ten minutes to four. That gave me forty minutes. If I hustled, I could have a shower and wash away the sweat and bad air before leaving for the train station. Leaping to my feet, I flung my clothes off. Twenty minutes later I felt like a new person. My hair was still damp, but the warm spring air would soon dry it as I walked the few blocks to the train station. Grabbing my handbag and the map from the travel agent I set off.

Rush hour was in full swing as I entered the echoing cavern of Gare de Lyon. Not having any idea what to expect, whom to meet or how to proceed, I wandered into the milieu and looked around. In three minutes it would be four thirty. My heart began to pound as I strode down the massive station toward the platform marked "Voie 5" and noticed from the corner of my eye a man approaching, heading directly toward me. I slowed down, but he turned away and stepped aboard the train bound for Dijon.

"Madame Moss?"

I spun around. A middle-aged man, tall, and with skin the colour of tea, grasped my elbow. He wore a black suit and carried a black umbrella, though there was not a cloud in the sky outside.

"You must come with me," he commanded in an accent not French, and headed toward the street. The acrid odor of French cigarettes drifted past me as I dashed after him. A gaggle of school children in navy blazers, their socks bagging around skinny legs and shirttails hanging from drooping waistbands, thronged into the station, laughing and shouting. Harried chaperones scurried to keep them in order. Leaping sideways, I darted around the group of children, while the tall man charged ahead. Suddenly, a hand grabbed my other arm and a voice hissed in my ear. "Neil Bryant has sent me. Come with me."

I staggered. "Wait a minute," I gasped, tugging my arm free from this stranger's grasp. "Who are you?"

"There is no time. Come now." A little man with a balding head tugged on my sleeve.

"Stop," shouted the man in black, lunging for me. The little man yanked on my wrist and began to run, dodging commuters, and hauling me along with him. I glanced over my shoulder. The dark man charged after us, dancing around the school children who scattered like a flock of chickens. Their two chaperones ran in circles around them. Then my pursuer stepped on the foot of a little girl who began to howl and her guardian let loose a stream of abuse at him. He ducked away from her tirade and tore after us. I sprinted down the platform, my arm in the bald man's steel-like grip. On our left, a train began to move and my companion lunged for the closing doors. Forcing them open, he dragged me up the steps behind him onto the moving train as the doors slid shut behind us.

My captor loosened his grip on my arm and I flung his hand off and peered out the window. I could see the tall man loping along beside the train as it gathered speed. Finally, he jogged to a stop, turned and stalked away.

"*Venez ici*," said my companion, motioning me to follow him as he headed toward the trailing end of the train. I didn't move. "Madame, come on," he urged reaching for my arm. Snatching it away from his grasp, I sighed. What else could I do but follow?

He walked swiftly, glancing back at me every few steps, as though I might disappear. Dodging standing passengers, pushing through knots of people with lap-top bags and lunch totes, babies and briefcases, he led me through three cars until we found seats. Wedging himself against the window, he tugged me down beside him.

"Oh, Madame," he cried, wiping a shirtsleeve across his shining forehead, "that was a close one, *non*? That man, you don't want to go with him. No, no, no." He shook his head emphatically, reminding me of the toy dog that had sat in the back window of my grandparents' car when I was a child.

"Who are you?" I asked.

"Oh, Madame," he exclaimed. "So many pardons. I am François Trouville. I know your uncle, Monsieur Neil, ooooh, long time. Yesterday, paff, he call me on the telephone, out from the blues. I do not see him since a long, long time. Anyway, anyway, he call me, he say he is in big fix and needs me to find you and take you to see a guy. Some guy I never heard of before. But hey, that's Neil. He always a little crazy!" He waggled his fingers next to his ear. Outside, the city flashed past, apartments followed by more apartments, cars stopped at crossings, finally suburbia. "The stories I could be telling you," he chortled. "One time in Morocco..." His calloused hands became animated and his pale blue eyes grew bright.

I interrupted. "Where are you taking me?"

"Oh, my," he said, his head snapping round to look out the window. "We get off at the next stop. Catching this train was not part of the plan, but Neil, he warned me about Menendez."

"Menendez?"

"*Oui*, the man who chase us. Neil said he might turn up and I should look out for him. I just didn't think he is turning up so soon. God only knows how he found out where you are." He clucked his tongue.

"Perhaps you had better tell me what you know," I demanded.

"Okay, okay," François Trouville said. "Neil and I go way back. We worked together in Egypt in the seventies and we keep in touch now and then. He's a great guy, Neil. Heart like gold." He thumped his chest. I nodded, hoping he wouldn't drift back into stories of past exploits, but he went on. "A few days ago I gets a phone call from Neil. I not see his face for ages, oh, since ninety-six, ninety-seven, I think since a big conference in Brazil. Way back. Anyway, he calls me and says he needs a favour. *Bien sûr*, I say yes right away. He ask me to meet you, to leave the message at the hotel, all secret like. I'm supposed to take you to see a guy, a Dr. Bernaud, the best expert on middle-Americas this side of the Atlantic. I say, 'Hey, easy. I meet you, pick you up and take you there, no problem'. Then Neil tells me about this other guy to watch out for, this guy Menendez who is after something Neil found. That one who chased us back there at the station, I figure he is Menendez."

"Who is he? Do you know anything about him?"

François shrugged. "Never heard of him before Neil telephoned. I don't know who he is or what he want. I don't know what you're doing either."

"That makes two of us," I muttered. Trouville regarded me quizzically. I went on. "Are we going to see this Dr. Bernaud now?"

He laughed, the corners of his eyes crinkling almost closed. "We would be if we weren't going in the wrong direction."

"Excuse me?"

"It's okay, it's okay. I came in my car to pick you up. I have no plan to get on this train. In fact, we have no tickets, so if you see the train guy coming, we go for a little walk." He winked and jerked his head toward the onboard restrooms. "We getting off at the next stop. We should be able to get a taxi back to Gare de Lyon. Then we can hop in my car and carry on."

"What if this Menendez is waiting for us?"

"How does he know what kind of car I drive?" he asked, throwing up his hands, and then he reached over and covered my hand with one of his. "Don't you worry, Madame Moss, we'll give that guy the slip, no problem."

I didn't share his confidence but kept that to myself.

Twenty-five minutes later, we were in a shiny black taxi racing through the back streets of Paris. The train, a commuter, had stopped not long after we got on, so we made a quick exit. François manoeuvred me through the crowd like a housewife pushing a shopping-cart, then hailed the taxi and deposited me in the back seat before sliding in next to me.

Around the corner from the main entrance to the Gare de Lyon, the taxi pulled up next to a green Fiat with a dented front bumper. François pushed me out the passenger door, tossed some bills to the taxi driver then ran to unlock his car. Menendez, or whoever he was, was nowhere to be seen.

"Hop in, Madame, hop in," he said with a grin. "We'll make like tracks and get out of here, just in case." With one swift glance behind us, he sped off down a one-way street. Gunning the engine and shifting gears in rapid succession, we tore through narrow streets and past corner green grocer shops with bins of flowers out front, neighbourhood patisseries, and local garages. On one street corner, a stout woman, with a hairdo like a helmet, yanked her Yorkshire terrier's leash as we raced past, lifting the little creature clear off its feet. *Trouville must be terrified*, I thought.

"Do you think we're being followed?" I shouted, hanging onto the door handle as the car skidded around right turn.

"Oh, no," François said, laughing. "That guy is nowheres here." Then it struck me. He wasn't driving this way out fear. He drove this way all the time! I shuddered and hung on.

"There's a map in there," he said, pointing to a compartment under the dashboard. "I don't go to this part of the *cité* so often. I needs directions."

I pulled the map out and unfolded it, staring at the maze of lines scrabbled over the paper like barn loft spider webs.

"Let me see," said François, leaning over to look at the map. My eyes widened as a delivery truck bore down on us. I pointed at it and squeaked.

"We're about here," he said ignoring me and jabbing the paper with a stubby finger. "We are at Rue...." he leaned forward to squint out the windshield as the little car streaked past the truck, "Fourchette. Rue Fourchette and Avenue Le Boucher. Ha ha. Fork and butcher. Pretty funny, *non*?"

I scrutinized the tiny writing on the map and finally located Rue Fourchette. With my fingernail I traced the street as it zigzagged and eventually met with Avenue Le Boucher at a fork. "Found it," I said. "Now what am I looking for?"

"This guy, Bernaud, has an office somewhere around La Sorbonne. Rue Danton. Can you find it there? You got to tell me where to turn."

As we dashed past, I caught the name of a street I had seen on the map so I shouted, "Turn right here. Now left at the next corner." François leaned on the gas pedal and roared down a short block, then swung left and tore down the next road.

"We are here, Madame," he shouted as he stood on the brakes in front of a three-storey stone building with an oval window over its imposing front door. Screeching to a halt and shoving the gearshift into park, François leapt out and slammed his door. I peeled my fingers from the door handle and followed.

Inside, a directory on the wall indicated that Dr. Bernaud's office was on the third floor so we set off up the curving staircase to find it. The hallway, dark and smelling faintly of cats, led straight from the top of the stairs, but halfway along went up two steps and continued. The yellowed walls were streaked with water stains. A dingy brass plate engraved with the inscription "Dr. Alain Bernaud, Docteur d'Archaeologie" hung upon a heavy wood door near the end of the corridor. The door itself stood slightly ajar and a thin streak of light drew a bright line on the worn black marble tiles at our feet.

I placed my hand on the door and gently pushed it open.

François muttered, *"Mon Dieu!"* Before us the office lay in utter ruin. Papers and fragments of antiquities lay strewn about like a tornado had hit and filing cabinet drawers stood open, their contents disgorged all over the floor. One cabinet lay on its side, empty but for one drawer containing nothing but a bent file frame. The remaining drawers lay upside down around the room. A fine, old, oak desk stood near the window, drawers hanging open and the top swept clean. A smashed lamp dangled from its cord over the front of the desk. We stepped into the room, edging around a broken chair, and tiptoed over encyclopaedias and Mayan figurines. I found a clear space in the centre of the room and stopped to survey the wreckage.

"Look," I whispered, nudging François, who had come up behind me. His eyes followed where I pointed to the side of the desk. A pair of brown leather shoes lay upside down on the floor. The owner's feet were still in them.

CHAPTER 4

The instant François and I realized that the pair of shoes protruding from beneath the oak desk contained a pair of feet, we rushed to kneel beside him.

"He's breathing," I said, watching his chest rise and fall with quick, shallow breaths. I gently placed my fingertips on the pulse point of his wrist. "It's strong and steady," I said, counting off the beats against the second hand on my watch. Crouching lower, I could see a gash above the man's ear, the grey hair around it matted with coagulating blood and the bashed ear turning blue in the light from the windows.

Suddenly the muscles under the white cotton shirt twitched and the man groaned. Without a word, François and I turned him gently onto his back. His eyes fluttered open and his hand reached for the injury on his head, but I stopped him while I dug around in my bag for a tissue. As Francois assisted him to a sitting position, I dabbed at a trickle of blood.

"What happened?" I asked, then switched to French and tried again. *"Q'est-ce qui ce passe?"*

"It's all right," he said, sending me a pain-filled glance. "We can speak English. I assume that you are Madame Moss," he said.

"That's right," I replied. "Are you Dr. Bernaud?"

"Yes," he replied, sitting up straighter, "but as you can see, I have recently had other visitors." He suddenly noticed François beside me. "Who are you?"

"Dr. Bernaud," I said, "this is François Trouville. He is an old friend of Neil Bryant's." They shook hands then François helped the doctor to his feet.

"My goodness," Dr. Bernaud exclaimed after settling into his desk chair and surveying the room. "What a mess this is!"

"Who did this?" I asked, staring at the destruction around us.

"I have no idea who they were," Dr. Bernaud began, "only that they rushed in here like commandos and began shouting and shoving me, demanding something, and when I didn't respond how they wished, one of them came after me with that," he pointed to a stone figure lying on the floor under the window. I bent and picked it up, turning it carefully in my hands. Near the base of the statuette I could see traces of blood, which I wiped with the tissue in my hand, then set it on the corner of the desk. "After that," Dr. Bernaud continued, "everything went black."

"Are you feeling all right?" I inquired. "We could call an ambulance or take you to see a doctor."

Dr. Bernaud waved this idea away. "I have a bit of a headache, but I will be fine."

"How many these guys?" François inquired.

"Just two." He looked around the room and sighed.

"Would you like us to help clean up your office?" I asked. The task looked gargantuan.

"Oh, goodness, no," replied the doctor. "I will have someone come in and help me tomorrow. I have an assistant who comes in twice a week. Too bad she is not here today. She is of formidable proportions, and has a temperament to match." He smiled briefly and put a hand to his battered ear. "Well, at least this has stopped bleeding. I will clean it up in a minute. However, Madame Moss," he said, turning his attention on me, "we must now discuss your mission." He picked up a pair of glasses from the floor under the desk and held them up to the light. Satisfied that they had not been smashed, he polished them with the front of his shirt and settled them upon the bridge of his nose, gingerly tucking the temple wires over his ears.

"Yes," I agreed. "What can you tell me?"

"Absolutely nothing."

"I beg your pardon, Monsieur."

"My instructions were to reveal nothing unless you came alone, which," he glanced at François, "you have not. I am not at liberty to divulge any information of any kind. I am sorry, Monsieur Trouville."

François stared at him then back at me. He threw up his hands, muttered something under his breath and stalked out of the room, slamming the door behind him. I watched him go, then spun back to Dr. Bernaud. "What is it? Have you talked to Neil? What do you know?"

Dr. Bernaud rose slowly from the chair, wincing slightly with the movement as he began to pick up papers from the floor. His slight figure stooped over the sheets of paper and files strewn about the room as he cleared a narrow path to the door. I followed, grabbing up handfuls of papers as I went. He placed the papers on top of one of the cabinets that remained standing, opened the office door, leaned out, then motioned for me to follow. Closing the door behind us he also locked it, then led me to the end of the hallway where a plain door opened to reveal a narrow flight of stairs up to the next floor. At the top of the stairs he opened another door and invited me into the kitchen of a charming, small apartment. Sunlight filtered through the skylights, sending bright dots of yellow dancing over a hardwood floor. A glass-panelled door led to a tiny terrace which overlooked a side street and gave a fine view of the Eiffel Tower. Pots of African violets, in every shade from pale cream through deepest purple, bloomed on all the windowsills.

"My hobby," Dr. Bernaud said when he saw me admiring the flowers. "Please have a seat, Madame." He indicated a rush-seated chair beside a small square table in the centre of the room. I sat down, dropping my bag on the floor next to my foot. Dr. Bernaud seated himself opposite me, placed his elbows on the table and studied me over the rims of his wire-framed glasses.

"Now, what can you tell me?" he demanded.

"Very little."

He smiled. "Would you like a cup of tea?" he asked. "I could use one myself." Before I could nod, he got up and began rummaging in a cupboard, produced a kettle and spread out tea things. "Neil told me not to expect much from you. Oh dear, that didn't sound right," he said. "What I mean is that he did not tell you what to expect."

"What do you know?"

"Quite a bit, as it turns out." He filled the teapot with boiling water and placed it on the table along with cups for both of us. "Madame Moss, Neil and I have been colleagues for many years. We have worked on numerous research projects together and spent many hours blowing dust off relics in some of the most exotic and unsavoury parts of the world. So when he contacted me with this important request, I naturally agreed. He has made a discovery in the jungles of Mexico, the likes of which archaeologists and treasure hunters have lusted after for centuries. As you know," he said, pouring the tea, "the Mayan language was a mystery for a very long time and it is only in the past half-century that scholars have had any success deciphering the figures enough to piece together a coherent code or hieroglyphics. Much of the history from the ancient times of the culture still remains unknown."

He took a sip of his tea, frowned into the cup and replaced it on the saucer. Then he rose to his feet and walked to the window, touching the leaves of first one of his African violets then another, rummaging in the planter pots. Bending to peer beneath the furry leaves of one of the plants he said, "Aha, there it is." In his hand he held what appeared to be a lump of dirt. "This is part of the secret," he said, gazing at it almost lovingly. Moving to the sink, he dusted the soil from the object with his fingertips, then blew on it gently to remove the last fragments of dust. He held it out to me. In the palm of his hand lay a small grey stone block, approximately the size of a child's wooden alphabet block, the kind that my children had played with when they were tiny. I took it between my fingers. It was not a perfect cube as one side was narrower than its opposite side, thereby creating a slightly wedged shape. On three of the surfaces, figures and forms had been carved, each one different and distinct.

"Beautiful, isn't it?" Dr. Bernaud said. "As you can see, the fascinating thing about this stone is not that it exhibits a classic example of Mayan writing, but that it also has these other two languages on it. I believe one of them is of Olmec origin. The Olmec peoples lived in similar regions to the Maya but their culture originated prior to the rise of the Mayan culture. The two civilizations overlapped for a while, so it is not inconceivable that these two languages might appear on the same artifact, although that in itself is extremely rare. What is surprising, no, shocking, about this stone is the third language. If I am not mistaken, it appears to be an ancient form of the Hebrew language. While there have always been rumours and conjecture that peoples from the Middle East, such as the Phoenicians, had the wherewithal to accomplish oceanic travel, the general consensus is that no one from this side of the globe visited the Americas until the Vikings, followed by Columbus. The mere age of this relic makes it a phenomenal find, but what your uncle has found here could rewrite the books on Middle-America's history."

"What am I to do with this?" I asked, turning the block over in my hand.

"I'm sorry, Madame, but I do not know. Neil sent it to me and asked me to keep it for you to collect. He stressed the importance of the find, a fact I had no trouble grasping, and that it must fall into the possession of no one but you. I am sure that this is what those men who ruined my office were seeking." He turned and walked to the window, tenderly touching the petals of a delicate pink violet. Suddenly, he leaned forward and stared down into the street below.

"Madame," he exclaimed, "we must go." He opened the narrow door to the miniscule terrace. "Please, Madame, come with me. We will take the back way."

I leapt up from my seat and dashed to the window. Below, next to his car, I saw François standing with two other men and François was pointing toward the office windows of Dr. Bernaud.

"Quickly, Madame, we have no time to lose," he said reaching for my arm.

"Are those the men who accosted you?" I asked, following.

"Who can tell from here?" he said. "Do you have the stone?"

"Yes, I have it," I answered, opening my bag and stuffing it in an inner pocket next to my passport.

"Then come." We dashed down a decrepit iron fire escape clinging to the side of the building, Dr. Bernaud showing surprising agility for a man clearly in sixties and who had recently been knocked out cold. The stairway ended in a sliding ladder. We clung to it then hit the ground running and dashed to a small white Peugeot tucked into a parking spot in the alley.

"Quickly, Madame, quickly," he said in a harsh whisper as he twisted the key in the passenger door lock. I yanked open the door and jumped in, then reached across the driver's seat and unlocked his door. Within seconds we were speeding down the alley, away from the street where François Trouville and his companions stood.

"Those men who attacked you," I asked when I caught my breath. "Do you know who they are?"

"No, Madame," he said, "but I think that you must be very careful. This find of your uncle's is a great one." He reached over and patted my hand, his eyes filled with concern. "*S'il vous plait,*" he said, "please, be very, very careful."

CHAPTER 5

A hand reached for the back of my neck and I screamed, wrenched away, and began to run. Darkness stuck to my sides like paste as I scrambled toward a circle of light in the distance, my feet slipping on muck and my hands clutching at the slimy sides of a tunnel, no, a culvert, under a road. As I ran, gasping, sobbing, the light grew brighter. It was hot, so hot. The sound of running feet pounded behind me as the light spread, grew, changed. Then I floated up out of sleep like a bubble in a glass, popping out of the horrible dream and onto the surface of wakefulness.

The bed sheets and my pyjamas twisted around my soaked body like seaweed and my hair stuck to my neck. I opened my eyes and pulled the blankets away, flinging them off the end of the bed. The early morning light leaked in around the thick orange draperies, and I could hear a bird outside the window calling to its companions.

"*Madame?*" said a voice from the other side of the door. Knuckles rapped on the wood.

I sprang out of bed, disoriented, and put a hand out to the wall. "*Oui?*" I called out reaching for the door handle.

"*Madame, ici le concierge. J'ai une message pour vous. C'est urgent.*" An urgent message? What time was it?

I pulled the door open and heaved a sigh of relief when I saw the night clerk standing there, dressed in his uniform. He held a small card in his hand. I took it from him, closed the door and staggered back to my bed. Flicking on the lamp, I squinted against the sudden brightness. The card read simply, "Change of plans. Call this number." It was followed by a telephone number.

The digital clock glowed a red 5:15 from the bedside table. I snapped off the lamp and rolled back onto the pillow, lying in the dark and listening to the muffled hum of the city. I didn't want to call; I wanted to sleep, but after I few minutes I groaned, turned the lamp back on and dialed the number.

"Is this Jill?" asked a cultured British woman's voice after the first ring.

"Yes."

"I'm Claire Jamieson. Neil's been in touch. Slight change in plans. I'll be there to pick you up in thirty minutes. Can you be ready?"

"I guess I can be ready," I replied, apprehension still clinging to the edges of my mind.

"Good. See you soon." With a click the line went dead.

Twenty minutes later I stood on the sidewalk outside the hotel, my luggage at my feet, breathed in the cool morning air and thought about the last time I had seen Paris. It was in those early days with Roger, when life was fresh and fun and I was so young. I felt a twinge of sorrow that they had gradually given way to the usual tread of daily living: the children, jobs, and schools, lawns that needed mowing, mortgages and motorcycles, traffic and tutus, puppies and pulled muscles and pancakes for breakfast. So much had changed since I had last seen this city.

Initially, the shock of Roger's death had sent me into a downward spiral that threatened to take both me and my two children, Tim and Julia, into a place from which we might never emerge, a place of grief so deep and dark I believed that we would all be damaged forever. I had kissed Roger good-bye one morning as he left for work and two hours later the police stood at the door informing me that he had been the victim of a horrific highway accident and was pronounced dead on arrival at the hospital. It was unbelievable, unthinkable, and so totally unchangeable. In an instant he was irrevocably gone.

That was three years ago. The children were now both grown and on their own. Julia was working her way through university, planning to conquer the world as a high-powered businesswoman of some description. Tim told me, "Asia is the new Europe, Mom," as he booked a ticket to Thailand.

The sun crept over the horizon and I thought about the small carved rock tucked in the inside pocket of the bag at my feet. It felt like I carried a hot coal that would soon sear its way through the sides of the bag and reveal itself to everyone. I reached down and squeezed the side of my bag again, reassuring myself that it was still there, still safe.

I thought about those two men on the sidewalk with François Trouville. Were they the same men who had ransacked Dr. Bernaud's office? And what about this character named Menendez? Who was he and why did he want the stone? "Lord, please give me some answers," I said. The sound of my voice drifted into the still morning air as I sat down on the curb to wait for Claire Jamieson. Though there was barely enough light in the newborn sky to read by, I pulled Neil's old Bible out of my bag and opened it anyway, flipping through the pages looking not only for clues but for words of comfort. It seemed like eons since I had sat staring at a computer screen and read that message from Neil telling me he had a job for me. Or, I wondered, was it actually God who had a job for me?

As my fingers idly turned the pages, I began to notice something. Every now and then, there was a mark in bright red ink, hardly more than a dot, beside a verse. I thumbed the pages more deliberately, scanning for marks. There did not seem to be any connection between them; they seemed entirely random. I opened again at the beginning to Genesis 1:1 and turned page-by-page looking for the marks. From my bag I pulled out my travelling sketch book to jot down verse references but before I could begin, a sleek black car rounded the corner at the end of the street and came toward me. When it drew up beside me, I got to my feet, stuffing the Bible and sketchbook back into my bag.

"Hi. You must be Jill," said the driver, pushing open the passenger door. "Get in."

Not so fast, I thought. I leaned over to get a good look at the long-legged blonde in low-slung designer jeans and an oxford cloth shirt. She wore gold hoop earrings that peeked from behind a sleek, chin-length, blunt cut, and several bracelets on her slender wrists. Dark brows and lashes framed deep blue eyes. "Who are you?" I said.

"Claire Jamieson," she replied, sticking out her hand. "Come on, get in."

"I think you need to explain a few things to me first."

"Sure," she said. "What do you want to know?"

I rested my forearm on the roof of the car. "Why are you here and how did you know about me?"

Claire sighed and placed her hand on the back of the passenger seat. "I'm here because Neil Bryant asked me to be. He even described you to me, though he didn't mention what great hair you have. Neil wanted me to pick you up and take you to Tours. Like I said, there was a change of plans."

"You sent that note to me?"

"Yes. Neil asked me to call the hotel and let you know. He told me where you would be and asked me to give you a lift to your next stop. I go down there regularly for my job, so it's no trouble."

I felt my resistance softening. "How do you know Neil?"

"I was one of his students several years back. We kept in touch because we have a mutual interest in Mesoamerican history and archaeology. Come on, I won't bite. Toss your suitcase in the boot. I'll pop it open for you." She reached down beside her seat and released the trunk latch.

"All right," I said. In the past twenty-four hours, I had become leery of just about everyone. As I lifted my suitcase into the trunk, I thought a silent prayer, asking the Holy Spirit to warn me of danger, but had neither a sense of peace nor a strong warning. I hesitated, then closed the trunk lid.

When I climbed into the passenger seat, I decided to let Claire Jamieson do most of the talking. Fortunately, she did not require prompting. I quickly learned that she had been born in Bournemouth, her parents emigrated to Canada when she was a young child, had become Canadians, then moved back to Britain by the time she was about to start school. When she finished school and decided to go into archaeology, she ended up in Vancouver and jumped at the chance to study under Neil.

As Claire talked, I gazed out the window at the passing French countryside. Outside the city, newly cultivated fields rolled away into the distance, interspersed with groves of trees and charming villages. The sky melted from lavender blue to pale blue then bright yellow as the morning light seeped over the horizon and cast long shadows across the road.

Claire told me that her years studying with Neil had been some of the most exciting of her life. She was now in her early thirties, and was passing through Paris on a business trip as part of her job in Manchester where she worked for a small, private museum. She rambled on, seeming not to notice the one-sided conversation but eventually she stopped talking. In the silence, I dozed off. I woke to the sound of tires crunching on gravel as the car drew into the parking lot of a roadside restaurant.

"I'm sorry," I apologized, stretching. "My body clock is a bit out of whack with the jet lag." Claire pulled the car up in front of the café, an unprepossessing place with vines straggling over a small terrace at the side of the building.

"I thought we might get a bite to eat," Claire said, glancing at her watch and reaching for her purse. Several delivery trucks and long-distance hauling trailers were parked along the side of the building.

A wall of cigarette smoke met us as I pulled open the café door. Five minutes in this Gauloise cloud and I would reek for the rest of the week. Most of the tables were occupied by rough men hunched over tiny cups of thick coffee, gnawing slabs of crusty bread, or attacking plates of unidentifiable foods glistening with fat. We threaded our way between the jutting elbows and slid into the single empty booth at the side of the room. Behind the bar, a stout, red-faced woman with hair the colour of maraschino cherries looked up and supplied us with a stony stare.

"*Watch the door*," said the Holy Spirit in my mind.

"Do you mind if we trade places?" I asked Claire, sliding out of the booth again.

She shrugged. "Whatever you like."

The maraschino woman rounded the end of the bar, grabbed a couple of plastic-covered menus and dropped them on the table between us. She spat out a stream of French, then strode away again.

"How is your French?" I asked, looking at Claire.

She shrugged with one shoulder. "Not bad. She said they have Croque Monsieur and something else. I didn't catch it all." She flipped open a menu then said, "I'll just have coffee."

I read the selections on the menu, silently thanking God for my high school French teachers. I hadn't eaten since the plane so decided on a complete trucker's breakfast and a *café au lait*. The flame-haired Madame circumnavigated the room, swinging her generous hips past elbows and booted feet. We gave her our orders, and she stalked off to the kitchen, hollering as she entered.

My coffee arrived in a ceramic bowl, brim-full with creamy foam, and I inhaled the aroma and took a sip. In a few minutes my breakfast followed, a plate heaped with eggs, thick dark sausages, ham, and bread.

"You're a big eater," Claire observed coolly.

"The last meal I had was airplane food," I said. "Most of it was plastic."

Her gaze wandered off around the room as she stifled a yawn and looked at her wristwatch.

"Are you in a hurry?" I asked.

"No," she said, fiddling with a fork, "I just don't want to spend any more time in this dump than I have to."

While Claire visited the ladies' room I finished eating and pushed my plate away. "The atmosphere may not be much here," I said when she returned, "but the food's good. I feel like a new person."

"You probably have to use the ladies' room before we go." She put her hand in her purse. "It's not spotless, but you probably won't catch anything."

I dropped my napkin on my plate and slid out of the booth, taking my bag with me. As I pushed open the restroom door, I heard the voice of the Lord. *"Look at Claire."* I turned my head toward the table. Claire was furiously jabbing the buttons on her cell phone and casting glances over the back of the booth toward the café's door. I slipped into the ladies' room and peered back through the door crack. Claire spoke briefly on the telephone then snapped it closed and hoisted herself up with an elbow to watch the front door of the café. Within moments, a man pushed the door open and strode in. Clearly not a trucker, he was dressed in a pair of dark pants and a black leather jacket. He sat down in the seat I had just vacated.

"What now, Lord?" I prayed silently.

"Lock the door." I locked the door, used the toilet, then freshened up at the sink, squinting at my reflection in a cloudy mirror screwed to the wall. The room had no windows, not even an air vent larger than a potholder. "Okay, Lord," I said. "What do you want me to do?"

His answer was swift and sure. *"You are in danger. You must leave here."*

I slid the strap of my bag over my shoulder and opened the door. Through the crack I could see Claire and the man with their heads bent together. At that moment, the proprietress sashayed up to a table near where I stood, balancing a tray on one hand as she loaded it with dirty dishes.

I ducked my head out the door, keeping a careful watch on Claire and her companion. "Madame, please," I whispered in French. "I need your help."

She turned her head toward me without stopping her work and said, "*Oui?*"

"There is a man," I began in French, nodding toward the table.

"Aaah!" she intoned, a knowing look passing over her face. "Is he your husband?" Before I could explain that the man I mentioned was *not* my husband, she said, "Come with me," and glanced about the room. Reaching through the restroom doorway she grasped my arm then, puffing herself up and using the tray of dirty dishes as further concealment, she marched me across the back of the room and through the swinging kitchen doors.

"*Voila!*" she said as the doors flapped behind us. Her previously emotionless face split into a grin so wide it revealed a missing molar. "Men, pah!" she spat and launched into a string of what I can only guess were invectives against all men everywhere. With a hand on my back, she shoved me past the gaping cook and a silent old woman in a shabby flowered dress washing dishes at a corner sink. Thrusting the back door open, she pushed me out.

"Marcel!" Madame bellowed at lanky young man with a blond crew cut who was reaching for the door of a delivery truck. His head snapped round and he raised a hand to shield his eyes from the glare of the morning sun. The lady dragged me over to where he stood and explained her imagined version of my situation to the truck driver. When she finished talking, he turned to me and gave me the most dazzling smile I have ever seen.

"*Oui, oui,*" he said, nodding vigorously and reaching for my hand to lead me to the passenger side of the truck.

"*Un moment,*" I said, holding back. "*Mes bagages sont là.*" I pointed to the black car whose back bumper could be seen from where we stood. I couldn't leave without my suitcase.

"No problem," said Marcel with another incredible grin. He reached into the cab of his truck and pulled out a tire iron, jogged over to the car, and within two minutes returned with my suitcase. My mouth dropped open. He tossed the case behind the seat of his truck, then handed me up to the passenger seat. Madame Flame-hair had retreated to the corner of the kitchen, her arms crossed over her sizable girth and a glow of satisfaction across her features. I had the distinct impression I had just done my bit to help settle a score.

Marcel turned the key in the ignition, the truck engine rumbled to a start and we rolled across the gravel parking lot and out toward the highway. As I took one last look at the café, I saw Claire and her companion burst through the front door. I leaned back in my seat as Marcel stood on the accelerator and we roared away. Within thirty seconds the café was out of sight.

"*Merci, Monsieur*," I said, reaching across the cab and patting Marcel's arm. He turned to me with a huge, happy grin and replied in thickly-accented English, "No problem."

CHAPTER 6

"Hi, Dad," I called into the pay phone receiver.

"Jill, where are you?"

"I'm in Europe right now." I said.

"You'd better talk to your mother," he said. "Neil phoned and now she has something to tell you. I can't remember all the details. I'll put her on."

My mother took the telephone and asked me where I was and didn't I know what day it is, and how did I get there; wasn't I supposed to be on my way to London or somewhere?

"Give me a minute, and I'll explain," I shouted, cutting her off. I watched the time on the pay card counting down while I told her, in as few words as possible, the events of the previous two days.

Marcel had explained to me that he had no plans to stop until Narbonne, almost at the Spanish border. I also discovered that beyond a few phrases like, "No problem, hey man, okay, and Coca Cola," Marcel spoke no English, yet in spite of our language differences, we managed to carry on a conversation. Marcel explained that he drove truck for his uncle's company during the summers while he was off from university where he studied architecture.

A couple of hours after our narrow escape from Claire and her companion, we pulled into one of those mega rest stops on the Autoroute. I thought that if Neil needed to find me, he might contact my mother so I called to see if she knew anything. Neil's message was simply to email Dennis.

"Do you know Dennis' email address?" my Mom asked.

"Yes, I do, and as soon as I find a computer, I'll email him." I wished her a hug, placed the receiver back on the cradle and looked around. A central walkway led through the main rest stop building and contained four pay phones, a news kiosk and a garbage can. Doors led off it to a cafeteria, a small convenience store and restrooms. Shouldering my bag, I went into the store and bought a bottle of water, a bag of salted almonds and two apples.

The metallic red cab of Marcel's truck glowed in the morning sun, making it easy to spot in the immense parking lot. Marcel had already invited me to join him for as long as I needed to because, frankly, I think he appreciated the company. Since I had no idea where to go next, I hoped that Dennis could help. I found Marcel under his truck with a wrench in his hand banging on the undercarriage. I leaned down and peered at him.

"Is everything all right there?" I asked.

"*Ah, oui, oui, Madame. C'est bon, oui*," he answered, rolling out from under the vehicle and brushing gravel from his clothes. "No problem. No *finis*, Madame," he said looking apologetic as he headed around to the far side of the truck and rolled beneath it again. I sat down on a nearby curb and polished an apple. The sunshine felt warm on my face and glinted off the apple's gleaming skin. Sinking my teeth into the crisp, fresh fruit, I leaned against a pole and closed my eyes. Marcel had told me he planned to arrive in Narbonne that evening. He would unload the truck, find somewhere to spend the night, then pick up another load in the morning and head north again.

I had to find a computer with internet to email Dennis. I had missed my trip to London and had no idea if I should stop in the city of Tours. Claire had told that me I was to meet someone there but who knew whether that was true? I would have to ask Marcel if he could help me find an internet café. For the moment, however, there was nothing I could do until Marcel was ready to go, so I thought I might as well relax and enjoy the sunshine. I opened my eyes, took another bite of my apple, and saw Claire's car pull into the parking lot.

I drew in my breath so fast that I choked on the bite of apple. Leaping to my feet, doubled over and coughing, I ran toward the truck. Dodging behind a nearby car, I called in a loud whisper, "Marcel, Marcel". He edged out from beneath the truck again, wiping his hands on a greasy rag, and lay on the gravel staring up at me.

"*Oui, Madame?*" he asked, registering my alarm.

"The black car," I squeaked between coughs, stabbing my finger frantically toward the parking lot entrance. "It's here," I said, crouching down beside Marcel.

Marcel got up and, shielding me from view, hustled me through the passenger door, closing it behind me with a soft click. I hunkered down and peered over the dashboard. With exaggerated calm, Marcel strolled around the front of the cab to the driver's side, scrubbing at the grease stains on his fingers, his lips pursed in a tuneless whistle. I could see his eyes slide sideways as he surveyed the parking lot and the building.

Claire slid her long legs out of the car door and stood with her hand shielding her eyes in the brilliant sunlight. Her companion hitched up his pants and looked around too, then motioned for Claire to follow him into the building.

Marcel jerked open the truck door and bounded into the driver's seat, tossing the oily rag over his shoulder, where it slid down behind the seat. He started the engine, slipped the transmission into gear, and the truck rolled out onto the highway. Our departure went unnoticed.

Though we had eluded Claire for the moment, I knew I had to find a computer with internet connection soon to find out what to do next. As the truck rumbled down the highway I turned to Marcel. Speaking French, I explained my problem.

He stared at me, bewildered. "Pardon?"

I took a deep breath and pulled a little French-English dictionary out of my bag. As I looked up the correct words I understood why Marcel was so perplexed. I had said, "Do you know where is a microwave coffee? I need to make a message to my pig." I laughed and started over, this time with the correct words.

"Ah," said Marcel, comprehension dawning. He reached into a compartment behind my seat and pulled out a laptop computer, then tugged a cellular telephone from his jeans pocket. "No problem," he said with a grin. In slow, simple French, he instructed me on how to connect to the internet using his cell phone. Once connected, I pulled up the site where I could check my email in case there was something there from Dennis, or better yet, from Neil. I scanned the list. There were two from Julia, one from Timothy, a couple from my mother, and at the top of the list, one from Dennis. I opened it first.

Hi Jill,
No one seems to know your exact whereabouts and things are heating up on Dad's end. He's asked me to get in touch with you. I'm in points North (sorry, not a good idea to say exactly where) for a couple of weeks and will send you instructions periodically. If you get this email, just reply to it, but don't tell me where you are. I'll let you know how to get in touch with me. Dennis.

I typed a reply stating simply that I was awaiting further instructions and clicked the send button, then opened the message from Tim. His last communiqué several weeks before had been from Kathmandu where he was about to set off on a series of hikes into some remote territory. I read eagerly through his rambling letter detailing his exploits and sensed the excitement and enthusiasm he felt for the country and the people. Hearing from him made me smile, but then Tim had always made me smile. I dashed off a reply to him, mentioning only that I was travelling in Europe while doing a little job for his great-uncle Neil and hoped he was somewhere that he would be able to pick up emails.

Next I clicked on Julia's messages. She asked how I managed to travel on my own at my age and let me know that Pianissimo was fine but he sure makes a mess of her kitchen when he gets in a flap. She also wanted to know how soon I would be home as she needed me to sew an outfit for her to wear to a conference. I replied that I was fine travelling on my own as I was not yet ready for a walker and support hose, and had hitched a ride with a really cute guy. I could imagine her eyes rolling at that comment, which made writing it all the more enjoyable. I mentioned that Pianissimo only gets in a flap when startled so try talking softly to him, and that she had better go buy an outfit if she really needed one, which I doubted.

My mother's email was filled with descriptions of what all her friends were up to in their small town; whose daughter had a baby boy, who had broken a finger while getting out of the car at the baseball tournament, and who was flying to Australia to attend a wedding. She briefly mentioned that Neil had called once but had not told her anything interesting at all, then went on to explain that Dad had been to see the doctor and everything was all right after all. I wrote a brief reply that I was happy everything was fine with Dad, and that I was fine, too, and would be in touch as soon as I had something to report.

I glanced at Marcel then checked my inbox again. A reply from Dennis had appeared. "Thank-you God, for satellites," I said as I opened the email. It instructed me to call a cell phone number immediately.

Dennis picked up on the first ring. "Hey, Jill!" he shouted. "How are you? It's been ages."

"I know, Dennis. What have you got to tell me?"

"Dad phoned this morning," he began. "I can't tell you where he is but he is on the move. Of course, you know that he made an incredible find. I don't know very much about it. The reason for the elaborate subterfuge is that certain criminal elements have found out about it. Evidently, they have the idea that there may be a big Mayan gold find involved. Dad said he wasn't sure who was behind it all, but there have been threats on his life. There is a particularly nasty Mafia crowd in Mexico and Dad thinks they got wind of it. What he found is way beyond a bit of gold, but they don't know that. They just know that the find is significant. Anyway, he's gone underground, which is why he put together this plan to get you to collect the artifacts."

"Can you tell me anything about the find, Dennis?" I needed to know just how much danger I was in.

"No," he answered. "I'd love to be able to, but Dad didn't tell me. All I know is that he believes this find will turn the Mesoamerican archaeological world on its proverbial ear."

"Dennis," I cried. "Neil sent me off on this wild goose chase all over who-knows-where. There are bandits and thugs after me. I don't know where I'm going or whom I can to trust."

"Listen, sweetie," Dennis said. "I understand that you missed the train to London, and that's okay, since there's probably someone watching for you there anyway. What country are you in now?"

I told him, explaining what had happened yesterday with Dr. Bernaud and this morning with Claire.

"I don't know who Claire is," Dennis said, "but I'm sure Dad knows." I told him what had happened at the truck stop and where I was now, heading south to Narbonne with a truck driver.

"Okay, Jill," he said. "Here's what you do. You have to stop in Tours before this Claire person gets there. Are you ahead of her?"

I told him I thought we were ten to twenty minutes ahead of her.

"I need you to go to the Best Western Central Hotel at 21 Rue Berthelot as soon as you can. There is a woman there who will be expecting you. Her name is Dr. Diederich. She's from a university in Germany. She has a piece for you to pick up."

"Okay, Dennis. Is there anything else?"

"Sorry, but you're on your own. If you can stay with your trucker friend all the way to Narbonne, go straight on to Madrid. You'll have to go there anyway, so you might as well go now since you're heading that way. If you have something to write on, get this address." I pulled my pen and notebook from my bag and scribbled down the address. "When you get there ask for Mariana. I don't know who she is, but Dad does and she's either supposed to give you the artifact, or take you to whoever has it. Dad went through the details so fast that I didn't catch everything. Then he hung up and I can't call him, so I guess you'll find out what to do when you arrive."

We said goodbye and I flipped the telephone closed, setting it back on the console beside me. Marcel raised an eyebrow and said, "Okay?"

I shrugged. "Well, no" I replied. I explained that I had to get into the city of Tours before Claire. He nodded gravely, checked the time, and drummed his fingers on the steering wheel. Then he asked me for the address in Tours. As I read it out, he keyed it into the global positioning system box on the dashboard.

"Okay," he said, grinning at me. "We go."

CHAPTER 7

According to Marcel, it would take nearly an hour to reach Tours. The truck sped south on the A10 and I drew Neil's Bible from my bag and spread it open on my lap. One by one, I turned the crisp, dry pages with my fingertips, beginning again at Genesis, as I had that morning, and searching for more tiny red dots. The first dot appeared at Genesis 6:5. I leaned over the page and read, "And God saw that the wickedness of man was great in the earth, and that every imagination of the thoughts of his heart was only evil continually." This passage referred to the era before the flood. Again there was a mark beside verse thirteen, which read: "And God said unto Noah, The end of all flesh is come before me; for the earth is filled with violence through them; and, behold, I will destroy them with the earth."

A little further along, "And it came to pass after seven days, that the waters of the flood were upon the earth. In the six hundredth year of Noah's life, in the second month, the seventeenth day of the month, the same day were all the fountains of the great deep broken up, and the windows of heaven were opened." Funny, I had never before noticed the part about the fountains of the deep. But it said here that underwater springs and wells gushed forth, too, causing the earth to flood abruptly. A cataclysmic earthquake might cause that to happen, I surmised.

A small red dot pointed out Genesis 8, verse 2 which read, "The fountains of the deep and windows of heaven were stopped, and the rain from heaven was restrained." Why were the windows of heaven and the rains from heaven mentioned separately? Curious, I read on. After ten months, the ark ran aground on a mountaintop but there was not enough dry land for Noah and the family to leave the boat. It would take several more weeks before the ground was dry enough to disembark.

Marcel began to hum to himself. I glanced out the window at the passing vehicles, then went back to reading.

In chapter nine, there was a tiny red mark next to the ninth verse. "These are the three sons of Noah: and of them was the whole earth overspread." These small red marks must be there to tell me something about the stone blocks. But what? I studied the page again and in the reference column I found another notation. Matthew 24: 37.

Marcel turned on the radio. A voice shot from the speakers like machine gun fire, too fast to translate. He switched the channel, stopping at the sound of a bluesy female singer, then looked over at me and said, "Okay?"

I nodded. In the passage in Matthew, Jesus was speaking to his disciples, telling them about things to come. He said that as in the days before the flood, so would things be at the time of the end of the world. There would be eating and drinking, marrying and giving in marriage just like up to the day that Noah went into the ark. In Noah's day, the people had no clue that anything was going to change until suddenly the flood came like a tsunami and swept them all away.

Staring out the window at the passing landscape, I visualized how that must have happened. As we drove along, I saw a couple of women standing outside a tobacco shop in a village, a farmer ploughing a field, and a couple of schoolboys with backpacks, riding bicycles on a narrow road. Outside a local bar, big-bellied men drank beer at sidewalk tables. Life was probably not much different than this in Noah's days. For everyone to be lost, the flood must have erupted as an instant deluge. Everyone would have been caught unawares. If the flood had been just a steady downpour, some of those people would have had time to bang together a boat, throw some provisions in it, and wait for the waters to rise. But waters had gushed from above and below. Unless they had already prepared, no one could possibly be saved. No wonder all but Noah and his family perished. I had no idea what this all had to do with the stones but there had to be some connection or why would Neil have sent me the Bible?

As we drew closer to the city, the road widened and traffic was heavier. I closed the Bible and placed it back in my tote as we crossed over the Loire River. Shallow boats slid over its surface and a stiff breeze flicked the water into ruffled peaks. The sky had clouded over and now threatened rain. Flags snapped along the ramparts of the bridge as we rolled into the old centre of the city. My pulse quickened.

Marcel slowed the truck as we edged through traffic and merged left to turn onto a one-way street then passed through another intersection and found the Central Hotel. The building stood back from the street on a semi-circular drive, attractively lined with flowering shrubs on either side of the glassed main entrance. Over the portico, three flags flew against an imposing, white façade. Marcel pulled in against the curb down the street from the hotel entrance and switched off the ignition.

"Okay," he said, hopping out. I grabbed my handbag and jumped out, too. We could just see the entrance to the hotel through the shrubs lining the street and were about to set off when we saw the black sedan manoeuvre onto the circular drive. Claire and her companion leapt out of the car, slammed the doors, and ran to the hotel entrance.

"Marcel, look," I whispered, grabbing his sleeve.

Crouching low, we both took off toward the hotel. Even if Claire got to Dr. Diederich first, she was not going to get away with snatching this stone from under my nose. It belonged to my uncle and I meant to get it. From behind the shrubs, we peered through the glass entrance and watched the two disappear into the elevator. When the doors slid closed, I yanked the front door open and ran to the front desk.

"Dr. Diederich," I demanded. The desk clerk, balding and middle-aged man, eyed me impassively.

"*Chambre* 312," he replied, "*le troisieme étage.*"

"Third floor," I said. "Let's go, Marcel."

"Wait!" Marcel pulled me away from the counter and into a seating area where tall windows looked out on a pretty garden. "We need a plan."

We deduced that Claire probably believed she had lost me, since she would assume I did not know the pick-up location in Tours. Marcel and I agreed to let Claire meet with Dr. Diederich upstairs, then when she came back down the elevator with the stone we would make our move. A pair of potted palms stood on either side of the elevator doors. I felt like I was acting in a two-bit detective show as Marcel and I concealed ourselves behind the foliage and waited. I hefted my tote bag over my shoulder. Inside it were Neil's Bible, an apple, my journal, the stone artifact, a language dictionary, plus a makeup bag and a wallet heavy with French coins. In a few minutes, the numbers above the elevator indicated its descent. My pulse began to race and I flung a quick, silent prayer to God, "Please help me make this count."

The elevators doors jerked open. Through the palm fronds I could see Marcel crouched and ready to spring.

Claire exited first, looking over her shoulder at her companion. She was laughing. *Smug cow,* I thought. *You're in for a surprise.* As the doors of the elevator closed and the two strode into the lobby, Marcel lunged. With one swift blow, he lambasted Claire's companion across the back of the head. The man sprawled into a small table and metal chairs in the breakfast area, sending the furniture flying, and landed with a thud, face down on the tile floor.

Claire let out a little shriek and spun around. On her face, a look of recognition then shock was followed by pure loathing. She whirled and headed for the door but before she could take two steps, I swung my tote bag over my shoulder. My bag struck her squarely on the side of her head. She screeched and staggered sideways, dropping her purse. When it hit the floor, the clasp popped open and out rolled a little stone wrapped loosely in tissue. Claire wobbled onto one knee and tried to push herself back to her feet, grabbing for the stone.

"Oh, no you don't," I snarled. Planting my foot squarely on her rump, I shoved with all my might. She collapsed on the floor. Marcel grabbed a nearby armchair and placed it on top of her, pinning her down. While I scooped up the stone, he leapt over Claire's legs and ran for the door. I heard Claire's companion moan as I clutched the stone in my fist and raced after Marcel.

A light rain had started, dampening the pavement. By the time I yanked the truck door open and threw myself up into the high seat, Marcel had already started the engine. He rammed the gearshift, jerked the steering wheel, and we surged into the traffic, barrelling down the busy street. As we rounded the corner, I stole a look back toward the hotel. I saw Claire run outside and her friend stumble after her holding his head. I grinned as she stomped her feet. Shaking her fists, she screamed at her companion, her face turning an unhealthy shade of purple. Then she smacked him on the shoulder and ran for the car door. He lurched for the passenger door and jumped in just before she spun out of the concrete driveway and turned our way.

Marcel cranked the wheel, taking the next right turn, and the truck swayed to a stop behind a girl on a yellow scooter. Leaning to my right, I stared into the rear-view mirror and watched for the black sedan. In a moment, the traffic began to move and the truck ground forward. On the street behind us, I saw the black sedan roar straight past the corner and disappear. Marcel saw it too.

"They didn't turn," I said, glancing over at him.

"Okay," he replied, flashing a wide grin at me as he stomped on the gas pedal. "No problem."

CHAPTER 8

A chilly wind licked at my face and bare hands and whipped a lock of hair across my cheek. Shivering, I tucked my jacket collar close around my neck and jammed my hands into my pockets as the sun slid below a stand of cypress trees edging the tracks, turning the sky lavender and gold. When Marcel insisted on dropping me at the train station in Narbonne, across town from his depot, I accepted gratefully. After setting my suitcase on the pavement, he surprised me with a hug and kissed both my cheeks.

"*Au revoir, Madame*," he said, smiling down at me. "God bless."

I caught the first train out of Narbonne bound for the Spanish frontier. Forty-five minutes later I was in Perpignan. Now I waited for the night train to Madrid which was supposed to arrive at 7:21 the following morning. A warm bowl of soup and thick chunks of bread purchased at a dingy little café across the street had warmed me a little but I was looking forward to boarding the train.

Light flashed across my face then I plunged back into darkness. Humming, tapping, a flash of light then black again. I flung an arm over my eyes and slid away into sleep again, into some velvet place as soft as a coat pocket. A picnic table stood on my back lawn and Julia was there in the twilight, wearing a yellow dress and asking why there was no mayonnaise. I tried to tell her that I would get some from the kitchen but suddenly bright streaks of light stabbed through the thick gloom and penetrated my eyelids. I hovered on the edge of the dream, then reluctantly swam into blurry wakefulness. Squinting, I rolled over and groaned. Pain stabbed my hip and my right arm prickled from the shoulder down and when I stretched it out to ease the kink I touched something soft and warm. Turning my head, I shielded my eyes from the brightness.

A child lay sleeping on a bench seat opposite me. My fingertips had brushed her cheek. She stirred, soft pink lips opening in a little sigh, and rolled onto her back, her dark hair falling away from a beatific face. Suddenly, it came back to me. I was on a train, sharing a compartment with two Spanish women and their children.

I glanced around the compartment. The women and a small boy also slept, their bodies draped over the seats like last night's laundry. Sitting up, I checked my watch. It was early, just past five o'clock. Through the grimy windows, mountains thrust upward against a deep blue sky and between gashes in the rock I could see winding rivulets of murky water far below. The train wheels clattered over a trellis then plunged into the roaring inky blackness of a tunnel before bursting again into the morning light.

I shook out my sweater, rolled it into a soft pillow again and closed my eyes. My arm was no longer asleep, but my hip still ached and I pressed the heel of my hand into the sore spot and drifted back to sleep, this time dreaming about eating spaghetti at a little restaurant with Roger.

After Roger died, I dreamed of him often, sometimes several times a night. In spite of the sleeping pills that my doctor had prescribed, I woke frequently, my pillow wet with tears and my blankets in knots. Anguish and bitter grief consumed me but some dreams came as gifts. One dream in particular I remember vividly. I was sitting on a picnic blanket in a mountain meadow. The sun warmed my face and bees buzzed in the wildflowers all around me. The hike back down the mountain was a long one and I would have to leave as soon as the afternoon light had begun to fade into the purples of evening. As I placed the dishes and left-over food into the backpack cooler, I became aware of someone near me and turned to see Roger standing there. Leaping to my feet, I ran to him and flung my arms around his neck, kissing his cheeks and his mouth and crying, "Oh, Roger, you've come back, you've come back! I have missed you so. Where have you been?"

Roger put his hands on my shoulders "I can't stay, Jill," he said looking into my eyes. "I'm sorry."

"But why, Roger?" I cried. "The children miss you so much. We need you to come back."

"I'm with Him now," he replied.

"Who?"

He glanced over his right shoulder. Farther up the meadow I saw another figure waiting, dressed in jeans and a white tunic-style shirt. I could just make out the expression on his face and I gasped at the deep tenderness I saw there.

"Is that Jesus?" I whispered.

"Yes," Roger had replied. "He let me come to tell you I'm alright. Everything will be fine. I can't come back, even though I miss you, too. But you will be okay. He will look after you. Tell the children that I love them."

"Don't go," I cried in desperation. "Don't leave again."

"It's okay," Roger said, stroking my cheek. "He will look after everything. Don't worry."

Then the dream began to unravel, paling as sleep disappeared like a vapour and I found myself suddenly awake as though someone had nudged me. I even sat up and looked around me, thinking that one of the children had come into the room to shake me awake. But there was no one there, only the faint glow of moonlight filtering through the blinds. I lay back down and closed my eyes, willing myself back to sleep and into the dream, but it would not return.

From that night on, the sorrow had begun to subside, its stinging knife-edged pain dulling a little more with each passing day. I began to pray again with thanksgiving and hope rather than crying in agony as I so often had. The children, too, had from that night, seemed to rise from the gloom of grief. Laughter began again, and Tim's silly sense of humour emerged from wherever it had gone the day Roger died. A miracle had taken place.

The train rocked and rattled around a bend in the track, flinging me away from the window and banging my head back against the pane like a swift punch. The jolt also wakened the little girl who sat up and blinked. Then she lay back down in the other direction, stuck her thumb in her mouth and fell asleep again. I took a drink of water from the bottle in my bag. We would be in Atocha station in Madrid soon.

Forty minutes later I sat in the back of a worn-out taxi; the only one I could find whose driver spoke English. At least, he said he spoke English, and though his proficiency exceeded Marcel's, he still had a lot of vocabulary gaps. I peered through the window and a blanket of pollution up a main thoroughfare in Madrid. I had no idea where Mariana's address was but the driver had assured me that he would take me there by the most direct route.

We crept through the city streets, finally drawing up in front of a tall, stuccoed building on a tiny square. A tinkling fountain stood in its centre and two small girls in brightly-coloured cotton dresses stopped skipping rope to stare as the taxi pulled to a stop. I checked the house number again, then got out and knocked on the heavy wooden door. One of the children said something.

"Señora," the driver told me, "this lady, she not home now. You come here. She over here." He pointed across the square to a blue door. "You want I go now, Señora?"

"Please wait a moment," I answered. One of the little girls grabbed my hand and pulled me toward the door. The heavy iron knocker struck the door with a sharp clack that split the still morning air like a whip. After a moment a woman pulled the door open and stepped into the sunlight. She was in her mid-thirties, short and round with sparkling black eyes. I heard the taxi driver inhale.

"Mariana?"

"*Sí.*"

"Neil Bryant sent me," I said.

Her hands flew to her head and she screamed, jumped up and down, and spun around, jabbering in Spanish.

"So sorry," she said finally. "I be waiting for you." She grabbed my hand and kissed both of my cheeks then waved at the taxi driver and said, "Shoo. *Salga de aquí.*"

He poked me on the shoulder with a stubby finger. "You pay now, Señora."

"Yes, *sí*," I said. I fished around in my tote for the amount that we had agreed upon and placed the rumpled bills in his hand. He eyed it pitifully. "Okay, okay," I muttered, peeling off another bill and handing it to him.

"*Gracias,* Señora," he said with a lisp. He hopped into his aged vehicle, took a spin around the fountain, and tore off down the narrow street, leaving my suitcase standing on the cobblestones. When the children saw it, they rushed to bring it to me, fighting over who would pull the handle, then dragged it, bumping along, to the house on the opposite side of the square.

"So, so, Señora," Mariana said, stepping out of the doorway. "You must come to my house now." We crossed the square and entered a dark hallway. After everything I had been through in Paris, all that had happened with Claire and Marcel, the night on the train, and the taxi ride, I had found the right place. Now perhaps I would be able to learn from Mariana when this escapade might end and when I could go home again. A wave of relief washed over me and it felt wonderful.

I only wish that the feeling had lasted little longer.

CHAPTER 9

A lazy fly buzzed past my arm and landed on the table next to a plate of sweet cakes that lay warming in the sun. I flicked my hand at it and watched as it lifted off, made a slow circle over the table top and landed on the other side of the plate. This time I waved it away for good.

Mariana had gone into the kitchen to make more tea, leaving me sitting alone except for the two little girls who had been in the square when I arrived. They had insisted on coming to play in the courtyard to make sure they didn't miss anything. Each child held a scruffy, well-loved doll beneath an arm and took turns jumping over a rope tied to a door handle while sneaking glances at me.

The bones of the wicker chair pressed into my back as I looked around me. After I had come into the house through the front door, Mariana had led me through a dark hallway and out into the blinding sun of the small interior courtyard. The day had already become hot and I fanned myself with a napkin as I waited for Mariana to return, but the telephone had rung and I now heard her chatting with the caller.

The relative quiet of the courtyard settled around me like down. I hadn't slept nearly enough on the train from the French frontier. I had hoped to see some of the passing scenery before the light faded, but by the time we pulled out of the station at the border it was too late to see much more than lights twinkling in the dark.

On the train I had purchased a bottle of water, a crusty roll filled with sliced meats and a factory-made, packaged apple dessert which I tossed out after a few bites. I slipped off my shoes and curled my legs up into my seat, pulled Neil's Bible from my bag and began again to search for his clues.

Opening the book in my lap, I had turned the pages one by one. My notebook and pen lay beside me on the seat and I made notes as I leafed through the Bible. In some instances there was only a small red dot, other places had certain words circled. I made a mental note to watch for patterns that might be revealed by the different markings.

I came across markings in the tenth chapter of Genesis. The text recounted the building of the tower of Babel, how the people believed that they were so smart and technologically advanced that they could build a tower and get to heaven whenever they wanted to. Unfortunately for them, God had other ideas. Because the people all spoke the same language it was easy for them to collaborate on the project so God simply changed their languages so they could no longer understand each other. Confusion reigned and the plan fell apart. It seemed like the salient point Neil had emphasized was that these people already had some pretty advanced abilities.

Now in Mariana's garden, with the sun warm on my face, my mind slid into a heat-daze and I had nearly dozed off when she sashayed back out into the courtyard, her green dress swirling around her legs. She plopped down in the sagging wicker chair opposite me and flung an arm across her forehead.

"Oh, my goodness, my goodness," she exclaimed. "Just when you think everything is good, she goes wrong. What am I going to do?"

Startled by this drama, I said, "What is it? What's wrong?"

"*De nada*," she sighed, waving a hand over her head. "It is my mother. She wants to come and stay with me, but she doesn't want to sleep in the bed we have. So she wants to bring her own bed, but wants to keep it at home, too. This is impossible. She can't have her bed at home and here, too!"

I tried to appear concerned, but the situation didn't seem particularly earth-shattering to me.

"I don't know what to do with her. Now she is by herself, my papa is gone. She phones me every hour. I know she is lonely, but my goodness, I have other things to do. Now she wants to come and stay but not come and stay, but she wants her own bed at her house and at my house. She doesn't want to live alone, but she thinks it is too busy at my house for her. The children make too much noise, but she's lonely without them."

"Your mama," I said gently, "where does she live?"

"Across the square!"

"Pardon?"

"You know the house across the street where you came first?" I nodded. "She lives over there." She flung out her arm toward the tiny square. Then she grabbed her head and wailed.

I bit my lip and tried not to chuckle. Mariana tilted her head and looked at me, then laughed.

"You are a smart lady, I think," she said. "What should I do with my mother?"

I thought for a moment. "Maybe she just wants to know that she is not forgotten, that she is still important to someone. It's probably not about the bed so much as just needing to be heard."

"Yes," Mariana said. "That's true. I will keep talking to her. And maybe I'll even get her a new bed for when she wants to come and stay at my house. Would you like more tea?"

I declined. "Can you tell me why I'm here?"

"Oh my goodness!" she cried, slapping her forehead. "I have forgot already why you have come here." She took a deep breath and blew it out, flattening her skirt with the palms of her hands. "There is someone you must meet. He is Señor Profesor Augusto de Alvarez y Delgado. He was my father's best friend and long-time college, no collaguy, oh, what is that word?"

"Colleague?" I offered.

"*Si, si.* Augusto is my father's colleague for many, many years. For decades they work together at the Museo Arqueologico Nacional here in Madrid. Augusto, Profesor de Alvarez, he is a wonderful man, and so smart. He knows everything about Mexico and Guatemala, all the history and geography. And he and my father also work one time in Mexico with your uncle, Doctor Neil. Then Doctor Neil, he comes here and stays with my father and my mother, right there across the square. I was young then, maybe sixteen. I love your uncle so much. He is such a sweet man," she sighed, pressing her clasped hands to her breast.

I nodded, "Please go on."

"Profesor de Alvarez, he is at the Museo. You must see him today. He is waiting for you now." She twisted the silver watch on her wrist and studied the time. "*Si,* now is good. I will call a taxi for you and this taxi he will take you to see Augusto for whatever you need to see him for.." She looked sharply at me. "No one has told me anything, why you come here, why you must see Augusto. I only get a call from Doctor Neil yesterday asking me to have you at my house and help you see Augusto." She paused. I said nothing. "Of course, I say yes! You can stay here with me and Paulo as long as you want to, or with Mama. She has a big empty house now. Maybe you tell me why your uncle has you to come here, I can help more..."

I shook my head and spread my hands in a gesture of helplessness.

She sighed. "Okay, okay, I stop snoping."

"Um, I think you mean snooping," I corrected.

Mariana grinned. "Okay, I stop snooooping. Anyway, I go now to telephone Profesor de Alvarez and you wait here. Have more to eat, tea, whatever you want, and I get a taxi and talk to him to take you to see my friend. Then when you finish, you come back here and stay with me and Paulo and Isabella.

My son, Oliver, is on holiday with his friend, so now it's more quiet. Okay?"

"Okay." It sounded like a good plan to me.

Mariana rose and went into the house. By now, the sun was almost directly overhead and heat beat down upon me. I picked up my chair and moved it into the shade, sat down again and rested my head against the top of the backrest. Everything was moving too fast. I felt like I had accidently stepped into a flooding river and been carried away like a piece of flotsam, not knowing where I might land next or even if I would make it out alive.

Twenty minutes later, after I had taken a quick shower, pinned up my hair against the rising temperature of the day and changed into fresh clothes, I stood waiting by the fountain outside while Mariana gave the taxi driver instructions.

"Don't give him any more than seventeen Euros, twenty tops. These taxi drivers they are what you call highway robberies."

At the Calle de Serrano, I stepped from the cab and walked through a pair of iron grillwork gates. The imposing façade of the Museo Arqueologico Nacional rose before me, the wide flight of stone steps leading to the entrance, flanked by a pair of winged creatures, part bare-breasted woman, part lion, and part warrior. A statue of the artist, Diego Velasquez, sculpted in white marble, but now blackened by soot and pollution stood next to the entrance, his painter's palette resting along his forearm, and one foot crossed over the other. In voluminous breeches, a fitted waistcoat with split sleeves, and beribboned shoes, he dressed up a lot more for painting than I ever had. At the opposite side of the entrance, the figure of the Spanish sculptor, Alonso Berruguete, stood dressed in a simple smock, vest, and baggy marble stockings.

The heels of my shoes clicked on the marble floor tiles as I entered the building. Inside, the interior was bright and cool and the long galleries were fitted out with minimalist glass cases containing pottery bowls and jugs, clay oil lamps, cloudy glass pitchers and vases, and ancient stone and wooden tools. In the centre of an open area, I stopped briefly to look at the famous Lady of Elche sculpture in a glass cube, staring with heavy-lidded, unseeing eyes out from between the twin wheels of her incredible headdress.

Drawing Mariana's scribbled note from my pocket, I followed its directions to Profesor Alvarez's office, using the map I had picked up at the front entrance. As I walked, I prayed, *God please protect me and guide me in this meeting. Help me to hear your voice and understand what it is that you want me to do.*

Pushing through a steel door, I entered a smaller hallway lined with offices. Alvarez's door was the third on the right. I rapped on it with my knuckles and heard a muffled reply so went in. The room looked like the anteroom for a suite of offices. It had a large mahogany desk in the centre and rows of filing cabinets against the walls.

A man, about my height but with at least twenty years on me, came toward me smiling, and reached for my hand. "Señora Moss, I presume," he said in a deep, rich voice.

"Señor Profesor Alvarez?" I inquired, unsure which title was correct.

"Please," he replied, "call me Augusto. I know that your uncle, Neil Bryant, would insist on it and so do I. I feel that I know you almost as part of my family already, so great is my love and esteem for your uncle."

"Then please call me Jill."

"Gladly. Now please come with me into my office and we shall have a drink and a little talk. My secretary is away today as are my colleagues, so we have the place to ourselves. I am so happy you are here."

I followed Profesor Alvarez into a small office and glanced out the windows to an inner courtyard clearly suffering from neglect. A few scruffy bushes clustered around a pool filled with murky, green water. *Too bad this isn't a natural history museum,* I thought. *Biologists would have a field day with that ecosystem.*

"Thank-you, Augusto," I replied as he offered me a seat in a worn, green leather chair. I sat down, dropping my heavy tote on the floor beside my feet and pushing it under the edge of my seat with my heel.

Profesor Alvarez poured coffee for both of us, then sat down behind an old wooden desk opposite me. I saw him unlock and open the desk drawer in front of his body and draw out a small object. Holding it gingerly in his fingertips, he looked at me and smiled slightly.

"I assume that this is what you are here for?"

Between his fingers perched another stone, similar to the ones in my bag right now, yet even from this distance, I could see that the markings were different. I reached out my hand to take it from him, but he stopped me. "Not just yet," he said, slipping the stone back into the drawer and closing it, but not turning the key in the lock. "Don't worry," he said. "I will give it to you. But first there is something I want to show you." He rolled his chair away from the desk and stood up. One by one, he closed the blinds on the windows, blocking the view from the courtyard and the windows on its opposite side, and plunging the room into semi-darkness. Profesor Alvarez placed the palms of his hands on the desk and leaned toward me.

"My dear, Señora Moss," he said. "What I am about to reveal to you may change everything about your quest." He paused and straightened up, his eyes grave. "In fact," he said, "it may even change the whole history of the world as we know it and the future of the world as we perceive it might be. Are you ready for that?"

I swallowed and stood to my feet. "I hope so."

CHAPTER 10

A dark, solid wood table stood against the wall next to the door where I had entered the office of Profesor Augusto de Dalgado y Alvarez. Stacks of papers, books, and peculiar artifacts lined the wall and a heap of rolled maps and charts lay on a cleared space in the centre. Augusto stood beside me with a large magnifying glass in his hand.

"This map is a copy of one by a Turk named Piri Reis." He smoothed out the curled edges of the heavy paper copy and set books on each of the four corners to hold it flat. "The original was drawn on gazelle skin in 1513 A.D. and was signed by the cartographer, Piri Reis, who was an Ottoman Turk admiral and general. He claims that he created it using a variety of documents from much earlier times. It was found in the Topkapi Palace in Istanbul in 1929, the year the building was converted into a museum. Regardless of his method, the degree of accuracy is remarkable." The map fragment depicted the west coasts of Europe and Africa, complete with rivers and geographical features, plus the Atlantic coastline of both North and South America. The cartographer had also included pictures of animals, some common ones like an elephant and other fanciful ones like a six-horned beast too indistinct to make out and a dog dancing with a monkey. People in various poses decorated the land masses.

Profesor Alvarez went on. "As you can see, the cartographer made copious notes regarding his map, unfortunately for us, written in his own language. What you see here is just a fragment of the work that he did to map the whole world. Including the maps drawn by Columbus, he used between twenty and thirty-four others to create his world survey."

I leaned over the map. "What do these circles represent?" I asked, pointing to a large, decorated ring in the centre of the north Atlantic from which numerous lines radiated. It had an exact twin in the south Atlantic.

"This represents a method of determining mathematical measurements using spherical trigonometry. The focal point is in Egypt."

"I see." I didn't really, not ever having studied anything as esoteric as spherical trigonometry. The interesting thing about this map, Alvarez told me, is that Piri Reis claims that he also used several maps from much earlier epochs. Evidently there are many maps and geographical surveys dating back to almost 4500 B.C. that survived until into the sixteenth century. They are credited to the Chinese, Japanese, Norse, and other people groups who were travelling and charting the whole world long before Columbus sailed the ocean blue. He pulled another map from the bottom of the pile. "This is called the Zauche map, which was created in 1737 and shows Antarctica."

"Wait a minute," I said. "I thought the existence of Antarctica was not even verified until sometime in the nineteenth century, and you're saying that this map was created in 1737. How could that be?"

"Good question. Not only does this map show the continent, but it is mapped completely free of ice. It is shown as two islands separated by a strait, as you can see here." He drew a stubby finger over the surface of the paper, delineating the coastline of the islands. "What's fascinating is that the fact there are two islands was not established in our time until 1968."

I frowned. "Are you telling me that the map is the product of a time before the ice-age?"

Augusto shrugged. "That's what it looks like, but studies are not conclusive." He pulled another chart from the pile and laid it on top of the Zauche map, pressing down the rolled edges. It showed a photo of what looked like a slab of stone with rivers, tributaries, irrigation canals, huge dams, and mountains carved in relief. "I think you will also find this interesting," he said. "This is a photo of an artifact discovered in 1999 by a Doctor of Physical and Mathematical Science, Professor Alexandr Chuvyrov of Bashkir State University in Russia. What you see here is an ancient relief map of the Ural region northeast of Moscow, which was found under the step of someone's house."

"How old is this map?"

"It is not really known, but it has been suggested that it is somewhere between three thousand years and one hundred million years old."

"That's a pretty big spread."

"No matter what scientists would have us believe, there really is no fail-safe method of dating ancient artifacts. I will say, though, that it has been agreed that the creation of this piece could only have been done from the perspective of high in the atmosphere. Today's military only now has maps such as this. There are also inscriptions on it that have never been deciphered. That means they could be of a language not currently known in the modern world." Profesor Alvarez stepped away from the table. "Let me show you something else," he said, pulling open the top drawer of a nearby filing cabinet and lifting out a compact portfolio. He laid it on the table and spread it open, then began flipping through sleeves of photos taken of various stone artifacts and archaeological dig sites. "Ah," he said, "here it is." He pushed the portfolio toward me. The photo was of a rock wall covered with primitive paintings in black, rust red, and ochre, featuring figures of round-bellied, four-legged animals and spear-wielding hunters. The opposite page sleeve contained another photo of similar figures in different poses. I failed to see the connection and said so.

"This is a recent discovery from Peru," he explained. "These inscriptions have been dated at approximately six thousand years old and were found in caves at an altitude of twenty-seven hundred meters above sea-level." He paused for effect. "Now, take a look at this one." He turned the page and I saw a photo of a semi-circular plaza of some sort, dug into clay or stone. Several people stood around the excavated area which extended beyond the edge of the photo. "This is another recent discovery in Peru, in the same region as the Nazca lines. I'm sure you are familiar with those." I nodded. The Nazca lines have been a source of mystery and speculation for centuries. Carved into the surface of desert sand in the high, dry mountain plateaus of Peru, these approximately three hundred figures, in straight lines like aircraft runways, geometrical shapes, pictures of animals such as a monkey, a spider and a hummingbird, are clearly visible - but only from the air.

"The Nazca lines have been dated at 5500 B.C. Do you know that's older than the pyramids in Egypt?" I could hear the excitement in his voice but still wasn't clear on where he was heading with this information. He must have read my thoughts.

"Jill, according to Bible scholars, the flood took place around the year 2304 B.C. They arrived at that date using information contained in the scriptures, genealogies, and ages of people. That means these recent finds pre-date the flood."

"I see," I answered, wanting more.

He smiled. "There are many different theories as to the origin of mankind on the earth, including everything from Darwin's theory, which is accepted as truth in many scientific quarters, to creation theory, which is believed to be truth by most religious communities." He shook his head. "No one knows exactly how it all came about. I'm inclined to believe in God and his story, since I am a believer as well as a scientist. I have to admit that it amazes me sometimes the lengths to which some researchers will go to avoid considering that there is a God who originally created the earth. Anyway, I won't go into that or you would be here all week listening to me drone on." He closed the book of photos and slipped it back into the cabinet. "Come. Sit down again, my dear."

He pulled open the desk drawer and took out the stone block, setting it lightly on the blotting pad before him. "This little artifact is still a mystery. As I'm sure you can see there is more than one type of language inscribed here on its sides." He turned the block so the widest part faced me. "This figure here," he said, indicating that side with the tip of a pen, "is not of the same language as this figure." He tipped the block so I could view the top of it. "And it's not the same as this side either," he continued, turning it so its bottom showed. "I believe what we have here is a translation stone. Unfortunately, ancient languages are not my specialty but it appears to be that one side shows figures from ancient Maya and the other looks to be Olmec in origin. These peoples populated the same areas around the same time period so it could easily be that this artifact depicts both their languages. The third side, however, is nothing like the others at all. If I were guessing, I would say it is either Hebrew or Gaelic. How many did you say there were of these?"

"I didn't."

"Would you mind telling me? No, never mind. It does not matter. I will let your uncle have his secrets, though I must admit that I am consumed with curiosity. This is the bane of the true archaeologist. I will ask, though, if you have any others like this that I might see."

I hesitated. There was nothing about Profesor Alvarez that made me uneasy but I looked away for a moment, mentally checking with the Holy Spirit and my own spirit to decide if showing him the other stones in my possession was wise. Instantly, I felt the calm assurance that I had nothing to fear. "Yes," I said, "I have two others." I pulled them from my bag, carefully removing the layers of tissue, and passed them across the desk.

He lined them up to form a slight curve. "I don't think these go together like this." He switched the arrangement several times and looked at them from varying angles. "My guess is that there are many more and that they fit in with these, but these three are not mates." He handed them back to me. "Take good care of them, my dear. I'm sure they are of great significance. I hope you will be so kind as to keep me informed as the mystery unfolds." He stood to his feet and held out his hand. "I wish I could ask you to stay longer, but alas, I have a meeting soon and must make some preparations before I attend."

I shook his hand as I rose to my feet.

"Oh," he exclaimed. "I nearly forgot. You are to visit with Mariana again today, are you not?" I nodded. "Your uncle asked me to tell you that you must take time to visit her mother, Señora Jimenez."

By the time I walked out of the building it was well past noon. Sweat trickled down my back in the hot sun. The national library occupied the other half of the museum building and faced a busy street, on the far side of which I could see a restaurant under the trees in a small park. I crossed the street and found a tiny table tucked in the shade, then ordered lunch. I slid my tote bag between my feet. The maps and photos that Profesor Alvarez had shown me, though fascinating, produced more questions than answers. So what if the cave drawings had been created before the flood? Did their location high in the mountains mean that the flood waters did not reach them, and therefore had not washed them away? If that were so, why was it significant and what did it have to do with the stones in my bag?

Two hours later I lifted the knocker on Mariana's door. No sound came from the interior of the house. I was alone except for a ginger cat sunning herself on the cobblestones. I raised the heavy iron door-knocker once more and let it fall against the solid, dark wood and pulled the map from the museum out of my bag and fanned myself as I waited.

Across the square, a door opened. I turned to find a small lady standing there eyeing me with a steady gaze. "You," she said. "You Neil Bryant girl?"

"*Sí.*"

She motioned for me to come. I stuffed the map back in my tote and crossed the square. She opened her door wider, reaching for my arm and drawing me into the cool shadows of the house. Her black hair, only lightly streaked with strands of grey, was pulled back into a thick knot at the base of her neck. She wore a blue linen dress and leather sandals. I guessed her to be around seventy.

"You are the *madre* of Mariana?" I asked.

"*Sí, sí,*" she said, nodding vigorously. "I Señora Jimenez." Pulling me into a small sitting room she indicated a large armchair for me to sit down in, and patted my shoulder. Then she seated herself in a small wooden rocking chair on the other side of the room. "My *ingles* is no so good," she said, folding her manicured hands in her lap. "My Señor Neil, he is good?"

I shook my head. "Not so good now," I said slowly. "I do not know where he is. I have not seen him for many months. Profesor Alvarez said I must come and see you. He had a message from my uncle."

"Oh. Señor Neil has send me gift. Is for you." She sprang from her chair and ran from the room. I looked around. A blue and red patterned Persian rug covered most of the tiled floor and a wide window looked out onto a little interior courtyard where bougainvillea tumbled over trellises. Across the room from where I sat, a small fireplace against the wall held a vase of fresh daisies in the hearth. Next to the rocking chair on a pedestal table covered by a lace doily sat a framed photo of one of the little girls I had seen this morning. A pastel-green, slip-covered settee sat to one side of the fireplace and another small table near my elbow was covered with an exquisite, antique lace cloth. All in all, it was a charming room.

Señora Jimenez re-entered carrying a tray with coffee and a plate of fancy bakery cookies. Beside the cookies lay a bulky padded shipping envelope.

"So," she said, placing the tray on the table next to my chair. "We have coffee and you take this…" she handed me the envelope. "Your uncle put letter in. I have Mariana read for me. It say I keep this for you and you come."

I thanked her and pulled open the envelope, turning it upside down over my lap. Out plopped number four in the set of sixteen stone blocks.

"What is this?" She looked intently at the block in my hand. "I think it must be secret stone. Why he send to me?"

I lifted my shoulders in a shrug. "I don't know. Señor Neil told me it is important for me to come and get this. So I came."

She laughed. "Men! They always say, 'Come here, go there, do this, do that'. And women? We do! We crazy." She shook her head as she poured coffee for me and I mentally kissed a good night's sleep good-bye. Señora Jimenez returned to her seat in the rocking chair. "Now," she said, settling her cup on the tiny table next to her, "You tell me all about yourself."

Our lively conversation covered topics that included the European Economic Community and its effect on Spanish politics, her now-deceased husband's relationship with my uncle, Mariana's job as an accountant for a plumbing firm, and her grandchildren. Señora Jimenez told me that she had had a long career in an architectural firm, was almost the sole parent for her three children while her husband was off around the world on archaeological digs, and had been widowed, like I had, for a couple of years.

Our discussion was interrupted by the arrival of a motorcycle outside, followed by a loud rapping at the door. Señora Jimenez threw her hand to her forehead in a grand, dramatic gesture, muttered something I didn't catch, and rolled her eyes to the ceiling.

"What is it?" I asked, surprised.

"It's Marco," she answered, exasperated. "He must drive the moto," she said, rising from her chair. Before she reached the door, a man burst in, grabbed her in a bear hug and lifted her off her feet. The intruder spun into the room where I sat. When he saw me he said, "Oh," as he set the protesting lady carefully back on her feet. She cuffed him on the ear.

"Señora Moss," she said ceremoniously, "please to meet my son, Marco." Then she introduced me and took her seat at the far side of the room. Marco Jimenez stood before me grinning like a golden retriever. He was tall and dark. His eyes were the colour of dark Swiss chocolate. Black hair curled around his forehead and ears and a row of straight white teeth flashed from a dimpled smile. He stuck out his hand, said something in Spanish and tentatively leaned forward to give me the usual kisses on both cheeks, assuming, I suppose, that any friend of his mother's was a friend of his. When I pulled away, he turned to his mother and spat out a string of Spanish which I had no hope of following. She answered with a simple, "No."

"Please forgive me, Señora Moss," he said in perfect, slightly-accented English. "I did not realize that you speak no Spanish."

"Not very much, I'm afraid."

"Then it's settled. We will speak English." He turned and dropped into the settee, leaning back and stretching his long legs out into the middle of the room. I sank into my chair and picked up my coffee cup. Marco appeared to be around my age but had a slightly rakish look about him that reminded me of someone who might land the part of a pirate in a made-for-TV movie. I had always leaned more toward the collegiate, leather-elbow-patches, tweed jacket type, hair optional, but this man got my attention. He wore a blue striped shirt; open at the collar, jeans, and a pair of tan leather loafers with no socks. There was something familiar about him that I could not place. I drew in a deep breath and gave him a shaky smile.

CHAPTER 12

Slivers of faint pink light seeping between the shutter slats painted pearly streaks across the bedspread and the floor. The temperature in the room had already begun to rise. Rolling over in bed, I pushed the sheets down my body and looked around, my barely-awake mind fumbling through the experiences of the past few days, searching for a reference point to explain where I was at the break of day. The tiny room, plainly decorated with a single bed, a bedside table with a candlestick lamp on it, and a black wicker chair in the far corner, had a ceiling that followed the slant of the rooftop from which hung a peculiar leafy metal chandelier.

In a heartbeat, it came rushing back to me. I could hear the sounds of traffic moving through the city and people rushing off to work in the distance. Occasionally, a car sped by on the street at the end of the cul de sac, but nothing moved in the street or courtyard below my room. Reaching for my watch, I pushed the hair out of my eyes and sat up. It was five minutes after six o'clock.

Somewhere far away in the house I could hear a telephone ringing. A door opened and closed, and finally someone answered it. A few minutes later I heard footsteps on the stairs and tapping on the old wood of the door to the room where I lay.

"Come in."

It was Mariana. "So sorry to wake you so early," she apologized, "but there is a telephone call for you. You must come now." I swung my feet over the side of the bed and stood up, followed her down the stairs to the kitchen and picked up the receiver. My cousin Dennis was on the line.

"Hi, Jill," he called out. "How's it going over there?" I tried to calculate what time it must be in his zone and became confused, so gave up.

"Dennis, how did you know where to find me?"

"Never mind about that," he said, his tone becoming serious. "You've got to get out of there now. I've been in touch with the boss and he's found out a few things. Time to move on, and I mean right away."

"Okay, whatever you say. But where am I supposed to go? Can I go home soon?"

"Not a chance, cuz. The job's not finished. I'm going to send your instructions to Chicky. I need you to get in touch with her from a different phone and find out what I will tell her. We can't be too careful. She's only one time zone over from me, so now would be a good time to get her." Chicky was Dennis' nickname for my daughter, Julia.

"Dennis, it is six o'clock in the morning here. I'm in my pyjamas and I'm staying at the home of people I met only yesterday. I have no intention of running out on the street at this hour to look for a pay phone. Surely this can wait a couple hours, or at least until I've had a chance to get dressed and have a coffee."

"Sorry, kiddo," he said, not sounding the least bit apologetic. "Do what you have to do and get right on it. I don't think I need to remind you that my Dad is in a tough spot. We're all counting on you."

I ran my hand through my hair. "I'm sorry, Dennis. That was thoughtless of me. I'm barely awake, tired, hot, and confused. I've got what I came for so far, but it hasn't been easy."

"I'm sure it hasn't, but it's important, Jill. Now, more important than we both know."

A jolt of panic surged through me. "What does that mean?"

"I managed to talk to Dad a little while ago. I have no idea where he is, so don't ask. He sounded worried and you know that's not like him. I don't think he was in immediate danger, but he stressed the importance of gathering up the... stuff, as soon as possible. Time really is of the essence."

"Don't worry, Dennis. I'll get on it right away."

I said good-bye and hung up the phone. Mariana had been hovering around the kitchen making coffee and now she held out a steaming mug for me. "Thanks," I said, sinking into a chair and stirring cream into my cup. "I need to find a telephone that is not in this house," I said. "I wish I could tell you why, but I can't."

She reached across the table and patted my arm. "I know you can't. It's okay. My papa sometimes had big secrets, too." She took a sip of her coffee. "You can go across to Mama's house and use the telephone there. Would that work?"

"Yes, it would," I answered, "but I need to call right away." I looked down at my cotton pyjamas with yellow daisies and laughed. "After I get dressed, that is."

She waved her hand. "Just throw my trench coat over your pyjamas. I do it all the time. And don't worry about my mama. She gets up practically before God."

After a quick trip to the bathroom and running a brush through my hair, I headed out the door, coffee in hand, my pyjamas disguised by Mariana's black trench coat. Señora Jimenez opened the door before I could knock, and drew me inside. She was dressed in a red silk blouse, black dress pants, with a pair of red patent pumps. Her hair was rolled into a perfect knot at the back of her head and she already had her makeup on.

My daughter Julia answered after the second ring and began chattering as soon as she heard my voice, explaining that

Dennis had called her, hardly talked at all even though, she pointed out, she hadn't even seen him for three years and he never calls. He had insisted that she write down his every word, and read it back to him. Then he had abruptly hung up without even asking about anything that might be going on in her life. I mollified her by explaining that Dennis was likely calling from some remote location where he didn't have much time to talk.

"But what's going on, Mom? Where are you and why haven't you come home yet?" She sounded a little frantic.

"I don't think I should tell you exactly where I am, sweetie. It's important that no one know that right now. Your great uncle Neil is still in some kind of trouble and needs my help. I don't think it will take much longer." To be honest, I had no idea how much longer this wild chase would go on, but I didn't want to alarm Julia unnecessarily. "Now, I need you to tell me exactly what Dennis told you, and don't leave anything out."

Julia read the message, and word for word, I wrote it down in my journal then read it back to her to make sure that I had missed nothing. When I felt sure I had every detail down, I took a few minutes to ask Julia if she had found a dress to replace the one she'd hoped I would have sewn for her by now.

"Oh, that thing was cancelled," she said lightly. "The main speaker couldn't make it because of a conflict or something, so they called it off." *Thank goodness, I hadn't knocked myself out trying to sew new outfit for her,* I thought. I gave her some time to talk about herself then I told her I loved her and rang off. Placing the receiver back on the hook, I re-read the instructions I had written in my journal.

Barcelona. How was I going to get to Barcelona today? Leaning against the wall of Señora Jimenez's kitchen I mulled over the possible options. I could take the train or fly, but part of Dennis' instructions involved staying out of sight and not leaving a trail. That meant I couldn't rent a car either. If I couldn't fly, take the train, or rent a car, my remaining choices seemed to be to walk, steal a bicycle, or ride a donkey. Señora Jimenez came into the room, a watering can in her hand.

"So, Señora Moss," she said with a tender smile. "You are good today, *si*?"

I shook my head. "I have to go to Barcelona," I said, "and I have to go today. But I can't fly or take the train. I do not know how I will go there."

"Barcelona?"

"*Si.*"

Wait, she told me then she grabbed the telephone, punched in some numbers and patted my shoulder. A second later, she launched into a one-sided conversation with minor breaks punctuated by, *si, si, si*. Then she placed the receiver back on the cradle and turned to me.

"My son, Marco, you remember?" I nodded. How could I forget? "He go to Barcelona today, in his car."

I gaped at her. "Today?"

"*Si, si*. You dress now. He come here in one half hours." I couldn't believe my good fortune.

"Why is he going to Barcelona?" I enquired.

She gave me a sly smile. "To take you there," she replied.

"Oh no," I cried. "You can't mean that he is going just to drive me there."

"*Si, si*," she repeated, turning me around and marching me to the door. Before she pushed me out into the street, she gave me a big hug, a kiss on each cheek, and looked into my eyes. "Go with God," she said. "He will protect you." Then she shoved me bodily out the door and closed it behind me.

Mariana had a better explanation. It seemed that Marco worked for a company that sold restaurant equipment. He routinely travelled all over Spain and Portugal and even into the south of France and the U.K. Since he had just had a few days off, he was ready to hit the road again. Evidently, he had the option of choosing his own routes, so rather than go to Seville today and Barcelona at the end of the week, he just switched it around and decided to go to Barcelona today. I couldn't contain my relief. God had suddenly made a potentially difficult situation so easy for me. All I had to do was take a quick shower and get dressed. For some reason that I decided not to examine, I spent a few minutes extra with mascara and lipstick. I put on the only dress I had packed, a white sundress with a splashy fuchsia floral print. I slipped my feet into a pair of strappy silver sandals, added silver hoop earrings and a bracelet then threw the rest of my things into my bag. Twenty-five minutes later, I was waiting at the door for Marco to show up.

Down the street, a mo-ped raced past, and for a fleeting moment I had visions of tearing across Spain on the back of Marco's motorcycle, the wind making shreds of my hair and my skin looking like a bronc saddle by the end of the day. I sincerely hoped he had a car.

A few minutes later, a snappy little red sports car pulled into the street and stopped by the tinkling fountain. Isabella had wandered out of bed while I was getting ready and now she stood beside me on the doorstep as Marco leapt from the car. With a grand flourish, he swept into a gallant, deep bow. "Marco Alejandro Ibarra de Jimenez at your service, Señora," he announced. Then he spotted Isabella, "and Señorita," he added, blowing her a kiss.

I looked down to see Isabella's reaction to this little drama. She lifted one eyebrow, glanced up at me, then over at Marco who was still bowed over, rolled her eyes and said with an air of exasperated disgust, "*Hombres!*" Then she raised both her hands in a gesture that indicated that she considered her uncle and all his kind to be beyond hope and stomped into the house. I burst out laughing.

"I hope," Marco commented pitifully, "that you are not as jaded as my niece."

Before I could answer, Mariana appeared at the doorway carrying a large paper shopping bag. "I make a little something to eat for you," she said, pressing the handles of the bag into my hands. I nearly dropped it when the full weight of the "little something" fell to me. I peered into the top of the sack. Inside were several neat packages wrapped in foil and clear plastic. It looked like enough food to feed a Boy Scout troop for an entire weekend.

"Oh, Mariana," I protested. "This is too much. You didn't need to make anything for me. I can't possibly eat all this."

"Is not just for you," she said lightly. "I put something in for Marco, too. Maybe today you find a nice place, by a river maybe, you have a little picnic, just you and Marco." She glanced pointedly at Marco. I followed her look. Marco was pushing a pebble around with the toe of his loafer. Something funny had just happened, but I wasn't sure what. I searched Mariana's face for clues, but she threw her arms around me and gave me a warm hug. "I feel like you are my sister," she said standing back with her hands still on my shoulders. The beginning of tears had seeped into the corners of her eyes. "You must come back again and stay with me. Next time, for a long time, when all this, whatever it is, is over."

I smiled and nodded and we did the cheek-kissing routine, then she wiped her eyes with her fingertips and hollered at Marco to get my bags and hurry up about it. At least I think that's what she said, judging by how he leaped into action. Within moments the car was packed and we waved good-bye to Mariana. Her mother had also come out at the last minute and given Marco an earful before he slipped behind the steering wheel and closed his door. Whatever she said had something to do with me, but no one translated for me and I didn't ask.

Leaving this early in the day meant that we travelled against most of the traffic coming into the city, so the morning rush hour seemed surprisingly light. Sunlight, slanting through a thick layer of grey-yellow haze that clung to the contours of the buildings, lit up the window glass of apartments and offices that burst into flashes of light like firecrackers as we passed. We edged out of the old city centre where the main roads, lined with attractive buildings wearing facades from a bygone era, gradually gave way to plain and rather ugly apartment blocks. Kilometre after kilometre of drab apartment buildings, three, four, or five storeys high rose on both sides of the streets. Even in these areas trees grew and green lawns edged some of the buildings. Subdivisions farther out, constructed more recently, had been designed in an updated reflection of old Spanish architectural style and many were quite lovely.

Marco and I spoke little until we had cleared the most congested part of Madrid. Even though we had taken a freeway out of town, we had driven at least an hour before the congestion of the city gave way to small farms with groves of olive and orange trees. Dry sienna fields, fringed in last winter's yellow grasses, stretched away to the horizon over rolling hills punctuated by industrial developments and silt-brown, winding rivers.

I stole a look at Marco as he manoeuvred through the freeway traffic. One wrist rested on the top of the steering wheel and his other arm lay on the armrest, his fingertips just touching the bottom of the wheel. Sneaking a look from beneath my lashes, I allowed my gaze to linger on his face. Thick, black hair curled down the back of his head and onto his collar in soft wisps that begged to be wrapped around a finger. His skin, tanned and smooth, showed the faintest shadow of a blue-black beard, freshly shaven this morning. His lips curved in an ever-so-gentle smile at the corners. Dark sunglasses wrapped around his eyes and hid them from sight, but I suspected that their deep, chocolate brown could melt polar ice and with a fringe of black lashes, a sidelong glance was enough to send my senses into a spin. I could not shake the feeling that I had met him somewhere before.

Suddenly he spoke and startled me out of my admiring reverie. "How do you like my city?" he asked, glancing toward me.

I cleared my throat and looked out the front window of the car. "It's...it's lovely," I stammered. "Well, most of it is lovely," I said. "There are lots of apartment buildings, aren't there?"

He laughed. "Every Spaniard's dream is a little place in the country, but most will never have one."

"Where did you learn English?" I asked. "You have almost no accent."

"I spent a year studying English at Cambridge in England and another year working in New Zealand on a sheep ranch. I even spent a few months in Canada travelling across the country, followed by half a year in California surfing."

"You have been around," I commented lamely, feeling as tongue-tied as an adolescent at a high school dance.

The corners of his mouth curled up in a grin, which, to be honest, was not helping. "You could say that. I wanted to see the world before I settled down."

A rock hit the bottom of my stomach. *He's married,* I thought, *and probably has a bunch of kids, too.* Why this hadn't occurred to me sooner I don't know, but I chalked it up to being totally dazzled by his good looks.

"So now you're settled?" I asked weakly.

At this he laughed out loud. "I was for a while," he said. "I was married for seven and a half years before my wife decided that she preferred her boss to me. We never had any children. She kept saying that we could always have them later, but later never came." I thought I detected a trace of bitterness.

"I'm sorry."

"Don't be," he said. "She wasn't easy to live with anyway, though I turned myself inside out to make it work. Her name was Antonia and she had the privilege of growing up the only child of older, well-off parents. They denied her nothing and she expected that from me, too. I've been on my own for about ten years now."

I didn't know what to say so I said nothing. A few minutes passed then Marco turned to me. "What about you? Are you happily married with children?"

"I was married until my husband was killed a few years ago in a bicycle accident. I have two children who have now left home. Julia is twenty-two and works in Vancouver, and Timothy is nineteen and is currently somewhere in Asia. Nepal, last I heard."

"Your husband died!" Marco exclaimed as though he'd been punched in the chest. "How tragic! How terrible for you! I am so sorry, Señora Moss."

"Thank-you," I replied. "It was very difficult." I didn't want to talk about Roger or his death. "How long does it take to get to Barcelona?"

Marco hesitated. "It takes about five hours driving if we go straight through without stopping," he said, grinning. "But we will want to stop for lunch. After all, we have to eat all that food that Mariana prepared or she'll chew my ears off."

CHAPTER 13

The black and yellow wings of a butterfly lifted and fluttered in the sunshine as it kissed each fragrant, white blossom on a tiny bush that stood just out of my reach. Above where I lay, a scruffy pine tree, long needles rattling in the hot breeze, shaded me almost entirely. I knew that if I pulled my feet up, I could keep them out of the sun for a few more minutes but only until the earth rotated a little, then they would be exposed again. Given that I'd already slathered them with sunscreen, I left them, because I felt too lazy to move. Behind me, limestone mountains covered in dark evergreens rose up from the plains, their peaks reaching toward the shimmering sky, an empty blue pan except for strands of cloud, like pale chiffon scarves, that floated high above. If I squinted, I could just make out a pair of buzzards circling slowly on the updrafts. Near my head, bees worked the flowering shrubbery along the banks of a meandering stream.

The remains of Mariana's picnic lay scattered about on a yellow fleece blanket that Marco had produced from the trunk of his car. A small army of tiny ants, intent on carting away the crumbs, scrambled about on the soft surface. Marco had insisted on taking a detour off the main highway, claiming that he knew the perfect spot for a lunch stop. The switchback road wound up through the mountains, past a reservoir and over several rocky gorges before reaching a small village called Tosos.

Marco pulled the car off to the side of the road and grabbed the bag containing lunch, plus cold drinks he had purchased from a corner shop in the village, then led me through a thicket to the side of the stream. Officially called "El Mirador," which I found out by reading the sign when we crossed over the bridge in town, the little river flowed down the mountain slope on its way to the valley we could see far below. The view from our perch on the hillside spread out before us like a visual feast in the noonday sun. The dark green of the mountain slopes was broken here and there by dry patches where the land fell away in rocky folds punctuated by shrubs and thistle. Bright red poppies decorated the edges of small olive groves clinging to the slopes and farther on we could see the wide, green, valley bottom where it melted into the shimmer of the noonday haze.

Marco had spread out the blanket, explaining that he carried it in his car in case he felt sleepy on his road trips and the weather was cold enough that he might need the extra warmth. Inside the bag of goodies, Mariana had included a small blue-checked tablecloth along with bread, cheese, fresh tomatoes, as well as cold wedges of *"tortilla de patatas,"* a kind of potato quiche without the crust. She had also included more sumptuous treats like marinated shrimps, tiny sausages, artichokes, fish, and cheese. Marco produced all of these delicacies with a flourish as though serving a queen, and indeed, made me feel like one. China plates and silverware, lacy cloth napkins and fragile goblets completed the meal. It was lovely.

With everything spread out before us, we settled into enjoying our banquet under the pines. In the shade of the tree, the air was soft and warm; the noise and hurry of the world felt far away. A squawking bird came by for a look, perching above us and raising a ruckus, until he tired of the view and took off in search of better prospects. We ate in a companionable silence, talking now and then about nothing in particular.

"More *ceviche* for you?" Marco offered, reaching for a dish of spiced, lime-bathed fish.

"It's delicious," I said, accepting another spoonful and smiling at him.

"Tell me about your life," Marco said, leaning back against the tree trunk and picking at his plate of food. "What do you do when you are not racing around Europe?"

I thought he had used a curious phrase, but let it go. "I'm a professional artist," I answered. "I create paintings that are sold in several galleries, and I also paint a lot of commissioned portraits, company CEOs and their wives, children, dogs, and even houses and boats, that sort of thing. It's not my favourite work, but it pays the bills."

"And where do you do this painting, Señora?"

"Please call me Jill," I said, dispensing with formality. I realized that I had thought of him only as Marco since we'd met. Well, that and "Hello, gorgeous," but I tried not to think about that one too much. "I have a studio space on the second floor of my house. I live alone in a small village."

Marco nodded. "And what do you do when you are not painting and travelling?"

"I don't really travel very much," I said, "in fact, hardly at all. This trip is an errand for…someone I know. When I've done what I came to do, I'll go back to my little house and resume painting. I was in the middle of a commission before I left." I took a bite of pale gold cheese.

"What did you think of Paris?" Marco asked. I stopped chewing. In my mind, I scanned through the interchanges of the past twenty-four hours from the moment I reached Mariana's house until now. Nowhere could I find a memory of mentioning that I had recently been in Paris. I couldn't imagine that either Neil or Dennis had let it slip in their communications with his family either. How could he have known this fact that I had not revealed?

"What do you mean?" I enquired, looking at him.

He seemed to hesitate, then purposefully composed his features into an impassive mask. "Nothing. I just assumed that someone like you must have seen Paris, either on this trip or sometime in your past. Is this not so?" He seemed to me to be feigning nonchalance now.

"Yes," I answered. "As a matter of fact, I have seen Paris before. My husband and I toured Europe before our children were born. That was a long time ago, though." I left it at that and did not mention that I had landed there and stayed overnight not three days ago.

Marco dropped the subject. He reached into the bag of lunch and brought out dessert, cold vanilla custard, my favourite, served on glass plates which had been covered with stretch plastic wrap. He handed me a silver spoon.

"All we need now is coffee," I said, carving a bite of the pudding with the tip of my spoon. "That would make this picnic just about perfect."

"I can think of a few other things that would make it even more perfect," Marco quipped, tilting a dark eyebrow up in my direction. I caught the innuendo from the mock-innocence of his grin.

"Such as?" I asked levelly.

"Such as spending the rest of the afternoon here," he replied.

I placed the spoonful of custard in my mouth. "Mmmm," I said, drawing the syllable out and letting my gaze linger on Marco's. "You should try this."

"I have," he said, biting the inside of his lower lip in studied seriousness. "There's almost nothing better."

"Is that so?"

"Almost."

The banter had a tantalizing edge to it, underscored for me by his undeniable attractiveness. I had assumed that Marco Jimenez came purely at face value. He was Mariana's brother, someone who was known to my uncle and he worked for a restaurant supply company as a travelling salesman. Other than what he had told me in the car this morning, I knew very little about him. For all I knew, that could have all been fabricated. I suddenly wondered if I could trust him.

I poked at my custard, mixing the caramel into the milky part. I always assumed the best of everyone, but since I had set out on this escapade for Neil, that assumption was on shaky ground. Someone was after the stones, and I had no way of knowing who might be the villains in this story. Since Neil's life might depend upon whom I chose to trust or not trust, it was of utmost importance that I not only keep in close communication with the Holy Spirit, but also trust my own intuition. Until a few moments ago, I'd had no premonitions about Marco. But if he was who he said he was, how could he possibly have known that I had just come from Paris? If he knew more than he was letting on, then had he let that slip on purpose, or was it a blunder? Maybe I was imagining something more to his question than what he meant. I felt a quiver of unease.

In spite of my propensity for trusting people, I was still a pretty good judge of character and was accustomed to the Holy Spirit's warnings. I hoped I had not been too pre-occupied to notice them this time. The past few hours had been the most pleasant and calm I had experienced since the travel agent had knocked on my door and I wanted the feeling to last, especially in light of what might await me in Barcelona. I pushed my suspicions out of my mind.

Just then a soft breeze picked up a lock of my hair and blew it across my lips. Before I could brush it away Marco reached out and with one finger gently lifted it away from my face, tucking it back beside my ear. Our eyes met and held. I could hear my heart beating in my ears and my lips open. Suddenly all my senses felt like they stood on tiptoes. He drew me towards him and for a moment I had no desire to resist. Then I blinked and dragged my gaze away from his.

"This, um, this is lovely," I said, reaching for another spoonful of crème caramel. "Mariana is quite a cook. She must have been up all night putting this picnic together for us. It was so wonderful of her to have me for the night. I don't know what I'd have done if she hadn't invited me to stay. Go to a hotel, I suppose." I was babbling and I knew it.

"Be quiet," Marco said, turning my face toward his. When my eyes met his again, I knew I was sunk. The magnet was too strong for me this time and as his lips met mine, first softly, then with more intensity, I leaned into his kiss, my body yielding as his arms came around me. I felt like a flame had suddenly ignited inside me, where there had been nothing but burnt-out cinders for a very long time. The heat from it began to flutter into a glow that spread from somewhere in the middle of my belly outward, reaching my limbs and making them fluid and heavy. Marco's fingers caressed my cheek and slid down the side of my neck as he cupped the back of my head in his hand. Compelled by something other than my will, I sought his mouth eagerly, almost hungrily.

How long we sat wrapped in each other's arms, I have no idea; only the cry of that raucous crow landing in the tree above our heads brought me back to earth. I blinked and pushed Marco away, sitting up abruptly and straightening my dress. Frantic thoughts raced through my addled brain. What on earth was I doing? *I don't even know this guy,* I thought. Oh, but that kiss felt wonderful. I took a deep breath and looked back at Marco. He regarded me thoughtfully.

"What's the matter, *mi amor?*" he said softly, reaching again to touch my hair.

I twisted away and stood up, brushing imaginary crumbs from the front of my dress. "I think we should go now," I said.

"But why? We don't have to be in Barcelona for hours. You told me so yourself."

"I know," I snapped, not trusting my voice to remain level. "But I think, oh, I think..." I sank to my knees and began to toss the remains of our lunch back into the bag. Marco reached over and pinned my arms to my sides.

"I'm sorry," he said, forcing me to look at him. "I should not have done that, and I wouldn't have either, except that you looked so beautiful there. Did you not want me to kiss you?"

I shook my head. "I did," I said. "I mean, didn't. Oh, Marco. I don't know what I want right now. You're the first man I have even noticed since my husband died, and suddenly I just wanted to be touched again and treated like a woman by…" I stopped, not sure what to say next. Part of me wanted to tell him how attracted to him I felt, how I wanted to be swept away by a power bigger than me. Another part wanted to get as far away from him as possible. Given that we were practically in the middle of nowhere in the Spanish countryside and a few miles walk to the nearest village, to get away from him right now was not feasible. After all, as nearly as I could tell, I wasn't in danger of bodily harm and I still had to get to Barcelona today.

"It won't happen again," he said solemnly, stroking my arms. "You have my word. Okay?"

I took a deep breath and nodded. "Okay."

"Now why don't you lie down and have a little rest. I have to make a few telephone calls to my customers so I'm going to walk up the road a bit and see if I can get a signal for my cell phone." He got to his feet and headed through the brush toward the road.

As I watched him go out of sight, I thought that the last thing on my mind at that moment was lying down, but after a few minutes alone, I suddenly felt very tired. I had been up early in the morning, and now had a stomach full for rich food. In the silence of the forest, with the tinkling of the stream running past where I sat, a nap began to sound like a pretty good idea. I brushed the remainder of the crumbs and the ants off the edge of the blanket and rolled onto my back on the soft fleece. Just about the time my eyes were fluttering closed, I remembered that I had not had the opportunity to take a good look at the instructions for my meeting later in Barcelona. I must get things clearly in my mind prior to reaching the city, since chances were I would not be able to stop and figure it out if things didn't happen to go exactly as planned.

I reached for my journal, bound in scuffed fuchsia-coloured leather. Holding it open with my thumb, while I rested my head on my other arm, I read again Dennis' instructions for picking up the next stone in Barcelona. Somewhere in the city there stood a small ancient cathedral named Sant Pau Del Camp. I was instructed to find the cathedral, park the car in a particular place under a tree next to a building housing something called the Adequacio del Centre d'Educacio Infantil i Primaria Collaso i Gil, whatever that was. After parking I was to enter the cathedral at the main entrance at exactly ten minutes after seven, proceed down the aisle to the front of the church and kneel before the altar. Presumably, on this day of the week there would be nothing else going on in the church. I was to wait there until approached and touched on the left shoulder by the resident priest, Father Francisco. Then I would rise and he would pass me the stone from inside the sleeve of his cassock. After that, he would bless me with the sign of the cross, I was to turn and leave, walk directly out of the building, straight to the car, get in and drive away by a different route from the one we had used in our approach.

I read the instructions over carefully until I had a clear picture of how it should all play out. I hoped that it all went as planned, but as I was soon to find out, even the best-laid plans sometimes go awry.

We pulled into the outskirts of Barcelona as the sun was slanting in the west. Long shadows from olive groves and the trees along the highway stretched across the landscape. Approaching the old part of the city from the southwest, we followed the curve of the Mediterranean on our right, past the international airport and through the ubiquitous procession of apartment blocks. Marco had set his GPS to guide us into the city and it spoke to him as we travelled – in Spanish, of course. Driving over a river, I had a flashback to our afternoon beside

El Mirador and felt myself flush with the memory of Marco's kisses.

After the airport we passed the train yards, ugly industrial sectors and oil refineries then shipyard docks with their rusty barges and container yards. Suddenly, we were at the waterfront, where an immense, long dock led straight out into the bay. Cruise ships rested at anchor alongside the terminal, a round white building occupying the far end of the dock. A metal tower with an observation platform stood on the dock in front of it. Beyond that I could see several luxury yachts and sailboats anchored in the harbour.

"That's called the Teleferic," Marco explained as we drove beneath the taut lines of a cable car. "It stretches from that tower over there," he said, indicating another one on a farther dock, "to this one." He pointed at the nearest metal tower with his right hand while managing to steer another turn around a massive roundabout with the other. "Then it goes on up to Montjuic over here," he said, bending slightly to point past my nose and up the mountain slope on the south side of the city centre. "It ends in a cactus garden. Sometime you should take a trip up there. It's very beautiful." Then he added, "Perhaps this evening when you have completed your rendezvous, we could go for a little walk and see the city lights."

"Perhaps," I replied.

Another spin on the roundabout and Marco took the exit into the city past a statue of Christopher Columbus atop a high stone pole and beside a stretch of the crumbling, vine-covered wall of the old city. The GPS was talking to Marco. Since trying to translate the few Spanish words I knew seemed like too much trouble, I didn't bother to listen and instead tried to memorize the route we were taking through the city, just in case I might require the information later. You never knew. The muscles along the top of my shoulders tensed in anticipation of the coming appointment. Within minutes we arrived at the designated parking area. It turned out that the church was within only a few blocks of the waterfront. Pulling into a short alleyway, Marco wheeled the car into the lot of the building with the long name and parked under the specified tree by the fence. We got out and stretched. Though it was still warm out, I pulled on a light cardigan sweater since I knew that these old stone cathedrals had a reputation for being chilly. It was two minutes past seven o'clock. I grabbed my tote bag from the floor of the car and headed toward the church.

"I'm coming with you," Marco announced, striding beside me. I considered telling him that he didn't need to come with me, but the thought of his company gave me courage, even if I wasn't sure whose side he was on.

"Okay," I said. "Perhaps you can wait by the door while I go meet with Father Francisco."

An opening in the wrought iron fence led into a stone courtyard and I slowed my steps as we approached the main entrance to the ancient Romanesque church. A lush palm tree stood in a crook in the stone walls and a towering cypress dominated the corner of the building. The two-level courtyard also contained a row of shrubs and a single olive tree, quite possibly as old as the cathedral itself. Under a perfect arch, guarded by a couple of weather-beaten gargoyles, a pair of heavily-studded black doors stood, one ajar. I checked my watch. The moment had arrived. I glanced up at Marco and he nodded. Ducking into the church behind me, he stepped to one side of the closed door and folded his arms across his chest, looking exactly like a nightclub bouncer.

Inhaling deeply, I started up the aisle of the church. The inside of the building was cavernous and cool; the air still as held breath. The walls around rose to high, vaulted ceilings and narrow shafts of pale evening light penetrated the interior gloom. My footsteps echoed off the stone floor as I walked slowly toward the altar, my senses all on high alert. The place was empty except for Marco and me, yet I couldn't shake the feeling of impending danger. It's easy now to say that I should have paid closer attention to that feeling since now I know that God was warning me. But at the time I was just following orders, driven by the goal of getting Stone Number 5 into my hands as soon as possible and high-tailing it out of there.

Since the church was not large, it took me only a few moments to navigate the length of the aisle and come to the altar steps. I glanced to my left and right but saw no one. Dropping silently, I felt the stone step beneath my knees and I bowed my head slightly as though in prayer. Actually, I was in prayer since screaming for help from the Lord in my own head definitely counts. My heart was pounding so hard that I could hear nothing else and I felt the dampness of sweat prickle under the hair at the back of my neck. I dared not close my eyes.

It seemed like hours that I knelt there, the cold stone digging into the flesh of my knees and the backs of my legs beginning to cramp from the awkward position. I decided I could never become a Catholic; kneeling on stone would do me in. Just when I thought I could bear no more and that this whole meeting was a hoax, a door opened and a figure dressed in black emerged. Barely turning my head, I saw the priest approach me. I didn't move until his fingers lightly touched the point of my shoulder then I rolled back on my heels and pushed myself to my feet, trying not to groan with the effort. This was a church after all. Groaning about my discomfort seemed, well, unseemly.

Turning, I looked into the face of the priest. With a jolt I saw that, rather than a gentle, kind-eyed man I expected, a thin face pierced by steel-grey eyes regarded me with an icy glare. I shuddered a little but held out my hand for the stone. When nothing dropped into my palm, I dragged my gaze away from the priest's face and looked down. There, pointed directly at my waist was the dark barrel of a gun.

"You are coming with me," the man said, in a voice thin and hard as the blade of a palette knife.

I took one swift breath and screamed, "Marco!"

CHAPTER 14

You know how people always say that when something cataclysmic occurs, it is like it happened in slow motion? What happened next was not like that at all. It happened so fast, it was a blur. But my senses, so heightened by pumping adrenalin, produced a memory that is still crystal clear.

The moment I looked into those cold eyes and saw that gun pointed at my middle, I just acted. As I screamed Marco's name, I swung my tote bag, books, stones and all, at the head of the man in front of me. If he had expected me to acquiesce in fear to his demand, he had picked the wrong woman. I felt incensed that anyone would have the effrontery to threaten me with a gun. I had no intention of going anywhere with this hoodlum. I had already gone through too much collecting Neil's stones to risk losing any of them now.

When my bag connected with this man's left ear, he stumbled sideways. At the same time a shot rang out, the crack ricocheting off the solid stone walls of the church. In an instant, Marco was beside me. He must have been on springs. Before my assailant could even regain his balance, Marco hauled off and pasted him in the nose, then gave him a hard left to the jaw. Blood spattered from the imposter's nose as his head snapped backwards and arms flailed. Marco snatched the gun out of the man's hand and passed it to me.

"Here," he said, with surprising calm. "Hold this for me."

I took the gun out of his hand and pointed it at the man who was weaving and staggering under Marco's blows to the head and stomach. A final punch to the jaw, and the man fell in a heap on the stone floor, his head making contact with a nasty whack.

"Come on," Marco said turning to me and grabbing the gun from my hand. He stuffed it into the back waistband of his pants just like the detectives on television. "This guy's not going to be out for long," he said. "I didn't hit him that hard."

"You could have fooled me," I remarked as Marco grabbed my elbow.

"We have to find the real priest," Marco said as we raced for a side door. Flinging the door open, we found ourselves in the cloisters, a small area with flagstone paving in the centre. A stone font resembling a bird bath stood in the middle of the open space. At the end of one passage of the cloister, we saw another door and charged toward it. Inside we found a small room containing an old wooden desk and a chair and a few other items that the priest might use for conducting services and ceremonies. A man wearing plain brown pants and a white shirt sat strapped to the chair with strips of duct tape. Another piece of tape covered his mouth.

"Padre Francisco?" Marco gasped. The priest nodded, his eyes wide. Leaping behind the desk, Marco muttered something in Spanish which I guessed was, "This is going to hurt," as he stripped the duct tape from Padre Francisco's mouth. The priest winced as the tape ripped away but began to talk immediately while Marco, whipping a small folding knife from his pocket, cut away the rest of the tape. *Was there anything this guy was not prepared for?* I wondered.

Once freed, the padre stood up and held out his hands toward me. "Señora Moss, *sí?*" he asked. He was a small, round man with kind, dark eyes and a bald spot on the top of his head. To me, he looked exactly like a good-hearted priest should look, like Friar Tuck only not as fat.

I nodded. "*Sí*." Then I turned to Marco. "Is he all right? They haven't hurt him, have they?"

"I checked," Marco replied. "He says he's fine."

"Come," he said, motioning me to follow him. He stepped to the side of the room where several robes hung from a tall coat rack. Lifting one of the robes to the side, he revealed a wooden box upon a waist-high stand. There was a slit cut into the lid. I gave Marco an enquiring look.

"I think you would call that the Poor Box," he explained.

Lifting the lid, Father Francisco put his hand inside and drew out a small package still wrapped in the brown paper in which it had been mailed. He held it out for me to take. Grabbing it from his hands I said, "Thank-you, *merci, gracias*," mixing up my languages. I dropped the package into my tote bag with its mates.

"Okay," Marco said, briefly shaking the priest's hand. "We have to get out of here now before that goon in the church wakes up." I felt like I should stay and make sure the priest was unhurt, or ask him how he came to have this stone, or something, but Marco had already turned me around and was ushering me out the door.

"*Viene esta manera*," Padre Francisco said, motioning for us to follow him. He led us out by a different way than we had entered and gave Marco instructions how to get back to the car.

Marco grabbed my hand, but I said, "Wait." Turning back to Padre Francisco, I gave him a quick hug then squeezed his hands. "*Muchos gracias*," I said. He patted my shoulder as Marco yanked my arm and we took off.

We ran out the back door into a semi-circular park, Marco pulling me and my bag flying from my shoulder. In a couple of seconds we rounded the corner onto the street then dashed up to the edge of the adjacent building. Marco skidded to a stop and peered around the corner, then took off again at a dead run while I stumbled along behind trying to keep up. He repeated the procedure at the next corner and off we went, this time around the perimeter of the wrought iron fence and into the parking lot. Just as we were about to jump into Marco's car, we saw through the trees the imposter priest run back into the church through the front door. With him was someone else, a tall man wearing a dark suit.

I gasped and covered my mouth with my hand.

Marco's head snapped around. "What is it?" he demanded.

"I know that man," I shouted in a harsh whisper. "I've seen him before."

"Get in," Marco commanded as the two men disappeared into the church. "You can tell me all about it while we drive."

We leapt into the car and Marco turned the key and slammed the gear shift into reverse, then spun the car around and jammed his foot on the gas pedal. Tires squealing, we raced out of the parking lot and onto the street.

"I saw him a couple of days ago," I said in a small voice. "In a…a train station, in France."

"Who is he?"

"I don't know. I think his name is Mendez or Mendosa, or something. No wait. It's Menendez. That's all I know about him but he was after me before."

"Not good," Marco said, gunning the engine of the car and narrowly missing a delivery van pulling out onto the street in front of us. Driving furiously with one hand, he pulled his cell phone out if his pocket, and punched in some numbers with his thumb. "Jose? Marco. *Si..si.*" He said something else in Spanish, then, *"dos minutos, si."* That's the only part I recognized – two minutes. He jammed his phone back into his pocket, cranked the wheel around a double-parked taxi then, hauling it back right, he stood on the gas pedal and screeched around the corner. Within seconds we were on a tree-lined boulevard, weaving through the traffic. In a few more seconds Marco zoomed off on another street to the right. I hung onto the door handle, my heartbeat drumming in my ears. My head felt suddenly dizzy and I had the passing impression that my side hurt as I clung to the door handle.

We sped into a narrow street then into a short alley between a couple of apartment buildings. A garage door stood open on our left and, to my surprise, Marco spun the wheel, roared into the empty garage space and killed the engine. The automatic door dropped behind us leaving us in blackness. Just then a door opened and man emerged from the building.

"Come on," Marco said, opening his door. "I'll introduce you to my friend."

I took a deep breath and peeled my fingers from the door handle. Marco bounded around to my side of the vehicle and opened the door. I swung my legs out slowly and pulled myself to my feet. The room began to spin and I stumbled a little but Marco took my hand, led me to where his friend stood waiting and introduced me to Jose Rodriguez.

"Come, come," Jose said, leading us up a set of stairs and opening a door on the landing. Suddenly everything started to go all silvery and my knees buckled under me. The floor rose up to meet me as I blinked hard. Before I dropped, Marco caught me with an arm around my back.

"Oh, my goodness," I said, suddenly feeling all out of breath. The room was swimming and my legs were jelly.

"What is it?" Marco demanded.

"I don't know. My side kind of hurts," I replied, trailing off weakly. Looking down, I pushed the hem of my sweater out of the way and gasped when I saw a blood stain the size of a dinner plate down the side of my dress. Marco took one look at it and swept me up in his arms.

"You're hurt," he said stiffly. "You need to lie down and we'll take a look at this." He strode directly to a pale green leather sofa under a wide window and laid me down, stuffing a cushion under my head. "Let me see," he said, reaching for the hem of my dress.

"Get away," I cried, slapping at his hand. "I'll do it. You turn around." He rolled his eyes and muttered something. "You too," I said to Jose, who was also reaching for me. He mumbled something under his breath to Marco and they both turned their backs. I looked down at my dress where the stain started and saw a hole in the fabric. "I think I've been shot. That jerk ruined my dress."

Both men spun around.

"Look at that," I said, tears springing to my eyes. "This dress is brand new."

"Get out of our way," Marco commanded, removing my hand from the fabric and placing it gently on my chest. "Jose is a paramedic."

"That's handy," I said, wiping away the tears that now slid toward my temples.

Marco lifted the hem of my dress up and away from my side. Then I had a completely silly thought. I was glad that I had decided to wear my white stretch-lace panties instead of my usual plain cotton ones. Marco gave a low whistle, and I threw him a furious glance.

"I meant the wound," he said. The look on his face reminded me of a little boy who had just been caught flipping through the bra pages of Sears catalogue. Jose knelt by my side to examine the gunshot wound, touching the area around it gingerly with his fingertips. I bit my lip and tensed. He said something to Marco and patted my hand, then got up and went off to another room.

"What?" I asked, searching Marco's face.

He knelt down beside me. "It's only a flesh wound," he said. "The bullet just grazed you. Jose will have you fixed up in no time." He spoke softly and gently stroked my brow, pushing the hair away from my face. "Don't worry, *mi amor*. You will be fine. I will take good care of you. Jose has gone to get dressings now." His kindness brought fresh tears to my eyes which he dabbed away with a handkerchief from his pocket.

Jose reappeared carrying a basin of water, a dark towel on his shoulder, and a medical case. He set about calmly cleansing the wound and applying the dressing as I lay there gripping the back of the sofa with one hand and the front of my dress with the other. When I could see that he was nearly finished I turned to Marco, who was still stroking my brow. "I need to change my clothes," I said. "Do you think you could bring my suitcase up from the car?"

He jumped to his feet and tore out the door.

"Señor Rodriguez, tell me. Is it bad?" I searched his calm face for truth.

"No, Señora," he replied. "Is not bad. Is small, small." Marco charged back into the room a couple of minutes later, before Jose had finished his gentle ministrations, and set my suitcase down at the end of the sofa.

"Are you okay?" he asked, concern still etching his features.

"I think so." Jose put away his medical gear and picked up several bloody tissues. "Would you mind opening my case and finding my jeans, please?" Marco whipped my suitcase out and zipped it open. In typical man-fashion, he began to paw through my things. "Hold on," I said. "Just lift up that top layer. My jeans are underneath the red shirt. In fact, give me that shirt, too. I'll put it on."

Jose came back into the room and said something to Marco. "He says that you must not put pressure on the wound now or it might start bleeding again."

"Okay, I'll leave my pants undone. Now if you'll help me up, I'll use the bathroom to change." I took Marco's hand and tried to sit up, but a fiery pain stabbed through me. Gasping, I persisted, slowly standing to my feet. Then everything went all shiny again, and I sank back down to the sofa. "Maybe you can help me," I pleaded, feeling pitiful.

Marco leapt to my aid, gently removing my sweater. He unzipped my dress down the side and carefully lifted it over my head. "Don't worry, I won't look," he said, "at least not at the good parts." He turned his head away but I could see him trying not to grin.

The wound in my side really hurt now, like someone held my flesh in a big nasty pinch. As Marco slid my jeans over my feet and up my legs, I put my arm around his shoulders to stand up, leaning on him as I yanked up the zipper. Then he helped me get my shirt on without twisting my torso too much and even did up the buttons like I was a little kid.

As I lay back down on the sofa I said, "I think I'm hungry."

Marco smacked his forehead with the palm of his hand. "No wonder you're so weak. It has been hours since we've eaten." A short conversation ensued between Marco and Jose then Marco got out his cell phone and made a call. "We will have food in a few minutes."

"How did you do that?"

"One of my clients owns a restaurant down the street. He's sending something over."

Within minutes, a knock came at the door and Marco brought in the restaurant take-out. Jose set the table in a cursory fashion and the two men spread out the food as I watched from the sofa. Jose was short and slight with fine, dark hair greying at the temples. He seemed as efficient in the kitchen as he was as a medic. I wondered if there was a Mrs. Rodriguez and a glance around the room told me that a woman definitely had a hand in the decoration. When everything was ready, Marco helped me to my feet, and clinging to his arm, I went and sat at the table. We asked the blessing for the food and Jose served. First, soup with little meatballs and chunky vegetables, then rice and seafood and bread. After the soup, I ate little. My appetite had vanished suddenly and I felt exhausted.

As Jose cleared the table, Marco's cell phone rang. He spoke softly to the caller for a few minutes then handed the phone to me. "It's for you," he said.

"For me? Who knows I'm here with you?" I took the telephone from his hand and put it to my ear. It was Mariana.

"I'm so happy that you are still with Marco" she said in her rapid-fire accented way. "There is a man who called on the telephone. He is looking for you."

I gasped. Too many people were looking for me. I didn't need any more.

"He says that he knows your uncle and you are supposed to go see him." She told me more about the call and gave me the telephone number. "He says that it is very urgent. His name is Gerhard Mueller. He lives in Switzerland. Oh, and he said to tell you that your uncle told him that you have a birthmark that looks like a peanut on the outside of your right knee. Is that true?" Yes, it was true, I told her. I wrote down the number in my journal. I hung up and punched in the number.

A young man's voice answered. "Gerhard Mueller?" I asked.

"*Ja, ja,*" said the voice on the other end. I introduced myself and he immediately switched to English. "I'm so happy you called, Frau Moss. I have something here for you. You must come and see me right away."

"Where are you, Mr. Mueller?"

"I am in Switzerland. My city is Thun." It rhymed with moon. "Can you be here in the morning? Where are you now?"

"Right now I am somewhere in Spain. I don't have any idea how I could get to Switzerland by morning, Mr. Mueller. And there is something else. I was shot tonight." There was an audible gasp on the other end of the line. "Don't worry," I soothed. "It's just a flesh wound, but I'm moving pretty slowly right now. I don't know how I would get there. Can I fly?" As soon as I said the words, I knew that it would be foolhardy to attempt to use an airport tonight.

Before either Gerhard Mueller or I could come up with a solution, Marco took the phone from my hand and spoke into the receiver. "My name is Marco Jimenez," he said, "and I am a friend of Señora Moss. I will see to it that she gets there by morning. Just tell me where to meet you and we will be there."

CHAPTER 15

"What are you talking about?"

Marco dropped the cell phone back into his pocket. "Simple. You have to go to Switzerland and I am going to take you."

"Why?"

"Listen, Jill. You are obviously in danger. You've just been shot so you can't go traipsing around the continent in the condition you are in now. That wound could open up and start bleeding again any time if you're not careful. I know that you can't go by train or plane, otherwise you would have taken the train to come here, wouldn't you? I'm assuming that secrecy is still an issue, since there are men out there trying to kill you for what you are doing. No one knows me and no one has seen my car. As a Spaniard and a gentleman, I don't see that I have a choice but to drive you to Switzerland, do you? And I don't see that you have a choice either."

"Well," I replied, leaning into a cushion, "when you put it that way…"

"Okay. Now come, I'll help you up and you can freshen up before we leave." He held out his hands for me to take.

"We're leaving now? But Marco you've just driven all day. Aren't you too tired?" I knew that I would be, even without a gunshot wound.

"I'm used to driving long distances, and besides, when I get tired we'll take a break and I will sleep a little. There is plenty of time." He turned to Jose, who was standing nearby, clearly not following the gist of the conversation. Marco asked a question. Jose shrugged and answered. Marco explained, "It's about eight or nine hours to drive from here, so we have a little leeway."

"Is that all?" I grasped Marco's hands and allowed him to pull me to my feet. I felt much stronger now that I had eaten something. Once he put the travel time in perspective, it made it much easier for me to accept. After all, I had driven from my home near Vancouver to Calgary, where my sister lived, numerous times by myself and the distance was farther than from Barcelona to Thun.

"Hold on a minute, Marco," I said. "Don't you have to get to work tomorrow? You told me that you were on a sales trip or visiting clients. Isn't your boss going to notice if you don't show up?"

Marco smiled and shook his head, "That's all taken care of for now," he said, "so don't you worry about a thing."

Ten minutes later, Jose pressed a package of painkillers into my palm and handed me a bottle of water. We said goodbye and pulled the car out onto the street in the twilight. It was nearly ten o'clock by now and the city was lit up. The night air, soft and warm, flowed through my window.

"Once we get out of the city, I can put the top down," Marco said, "but I think we should stay out of sight for now, just in case." Marco explained that he would leave town by way of smaller roads which would keep us off the toll-highways.

I wasn't aware that I had fallen asleep until the car began to bounce and jostled me awake. I sat up straight and looked around. The night was completely dark; there were no lights around us at all other than the headlights of the car. Marco steered the car off the bumpy side road and into a field. In the light from the headlights, I could see a crumbling stone wall looming on both sides of the grassy track. *He is going to steal the stones, murder me, and hide my body under that hay stack up ahead,* I thought. "Where are we?" I asked, barely able to keep the quiver of fear out of my voice.

"I was getting sleepy so I thought I would pull over here where it's quiet and have a little nap before we carry on. We're near Avignon."

"Oh," I said, breathing a long sigh of relief. If he was planning to do away with me, he sure seemed calm about it. Mentally, I checked with the Holy Spirit to see if there was anything to be alarmed about and all was peace, so I relaxed.

Marco had put the top of the car down and now he leaned his seat back to a reclining position. "Lay your seat down," he said, "and we can look at the stars."

"Oooh, ouch," I said, wincing as I dropped my seat back and a stab of pain burst through my side.

"Be careful, *mi amor*," Marco said, reaching to help me. "Maybe you should take another painkiller." *Did he call everyone that or was it reserved for me*, I wondered.

"Good idea." I found the water bottle and packet of pills and popped one in my mouth, swishing it down with a gulp of water. Then I lay back down, carefully this time, and gazed at the heavens. The cloudless sky covered us in an inky blanket hung with millions of twinkling stars. The moon, just a sliver away from full, sailed high overhead illuminating the countryside in a soft, silver glow. We had stopped in what appeared to be an old cow yard. The crumbling remains of a stone barn stood a short distance off, a tree growing up in the middle of it. The car was concealed from the road by the remains of the old stone wall, but since there was no traffic out here anyway, it seemed a moot point.

"It's a beautiful night, isn't it?" Marco said. "Look, you can see the Milky Way."

"God made an incredible universe."

"Yes, he did." Marco turned in his seat to look at me. "You look beautiful in the moonlight, Jill," he said.

"That's a nice thing to say, Marco."

"I mean it. I've never met anyone like you. You are amazing."

I smiled ruefully. "No, I'm not. I'm just an ordinary person caught up in an extraordinary situation."

He reached out and touched my cheek, drawing a finger softly down the side of my face. "You take my breath away," he said. Then he let his hand drop and within seconds was snoring.

I gazed at his sleeping profile in the moonlight. The truth was, I had never met anyone like him either. He was smart, thoughtful, masculine yet gentle, and so good-looking that he took *my* breath away. I hoped he was for real.

I woke sometime later when Marco's car door closed. "Hey," he said quietly, "it's time to hit the road again." I propped my seat back up and blinked.

"What time is it?"

"About three."

"Can we stop somewhere to use the restrooms?"

Marco nodded. "I could use a coffee. We'll find someplace soon, I hope." *Me too,* I thought as he pulled the car out of the cow pasture and onto the potholed lane. In no time we were sailing along through the night on the A7 north of Avignon. Marco had put the car top up as the night air now felt cool with the dew of morning. Within about ten minutes, we spied an all-night rest stop and pulled in.

As we drove on through the night, I wanted to stay awake so I could help Marco stay awake. But I kept drifting off, only to wake and find the clock on the dashboard showed an hour or two later. As dawn broke, we stopped near Saint Julien-en-Genevois, which was just inside the French border with Switzerland, parked the car and got out to use the restrooms, buy gas, and find something to eat before crossing into Switzerland at Bardonnex. Marco looked exhausted and I told him so, but he waved away my concern like it was nothing and kept driving. We skirted Lake Geneva as the morning sun glinted off its rippled surface and slanting rays lit up the mountains in a blaze of purple and apricot.

We pulled into the pretty city of Thun at about nine-thirty. The centre of the old town was dominated by a medieval castle which looked like Rapunzel may have tossed her hair from one of its towers sometime in the past. The ramparts of the Alps rose up behind the town like a symphony in stone and snow. Winding streets crammed with rush-hour traffic had us driving in circles trying to find the address that Gerhard Mueller had given me. He said he worked in a bank and we were to meet there whenever we arrived. We found parking in a narrow lot behind the Berner Kantonalbank building. Marco unfolded his long legs and stood up. Stretching his arms over his head, he turned and rested his body on the roof of the car.

"I'm tired," he groaned.

"I know," I said, walking to his side of the car and taking his arm. "Come on, cowboy. We've got someone to meet."

Inside, the bank was the picture of efficiency and glossy order. I scanned the nameplates of the bank staff, each one on a little stand visible from behind the glassed-in wickets. Gerhard Mueller's station stood at the end of the row farthest from the door. Tall, with short, sandy-brown hair and wire-framed glasses, he wore a pale-yellow shirt and a coordinating tie. He looked so young that I wondered if his mother still chose his clothing. I led Marco over to his wicket and said, "Hello, Mr. Mueller. I am Jill Moss."

Gerhard Mueller gave me a non-committal little smile from behind his glass shield and said, "I am happy to meet you." Then he turned his name plate around to show *Closed*. Coming out from behind the barricades, he shook hands with us as I introduced Marco. "Frau Moss," he said with all the seriousness of a banker, "I must speak with you alone. I apologize, Señor Jimenez, but those are my instructions." He spoke excellent English with a lilting Swiss accent. Marco shrugged and lowered himself into a brown leather chair.

"Before we can go any further, Frau Moss, I must ask you to show me your passport and also to reveal the birthmark I mentioned on the telephone," Gerhard Mueller said when he had closed the door to a small office cubicle.

"Of course," I replied, digging out my passport and handing it to him. He held it up and compared the dismal photo to my face, then nodded and handed the passport back. Thankful that I no longer owned skinny jeans, I pulled up the right leg of my pants to reveal the birthmark above my right knee.

"Thank-you, Frau Moss. That is sufficient." His excitement seemed to crank up a notch, now that he felt convinced of my identity. "I have to tell you, it was wery difficult not to open this package," he said, his accent thickening. Taking a small box out of the desk drawer he slid it toward me with his fingertips. "Herr Bryant is one of my big heroes, so when this came in the post for me, I was over the moon. But before I could open it, someone telephoned me and commanded me to leave it intact until you are coming to get it." He started to fidget as though trying to remain professional while barely containing his anticipation.

I took the box and held it in my hands, mentally weighing it in comparison to the others I carried.

"The person who called also asked me to recommend that you take out a safe deposit box here at the bank. I am prepared to help you with that. I assure you that it is very secure. This is Switzerland," he added, as though that information was all I would need to give me confidence.

"Who called you?"

"I do not know, Frau Moss. It was a man's voice, but he did not give me his name."

"But," I began, perplexed, "why would Neil Bryant choose to send something to you, Mr. Mueller?"

"Please, call me Gerhard," he said. "I have been a follower of Herr Bryant's work for many years. I have read all his papers and have even spent my vacations working with him in the jungles of Central America. I know I am just a bank employee, but my true passion is Mayan archaeology. Without any formal study, I have become very knowledgeable about Herr Bryant's work and have even written some papers of my own." I detected chest expansion. "I will be finished here at one o'clock and invite you and your friend to join me for lunch then. We can talk about Neil Bryant together."

I thought of Marco waiting in the lobby. "Gerhard, we have just driven all night across France and we are both very tired. As I mentioned when we spoke on the telephone last night, I was the victim of a gunshot and am feeling the effects of too little sleep and too much excitement." I glanced at the clock on the wall behind the desk. "I would love to join you for lunch, but we need somewhere where we might rest for a few hours and freshen up. Can you recommend a hotel or inn close by?"

Gerhard clapped his hands together with a look of glee. "I know the perfect place. You can go to my parents' flat. They are in Turkey on a tour right now and I know that they would insist you come and stay. The place is empty and you would have everything you need. Once you have taken a rest, we can meet again and have something to eat. I want to show you my collection of Mayan artifact photos. I have recently discovered some very interesting information which I think you will want to know about." He was fairly vibrating with excitement.

"That sounds lovely. I accept. Now, what about a safe deposit box?"

Ten minutes later the transaction was complete and I had the keys to Gerhard's parents' apartment in my hands and the key to the deposit box in my wallet. I found Marco slouched in a chair, fast asleep, and the other tellers shooting disapproving looks in his direction. Thankfully, he wasn't snoring. I nudged his knee with mine a couple of times and got no response so I shook his arm. He sat up abruptly and rubbed his face.

"Come on, sunshine," I said, smiling at him. "I've found somewhere that you can crash lying down." He got up and followed me out the door.

We found the Mueller's apartment in a fine, old, traditional Swiss house situated on the hill leading up to the castle. A pristine living room decorated in yellows and blues offered a magnificent view of the river flowing into the Lake of Thun. Arrayed around the lake's perimeter were the famous Swiss Alps. It was breathtaking. I opened the old-fashioned window, hinged along the side, and leaned my elbows on the sill, drawing in deep breaths of cool mountain air.

Marco had come to stand behind me and leaned out the window over my back. "That's the Eiger," he said pointing to one of the far mountain peaks, "and that one is the Monch and here is the Jungfrau. I have been skiing at Grindelwald once, up the lake."

I stood up and found myself in the circle of his arms. "How are you feeling?" he asked, nodding toward my waist where the bandage covered the gunshot wound.

"I'm all right," I said. "I'll check it in a minute. How are you feeling?"

"Like I've been run over by a truck."

"Then go find a bed and get some sleep. Gerhard will be calling in a few hours to take us to lunch."

He dropped a soft kiss on my forehead and wandered away. I turned back to the window, leaned against the sill and stared out at the beauty that lay before me. "Thank-you, God," I whispered, "for getting me here safely. Thank-you for sending your angels to protect me. And thank-you that that jerk in the church in Barcelona didn't kill me. I'm not ready to go just yet. And, please keep showing me what to do. I'm lost without your help."

I pulled the window closed and latched it, then went to the bathroom and took a look at my injury. Other than a little dried blood that had oozed from the cut line, it looked fine. I cleaned it up with a tissue and re-applied the dressing. Jose had done a good job.

I found Marco flaked out in one of the bedrooms, sound asleep. I crept in and covered him with a shawl I found on a chair in the corner. He didn't move.

Back in the living room, I found a telephone and made a collect call to my mother. Strictly speaking, I should have been more careful, but I needed to connect with some semblance of stability in my life today, and my mom was it.

"Hi Mom," I said when she picked up. "It's Jill. How are you?"

"For goodness sake, Jill," she nearly shouted into the phone. "Where on earth are you? I've been absolutely frantic."

"Why? What's happened?" Instantly alarmed, my hand flew to my throat where I could feel my pulse suddenly increase.

"Dennis has disappeared," she cried. "We think he's been kidnapped."

CHAPTER 16

Gerhard Mueller's apartment was barely bigger than a walk-in closet, but he had managed to store an amazing amount of stuff in it. Souvenirs of his trips to Central America adorned all the surfaces. Masks, clay figurines, bowls painted bright colours, woven rugs, blankets, and wall hangings covered every square millimetre of space. A pine table stood next to the tiny galley kitchen and on it was a photograph of the complete ring of stones, all the pieces to the puzzle.

While alone in the bank vault, I had removed the wrappings from the stone Gerhard had given me and, taking the rest of them from my bag, I lined the six pieces up against each other on a small table. The indents in the sides matched perfectly but their placement and message was still a mystery. I stared at them for what seemed like a long time, wishing for them to speak and reveal their secrets, then wrapped them carefully in tissue and placed them in the deposit box. I did not know when I would see them again.

Now I picked up the photograph. "Where did you get this?"

"Herr Bryant sent it to me. I'm not really sure why, but it's interesting, isn't it?"

"Yes," I replied, studying the photo, "it is interesting." I, too, wondered why Neil had sent this photo to Gerhard Mueller. On close inspection, I could make out where the stones which I had already collected belonged in the ring.

There were still ten stones required to make up the circle. Where were those remaining stones now? I turned the photo over and saw that I was holding not one photo, but two. At first I thought they were identical, but as I examined them side by side, I saw that the inscriptions on the top of the stones did not match. Then it dawned on me. The second photo was of the opposite view with the second hieroglyphic linguistic style visible. The side of the stones that formed the interior of the circle had only a faint line travelling through the centre of each stone that matched them all and ran the whole way round the circle while the outside surface of the circle showed a third language, which was not at all like the other two.

"Was that one of the stones in the box that I gave you?" Gerhard asked. "Do you have the rest? Can I see them? Do you know what they mean?"

I held up my hand. "Yes, that was a stone in the package," I said. I didn't see any point in trying to hide that fact. "No, I do not have the rest, and no, I don't know what they mean. I think for now it would be better if you do not see them. I'm not sure who else may be trying to get their hands on them, so the less you know the better." He sagged visibly. "May I keep these photos?"

"I guess so." He looked so disappointed that I felt sorry for him. Then he brightened again. "Do you want to see some of the rest of my collections?"

When Gerhard had called on us at his parents' flat after work, Marco was still sound asleep. I thought it best to leave him sleeping for two reasons. First, he was dog-tired and would have to drive back to Madrid soon. And second, even though he had made it pretty clear he was attracted to me (and believe me, the feeling was mutual), I still had doubts about his real motives. He could be faking the whole "*mi amor*" thing. I had no way of knowing why he was suddenly so involved with me. For all I knew, Marco could be one of my enemies. The less he found out about me or the stones, the better. I had slipped out with Gerhard for a quick lunch then gone with him to his apartment to see his collection of archaeological treasures.

Now Gerhard dashed into his miniscule bedroom and I could hear him rummaging around in a closet; then I heard the drawers of a metal filing cabinet open and close. He came back into the tiny living room with his arms full of stuff and dumped it on the table. Sorting through a mound of papers, rolled up charts, and photographs, he pulled out a small paper-bound book and opened it.

"These are the field notes from my last trip to Mexico when I volunteered to help Herr Bryant with his dig. Look at this." The book was full of photos and notations written in tight, precise script. He pointed to a photo of himself standing next to Neil in front of a mound of dirt with trees growing out of its top. "See this? That's what it looked like before we started." He flipped the pages and stopped again near the end of the book. "Now look what we uncovered after the excavation." The two of them stood beside a small step pyramid shape, each with a foot on one of the steps leading up to the first ledge, shovels in hand and looking enormously pleased with themselves. "Isn't that incredible?"

I thought Gerhard's shirt buttons would pop.

"There is something funny that happened when I was there, though," he said, suddenly serious. "We found an artifact that didn't seem to fit in that location or the time period for the pyramid."

"What was it?"

"It was a sculpted head that was not Mayan or Olmec in style, which would commonly be found in that area. It looked very much like a bearded Jewish man. We discovered it when we pried away a couple of blocks which sealed the opening of the pyramid. Inside, we found a cache of the usual burial stuff like bones and pottery, but also this head. I've got a photo of it here somewhere." He paged through his field notebook. "Here it is. What do you think of that?"

The blank eyes of the sculpted head stared out of the photo at me. It definitely did not resemble the facial features from any Mayan art I had ever seen with the prominent nose that began in the middle of the forehead, or of the Olmec sculptures I had seen, which seemed almost African in their characteristics, with broad noses and thick lips. This figure looked like the father of a Jewish kid I had known in high school. I shook my head. "That's amazing. When do you think it was put in the pyramid?"

"Our educated guess was approximately fifteen hundred B.C."

"But that's impossible! Middle-easterners were not known to visit the Americas until sometime after Columbus made his discovery."

"That's what most people think, and it is what we're taught in school, but there is a growing body of evidence that suggests a different story." He shuffled through the pile of papers and pulled out a handful of sheets that looked like they had been printed from a website. "Once Professor Bryant told me that he thought there was world-wide travel just after the flood so I started doing my own research. You will be amazed what I have found."

"Hold on a minute. My uncle told you *he* thinks there was world-wide travel after the flood?" I remembered the verses in Neil's Bible that had been marked. Many of them referred to the time following the flood.

"Herr Bryant is your uncle?" Gerhard's eyes bulged and he took a step backward as I nodded. "That's so cool!" he cried.

"I don't know how cool it is," I replied, "but it's true. Now tell me, what do you know about the flood?"

Gerhard shrugged. "Just about everything there is to know," he said. "For starters, my father is a pastor so I grew up in church. But I have learned a lot more about that time period from my own archaeological studies. Do you know that when Noah and his family left the ark, the world was a total mess?"

"I kind of imagined it would be," I answered. "After all, they would see nothing but receding water everywhere, filled with dead people and animals floating around, trees, dirt, debris, you name it. The world was a cesspool."

He gave me a funny look. "What is this, cesspool?"

"A sewer, you know like when you flush your toilet, and it goes, swoosh…" I said, using hand motions for emphasis, "out to the pipes under the streets? A cesspool is where it all ends up; in a sewage treatment plant before the treatment."

"Aha, *ja*," he said, comprehending. "Okay, so the world was like a big cesspool for a while. But then they had to get on with life. There is something peculiar about that time just before and just after the flood. Think about this: Almost every culture on earth has a spoken history or some kind of writing about a great flood that covered the earth. They all agree that it took place about three thousand years before Christ was born. All of these peoples groups agree about that. Don't you think that is interesting?"

"Very."

"I think it is, too, but that's only the start. The Tower of Babel was built approximately one hundred years after the flood. How do you think those people had the technology to build such a tower?"

"I don't know. I have never given it much thought."

"No one really knows for sure, but maybe those people had better technologic than we have today."

Overlooking his terminology, I cocked an eyebrow. "What would make you say that?"

"Take a look at scriptures about the time right after the flood and until the Tower of Babel caused all the people of the world to have their languages mixed apart. There was huge population growth because people were living for hundreds of years. If they all stayed in the same area, it would be like a micro, um, culture situation."

"A microcosm? It's a miniature world."

He snapped his fingers. "Exactly! But God said in Genesis six, verse three, that he would limit man's length of life to one hundred twenty years. In not many generations after the flood, man was living only that long. Moses lived only one hundred and twenty years. I think God did that because man was becoming more and more evil and wicked. "

"What does this have to do with Mayan ruins, Gerhard?"

"This will surprise you, I think." He sifted through some sheaf of papers and pulled one from the pile. "Here is the short version. Many scientists and archaeologists believe that there were very developed cultures on the earth before the flood destroyed everything."

"Why is that?"

"Here is an example. In Baalbek, Lebanon there are three Roman temples and three courtyards built on an ancient tell that scholars believe dates back to before 3000 B.C. It is made from stones so huge that even now it would be almost impossible to move them. For example, there is one stone that weighs almost two thousand tonnes and could not be moved by a modern-day train. That is one stone! Some of these stones have been lifted up to seven meters above the ground. And they have been fitted so tightly together that a knife blade will not go between them."

I had always had an interest in history, but Gerhard's fascination was contagious. As he unfolded charts, unrolled maps, and opened books, he showed me example after example of ancient architectural and artistic wonders of such magnitude that the scope was staggering. For example, twelve thousand feet up in the oxygen-poor, high plains of Bolivia at a place called Tiahuanaco, stands a gateway hewn from a solid piece of stone ten feet high and six feet wide. It had been moved from quarries over ninety miles away.

"It seems like most cultures appeared quite suddenly, complete already. There seems to be a connection between different cultures, and they all seem to have started at Noah. They all say that before the flood mankind was evil and very bad; a special boat was built for the survival of a certain family and animals; and eight people survived in the boat and also some animals. The rainbow and the boat landing on a mountain top are the same, too."

"It certainly makes a convincing argument, doesn't it?"

"These people, Noah's family who came out of the ark, started the new population," he said. "But as time went on, Noah's descendents became extremely wicked. Then they decided they would build a tower and go up to heaven whenever they wanted. Can you imagine how God must have felt about that?"

"Thoroughly exasperated, I shouldn't wonder," I agreed. He gave me a quizzical look.

"Of course, you know what happened. God messed up their languages so they could not understand each other. Once they were separated into hundreds of different small groups by language, they would not be able to group together against God anymore."

"You mentioned earlier that there are lots of artifacts that point to a technologically-advanced civilization in the distant past. What are they?"

"Stonehenge is one example. It was built between 2800 B.C. and 1700 B.C. and has stones weighing as much as five tonnes which were carried nearly two hundred and forty miles. All the ancient stone sites all over Britain line up in a special geometric pattern in relation to each other at an angle of twenty-three and one-half degrees, or a multiple of that angle. This just happens to be the angle of inclination of the earth's axis. Are you familiar with the Nazca lines in Peru?"

I nodded. Spread out over the high, dry plateaus in southern Peru, the earth there had at some time in the distant past been carved with numerous figures and lines, the origins of which no one knows. Many of the lines are straighter than arrows, and are laid out like airport landing strips of today. Giant depictions of animals and other unrecognizable creatures also dot the arid landscape.

"One of the carvings is of a spider," Gerhard said, digging around in his pile of stuff and pulling out a photo he said, "Do you notice how this leg is so much longer than the rest?" The right hind leg was more than twice the length of the others and was bent at a sharp angle away from the body. "This shape is like an actual spider that lives in caves deep in the Amazon jungle. It is extremely rare. It uses the long leg in mating. This spider it is so tiny that it can only be seen with a microscope. Those people must have had ground optical lenses."

I pulled out a chair and sat down. "But how does this all connect with the ring of stones? These stones were found in Mexico. What's the connection between them and all of these other places and finds? Or is there one?"

Gerhard took the chair opposite me and pushed his pile of papers into the centre of the table. A mailing tube rolled off the top of the pile and bounced onto the floor. "Here's what I think," he said finally. "All this evidence shows that before the flood, civilization was already pretty advanced, but they were also very horrible people. After the flood, only Noah and his family lived, but they did not forget everything they knew from before the flood. Once they could live on land again, they just used what they knew and developed more. How else would the people in Babylon be able to build a skyscraper only one hundred years later? The Bible says that God then scattered them all over the earth. If that's true, then those groups of people left what is modern-day Iraq and travelled all over the world. To do that, they must have known how to build great boats. Look at the ark. Noah built it at God's instructions, but that doesn't mean that no one else knew how to build one."

"I can see that," I agreed.

"They took their knowledge with them and each group developed from there. Gradually the knowledge seems to have declined. No one is sure why. However, I believe that there was international travel for centuries before the technologics went lower, which brings us to this ring of stones. I'm no epigrapher," Gerhard said, shaping each syllable, "but I think we have three distinct languages here. One is certainly Mayan, the other looks to be Olmec and the third resembles Hebrew. This makes me ask a couple of questions. One, is this a translation of the same message into all three languages, something like the Rosetta Stone? I can see why there might be Mayan and Olmec on the blocks because these two people groups occupied the same area in Mesoamerica. But the Hebrews did not live there, that we know, so how did Hebrew get on these blocks if there was no world-wide travel in ancient times? It's a puzzle, isn't it?"

"What is your second question?" I asked.

"Oh, yes. If these stones are not the same message translated into all three languages, then it is possible that the reader must know all three of the languages to decipher it. What message is so important that it would require this kind of knowledge to be understood?"

We were both silent for a moment, then Gerhard spoke again. "Here is a third. What were the ancient Hebrews doing in Central America?"

CHAPTER 17

Soft afternoon air caressed my skin and ruffled my hair as I walked along the main shopping street in Thun. Beautiful designer clothes, lacy underwear, fabulous leather shoes, and exquisite chocolate creations all beckoned from pristine store windows. As tempted as I felt to forget my current situation and just go shopping for a few hours, I kept walking. Passing through a walkway between the picture-perfect, painted buildings, I crossed over the river on a narrow footbridge, pausing to watch a family of water fowl chicks learning to dive, then continued on through another narrow passageway and emerged into a shaded square. A sign on the side of a building informed me that it was the Rathausplatz and I knew from somewhere in my past that the Rathaus was equivalent to the town hall. I turned right and set off up the ancient high street called the Hauptgasse. Arranged in two layers, with an upper level above a lower street-level set of doorways that must once have held the carriages of the town's well-to-do, the street brimmed with shops, restaurants, and chic salons. Bright red geraniums tumbled from window boxes mounted on wrought-iron grillwork and Swiss flags alternating with the yellow, red and black Bern flag, featuring the stylized namesake bear, fluttered in the breeze.

As beautiful as this old street was and as much as I wanted to pretend that I was merely on vacation and enjoying the sights, I could not stop thinking about my recent telephone conversation with my mother. I had managed to put it out of my mind while poring over maps and photos with Gerhard, but now that I was alone again, all the anxiety came rushing back. Her announcement that Dennis had been kidnapped shook me to the core. How was this possible? Who was behind it? Dr. Bernaud had mentioned that Mexican organized crime might be in pursuit of Neil, trying to get their hands the stones in hopes of finding riches in Mayan gold. Were they planning to use Dennis to draw Neil out of hiding? I hated to admit it, but that would probably work. Neil would never sacrifice his only son for the sake of an artifact, no matter how important it might be. Or would he? No. No.

Needing a quiet place to think, I stepped into a small tea room, found a table overlooking the river below and ordered a cup of tea from a red-haired girl who spoke only a few words of English. The lowering afternoon sun tinted the mountain peaks in rose and violet and slanted through the town centre, painting rooftops with splashes of gold. My tea arrived in a pretty porcelain teapot and, while it steeped, I reviewed the telephone conversation in my mind, word by word, sentence by sentence.

At first my reaction was to stifle an anguished cry, then I had taken a deep, slow breath and said, "What makes you think he has been kidnapped, Mom?"

"Well, he disappeared," she said, as though that explained everything.

"Mom, he disappears for weeks at a time with his work and no one thinks anything of it. What's different about this time?" I was asking as calmly as I could.

My mother gave a huge sigh, like she couldn't believe I could be so dim-witted. "What's different is that Emily phoned me to tell me that he had been abducted. Dennis was due back from one of his trips out into the hill country, but before he returned, these two guys showed up in the middle of yesterday afternoon. She said they were dressed in suits and had nasty dispositions. When she told them that Dennis wasn't there, they said they would wait. So they sat around her office for several hours, then when she closed up and went home, they waited outside for him to come home. Emily tried to call Dennis but he was out of range. You know how that is. And she couldn't call the police because there aren't any of them way out there."

Dennis' work among the indigenous people often took him out into the hills for days or sometimes even weeks at a time. He helped dig wells, build houses, and conduct church services. Since he possessed more than a rudimentary knowledge of basic medicine, he often helped the villagers and farmers with injuries and infections and carried a well-equipped first-aid kit with him at all times. He travelled in an old pickup truck as far as possible and when the roads petered out, he continued on foot with his equipment on his back. His wife, Emily, ran the mission headquarters in his absence, with a staff of two or three for most of the year, but hosted groups of teenagers on goodwill missions in the summers. Emily, a no-nononsense woman not easily rattled, would have been home at this time of year getting ready for the seasonal influx of youth groups. I could easily imagine her attempting to dispatch a couple of thugs from her premises, and when that proved impossible, kicking them out of her office, locking the doors and going home to bed. She kept a large, well-trained guard dog with her at all times, a mutt of indefinable parentage, who was loyal to the death.

"Poor Emily didn't know what to do," my mother continued. "She was all alone so she took that mutt of hers, locked herself in the house, and slept with the loaded gun beside the bed."

"Did those two guys sit outside there all night?"

"Yes, they did, the scoundrels."

"And she was there inside all by herself?"

"That's what she told me." I had to hand it to Emily. The woman had pluck.

"Dennis arrived home around eight in the morning, having travelled since before dawn and no sooner had he pulled into the mission compound than those two hoodlums jumped him, dragged him into their car and took off. Apparently, Emily was in the kitchen when she heard Dennis drive up, and she saw the whole thing. Before she had a chance to grab her gun and blow out the tires, they were gone."

"Why didn't she think to blow their tires out earlier?" I asked.

"Why do you think? She was probably afraid of them. Who knows what they might have done. Emily called here because no one knows where Neil is, and she didn't know what else to do. Her mom and dad are so old now that telling them would just scare them, so she called us. We're trying to think of how we can help, but don't even know where to begin. I thought you might know something."

"Did Em describe the attackers, Mom?"

"Well, let me see. I answered the phone when she called. She was pretty worked up. I managed to get her calmed down a bit and she told me what happened. Okay now, wait a minute," she paused. "There was something she said about those two men. She said they weren't Mexicans. That's odd, isn't it? She said they spoke English but they had an unusual accent. She didn't feel very afraid of them when they first came into her office because she didn't have the sense that they meant to hurt her."

"Did she say anything else about them — what they said, what kind of accent they had?"

"Nothing that I recall," she hesitated. "Wait, there was something. She said that while they were waiting in her office, one of the men kept fiddling with the car keys, like he was nervous or agitated. It started to get on her nerves so she asked him to stop."

"What's strange about that?"

"The keychain had a Star of David on it."

The waitress came back to my table, startling me, and asked if I wanted more tea. I shook my head. It was nearly five o'clock and the sun was about to slide behind the mountains at the side of the lake. I had no answers about Dennis' abduction and could think of no way that I could help. Sighing, I picked up my bag, paid my bill, and stepped out into the street.

Climbing a set of stairs leading to the upper arcade, I wandered along while my mind worked away at the problem of Dennis' disappearance like fingers unknotting a necklace chain. I tried to picture the scene that Emily had described to my mother, but I had never been to their home in Mexico. I could only imagine her there alone with no help but the Lord to call on, which, let's face it, was considerable. But still, why had Dennis been taken at all and who were those men? What was the significance of the keychain, if any?

Then I remembered the photo of the carved stone head that Gerhard had shown me. It appeared to be Jewish, too. Was it possible that there a connection? I couldn't see what Israelis could want with Dennis. It just didn't add up.

I stopped before a jewellery shop window where a gold and diamond bracelet caught my eye. The piece was exquisitely crafted and for a moment I considered going into the shop to ask the price. That's when I felt the little quiver of apprehension; the kind that shimmies up the spine and parks itself on the back of your neck just below the hairline. Without moving away from the window or turning my head, I glanced first to the left then to the right. I could see nothing unusual and no one but a few shoppers on daily errands.

I stood up straighter as though to examine another item in the window and saw in the glass the reflection of a man standing in front of a décor store on the opposite side of the street, staring straight at me. Moving slightly to get a better look at him in the window glass, I could see that he was about my height, had brown, curly hair, and wore tan pants and a navy jacket. Upscale casual, you could say. At that moment, he seemed to realize I had seen him, because he took a newspaper from under his arm, flipped it open, and pretended to read it. I mean, really, who stands on a street reading the paper? Some disguise!

Feigning ignorance of the man's presence, I turned and continued up the street. On my left I could see the parapets of the castle on the hilltop. I knew that the flat where I had left Marco earlier in the day was a good ten or fifteen minutes hike from here, round the back of the castle and on toward where the river flowed into the lake. Meandering from shop to shop, I tried to keep the man in view. When I walked, he walked and when I stopped, he stopped. I was being followed.

I had to get back to the flat without being seen or I would lead him straight to Marco and we would have no hiding place. With a quick glance over my shoulder, I saw that the man had taken out his newspaper again, attempting to conceal himself behind it. At a moment when I felt sure he would not see me, I ducked into a tiny accessories boutique and headed toward the back of the store. The clerk, a thin girl with dyed black hair that looked like it had been cut with hedge clippers, looked up and greeted me. I smiled and headed for a sale rack with big signs advertising a *Pries Hit!*

Flipping through the shirts and jackets, I pulled out a loose-fitting, long-sleeved shirt in bright pink and slipped it on over my blue and white striped top, then found a colourful scarf and wrapped it around my head. This would have to do as a disguise. When I paid for the purchases which were breathtakingly expensive even on sale, the clerk offered me a bag for the scarf. I took it and placed my tote into it before heading for the door. Peering through the window, I could see my follower lurking in front of a china shop across the street. Just then a gaggle of teenage girls came along, so I slipped out of the store and matched step with them, keeping to the inside of the sidewalk. When we came to the corner, I crossed the street with my new girlfriends then while they continued on the Obere Hauptgasse, I headed up the road past the castle. One backward glimpse showed me that, for now at least, I had given my pursuer the slip.

The medieval castle and the old church stood on top of the hill overlooking the town and the valley below, their turrets and spires stabbing the purpling sky. But my desire to go exploring had been thoroughly extinguished so I gave the fairytale buildings barely a glance. Walking fast, I strode up the street, fighting the impulse to break into a run and put as much distance between me and the stalker as possible. If there was any chance he was still tailing me, running would only attract attention. The only other people on the road were housewives coming home with full shopping baskets and a few tired-looking office workers in suits. Gasping for breath, I turned the corner for the last stretch and checked the hand-drawn map that Gerhard had made for me with directions to the flat. My side hurt so that every step made me want to cry out, but I pressed on. I knew that we were all involved in a dangerous game, the end of which remained a mystery. I thought of Dennis and Emily and felt helpless and angry. The sooner I gathered the rest of the stones, the sooner it would be over and we could all get our lives back to normal. I thought about the remainder of my conversation with my mother. I had been so upset over Dennis' disappearance that I had sobbed into the phone.

"What am I going to do now?"

"Go to Geneva," Mom said firmly.

I sniffled. "What?"

"Go to Geneva," she repeated.

I wiped my eyes with a tissue. "What am I supposed to do in Geneva? Where do I go?"

She sighed. "Jill, listen to me. Go to Geneva. You know…Geneva. I can't say any more than that. You understand. Think about this. Do you know what I mean now?"

I stopped sniffing and thought about her words. Then it clicked. "Oh. Geneva. I get it. I have to go… to Geneva?"

"Yes, now go buy your ticket. It's all arranged." Which is exactly what I had done the minute I left Gerhard's flat.

Now as I reached the apartment, I turned the key in the lock and quietly opened the door, not wanting to wake Marco then gently closed it and placed my bag on the kitchen counter. Slipping out of my shoes, I tiptoed into the living room and was just about to set the keys on the dining room table when the bathroom door opened and Marco strode out wearing nothing but a small white bath towel clutched around his loins.

"Aaaa!" I cried, jumping backward and ramming my right hip into the corner of the dining room table. Yelping in pain I twisted away from the table, tearing the bandage off the gunshot wound at my waist. "Ooowww," I wailed, dropping the keys on the floor.

Marco let go of his towel and reached out to help me. "Oh, oh," he said, grabbing it just in time. "Sit down, Jill." He patted my shoulder with one hand while clutching the towel with the other. "I will be right back." I edged carefully toward the sofa while Marco fled down the hall. I pulled the scarf from my head and sat gingerly on the edge of the couch. Lifting shirts, I checked the wound. The bandage had pulled away from my skin and re-opened the wound. Dark blood now oozed from the ragged edges of the gash.

A moment later, Marco reappeared, this time fully clothed, his dark hair wet. "Let me take a look," he said, moving my hand away and lifting the bandage. I winced as it pulled more of the cut open. "Stay here and don't move," he said, replacing the gauze and dashing into the kitchen. With damp paper towel he dabbed the blood away, then he ran to the bathroom. I could hear him rummaging in the medicine cabinet, where he found clean gauze and surgical tape. Instructing me to lie down, he gently dressed the wound, all the while muttering softly in Spanish, his fine, black eyebrows drawn together in concentration.

"What are you saying?" I asked.

"*Que?*" His eyes flickered in my direction.

"What are you saying in Spanish?"

"Oh, *nada*," he replied, peeling a length of tape from the roll and tearing it between his teeth. "You have to take better care of yourself," he said, applying the tape to the bandage and pressing it onto my skin with his fingertips. "Where were you anyway?"

"I went to Gerhard Mueller's place."

"I should have come with you."

I lifted one shoulder and let it fall. How could I tell him that I hadn't wanted him there with me? "I didn't want to wake you. You had been up all night and I knew that you would have to drive back to Spain soon. You needed the sleep." That was all true.

"You could have let me decide about that, you know." He took the supplies back to the bathroom, then came and knelt by the sofa where I lay, checking his first aid handiwork. His damp curls tumbled all over his head but his chin looked freshly shaven.

"Someone was following me," I said.

He stared at me. "What are you talking about?"

"I walked back here from Gerhard Mueller's place just now and someone was following me."

"Who?" he barked.

"I don't know who; I just know he was following me."

"Does he know you are here now?"

I shook my head and pushed myself up to a sitting position, wincing from the pain. "I managed to lose him."

"How did you do that?" Marco looked thunderous, gripping both my arms in his hands as though I might evaporate before his eyes.

I twisted out of his grasp and sighed. "I went into a shop and bought that scarf," I said, indicating the wisp of silk that now lay on the floor, "and this shirt. I hid my tote in the shopping bag from the store. Then I waited until a group of noisy young girls walked by and slipped out of the store alongside them. When they crossed the street, I went the other way and walked as fast as I could all the way here."

Marco ran a hand through his wet hair and sat on the sofa beside me. "Tell me about this man who followed you. What did he look like?"

I hesitated. Perhaps I should have kept my mouth shut but I was scared and needed a friend. At the moment, he was the only one I had. I gave him what details I could and watched his face.

"We have to get you out of here," he said, standing up.

"I know."

"Get your things now and let's go."

"No," I said, not moving. "I'm leaving tonight on the train."

Marco blinked. "What do you mean? Where are you going?"

"Sit down, Marco," I said. He grabbed a dining room chair, swung it around and sat opposite me. With elbows on his knees, he leaned toward me and waited, his eyes fixed on mine and his lips in a thin, grim line. "I am leaving this evening and I can't tell you where I'm going. Something has happened that has upset me a great deal, but I can't tell you what it is."

He hung his head for a moment, blowing out his breath, and then looked at me again. "You shouldn't take the train. Let me take you where you have to go."

"No. That's not possible. I have been instructed to take the train this time. Besides, you have to get back to Madrid and to your work. I have to continue on my own."

He reached out and took my hands in his. "I know that what you are doing is very important, and that it is dangerous. I respect that, and I have tried not to pry. I think you also know that I have come to…to care about you a lot. I don't want you to walk out of my life today and then I will never see you again. You need someone to help you. You're not well. There must be something I can do. Please tell me." His dark eyes shone. I longed to throw caution to the wind and say yes, drive me where I have to go, drop me off at the door and kiss me good-bye, but there was too much at stake.

I shook my head and looked down. His strong hands with their sun-burnished skin gripped mine tightly as though he might refuse to let me go anywhere without him. "I don't know how this is all going to turn out so I can't..." I stopped, and looked away.

"Come here, *mi amor*," he said gently, sliding onto the couch beside me. Putting his arm around my shoulders, he kissed the top of my head. "It will all work out," he said gently. "There is a reason why we met and I know that you and I are meant to be together. Just wait and see," he said.

I hoped he was right.

CHAPTER 18

In spite of the language difficulty, I managed to order take-out pizza which had been delivered by a young man with more stainless steel hanging from his face than a kitchen utensil rack. It was safer to stay in and eat than go out to a restaurant and risk being seen again. I paid for the pizza with money I had exchanged at Gerhard's bank and Marco and I helped ourselves to dishes, cutlery and bottled water from the kitchen.

My train was scheduled to leave at 10:15 and Marco promised to take me to the station. From there he would head back to Spain, driving all night again. Now he sat across the table from me as we picked at the remains of our meal. We talked about everything but the fact that in a few hours we would part, not knowing when we might ever see each other again. Absently twirling his fork, Marco shared his hope of one day owning his own restaurant on a beach somewhere, a dream that closely matched mine of one day owning a house with a studio overlooking the ocean. Then we moved into deeper subjects as I described my faith and how my romance with Jesus Christ underscores everything in my life. Once we began to talk about spiritual matters, time flew by.

Now the sky was dark and the lights from the villages edging the lake glittered and danced on the black surface of the water like fireflies on a sheet of satin. As we cleared up our dinner things and were washing the dishes, we heard a sound outside the door.

"Shhh," I whispered, touching Marco's sudsy arm. Then I heard a soft rapping on the wood door.

"Ja?" I said through the door

"It's Gerhard Mueller. Please could you let me in?"

I twisted the key in the lock and opened the door. Gerhard leaned against the door frame, pale and shrunken. "Gerhard," I cried. "What is it? What happened?"

Gerhard stepped into the room and closed the door behind him, locking the deadbolt and turning to face us. "I went out this evening for dinner with my girlfriend, Rachel, and when I came home, my apartment had been sackranned!" he intoned, disbelief twisting his features into a stiff mask.

"I think what you mean is ransacked," I corrected, taking his arm and leading him to a chair. "Sit down here and tell us everything."

Marco dried his hands on the towel and took a chair opposite Gerhard. I sat beside him on the sofa and placed my hand on his shoulder. He trembled ever so slightly.

"When I comed home this evening, my apartment door was not locked, even though I know that I locked it when I go out. When I open the door, there is stuffs everywhere." He waved his hands to indicate the whole room. Clearly, his state of mind had affected his facility with English. It didn't matter. "Everything is torn apart; there are papers everywhere, and all my collections they throw on the floor. My files and maps they fling all over the place. I could hardly walk without stepping on important papers. The place is a big mess, a big mess." He stopped and rubbed his eyes.

"Gerhard," I urged, "are you hurt?"

He seemed to snap back to the present. "Oh, no, Frau Moss. They are gone by the time I goes home. I did not know what to do, but I thought maybe they are still around, you know, and might come back. So I think I better get out of there. I took my car and drove to Steffisburg where my friend, Hans-Ruedi, lives. There I put my car behind his house and go in and stay for a little while. When I leave, I drive his car and take lots of roads before coming here. I drive down the lake to Oberhofen and Hilterfingen and take all kinds of crazy streets, you know, in case someone follows me. Then I come here and park on the next street. I walked in the shadows to come up here.

"Marco spoke up now. "Do you think anyone was following you?"

Gerhard shook his head. "I don't think so, but I thought I should be careful, for you." He gestured toward me.

Marco nodded and bit his bottom lip, then said, "Could you tell if anything was taken from your flat, Gerhard?"

Gerhard looked so bleak that I felt like hugging him. He looked at me again and nodded. "The photos. The ones I gave you today, remember? I had my copies and they are gone. There does not seem to be anything else gone. When you left today, I cleaned up all of the papers that we looked at and filed everything back in its place, except for my field notebook. I put that into my bag when I went out because there was something else I wanted to show you. I thought I might come over this evening anyway, but now I don't think I can go back to my place. I have to stay here."

"What are you talking about? What photos?" Marco demanded, leaning toward Gerhard with a look so menacing that Gerhard backed away.

"Marco, please stop it," I said. "Can't you see the poor guy is rattled enough?" Marco glowered at me but leaned back in his chair, though I could see that his knuckles where he gripped the arm rests were nearly white through his tan. "Gerhard gave me some photos today. We can't divulge what they were, and you don't need to know. Suffice it to say that something of value and importance is missing and Gerhard may be in danger." I turned to Gerhard. "Of course you must stay here until you feel that the danger has passed. I am so sorry that this has happened to you. I am sure that my uncle never intended for you to encounter trouble like this, or he never would have involved you." Gerhard seemed to relax a bit now. "I have a feeling that whoever ransacked your apartment has found what they were looking for and won't be back."

"You are probably right, but what if they also wanted my field notes?"

"Chances are they don't know that your field notebook exists. If I were you, I would take out a safe deposit box in your bank and keep all the information regarding your work with my uncle in that box until further notice." Gerhard nodded and looked relieved. "There is something you need to know, though," I said gently. "I am leaving tonight on the train, and Marco is driving back to Spain. I wish I could stay longer, but I think that my presence here would make your situation even more hazardous. I will try to stay in touch with you, but I can't promise anything."

"I understand," said Gerhard.

"I don't," said Marco.

"I'm sorry, Marco," I replied, suddenly irritated. "There are things that you don't need to know. You would think, given what has just happened to Gerhard that you would realize that the less you know, the better." I drew a hand over my tired eyes. I looked at Marco and saw that he stared back at me with a steady gaze, exhibiting neither understanding nor rancour. "Oh, Marco," I said. "I'm sorry for snapping at you. But it's true, just the same."

He reached for my hand. "Forget it," he said. "I know you have a lot on your mind."

I smiled and thanked him, then stood up. "I need to gather my things," I said wearily. "It's almost time to go."

"But wait," Gerhard said, "I have something to show you." He glanced uncertainly at Marco.

Marco nodded. "I should wash my hands," he said, then he stood up, went to the bathroom and closed the door.

Gerhard reached into the newsboy bag at his feet and drew out his field notebook. "Look at this," he said, flipping the pages. "The light wasn't very good, I'm afraid." He stopped at a photo that at first looked like nothing more than a slab of rock. Taking the notebook from his hands I leaned toward a lamp and saw faint inscriptions carved into the rock. They looked like most other illustrations of Mayan codex that I had seen except that between each row of square glyphs were smaller inscriptions, perhaps one quarter of the size of the Mayan script, but in an entirely different style. It was hard to make out the shapes.

"What is it, Gerhard?" I asked handing the notebook back to him.

"To be honest," he replied, "we're not sure, but the style of the inscriptions resembles the one on the blocks. We found this before the blocks came to light and Neil and the whole crew were mystified. There hadn't been time to get in an epigrapher to give us an opinion on the language before I had to come home, so I don't know if Neil has yet found out what it says or what it means. I remembered it after you left. I haven't had a chance to look at the photos very closely but now that my copies are gone, I wondered if we might compare them to yours."

I pulled my copies of the photos from my tote bag and unrolled them. Holding them beside Gerhard's notebook photo, we examined the two sets of images. Sure enough, some of the characters on the wall frieze looked remarkably similar to the pattern on the stones.

"So these stones are not the only example of this style of writing," I stated.

"Evidently not," Gerhard replied. "Perhaps these people of another land spent more time with the Maya than we previously guessed." Marco emerged from the bathroom and Gerhard snapped his notebook shut and jammed it into his shoulder bag while I rolled up the photos and deposited them back in my tote.

Twenty minutes later we said good-bye to Gerhard and walked out to Marco's car, keeping to the shadows and dashing across the street toward the vehicle. The street was quiet and we saw no one. We parked next to the train station and Marco carried my suitcase up the steps. At the doors I turned and stopped him. "I don't know how to thank you for everything that you have done for me," I said facing him in the dim light. "I can never repay you."

"Shhh," he said, touching a finger to my lips. "You don't have to. I'm God's gift to you," he said with a grin. "We will meet again, I know. But for now we must go separate ways."

"Oh, Marco," I murmured. "Please kiss me good-bye." In an instant, his arms were around me, drawing me toward him as his lips found mine. After a long moment I dragged myself away. "I must go now," I said. "When this is all over, I will call you."

He brushed a finger down the side of my face. "Promise?"

I nodded. "I promise. Besides I've already given you my phone number, so if I ever get home again, you will know where to find me."

"You'll get home," he said. "I will be praying for you." With that he kissed my cheek and turned away.

On the platform I pulled the collar of my coat up around my neck against the night breeze and waited. The train rolled to a stop exactly on time and I climbed aboard and found my cabin. I had to change trains onto the French system at the border. From there, I had reserved a small sleeper cabin. I couldn't face the prospect of spending the night crammed into a compartment with five other people.

My destination was not Geneva, the city, but rather the home of my mother's childhood friend, Geneva Connolly, who lived in an eighteenth-century chateau in Provence. Geneva was like an aunt to me and had lived down the street from me where I grew up. Her daughter, Cynthia, and I had also been friends. Once the kids had grown and left, Geneva's husband, Stanley, decided it was time to indulge his lifelong dream of living in the south of France. He and Geneva sold everything and moved overseas.

Once on the French train, I found my cabin, kicked off my shoes, changed into my pyjamas and climbed onto the narrow berth. It was past midnight. I pulled my journal and Neil's Bible from my tote and closed my eyes. "Jesus, it is so nice to spend time alone with you again," I said. Never able to carry off long, religious-sounding formal prayers anyway, I had always felt on a first-name basis with Jesus. "You know what I have been going through and I know that you sent me to do this, but I'm tired and my side hurts where that creep shot me, so please take this pain away. I want to thank you for bringing Marco into my life when I needed someone. He is something else, isn't he?" I stopped. I hadn't felt like this about a man for a very long time and though it felt delicious, it was also a little nerve-wracking. "Please keep leading me in the way you want me to go." I prayed for protection and deliverance for Dennis, wherever he was, and Emily, too, and for special protection for Neil. I opened my Bible and slowly read Psalm 91 out loud, applying each verse to myself and the others involved in picking up the pieces of this stone artifact. I imagined us all under God's wings like chicks under the wings of a mother hen. According to the tenth verse, God orders his angels to protect me wherever I go. I leaned my head back against the wall of the moving train and allowed the lullaby of the track to rock me. I had just begun to drift off to sleep when I heard the Holy Spirit. I shook the sleep from my groggy head and picked up my journal and pen and began to write the words that appeared across the screen of my imagination.

"Have no fear, my child. You are always protected by my angels. Even though what you are going through is difficult at times, you can rest in the assurance of my protection. The mission you are on is not yours, nor it is your uncle's, but it is mine. These perilous times are drawing to a conclusion and these stones are part of the puzzle which will one day soon all become clear as the pieces come together. Never be concerned about those who doubt the way I speak to you. This is how it should be, yet most people never come to me and ask to hear my voice. When I speak they do not listen or they disregard my direction. Do not be that way for it is the desire of my heart to be in touch with those who love me. There is no nourishment for the spirit in empty religious practices. Like my word says,

those things are like filthy rags for all the good they will do you. Only true communion with my Spirit will feed your soul and give you rest. I promised green pastures and still waters and rest for your soul, yet most of my children knock themselves out going through the motions of religion. Take time to come and sit with me and I will lead you. I will refresh you. Trust in me alone and have no fear. I am looking after you."

I took a deep breath and a blanket of peace settled over me as I tucked away my journal and Bible and turned out the light. Snuggling down into the crisp cotton sheets, I fell into a deep, untroubled sleep, lulled by the rhythm of the rails.

Persistent, high-pitched beeps roused me from dreams and I rolled over to find my little travel clock squawking away on the floor next to my berth. I stopped the noise, then squinted at the time. Five after five. In less than an hour this train would pull into Aix-en-Provence and from there I would have to find a bus. I assumed that Geneva knew I was coming, but I had no instructions about how to get to her place.

I pulled on a pair of clean white jeans, a fuchsia t-shirt, and sandals. The sun had risen clear, bright and hot. Twisting my hair into a clip, I packed up my belongings and watched the French countryside slide past the windows of my cabin. Twenty minutes later, the steel wheels screeched to a stop in Aix-en-Provence. After stepping off the train, I found a small bakery café and ordered a cappuccino and a huge croissant, warm from the oven, which I slathered with butter and red currant jelly.

When I arrived in Lambesc, the tobacconist on the corner had just set out his sandwich board signs. The ancient main street lay still under the slanting early sun and a couple of old men hunched, leaning on their canes with flat hats pushed back on hairless skulls, watching nothing in particular through weary eyes. Yanking up the handle of my suitcase and giving the bottom a kick as I tipped its weight onto the wheels, I strolled down the sidewalk in search of a pay phone. At the tobacco shop my request was met by a surly grunt from the proprietor, a sloppy character with a huge belly straining against the buttons of his filthy shirt. He stared at me through red-rimmed eyes and told me no, I could not use the telephone and no, he had no phone book.

Through a haze of smoke from a foul-smelling cigarette hanging from his greasy lip, he mumbled something about the bar across the street so I left him to his self-inflicted misery and went to find out. A curling sign taped to the inside of the grimy, front-door window informed me that this establishment would not open until ten o'clock. I wondered who on earth started drinking at ten in the morning then decided that I would rather not know.

Shading my eyes with my hand, I looked up and down the street, contemplating what to do next. Down the block I could see a service garage that looked open and in front stood a couple of motorized scooters.

Parking my suitcase outside, I walked through the open garage door and greeted a young man who was sweeping the floor with immense enthusiasm. It turned out that he was Polish but he spoke a little English so I managed to communicate that I needed to find a telephone number. Running into his tiny, spotless office, he returned with the local phone book in his hands, yet we failed to find a number for the MacIntyres. Did he know the estate, I asked and he nodded vigorously, explaining that only yesterday Mr. MacIntyre had to take his wife for a ride in the country on one of the Vespas parked out front. After a bit of haggling, a lot of gesticulations from both of us, and a hand-drawn map to La Chalonnaise, I sped off down the road out of town on the scooter, my suitcase safely stowed in the garage's office.

The morning sun seemed to sparkle off the stone walls and houses, the grasses and wildflowers growing on the sides of the narrow country road. Once out of town, I slowed down to navigate the gravel ruts on the dirt lane. The track led past ancient stone fences craggy with lichen and fields of sunflowers about to blossom with bright yellow faces. The air, dry and shimmering with summer light, felt fresh and invigorating. In spite of not having had enough sleep, my soul lifted in joy and gratitude for this beautiful day in such a lovely place. It seemed like I had the world to myself.

At a fork in the road, I stopped to consult my map and turned right. I glanced in the bike's tiny rear-view mirror and noticed a car some distance behind me. It was red and looked a lot like Marco's. As I edged around the curve, I twisted around for a better look. The vehicle slowed, too, keeping pace with me. Gunning the throttle on the bike, I raced off in the direction of La Chalonnaise. Just before a small hill, I took a quick look back over my shoulder and saw the red sports car stop at the fork in the road, then roll into the turn and go left. With a sigh of relief, I headed over the hill to my next destination.

CHAPTER 19

The barking began even before the bell rang. Pulling to a stop next to a high, pale stone wall I edged up to two enormous, wrought iron gates. On the other side, two snarling dogs waited, one a German shepherd who appeared to take his guard duties seriously, and the other a mixed-breed, black mutt who looked like he simply enjoyed being mean. Inside the gate, a sloping, stone-paved drive led between two lower walls and on into a wider, open courtyard. Along the right, the wall enclosed the tiny courtyard of a cottage and behind it the main house rose up against the pale blue sky, an imposing gold-stuccoed structure with tall chimneys and windows high up under the eaves. Faded blue shutters bordered the tall windows of the lower floors. To the left of the drive, the ground dropped straight down probably twenty feet to peaceful gardens. Through the treetops I could see raised ponds and flower beds laid out in classical French symmetry.

A twisted wire ran through a loop embedded in the top of the stone wall and hung down along the side of the gates. Yanking on it produced a chain reaction that wound away into the inner courtyard and culminated in the jangling of a bell somewhere deep in the property.

I waited. After a few minutes, the dogs got bored with me and lay down. I gave the bell wire another good tug and listened for its clanking.

"*Oui, oui, je viens,*" muttered a voice coming from around the corner of the cottage garden wall. "I'm coming." Slightly stooped and wearing a pair of baggy brown shorts and a faded blue shirt with the sleeves turned up to the elbows, the man looked to be in his mid-sixties. A battered hat sat on his mop of grey hair; on his feet were a pair of scuffed clogs, and he carried a trowel. He sauntered up to the gate. The dogs leapt to their feet and bounded around him, tongues wagging. "Madame Moss?"

"*Oui.*"

"*D'accord. Venez-vous.*" He inserted a key the size of a dinner fork into the lock on the gate and swung the enormous iron structure open just far enough for me to walk the bike through, then closed and locked it.

"*Merci,*" I said holding my hand out. He took it in his dry, leathery palm and gave it a perfunctory shake. "Pascal Descartes," he said, setting off down the paved drive. The dogs sniffed my ankles, then they too sauntered away and plopped down in the shade. I parked the bike at the bottom of the drive. In the centre of the courtyard, a beautiful fountain stood with clear water trickling over the edges of three moss-covered stone bowls. Opposite the cottage stood another water garden, this one filled with towering trees in full leaf. At the sound of my arrival, five small spaniels rushed out of an anteroom and lined up along the iron railing of the wide terrace, each one poking its sweet face through the bars and regarding me solemnly.

Just then the shutters on a second floor room creaked open and Geneva leaned out. "Hello, stranger," she called. I squinted up at her and waved, breaking into a huge grin. "I'll be down in a minute, as soon as I get something decent on. Just come up on the terrace. The dogs won't hurt you."

A couple of minutes later she opened a set of shutters on the main floor and stepped into the morning sunlight, arms open wide. I rushed into her embrace.

"It is so wonderful to see you," I cried. "It has been too long."

"For me too, darling," she answered, standing back to look at me. "How are you?"

"Sometimes great," I replied, "and sometimes…not so great."

"I'm not surprised," she said, "but we can talk about that later. Come in and I'll fix some coffee. Have you had breakfast yet?" Without waiting for an answer, she said, "I'm sure you're ready for my special coffee and some croissants. They are fresh from the boulangerie this morning. Pascal picked them up when he came in." I didn't tell her that I had already had one. Another wouldn't hurt. She began making coffee then stopped. "Oh, my goodness. If we had realized when you were coming, Pascal could have picked you up this morning at the train. He was probably in town the same time you arrived. What a shame."

"I didn't have your phone number," I explained, "and couldn't find it in the book when I stopped at the garage. But the guy knew where La Chalonnaise was so he drew me a map, rented me a motor bike and here I am."

Out on the terrace, we moved the green metal table and chairs into the shade and Geneva went back into the kitchen and brought out a tray laden with white lace napkins, china coffee cups and small plates. In the centre sat a plate heaped with warm croissants, plus a bowl of butter, three pots of jams, and cream and sugar for our coffee.

She was almost exactly my mother's age, early sixties, but Geneva had always been the glamorous one compared to my mother's homespun prairie style. Now, when most women her age had long since lost their bloom, Geneva still presented herself with style and panache. This morning she was dressed in a trim, white dress with turquoise beaded trim, and a pair of chic white patent leather sandals. Her honey-blonde hair was held in a loose knot with a simple gold clip and she wore dangly gold and turquoise earrings.

"It's so beautiful here, Geneva," I said. From the corner of the terrace I could see a swimming pool below with a burbling fountain in the centre. Farther on, a field of purple lavender stretched toward a row of Lombardi poplars swaying in the morning breeze. From the terrace I also saw the sunken garden with stone statuary, raised semi-circular ponds and flowering trees. In the opposite direction, an alley of plane trees led away from the swimming pool and at the far end of the row I could just make out a stuccoed cottage.

"It is, isn't it?" she replied, pouring the coffee. "We love it here so much, and though sometimes we miss our home in Canada and being closer to family, we haven't regretted for a moment selling up and moving here."

"Where is Stan this morning? Isn't he joining us for breakfast?"

"Stan is in Hamburg looking at water pipes," she replied. "He left yesterday, so you just missed him, and he won't be home until sometime next week. I know he will be disappointed that he didn't get to see you but what can you do? *C'est la vie.* This whole property was built on a spring in the eighteenth century so the pipes are not exactly current."

We finished our breakfast and reminisced about our shared past and family news. Eventually, the sun came around so that we found ourselves in its direct glare and Geneva offered to show me the house. Gathering up our tray and dishes we went inside to the cool, dark interior of the little kitchen. The dogs followed our every move until Geneva insisted they stay outside so they wandered away and curled up in shady corners to snooze.

After days of tearing around the continent with villains on my tail, it felt wonderful to be safe and with someone I loved. We toured the house, starting on the main floor in the grand salon with its stone tile floors, fourteen foot ceilings, and towering French windows. Geneva explained that the house had originally been built by some member of the French aristocracy as a country house and before the citizenry began chopping off heads with the guillotine.

Taking the stairs up to the next floor, Geneva showed me the library, a green-painted room lined with antique books and the master bedroom which held a polonaise bed hung with more Provençal fabric.

"Come and look," Geneva said, leading me to the window where the courtyard and the water gardens lay before me like a picture. Beyond the perimeter of the garden I could see the rolling countryside.

"It is so beautiful," I sighed. "I could look at that view for the rest of my life and never grow tired of it."

"It gets pretty hot this time of year," she said, pulling the shutters in, "so it's important to close up early. But come and look at the view this way," she added. "This one faces south so we have to keep it closed in summer or we'd cook in here." She pulled open the glass windows and pushed the shutters out to reveal another perfect view, this time of the swimming pool filled with pale green water. Rows of fruit trees stood along each side of rows of lavender. "We have apricots, plums, apples, cherries, peaches, pears, and even a mulberry tree, should we decide to go into silk production," she said, laughing.

Later on, we arranged to return the motor bike and pick up my luggage. Geneva followed me in her car, a little Fiat, and after that we stopped at the shops to buy fresh food for supper.

When we returned home, I begged for a nap and Geneva offered me a little room above the kitchen. "That way if you get up early, you can go downstairs and make yourself a coffee. We live at a pretty relaxed pace here."

We shared a quick lunch, then I went for a nap. I woke at three o'clock, took a quick shower and changed into a pale green and pink sundress, the only dress I had with me that didn't have bullet holes in it. I found Geneva lounging on a chaise in the grand salon reading a book.

"Feeling better?" she asked, putting it down.

"Much better, thanks. I didn't get much sleep last night on the train, or the night before. It was definitely catching up with me."

"Come and sit," she said, offering a seat on a peculiar couch with high arms but no back. "I have something for you."

She walked over to a tall chinoiserie escritoire desk and opened the drop leaf. Reaching inside she pulled open a tiny drawer and drew out a square package and thick envelope and handed them to me. I set the package on the settee and slit open the envelope.

Geneva placed a hand on my shoulder. "I'm going to go make some phone calls and leave you alone while you read your mail." I nodded absently as she left the room.

Inside the envelope was a letter from Neil and a credit card in a smaller envelope. I opened the letter and read.

Dear Jill,

First of all, there is no way I can begin to thank you for what you are doing for me. By now you will have a pretty good idea of the magnitude of the request. In the interest of safety, I have tried to keep as much information as possible secret from all parties concerned but I'm sure after speaking with G.M. you have started putting it together. What you don't know is that there is much greater significance to this find than any of us had originally thought. It will all be revealed when the time is right.

Jill, I want you to know why I chose you to undertake this assignment for me. I realize that there are plenty of others who might have more stamina and more interest, but you have something that no one else has. Because you have dedicated your life to learning to listen to the Holy Spirit, you are in the best position to make the right decisions and take correct action when you have no one else to consult. Because you have taken the time to develop your ability to hear God's voice and you have an open mind about spiritual matters while still being immensely practical and capable, you were really my only clear choice. Needless to say, I gave this matter a lot of prayer once I could see what was coming down the pike and time and again the Lord brought you to my mind. I wish I could promise you that you won't regret this but I guess that will be up to you.

I understand that there are some nasty characters from Mexico who are trying to get their hands on the goods so be on guard at all times. What has only recently come to light is that another group has an interest of an entirely different nature. So if it seems like the woods are crawling with vermin, you're not far wrong. I don't want to give you any other information about this group yet because the less you know at this juncture, the better.

I have heard from other contacts that things are going well with the roundup of the items, and you are nearly halfway there. You can't know how much it pleases me that things are working out so well.

I am fine and am well-hidden so there is no need for you to be concerned about my safety. This will all be over soon and you can go home and get back to painting (I hope!).

I know that you will have incurred some expenses so I am including a credit card here for you to use. All you have to do is sign it and use it however you see fit. Be sure to reimburse yourself for everything that you have spent and don't be afraid to treat yourself, too. It will all be taken care of.

I have timed this letter to get to you and act as instructions for your next move. Ask Geneva to drive you to the nearest town that starts with P. There you will find a special delivery letter addressed to Geneva at the Post Office at Poste Restante, the French equivalent of General Delivery.

Don't stay in any one place too long. I'm sure you are tempted to hide out with Geneva, but the next links in the chain are waiting. The faster you move, the less likely that you will be observed.

Be careful and go with God. My prayers are with you. Psalm 91.

Love Neil

I folded the letter and placed it back in the envelope then took the credit card out and turned it over. It seemed clear that at the time of writing this letter Neil did not know what had happened to Dennis. How could he? He must have mailed this before I even left home. But no, he mentioned that he had contacts who were keeping him informed and knew of my progress. Who could that be? Perhaps he had been in touch with Dr. Bernaud already or Profesor Alvarez. He couldn't possibly have heard from Gerhard. My visit with him had been too recent.

Unless.

I had assumed that Neil was hiding somewhere in Central America, but if he was nearby he could have mailed the letter within the past couple of days and it would have arrived here before me. Was it possible that he was following me around making sure I did the job? That seemed unlikely. But if not Neil himself, who might it be? Could the man on the street in Thun be working for Neil? And what about Marco? Whose side was he on? Was it possible that he too worked for Neil and had latched onto me in order to keep an eye on me? It was all too crazy.

I placed the credit card in the envelope with the letter and went up to my room, signed the card, and put it in my purse. I had no doubt that Neil would help me with the cost of this trip but I had wondered how he would go about it. A credit card provided the simplest method. I just hoped that when the bill came, there would still be someone to pay it.

CHAPTER 20

After a dinner of salad and shrimp, with the soft evening air folding around us, Geneva invited me on a tour of the estate. It was named for the wife of an aristocrat from some past century who hailed from Chalon-sur-Saône, a small city in eastern France.

The gravel crunched under our feet as we wandered past the swimming pool. "Tell me what's going on in your life," Geneva said. "I don't mean what you are doing with Neil since that's temporary. I mean your personal life. How have you got on without Roger?"

I sighed. "It hasn't been easy, Gen," I replied. "The kids suffered a lot. Knowing that they were in so much pain compounded my suffering. But they seem to have bounced back a lot faster than I have. I still miss him, even though we had our difficulties."

"I'm sure you do. I won't say, 'life goes on' even though it does, because we know that it never goes on in the same way again. What sort of difficulties do you mean?"

"You knew Roger from the time he was a teenager." I answered. "He was so full of life and energy when he was young. That's what attracted me to him, but as time went on things changed. Maybe it was the responsibilities of marriage and a family, or that he wasn't very happy in his work, but he became kind of bad-tempered as though he carried around a smouldering anger at the world."

"I know what you mean. It's difficult to deal with a people who are unhappy, but who won't help themselves."

"He was basically a kind-hearted person, but so wound up in his own emotions that he couldn't talk things out. He came from a pretty messed-up family, as you know. His dad was a mean-spirited character and his mother was just defeated. When Roger was happy and feeling good, he was the loveliest man, but if things weren't going well with work or his health or whatever, he could be pretty unpleasant to be around. Sometimes it was very hard."

"So when he was killed...?"

"I was torn apart. I always thought there would be time to straighten things out, to help him get to the bottom of his anger and perhaps find peace, but it never happened. That's what hurts the most, the unfinished business. I prayed for him a lot, and I saw the Lord work in his life, but there was only so much I could do. The rest was up to him." We walked in silence for a few minutes. The fountain in the centre of the swimming pool splashed softly as we rounded its corner and began down the long allée of plane trees.

"I've prayed about it a lot since Roger died, too," I said, "and the Lord has given me peace about the whole situation. In fact, I don't know how I would have survived had it not been for the gentle compassion of Jesus, but that doesn't mean I don't still have regrets. My life has changed in so many ways, and since he has been gone I've often felt at loose ends. I feel like I'm trying to pick up the pieces of my life, but I don't know what or where they all are."

"We all have regrets, my dear," Geneva responded. "We just have to learn to let them go."

"I know. God has talked to me a lot about that." Out of the corner of my eye, I saw Geneva's body stiffen almost imperceptibly.

"Don't start talking about hearing God," she said, her voice tight. "You know that most people who think God talks to them are psychopaths or kooks. He doesn't do that nowadays, no matter what the television preachers say."

I knew that lots of people held that opinion, but just as surely I knew they were mistaken. Choosing my words carefully I said, "I agree that there are people who are mentally ill who claim to hear voices and are certain that it is God who is telling them to do horrible things. That's not what I'm talking about. You are a believer, so you must know that Jesus said in John 10:27 that his sheep, meaning his followers, hear his voice. I don't think he just meant when he was alive and walking on the earth, do you? It doesn't make sense that God talked with people all through the Old Testament and even the New Testament, but stopped after the book was published."

"Well," she replied stiffly, "that may have happened to Moses and Abraham, but I don't know too many people today who go around saying that God talks to them, do you?"

I laughed lightly, "Actually, yes, I do. The problem is that most of us have never been taught how to listen and hear God or the Holy Spirit speaking to us. We don't know what to expect so we have come to believe we shouldn't expect anything. It is a great deception perpetrated on the people of God because without knowing how to hear God, we cut ourselves off from much of his leading and direction. Most of us who do know that we hear God's voice don't go around telling everybody we meet about it for the same reason you just mentioned. People will think you are sick in the head." I stopped, bent down, and picked up a deep pink rose petal. "Come to think of it, I suppose that many people actually do sense the leading of the Spirit in their lives but simply don't recognize it as God's leading. They chalk it up to a hunch, or a feeling, or intuition. When we learn how to zero in on the voice of the Jesus, a lot of confusion goes away."

"Well," Geneva said, sounding quite defensive now, "I was taught that all that had passed away and now we have the Bible. That's where we are to go for God's direction."

"Of course, that's partly true. We are to use the Word of God for our direction, but we've all been in situations where the direction we seek may not be specifically addressed in the scriptures yet we still need God's input to help us. Things like whether to buy this house or that house, or even to buy one at all; what to say to your friend in a crisis, and how to make the right business decisions, often need specific answers. So then we pray and ask for the Lord's help, yet never sit still long enough to wait for an answer because we don't really expect one. We look for the circumstances to change or we think that we will get a sign or an impression, which, granted, are methods that the Holy Spirit will use. But I think that sometimes he is forced to use those methods since we don't actually take the time to listen for his voice."

"I never thought of it that way before," Geneva replied, her protective shield dropping a little. "But how do you know it is God talking to you and not just your own thoughts?"

"That's a good question and one that I'm sure everyone in history who has sought God has grappled with at one time or another, including me," I said, laughing. "I can only tell you what my experience has been. Years ago, long before Roger died, I realized that every day I needed help, direction, and wisdom for how to respond to situations, the kind that come up for all of us. It's great to have a friend or a spouse to talk things over with, but sometimes you have no one. And let's face it, sometimes the advice of those close to us is not that good simply because none of us can see into the future. But God can."

"Okay, that makes sense."

"One day I just sat down and told God that I needed to hear from him and from then on I would take time to listen. I also said that if I thought I heard his voice or direction, in whatever fashion, I would act on it. That way, even if I made a mistake, he could re-direct me. Sometimes I get his leading by just a sense or a feeling of peace or certainty that I should do or not do something, and other times I will hear him speak actual words, sentences and paragraphs into my mind. I usually use my journal to write down what I'm hearing so that I don't miss anything and so I will have a record of what he has told me to refer to later."

"But isn't that kind of like automatic writing?"

"I don't know. I just know that it works for me. I always start by using the authority that we have in the name of Jesus and commanding that every voice except for that of God, Jesus, or the Holy Spirit to be silent and leave my presence. The enemy will try to speak into our lives, but Jesus gives us authority over those evil spirits, so we don't have to put up with listening to whatever they want to say."

Geneva stopped and turned to me. "Jill, I have never heard of that in my life and I've been going to church since I was a little wee girl. How do you know that is true?"

"Because it is in the Bible, Geneva. Jesus himself said that he gave us power over all the works of the enemy."

"How could I have missed that?" Geneva asked almost to herself as we turned to continue walking. By now we had reached the end of the long alley which opened out into a small courtyard. In front of us stood the cottage that I had seen earlier from the terrace. It was divided into two compact dwellings. Attached to the front of the building stood a semi-circular pool with another fountain and in it floated several white water lilies. Beneath them I could see the flash of goldfish swimming in the tiny pond.

"Does someone live here?" I asked, looking up at the charming dwellings.

"We've been fixing up these cottages to rent out as guest accommodations. We're going to be starting a small-scale bed and breakfast operation once we get the plumbing updated."

"I would love to come here and bring my kids someday," I said, imagining us enjoying Provence with La Chalonnaise as our base. We turned and walked down a short stone stairway which led to the orchard level and started back toward the lavender field.

"You haven't answered my question, Jill."

"Which one?"

"What your life is like now that you are single. Is there anyone special in your life? Are you looking to get married again?"

I smiled and looked off toward the canal for a moment. The leaves of the soaring poplars along its banks fluttered in the warm evening breeze. "Until now," I began, "I haven't been interested in having another man in my life. I had to finish raising my children and I had to provide an income for us. My career has been going well, but it can be up and down, as I'm sure you are aware. It seemed like all the energy I had got used up just getting from day to day. Things are a little different now. The children are grown and off on their own and I have had several large painting commissions, plus my work has been picked up by a couple of successful galleries. Except for this episode working for Neil, my life is pretty peaceful - lonely sometimes, but peaceful."

"But, my dear, you are still young. You don't want to spend the rest of your life alone." She said it as a statement of fact. "You need to find yourself a man."

"Funny you should mention that," I replied, "because I have recently met someone here in Europe. I don't know him well, but um, there is certainly some chemistry going on."

Geneva grabbed my hand. "Tell Auntie G. all about him," she said, eyes shining.

"There's not much to tell. I met him a few days ago at the home of Neil's friend. He's Spanish and he's extremely good-looking, and..." I trailed off, not wanting to go into any more details.

"All right, dear," she said, relenting. "I won't press you further. But don't let too much water flow under the bridge before you move on. You're not getting any younger, you know."

"Thanks for the reminder!" I said, laughing as I took her arm and we headed back to the house.

The next morning, immediately after breakfast we drove to the nearby town of Pélisanne and found the Post Office. Outside, after picking up my letter from Neil, Geneva and I stopped at a sidewalk café and ordered lattes and, since no one makes them like the French, fruit tarts. I slit open the envelope and pulled out a single, slim sheet of paper.

Dear Jill,
It is time to move on again. I expect things are getting warm in Europe by now and I have heard through my friends that you have been followed. Here is what I want you to do:
Before you leave France I need you to go to Arles. Don't ask Geneva to drive you. Take the train. Don't make a reservation; just buy a ticket at the nearest station. When you get off the train in Arles, go find the Roman Arena. Go around the arena to your left and you'll find a restaurant called Hostellerie des Arènes. Take a table outside by the street at six o'clock Thursday evening and wait. A young woman named Rebecca will meet you there and give you the next instalment plus further instructions. Be sure to make her tell you her name. She will also mention a phrase which only the two of you will know. That phrase is, "East wind and rabbit tracks".
Burn this letter when you have finished reading it.
Love Neil

I read it over a couple of times until I had memorized its contents then burned it in the ashtray, making sure that nothing but grey ash remained.

"That must have been important," Geneva commented. "Are you on some kind of spy mission?

"No, nothing like that," I said, though there were distinct similarities. "Let's go now," I said, getting to my feet. "I need to get packed."

We would have just enough time to get back to La Chalonnaise and have a quick lunch. I asked Geneva if she could drive me to the train station at Salon de Provence. "I love Salon," she claimed. "The market is on today, so, if you like, we can go back to the estate, you can pick up your things and we can go straight on to Salon, have lunch there, wander the market, and you can catch the train after that. Would that work for you?"

Once back at the château, we checked the train schedule on the internet then set off. By three o'clock, we had walked the market and eaten lunch at a shady outdoor café in the main square. I had also bought a pair of pink polka-dot sandals and still made it to the station in time to catch the train to Arles.

"Thank-you so much for everything," I said, giving Geneva a hug.

"Let me know how everything goes," she said. "I can't wait to find out what this is all about, but Neil told me I wasn't to ask." Her eyes crinkled at the corners as she smiled at me. "And all the best with your new romance!" she said, kissing my cheek.

The sun was sinking toward the horizon when I stepped off the train in Arles and hailed a taxi to take me to the Roman arena. At the main entrance, I paid the driver, picked up my bag, and headed around to the side of the towering stone edifice, sorry that I had no time to explore it. I glanced at my watch and saw that I might have five minutes to spare so I ran up the long stone stairway to the base of the arena. Gazing through the soaring arches, I could see the centre oval where bullfights still entertained roaring crowds.

The restaurant was directly across the street from the side of the arena. I found a corner table under a huge green umbrella, behind a couple of planters overflowing with frilly greenery and hidden from the view of passersby. It was five to six. I ordered an omelette with cream cheese and herbs and a mineral water. The waiter, a short, sour-faced man, poured my water, set down the bottle, and strode away. Down the street I spied a tall, young woman coming toward me, gliding effortlessly along on a pair of inline skates. Her hair, a sun-streaked golden brown, fanned out around her shoulders and her skin was the colour of clear buckwheat honey. She wore a pair of knee-length jean shorts and a yellow tank top. *This has to be Rebecca,* I thought. When she skidded to a stop on the other side of the planter, she plucked an ear-bud from one ear and said, "Hi, are you Jill?"

I tilted my head and looked up at her. "Who are you?"

She rolled her eyes and pulled the ear-bud from her other ear. "I'm Rebecca," she said. "Oh yeah, I'm supposed to say, 'east wind and rabbit tracks,' whatever that means."

I nodded. "Please join me."

She wrapped the cord from her music player around her fingers and stuffed it into a pocket, then came around the planter and sat down opposite me. "So," she said, leaning toward me and dropping her voice, "I have something for you but I'm not supposed to let anyone see it." She shrugged a baggy backpack off her shoulder and dropped it on the pavement beside her skates.

"Would you like something to eat?" I asked, seeing the waiter head in our direction.

"Yeah, okay," she replied. "I'd love some quiche or something."

"My treat," I offered. She looked delighted and promptly ordered quiche and salad with strawberries, plus a glass of white wine.

When the waiter left again, she reached down and while she unzipped her pack she whispered, "I'm going to pass this thing to you under the table so you can put it straight into your bag."

"Good thinking," I agreed, smiling. I took a sip of water as I leaned forward. The box in her hand rapped my kneecap, but I wrapped my fingers around it and dropped it into my tote bag. Rebecca sat up and casually ran her fingers through her hair, flipping it down her back as though a little espionage was all in a day's work for her.

"Don't look now," she said later as she mopped up the last lick of salad dressing with a sliced strawberry, "but there's a man across the street who has been staring at us for the past ten minutes. Anyone you know?"

I laid my fork down and leaned back, peering through the plants next to the table. "Nope. I've never seen him before in my life. Are you sure he's interested in us?"

"Probably you more than me," Rebecca replied. "Is this someone we want to meet, or should we give him the slip?"

"The slip, I think."

She nodded. "Got a plan?"

"No. Have you?"

"Yeah."

"You have?"

She rolled her eyes again and signalled the waiter. I paid him as she picked up her backpack, pulled a scrap of paper and a pen out of it and scribbled something on it. "I'll go over there and create a diversion. While I have him occupied, you slip out past those people over there." With the pen in her hand, she pointed to a spot over my right shoulder. A tour group of elderly ladies milled around on the sidewalk, chattering like a flock of starlings. Rebecca handed me the paper as she slipped her arms through the straps of her backpack. "Follow this map and go to the address written on it. It's not far, just up the street. The **X** is where we are now, so it won't be hard to find. The door is open. Just go on in and wait for me. I won't be long."

Rebecca got up and skated away while I grabbed my bags and headed toward the gaggle of tourists, ducking out of sight as I passed them and following the map to a blue door leading into a tiny upstairs flat. I hauled my suitcase up the stairs, opened my tote bag and pulled out the small box wrapped in brown paper. Inside it lay another stone in the collection, plus a folded note which read:

Fly to London Gatwick as soon as possible. Don't waste any time. Call this number from the airport before you leave and someone will meet you at the arrivals level. They will find you, so wait outside the doors nearest to where you go through customs.

As soon as you can after this rendezvous, get on the next flight out to Miami, Florida. When you get to Miami, I will have a car waiting for you at the airport. The driver's name is Jim Escobar. Make him tell you his name and show you picture ID. He will take you to the next destination. You are to meet an old friend of mine. Prepare yourself. Neil.

A telephone number was scrawled along the bottom of the paper. I folded the note and stuffed it in my bag when I heard Rebecca come in. She clomped up the stairs and dropped her pack on the floor at the top.

"What happened?"

"I created a diversion," she replied, grinning.

"Okay. Tell me what you did."

Shrugging one shoulder, she flopped down on a worn, flowered sofa and began to remove her skates. "I just skated into the guy. He fell on the rack of magazines. The kiosk owner threw a fit and in the commotion, I just took off. Simple."

I laughed. I liked this girl. She had aplomb.

CHAPTER 21

The Rhone River glistened like a sheet of steel in the slanting rays of the rising sun. Barges and riverboats slid across its flat surface as the taxi pulled into the train station parking lot. According to the schedule, I should be able to take a train from Arles to Marseilles, then another out to the airport at Marignane, giving me plenty of time to catch the flight to Gatwick.

I had been unable to get a flight out of Marseilles the previous evening. Rebecca looked up the schedule on the laptop she carried around in her backpack and stated in her matter-of-fact way that there was no point trying to go anywhere that evening. When I announced that I had to find a hotel for the night, she rolled her eyes and said, "I know you're old enough to be my mother but if you want, you can have the couch."

Stifling a grin, I said, "All right. I accept." I could take an early train and get to Marseilles in time to board the ten o'clock flight. We spent a surprisingly pleasant evening eating popcorn and talking. Both her grandfather and her mother had worked with Neil at one time or another. Rebecca was perplexed about her role in Neil's escapade and asked me a lot of questions, most of which I answered with vague responses.

The next morning, I rolled off the lumpy couch to the alarm clock's squeal. The bandage on my side had come loose in the night and I could see that the skin around the slash left by the bullet had turned an ugly purple-red but there was little pain and no infection.

Twenty minutes later, showered, dressed, and cleanly bandaged, I was ready to go when Rebecca wandered out of her bedroom, yawning and rubbing her eyes.

"Leaving already?" she asked, hitching up her low-slung pyjama pants with one hand and running her fingers through her hair with the other.

"I'm aiming for that 10:00 a.m. flight out of Marignane, remember?"

"Oh, yeah." She ambled to the petite galley kitchen and pulled the refrigerator door open. "Did you have something to eat?"

"No," I replied. "I'll pick something up at the train station."

She looked at me like I had sprouted horns. "Are you nuts? Train station food is the worst. Here, let me fix you something. Let's see…" She stuck her head in the refrigerator and pulled out an orange, a lump of cheese wrapped in wax paper, and a half-empty jar of strawberry jam.

"I really should be going."

"My mom would break my arm off and beat me with it if I let you leave without feeding you," Rebecca said frankly. "This will only take a sec', then you won't have to buy anything."

"All right," I agreed, leaning against the wall and watching her spread butter and jam on a slab of a baguette. She hacked off a chunk of cheese, wrapped it in stretch film, and stuffed everything in a used paper bag.

"Here," she said, handing me the bag. "If you want, you can get a coffee at the train station. At least they do that right."

"Thanks," I said. "I've already called a taxi, so I had better go now." I hoisted my tote to my shoulder. "Thanks for everything."

"Hey, no problem," Rebecca replied, waving a hand. "Next time you're in town, look me up," she hesitated, "if I'm here." She reached out and gave me a quick hug. I left her standing at the top of the stairs hanging onto her drooping pyjamas.

At the train station, I checked the schedule for the right track then pulled my bag out onto the platform. I had ten minutes. A regional train sat on the nearest track. I glanced at my watch and sat down on a bench to wait. As the bustle of commuter activity swirled around me I felt, for the moment at least, solitary and calm. I took a deep breath and exhaled slowly, closing my eyes and allowing my muscles to relax as a gentle breeze fanned my skin.

"Madame," said a deep voice beside me. "We meet again."

My eyes flew open and a jolt of adrenaline shot through me as my head snapped round. Menendez! The same man who chased me at the Gare de Lyon in Paris.

"What do you want?" I said, hiking the strap of my tote up on my shoulder and reaching for my suitcase. I slid closer to the edge of the bench.

He fixed me with a cold stare. "I think you know what I want, Señora." How had he found me? And how was I going to lose him? I glared at him.

"Give me the stones, Señora." His voice cut through the air like a knife blade.

"I don't know what you're talking about." I said, leaping to my feet. With a lunge, Menendez grabbed hem of my jacket. I wrenched away from him. Something wild flared up in me. There was no way I was going to give in to this guy. Not now, not ever. I had been through too much to lose it all now. Yanking the tote bag from my shoulder and putting all my strength behind it, I smacked him across the side of the head with it, books, rocks, and all. He stumbled backwards a few steps, but it gave me just enough time to grab my suitcase and run. The wheels of nearest train had just begun to roll and an SNCF employee strode along the platform checking the doors. *If I can just get there before the doors close*, I thought wildly. Out of the corner of my eye I saw Menendez regain his footing and spring after me.

Then the unbelievable happened. A troop of school children tumbled out of the station doors onto the platform, three or four classrooms of them, all with backpacks and drink bottles in hand. Exuberant and high-spirited, they fanned out across the platform like a swarm of bees from a hive.

As the train on the track picked up speed, I leapt for the only remaining open door, pulling my suitcase aboard behind me. I glanced back at the platform and saw Menendez dodging and weaving after the train and surrounded by a sea of bouncing, chattering children. It was too late. As I rolled past him, I laughed out loud at his livid, purple face then, giving him a little wave, I picked up my bag, found a seat and blew a kiss heavenward.

"Thank-you, thank-you, thank-you, God," I said, "for getting me out of that fix."

"That was heartfelt," commented a voice from across the aisle. A woman about my age stared back at me with one eyebrow raised.

"Absolutely," I replied, reaching across the aisle and offering my hand. "I'm Jill Moss."

"Caroline Alexander," she replied, shaking my hand.

"You wouldn't happen to know where this train is going, would you?" I asked.

"You mean, you don't?"

"No. I was waiting for the next train to go the airport at Marseilles, but I suddenly had to get away from that platform."

"And that odious man?"

"You guessed it."

"He your husband or something?"

"No, nothing like that," I replied. "He's just a menace." She nodded but didn't ask for more. "So, where does this train go?" I repeated.

"Avignon."

"Oh, dear. I think I'm going the wrong way." Caroline pulled a map from her handbag and handed it to me. Unfolding it across my lap, I traced my fingertip over the rail lines. I had to go south and Avignon was to the north. Now what? Though it would be the quickest route to Marseilles, I didn't dare get off in Avignon and go back south the way I had come. I scrutinized all the squiggly lines on the map and discovered another rail line that led away from Avignon to the east through a town called L'Isle sur la Sorgue and then continued on south from there through Cavaillon and Salon de Provence. From there I would go on to Miramas where I could change trains again and get back on the route to Marseilles. I felt certain I could avoid another run in with Menendez if I took that line. There was no telling how long it would take me to get to the airport, but there didn't seem to be any other choice. I would miss my flight. I handed the map back.

In no time the train slid to a stop in Avignon. I left the train only long enough to change my ticket at the wicket of a sad-faced, chain-smoking woman who refused to answer any questions. Within fifteen minutes we pulled out of the station and left the city behind in favour of the French countryside. Before long, the train squealed to a halt at the quaint station of L'Isle sur la Sorgue. Everyone in the car except me got up and left the train.

"Aren't you getting off?" asked Caroline as she hauled a bulging bag from the overhead rack. "It's the end of the line for this train."

"Pardon?"

"This train stops here then goes back to Avignon. The one going on south doesn't come through until this afternoon. I know it doesn't make sense, but this is France; it doesn't have to. But this is a pretty town, lots of antique shops, so if you want to look around and have some lunch you'll have time." She reached over to shake my hand. "Good luck with your connections."

I stepped off the now-silent train, checked the schedule on the wall, and found the ladies' room in the station. There I changed my clothes. Slipping on a pair of black walking shorts and a plain white blouse, I twisted my hair up into a knot and secured it with a clip. It wasn't much of a disguise, but it might help, should Menendez come looking for me here. I walked through the station and out into the street.

Two hours later, I had eaten an early lunch, browsed the shops and was tired of dragging my suitcase around on bumpy cobblestone streets. Everything but the dingy bars had closed for the afternoon.

Back at the silent station, I sat alone waiting for a train that was not due to depart for another two hours. I had my pick of seating and chose a high-backed bench facing the ticket wicket. Though tempted to lie down and take a nap, I chose instead to pull out Neil's old Bible and look for more clues about the stones. I could not remember where I had left off, so I opened it in the book of Deuteronomy and scanned each page for markings. I came upon the first one in chapter two, verses ten and eleven, which read:

"The Emims dwelt therein in times past, a people great, and many, and tall, as the Anakims; which also were accounted giants as the Anakims; but the Moabites called them Emims."

And a little further on in verse twenty I read: "That also was accounted a land of giants: giants dwelt therein in old time; and the Ammonites call them Zamzummims: A people great, and many and tall, as the Anakims; but the Lord destroyed them before them; and they succeeded them, and dwelt in their stead."

I could not remember reading these verses before. Turning the page, I came across another marking in Chapter three, verse eleven. "For only Og king of Bashan remained of the remnant of giants; behold, his bedstead was a bedstead of iron; is it not in Rabbath of the children of Ammon? Nine cubits was the length thereof, and four cubits the breadth of it, after the cubit of a man." A bit further down I saw, "…and all Bashan, which was called the land of giants."

I leafed through the pages, scanning the margins. In chapter nine I saw another reference to the giants called Anakim. What was Neil trying to tell me about these giants? How could they be of any significance today? I looked again at the length of the bed mentioned in verse eleven. I had learned that the length of a cubit equalled the distance from the elbow to the fingertips but it differed in length depending on the stature of the person. A rough calculation meant that the bed measured between thirteen and a half and fifteen feet in length and approximately six feet in width. By anyone's measure that was one big bed!

If there was a connection between these verses and the stones, I couldn't see it. And I was feeling sleepy. The afternoon lay heavy and quiet, punctuated only by the sound of an indolent fly batting against the window. I rested the book on my lap and took the clip out of my hair, letting it fall around my face as I absently rubbed the spot on my head where the teeth of the comb had pressed. Leaning my head against the hard, wooden bench, I closed my eyes. I must have dozed off, for some time later I was startled awake by the raucous cacophony of a flock of crows squabbling in the trees next to the tracks. Sweat dampened my neck and my blouse stuck to my back. I sat up and tugged the shirt from my sticky skin, then twisted my hair up again.

That's when a car roared up outside. I heard the Holy Spirit warn me to duck. A man ran through the building and out onto the platform while I held my breath. I managed to catch a glimpse of him but through the dirty window and in the glare of the sun, I could not recognize him. Menendez must have found me but I was not sure. Something different yet familiar showed in the angle of his shoulders. Before I could get a better look, he was gone. I heaved a sigh of relief when the car sped away.

I arrived at the airport in Marignane, outside of Marseilles, barely in time to buy a ticket and get on the 5:20 flight to Gatwick. Before I boarded, I found a pay phone and dialled the number Neil had asked me to call. An answering machine picked up and a woman's voice asked me to leave my flight number and time of arrival. I recorded that and nothing more.

The south of England lay under a soggy, grey blanket of cloud which the airplane bumped through on its descent into Gatwick, touching down and screaming to a halt on the wet tarmac. Inside the airport, I pulled my bag through the mobs of people and stepped into the line snaking toward customs. Twenty-five minutes later, I stood on the rain-soaked sidewalk outside the terminal doors and waited in a steady drizzle for something to happen. I didn't have to wait long.

A sleek, silver car wheeled toward me and braked at the curb where I stood. I bent over and peered into the darkened windows and could make out two figures inside. Suddenly, the passenger door flew open and out leapt a woman in tall black boots and a black leather coat. Around her neck she wore a bright red scarf and above the scarf the familiar, arrogant face of Claire Jamieson regarded me with cool disdain.

"Hello again, Jill," she said with a smile that did not reach her eyes. "Let me take your bag." She dove for my suitcase but I snatched it away and backed toward the terminal doors. On the other side of the vehicle, the door opened and a man stood up, the same slimy character I had seen at the roadside café in France. He dashed around the front of the car and made for me as I ran for the glass doors.

"No you don't!" he shouted, his voice heavy with accent. "You're not getting away from me this time."

"Help!" I screamed, hoping to alert security or an altruistic passerby.

Claire bounded after me. Just as I neared the sensor the automatic door opened and someone streaked past me. A dark-haired man wearing sunglasses charged through the door, coattails flying. His arm shot out like a piston and his fist connected with the jaw of my swarthy pursuer whose head snapped around like a ball on a string as he reeled and fell to the pavement. Claire let out a little squeal and jumped sideways, then lunged for me. She took a swipe at my bag, but my mysterious helper grabbed her by the arm and with a swift backhand to the mouth sent her spinning to the concrete.

"Come on," the man said. Grabbing my suitcase with one hand and my wrist with the other, he hauled me down the platform. I stumbled after him as a white Volkswagen screeched to a halt at the curb. The man yanked open the door and shoved me in, throwing my case in after me and leaping in behind it. Before his foot left the sidewalk, the car careened away from the curb and sped off down the ramp from the terminal building, weaving through traffic like a pursued rabbit. The corner of my suitcase dug into my leg and I heaved it off me and looked at my captor. He had twisted around to look backward out the window, allowing me to see only the side of his face. Black hair curled around the bottom of his ear. My breath caught in my throat.

Then snapping his seatbelt into the buckle he turned to me and smiled. "Hi, *mi amor*," he said.

"Marco!"

"Mmhmm."

"What are you doing here?" I shrieked.

"Aren't you happy to see me?"

I grabbed the sleeve of his jacket with both hands and shook him. "How did you get here? How did you know I was here?" Then I stopped. "Are you following me?"

"Let me introduce our chauffeur for today, my dear," Marco said smoothly. "Please say hello to Eddie MacIntyre. Eddie, meet my friend, Jill Moss."

Eddie touched a fingertip to the frame of his aviator sunglasses and gave me a quick glance in the rear-view mirror. I could see only the crown of his glossy, shaved head over the car seat back. "Ma'am," he said, jerking the steering wheel hard left around a delivery truck, then pounding his foot to the floor as we tore down the street. "I think it's time to lose them, Marco." His eyes flickered back and forth from the rear view mirror to the road ahead. I clutched the door handle with both hands as the car wove through the congested traffic.

"Do what you have to do, Eddie," Marco answered, throwing a glance over his shoulder.

"Are they following us?" I twisted in my seat and gawked out the back window. I could see the big car about six vehicles back. Claire and her mate had wasted no time.

"I'm afraid so," Marco answered, reaching out to stroke my hair.

"You haven't answered my question yet," I said, pulling away from him.

"Hang on," Eddie said, cranking the wheel. The tires squealed as the car drifted around a turn into a short alley, then protested violently as we screeched to a stop.

"Come on, Jill," Marco commanded, throwing his door open and grabbing my suitcase. "Get out now!" I flung my door open and leapt out, gripping my tote. Eddie was running down the alley toward a scuffed metal door. Marco seized my hand and pulled me along at his speed. Eddie jerked the door open and held it open just long enough for us, then slammed it behind us. We were in a parking garage running headlong down a ramp to the underground level.

Eddie, several paces ahead, skidded around the corner at the bottom of the ramp. Through the concrete supports I could just see him dash to a pale green Renault, leap in, and start the engine. By the time Marco and I caught up, he had already thrown it into reverse and backed out. Once again, Marco shoved me in and threw my suitcase in on top of me before diving in behind me. Eddied gunned the engine and headed for the exit. Within seconds we burst into the grey light of day and careened down a completely different street, dodging a young mother pushing a pram and a milk truck double parked in the road.

"That should do it," Eddie commented, looking pleased. "Where to now, boss?"

CHAPTER 22

Gravel crunched under the car tires as it bumped through potholes and wash-boarded down a crooked lane bordered by ferns and hedgerows. Patches of blue sky emerged between bundles of cloud jetting off toward the southwest, tinted pink by the setting sun. The front right tire of the car plunged into another abyss in the road, throwing me against Marco's shoulder.

"Umph," I grunted, reaching for my door handle. Ahead lay a small clearing in a grove of trees and through it I caught sight of a perfect English cottage. White-washed walls, thatched roof, and with a scarlet climbing rose hugging the front door frame, the house looked like it had magically appeared out of a fairytale. Eddie pulled up before the front stoop. Before we could get out of the car, the house door opened and a flurry of small dogs poured out followed by a short, round lady with grey curls, wearing a mauve floral apron. Where it stretched over this woman's bulky waistline, the fabric was coated in flour.

Eddie leapt out of the car and the woman threw her arms open wide and folded him in a hug against her ample bosom. Eddie introduced Marco and me to his mother, Jean McIntyre, who promptly invited us inside for tea and fresh scones. *How very English*, I thought, as I stepped over the dogs and took a seat in the low-ceilinged front room. An electric heater glowed from an old, cavernous hearth and sent waves of warmth over my feet.

Mrs. Mac, as she insisted on being called, served us warm scones with clotted cream, plum jam, and scalding hot tea. It all tasted divine.

"Eddie," said Mrs. Mac when we had nearly finished eating, "why don't you take Marco out and show him the garden?"

"But, Mum," Eddie protested, "it's almost dark out."

"Then take the dogs for a walk. I need to have some time alone with our lady friend." Eddie sighed and looked at Marco. "Come on, mate. General Mac has spoken."

The two men rounded up all five dogs who, once the first leash came off the hook on the wall, clamoured to be let out. Marco flung his jacket over his shoulders and followed Eddie out the door.

Mrs. Mac walked over to a dark wood sideboard and pulled open one of the top drawers. From it she drew a small package, still in its postal wrappings, and handed it to me.

"You'll know what this is about, won't you, dear?" she said. "I thought it best to clear those two blokes out of here just in case this is something they don't need to know." She lowered herself into a sagging arm chair opposite me and stretched her stocking-covered legs toward the radiant grill. "How well do you know this Marco fellow?" she asked, pushing her glasses higher up her nose.

"Not particularly well, I'm afraid."

"Hmmm," she replied. "I'd watch out for that one if I were you."

"Why?"

"For one thing, he's too handsome for his own good." The hint of a twinkle entered her left eye then just as quickly disappeared. "And he's smitten with you."

"And your point would be?" I asked with a twisted smile.

"That's what I thought," she said, nodding. "Well then, never mind. Just be careful until you're sure which way the wind blows." Her motherly advice amused me. I nodded solemnly. "I wanted to talk to you alone because I have a story to tell you." She picked up the teapot and re-filled my delicate china cup and settled back into the comfortable old armchair.

"I hardly know where to begin," she said. "It was all so long ago."

"Why not begin with what comes to mind first," I suggested.

"Good idea." She smacked the arms of her chair with her palms, releasing puffs of dust that hung in the lamplight. "I first met Neil Bryant when I was a young student at Cambridge. He had taken a semester to study there under a visiting professor whose name now escapes me. That summer was my first year away from home and the confines of my mother's apron strings and my father's overbearing manner which discouraged all suitors and promised to render me a spinster for my entire life.

I met Neil one day in the dim recesses of a library. I'll never forget my first sight of him. I came around the corner of the shelves, drawing my fingertip along the spines of the books as I searched for some volume. Neil sat on the floor amidst a stack of crumbling volumes piled nearly to his ear tips. Scuffling away in the bottom shelf of the section on Hebrew history, there he was. I would have tripped over him if he hadn't reached out his arm to protect himself from being trampled. I yelped and gave him a swift kick in the pants, at which point he leapt to his feet and backed away, tripping over his piles of books, flailing madly, and landing on his backside. He looked so funny that I started to laugh. Eventually, I found my book in his pile."

She paused, staring into her teacup. "After that day, Neil and I were rarely apart. We found that we shared a passion for ancient Hebrew languages and Bible history. Those few months that he lived in Cambridge were magical for me, months of intense discovery and fascination, both in the subject of our research and personally. It turned out that I had a passion for more that archaeology. In fact, I fell in love with Neil in those days we spent together exploring musty old books." For a moment she looked almost abashed, as though she had never said those words out loud before. "He was the most exciting person I had ever met and I wanted him almost as much as I wanted to know the secrets of time." Her eyes swivelled back toward me. "Alas," she said, "it was not to be. Before long, Neil revealed to me that he was engaged to someone back home and at the end of his study semester he planned to get married. I have often wondered how different my life would be if he had married me instead."

I knew she could tell me much more, but my energy was waning. "What kind of secrets did you discover about ancient history?"

"Oh my," she replied, sitting up straighter and tugging her cable knit sweater down. She had removed the flour-dusted house apron over her plaid skirt and dark green pullover. "I'm sure you have heard of Sir Isaac Newton."

"Of course," I replied. "Gravity, the apple and something mathematical."

"Newton was the foremost scholar of his time. He was a scientist, certainly, but what most people don't realize is that he was also a Bible scholar without parallel."

"I didn't know that."

"They didn't want us to know."

"Who didn't?"

"The established church bigwigs of the day didn't want anyone to know what Newton knew."

"Which was?"

"Most people think of Newton as only a scientist, but he actually spent over three quarters of his years of study in theology. However, most of his notes and materials never saw the light of day until recently. You see, what he discovered would have turned the whole church establishment on its ear and upset the balance of power. Newton wrote about his theological thoughts for several decades but these works remained a secret. It seems like he intended for his research to be found after his death."

I leaned my chin on my hand. "What was it that Newton discovered that caused such a furor?"

"Sir Isaac Newton had risen to the position of professor at Cambridge and worked there until the bubonic plague came along. As the plague spread outside London, twenty-three year old Newton went home to live with his mother in a little place called Woolsthorpe. During this time in the country he devised calculus, came up with his theory on gravity and studied the works of ancient prophecy. While he'd been a student at Cambridge, Newton had learned Hebrew. A very clever fellow was our Mr. Newton. Several years after his discoveries about light, gravity, and how time related to prophecy, Newton wrote a book called *Observations upon the Prophecies of Daniel and the Apocalypse of St. John*. Newton centered his studies on what he called *"prisca sapientia,"* which means pristine knowledge. With *prisca sapientia*, Newton and his cronies sought to rediscover the vast body of knowledge they believed had been lost over the centuries. They recognized their own knowledge as vastly inferior to the knowledge of ancient intellectuals. Ancient texts had come to light in fragments and references in these works that had not been found heightened their drive to find out the hidden secrets."

"I see," I said, though I did not see clearly at all.

"The assumption today is that civilization has developed in an ever-rising standard of intellectual development, but a closer look reveals that the opposite is true. Newton believed that ancient civilizations were intellectually and scientifically superior to modern day cultures. The discovery of the New World by Columbus stimulated the desire for more adventure and knowledge; however, the perception that the New World had never been discovered before by ancient civilizations persisted and still does, even in the face of evidence to the contrary."

She took another drink from her teacup. "Oh, dear," she said, frowning, "that's gone as cold as a dead man's foot."

She pushed herself out of her chair, went over to the sideboard, and pulled open a drawer. Rummaging around in a mess of papers, she tugged out a sheaf of ten or so pages stapled together at the corner then sat back down.

"During this time, men trying to reconstruct the lost works of antiquity were in great competition with each other. Each wanted to be the only one who knew." She flipped through the sheets, running her finger down each one. "Ah, in Newton's own writing he says that the ancient geometers claimed no one else's work was worth anything and they deliberately concealed their own analyses from other scientists of the day."

Fatigue clouded my thinking. "I'm having trouble seeing the connection," I said, hoping Mrs. Mac would not take offense.

"This is it," she replied, unfazed. "Newton figured out that there was a lot of knowledge from the ancients that had been buried by time and, unlike his contemporaries, believed that it should be recovered and shared. He just had to do it so as not to jeopardize his job."

All of these bits of information had begun to fit like pieces of a jigsaw puzzle but many pieces were still missing. Each piece that clicked into place presented me with more questions. Gerhard Mueller's findings from his expeditions, Profesor Alvarez's maps and charts, and even what little Dr. Bernaud had shared with me in Paris seemed to agree with Newton. There was much more to the past than met the eye. The passages in the Bible that Neil had marked led to the same conclusion. How did what Newton understood about ancient knowledge fit with the mysteries of building construction in antediluvian Central America, for instance? What was the link between the languages on the stones and the knowledge that ancients had? And how much of the puzzle had Neil already solved?

Suddenly, the front door burst open and a bevy of dogs roared in, barking, panting, and leaping over each other. Marco and Eddie followed, each holding a tangle of leashes. With cheeks flushed from the cool night air, they released the dogs from their collars.

"Don't take your coats off," Mrs. Mac called out, pushing herself out of her armchair. "You can't sleep here tonight."

"What are you talking about, Mum?"

"I've given your room to Mrs. Moss," she replied, "so you take our Mr. Marco here and the two of you go on down to The Horse and Hounds and get a room or two. I am sure Geoffrey Bains has an empty house tonight, but you can give him a call first if you want to make sure. If he's full, go on over to The Seagull Inn."

Eddie sighed and shot a glance at Marco. "That's fine with me, Mrs. MacIntyre," Marco said. "We will be back bright and early to take Señora Moss to the airport again. Are you sure the two of you will be all right here?"

"We have five yappy watchdogs," Mrs. Mac said dryly. "I think we'll be all right."

The room that Mrs. Mac led me to under the thatched eaves held a simple double bed, a plain white-painted dresser, and a bedside table with a glass lamp. "Eddie only stays here when he is around," she explained. "He works for a power company and they have him tearing all over the country all the time. He has a flat in Salisbury, but sometimes he comes by when he's working in the area and stays overnight. The loo is down the hall on the right." She handed me a pile of folded towels. "There you go, love. You have yourself a good sleep."

"Thank-you so much, Mrs. Mac," I said, stifling a yawn.

"Do you want me to wake you in the morning, dear?"

"I have my own little travel alarm clock, but my flight leaves at ten forty-five," I said, making a mental calculation, "so I had better be up by around six, don't you think?" She agreed and promised to have breakfast ready.

Ten minutes later, I crawled into bed, turned off the lamp, and tugged the down-filled comforter up under my chin. A lace curtain on the window had been drawn back and a bright half-moon sailed through thin tresses of cloud against an ink-black sky. As I lay staring up at it, I thought about the wild ride from the airport with Eddie and Marco earlier. Mrs. Mac's house was not far from Gatwick and after a series of twists, turns, corners, and sudden veers behind hedgerows we had arrived at her farm. Though I had asked Marco again how it came that he happened to be at the airport at the same time as I, he somehow managed to dodge directly answering my questions. On a business trip; seeing a client; just happened to be in the right place at the right time, was all he said. I knew he was hiding something but could not pull it out of him.

Now I lay curled in my cozy bed staring out at the moon as my thoughts swirled. It seemed hard to believe that only this morning I had said goodbye to Rebecca in Arles. A shiver ran through me when I recalled my encounter with Menendez at the train station. Who was he anyway? Clearly, he was after the stones and I assumed he was with that Mexican Mafia contingent that Dr. Bernaud had told me about, but I had no way of knowing for sure, and I did not want to chance stumbling upon him again just to find out. If his demeanour was any indication, he enjoyed ruthlessness and brutality. Was Claire really who she had said she was, or had she lied to me about her past connection with Neil? And that horrible man she hung around with! Oozing evil, his hollow black eyes glittered with hatred. The mere thought of him sent a wave of nausea through me. Shuddering, I snuggled deeper into the bed. God help me.

It seemed with each passing day, more players entered the game of tracking me and trying to snatch the stones from my possession. Somehow the Israelis had become involved, no doubt because the stones themselves held a secret carved in ancient Hebrew inscriptions on the stone pieces. What could that message be that they wanted so badly? And how had they found out about it in the first place? All this cloak and dagger stuff was wearing me down, but I knew that I couldn't quit now. Too much was at stake, possibly even the lives of Dennis and Neil.

With everything that had happened, I had not thought of Dennis all day. I longed to call my mother and find out if she knew anything or had received any news of his whereabouts. What if Dennis had been killed? Resolutely, I pushed that thought away. If I allowed discouragement to enter my thinking now, I would not be able to carry on.

I sat up in bed. "In the name of Jesus," I said, "I come against discouragement and trouble. I ask God, my loving heavenly Father, to continue to look after me and keep me safe from harm until this mission is complete. I also ask you, Father, to look after Dennis and Neil wherever they are. Protect them from the enemies who are seeking Neil and holding Dennis captive. Lord, I pray that your angels will surround them both, and like it says in Psalm 91, lift them up with their hands so they don't so much as knock their feet against a stone." I stopped and thought for a moment. "Lord," I said now, softly, to my friend, "please, help me to understand what you want me to know, and to do what you want me to do. My life is totally in your hands. Thank you for the people you have sent to help me and to guide me. I don't pretend to understand what these stones mean, but I know you'll tell me what I need to know when I need to know it. Thank you for your goodness and kindness toward me and those I love and care about."

I lay back down and tugged the duvet around my ears as I turned over on my side. My eyes felt edged in gravel. Just before sleep overtook me, I uttered one more prayer. "Please keep Marco safe, too, Lord, and out of trouble. I think I'm falling in love with him."

In the quiet of my drowsy mind, the sound of a gentle voice floated to the surface. "*Don't worry. I will.*"

CHAPTER 23

Jim Escobar, a slight man with thick black hair to his collar, leaned against a pillar in the arrivals area and polished his sunglasses. When I emerged from the glass doors leading out of Customs and Immigration and into the main concourse of the Miami airport, I spotted him immediately. I marched up and asked to see his ID and he handed it over without a word. He reached for my suitcase and I followed him out of the crowded airport into a brilliant, sub-tropical evening. The sky had turned to lavender around the edges and a golden glow lit the western horizon.

Escobar deposited me in the back seat of a white Ford the size of a cruise ship then manoeuvred through the tangle of roads around the airport and headed south. As I watched the city glide by the window in the waning Florida sunshine, I couldn't keep my mind off Marco.

Marco and Eddie had driven me to Gatwick Airport that morning. Marco walked me to the check-in counter. At the line-up for security, his hand touched my back. He turned me toward him.

"You must be careful, *mi amor*," he said, softly. "What you are doing is very dangerous and becomes more perilous every day. There are people who would not hesitate to harm you."

For a fleeting moment I wondered if he might be one of them.

"Who are they, Marco, these people?"

"I can't tell you that, *mi amor*. I don't know enough about them, only that you must be careful. Promise me," he pleaded. "Watch everyone closely and distrust them all. Everyone is a suspect," he paused, "even me."

My heart skipped a beat. "Okay, Marco," I replied.

"Good. Now kiss me good-bye." He pulled me into his embrace and his lips met mine. My body melted against him as I wrapped my arms around his broad back.

Afterward, I leaned back against his arm and looked into his eyes. "You wouldn't just happen to be going to Florida on business now, would you?" I asked.

He gave me a boyish grin. "You just never know where I might turn up next," he replied, releasing me. "Now you go and get on that plane. And don't worry. I will see you again soon." With that he turned and strode away.

Now, riding along in the plush back seat of the car, I nudged my tote back over beside me and felt the hard lumps of stone wrapped in tissues inside. Packing my bag that morning, I had taken the stones from my tote and placed them in the centre of the clothes in my suitcase, first enveloping each one in tissues, then swaddling the three of them in a t-shirt. The thought of going through airport security and being hauled out of line by customs officials for smuggling antiquities filled me with trepidation. But rather than worrying about it, I prayed for God's direction. Convinced that the stones represented a vital part in a global picture of a prophetic nature whose magnitude exceeded my understanding, the importance of collecting and transporting them across oceans posed interesting problems. I thought about leaving them with Mrs. Mac, since, if Neil trusted her I could too, but that might have put her in danger and I could not take that risk.

Waking a full hour before my alarm, I lay in the pearly-grey dawn light and prayed for guidance. Though I did not hear God's voice directly this time, the thought of placing the stones in my luggage and sending them through the baggage handling system with the airlines kept coming to mind. As I meditated on this course of action, a sense of peace pervaded my spirit and the tension in my body relaxed as I decided to follow through with it. Of course, I also prayed that my luggage would end up at my destination as well. I asked God to assign a special contingent of angels to look after my suitcase in transit. Once I arrived in Miami and collected my bag, I slipped into the ladies' room, retrieved the stones from my case, and dropped them into my tote bag.

In spite of the ubiquitous roadside signs and businesses that mark every highway in North America, the view from my back window was enchanting. After leaving the city behind, we passed through marshy everglades before setting out across the first expanse of water toward the Florida Keys. With land now behind us, the Caribbean stretched away to the horizon in all directions. The sun sank into the water like a luminescent pumpkin and streaked the sky with strands of orange and purple, making the water a sea of fire. We passed through key after key, many not much bigger than small villages, but all with marinas and boats everywhere.

By the time we cruised into Key West, the sun had disappeared in a blaze of glory, leaving an indigo velvet sky pin-pricked with stars. Jim turned the car into the entrance of the Hyatt Key West Resort and Spa. Sliding the gearshift into park, he switched off the engine and turned toward me.

"Please wait here, Mrs. Moss," he said. "I will be registering in my own name and then I will come and escort you to your room. If you have a head scarf and glasses, please put them on, just in case." He reached for the door handle. "I will be back in a minute or two."

It turned out to be ten minutes before he opened the car door and reached for my hand. I had draped my head with the scarf in my bag, pulling it close around my face and throwing the ends over my shoulders. I felt silly wearing sunglasses in the dark, but decided that if the movie stars could do it, so could I. Jim led me to the elevator and up to a room on the third floor. He slid the key card through the lock and pushed open the door, instructing me to wait in the hallway while he checked the room, then motioned for me to enter and locked the door behind us.

"Mrs. Moss," he said, "it is important that no one know you are here. My instructions are to tell you to speak to no one and not to leave your room under any circumstances." I gazed longingly toward the roomy balcony overlooking an azure pool and the lights of the harbour. Jim shook his head. "No, Ma'am, you must not go out there." He walked over to the expanse of glass and yanked the drapes closed, cutting off the view. I sagged. To be in such a beautiful place and have to hide indoors seemed like a crime.

Jim informed me that he would return in the morning and suggested I wear something cool and casual and bring along a swimsuit. He also said that I would be checking out in the morning, and I should use the room safe for my valuables. His politely expressionless face gave nothing away. After he left, I secured the door and set my suitcase on a rack. It was late, and I was still on London time. Though I had napped on the plane, it wasn't enough. I wandered to the window and moved the drapes aside with my fingertip, peering out at the lights along the beach below. Out in the water, a sailboat rocked gently on a softly rippling sea, the faint glow of its lights twinkling in the water. *This place is paradise*, I thought. I slipped into my pyjamas and crawled under the covers of the luxurious bed, plumped up the biggest pillow ever and was asleep in thirty seconds.

The shrill ring of the telephone woke me shortly before sunrise. Flinging my arm out from beneath the quilt, I groped for the receiver, lifted it and let it drop. Sinking back into the pillow, sleep overtook me, yet within a minute the confounded phone started up again. This time I reached over and answered it.

"Moss?" A deep voice growled at me through the line.

"Yes?"

"Quentin McSweeny here. I'm sending Jim to get you in twenty minutes. Be ready. Don't worry about breakfast. I'll feed you. Bring all your gear. When he knocks on the door, he's gonna say, 'Marlin'r jumpin''. Got that?"

"Yes, Mr. McSweeney." The line went dead. I peered at the clock. It was 5:45.

I pushed the covers off my sluggish body and rolled out of bed. Twenty minutes later, I sat in a low, armless chair gazing through the semi-sheer drapes, my suitcase and tote bag on the floor in the hall. There was a knock on the door. "Marlin are jumping," said the voice from the hall.

I put my sunglasses on, wrapped my scarf around my hair and followed Jim out of the hotel. Wearing tan walking shorts, an aqua t-shirt, and a pair of sandals, I slid into the front seat of the car that waited at the lobby doors.

In a few minutes we pulled up beside a marina and Jim asked me to follow him as he led me along the dock, past beautiful sailboats and muscular sport-fishing vessels to the most beaten-up, derelict-looking boat in the whole bay. On the side, in white letters against dark green, someone had painted the name Angela. Beside the sleek, white cruisers and speedboats, this one looked like a back alley mutt in a pack of racing greyhounds. At the stern of the vessel, a pair of massive sheet metal tubes protruded out over the water. I would have to ask about those.

The first bright fingers of the morning sun reached over the edge of the sea and streaked across the water as we stopped beside the dubious-looking craft. I could hear noises coming from somewhere in the belly of the vessel, banging metal on metal, and gruff muttering. Then a loud roar erupted from the hold and a heavy wrench flew out and landed with a clank on the junk-strewn deck. A second later, the figure of a man appeared, stumbling from the hold and gripping his thumb with a dirty handkerchief.

"There you are," he said in a Scottish cum Texan accent, fixing me with a glare. "It's 'bout time you got here. Get on board and let's get goin'. I ain't got all day."

"Mr. McSweeney, I presume."

"Of course, I'm McSweeney. Who else would I be? Now get on up here and help me. I just banged my thumb with that wrench and I need help to get this rig outta here." He jerked his chin toward Jim, "You comin'?"

"Not today, Quentin," Jim said. He lifted my suitcase on board and waved as he walked away.

McSweeney reached down with a hand the size of a catcher's mitt and gave my arm such a yank that he nearly sent me flying over the opposite gunwale. A big, powerful man in his late fifties, he reminded me vaguely of Ernest Hemingway the way his clipped grey beard curved around a square jaw. A full moustache covered his mouth but for the bottom lip and steel grey eyes looked out from under a pair of flyaway brows. He wore rumpled shorts and a bright green t-shirt with "Margarita's Bar and Grill" emblazoned across the front with a picture of a parrot. His feet were bare and deeply tanned, but a pair of scuffed, rubber flip-flops lay on the deck. With one hand he lifted the weather-beaten baseball cap from his brow revealing a full head of grey curls. He scratched the back of his skull with one hand as he held up the other with its handkerchief-wrapped thumb.

"Here," I said, reaching for his hand. "Let me take a look at that." To my surprise, he stuck his hand out toward me and allowed me to remove the blood-soaked kerchief and examine his self-inflicted wound. The thumb had already begun to swell and turn a ghastly bluish purple. "Have you got a first aid kit?" I asked. He answered with a nod. Having a son who played sports in high school had given me a lot of experience in dealing with minor scuffs and bruises. I fetched the kit from a cupboard and dressed the wound.

"You're kind of handy to have around," McSweeney said when I had finished bandaging his thumb. "Maybe I'll keep you for a while." He grinned and winked at me.

"We'll see about that," I answered. "Now what do you need me to do, and where are you taking me?"

McSweeney began barking orders. Within a few minutes we were under way as he manoeuvred the craft out of the marina and into the shallow blue waters of the Caribbean. I've never spent much time on boats but my love of the sea made this work thrilling and I dove into carrying out McSweeney's directions with vigour and enthusiasm. Heading across the sparkling water with the morning sun heating up the day, I stood next to McSweeney in the wheel housing as we jetted across the flat water.

Once we were away from land, he offered me some breakfast, which I had to go down into the galley and get for myself. I found bread and jam and a toaster, plus McSweeney had made fresh coffee while waiting for me at the dock, so I helped myself to a cup and waited for my toast to pop up. The cabin of the boat was clean if not neat. Nautical charts covered every square inch of the walls and diving gear hung from hooks attached to the ceiling. Another pair of worn flip flops lay discarded under the table.

When I had finished my toast, I poured a second cup of coffee for myself and another for McSweeney and went back up. Handing it to him, I said, "I wasn't sure if you took cream and sugar and since I couldn't find any, I assumed you like your coffee black."

"Perceptive," he remarked, taking the cup from my hand.

"Perhaps you can tell me where you are taking me, and why. What are we doing out here?"

McSweeney started in. "A coupla years ago I was doin' some research on the Spanish treasure ships and I came across a passage with a quote in some old documents. It was from a diary kept by a seaman who was a quartermaster for a pirate ship called The Bartholomew. Since most seamen were uneducated, and only the captain and quartermaster might be able to read, the existence of a written record of any kind from the point of view of the sailor is really somethin' and that it came from a pirate is even rarer. In fact, according the book I found, only a few pages remain of this man's writing. His name was Charles Finstead. D'you know what a quartermaster is?"

"Isn't he the person who makes sure the ship is stocked with provisions?"

"Somethin' like that, only on a pirate ship the quartermaster ended up being second in command after the captain and was also in charge of disciplining the crew."

"I see."

"In Finstead's diary, he mentioned an encounter with a Spanish gold ship. He gave no details except a vague description of where the encounter took place. I'm thinkin' the reason for this was that they had blasted a few holes in the Spanish ship, but hadn't managed to sink 'er because a storm blew up and the galleon got away. My guess is that he didn't wanna take a chance of givin' anyone any clues until the pirates had chased it down and stolen the cargo. Too bad for them, that never happened because the damage their cannons inflicted on the Spanish ship, along with the raging storm, caused the gold ship to run aground on a reef and sink in heavy seas. Far as I know, she was never seen again by the pirates or anyone else."

Only a sip of coffee remained in my cup so I offered to make some more. When I returned, McSweeney continued with his story. "I've spent the winter scouring libraries and museums for information on this shipwreck, and I figured out her basic whereabouts and started searchin' whenever the weather permitted. I've been at it nearly every day for the past two months and just this week I came across the first traces of the site. The Spanish used cargo ships to transport their loot back to Spain in order to prop up their sagging economy during the Thirty Years War. The king of Spain's plan to bring in massive amounts of gold from the Americas was messed up again and again as hurricanes, roving pirates, or privateers sanctioned by enemy nations, caused lots o' that gold to disappear before it ever left the Gulf of Mexico. Since the shipping routes were well mapped to avoid the treacherous shoals around Florida, the ones that ended up in these waters had taken the north route past the Dry Tortugas with a plan to meet up in Havana with the rest of their fleet, fresh from looting South America, before all sailing back to Spain together."

McSweeney had begun slowing the boat and checking gauges. "We're nearly there," he said without explanation. "Anyway, the ships that sailed the north route usually ran aground in about seventeen feet o' water or less, since their hulls, when fully loaded, had a draft of eighteen feet max. They cracked up on the coral reefs in the shallows. This made 'em pretty easy to find for the Spanish salvage expeditions of that day. 'Course, Spain wanted to get back as much of its booty as possible. But, there's a lot of Spanish gold still in these waters since sometimes the very storms that took down the ships also scattered the wreckage all over the bottom of the sea. On top of that, there have been three hundred years of hurricanes, give or take, to stir up the wreckages and spread everything around. It's not easy to find a wreck and mostly requires a ton of money, years of research and search diving, and the determination of a bulldog. You've probably heard about one of the more famous ones, the find of the Atocha."

Though I didn't remember the details, I nodded. I wanted McSweeney to get to the point of his story.

"Sometimes, though, the find of a wreck is purely random. Some tourist is taking pictures of the fish and finds a gold or silver coin. Or a Sunday diver just happens on a bronze cannon in ten feet o' water. Most of the gold and silver had been taken from the Aztecs and the Mayan people during Spain's conquest of the Americas. The first mint was established in what is now Mexico City and crude coins were created for transport to Spain where they would be re-smelted into Spanish coins. But something else went on that isn't widely known, and that is, sometimes an artifact managed to avoid the smelter fires and remain intact in its original form. These artifacts are extremely rare since they belonged mostly in the private collections of greedy high-rankin' government officials, wealthy land-owners, traders, or ship captains of the day. Any stuff that still exists is now in museums, since most o' those things were kept on land. But, now and then something turns up that doesn't fit the pattern of smelting down the gold on land. An artifact that stayed in private hands and was in the process of being transported back to Spain as a keepsake, somehow wound up on the bottom of the sea."

"In water seventeen feet deep," I guessed.

"You're quick." He checked our location on a global positioning device and cut the engine. "We're here," he announced, leaving the wheel and dumping an anchor off the stern.

"What happens now?"

McSweeney grinned. "Follow me. I wanna to show you somethin'." He led me below and pulled open a drawer next to the stainless steel sink. From it he took a balled-up tea towel, laid it on the table and began carefully folding back the layers. Inside the cloth lay a small gold block about the size of the end of my thumb. On its sides I could see the remnants of designs stamped or inscribed into the gold but the shapes were indistinct.

"May I?" I asked, reaching for the object. McSweeney nodded and I picked it up, placing it in the palm of my hand. A hole ran through the centre of the piece like you would find in a bead and I could see faint markings on three sides. I turned it over in awe. It was an exact miniature replica of the stones I had collected, but in pure gold. I inhaled deeply, bit my lip and looked up at McSweeney.

"Recognize it, then?"

I nodded. "Where did you find it?"

"Down there," he said, pointing toward the sea with his thumb. "I'm convinced there are more of 'em, too, and today we're gonna go lookin' for 'em." He took the gold block from my hand, re-wrapped it, and returned it to the drawer.

Eyeing him warily, I said, "I don't dive."

"Time to start," he replied. "I've got all the gear you need, and frankly darlin', you don't wanna miss this." He stated it with such finality there was no point arguing with him. Besides, I was willing to give it a try. He opened a closet and began pulling out diving gear.

"Here," he said, handing me a wetsuit. "This should fit you. It belongs to my daughter Janice and she's about your size."

After donning the suit and emerging from the hold, I expected to find a tank ready to strap to my back. Not so, McSweeney informed me. He used an alternate method for breathing apparatus. A small air pump floating on the surface in an inflated ring would force compressed air through hoses to the divers. My first diving experience began with an abbreviated ground school. We would be diving in about twelve feet of water, and when I peered over the side of the boat, I could see the bottom so clearly that the water looked only waist-deep. McSweeney explained that the large metal tubes at the rear of the boat were giant sand blowers called mailboxes for their similarity to the roadside version. When tilted into place, they converted the wash from the boat's propellers downward toward the sandy ocean floor and blew sand away from the dive site.

"I don't think we'll use the mailboxes today," McSweeney informed me. "I found that block sittin' right on the surface, so it's possible that there are others nearby. I think the storm last week stirred up the bottom. Let's go have a look, how 'bout?" As he began hooking up my breathing apparatus, he added nonchalantly, "By the way, we may run into the odd shark down there."

I spun to face him. "The odd *what*?"

"Shark," he answered, turning me back around so he could adjust the head strap under my ponytail. "You know, big dorsal fin, ugly mug, lots of teeth. Don't worry, they don't usually bother anybody."

"What do you mean, 'usually'? What if one gets the notion that I look like a nice, light lunch?"

"First of all, we'll stay close together so pay attention and don't wander off, so to speak. Stay calm and maintain your position. They usually just want a look and will swim away, especially since we won't have any fish or food on us. If they seem too interested, then we leave and head for the surface. It's important to swim away calm and smooth-like, but keep your eye on the blighter the whole time. Swim to me first if I'm not right beside you, okay?"

I gulped and nodded.

"If the beast gets aggressive, rushing, hunchin' its back, or swimmin' zigzag, we get close together, or back to back, and slowly come to the surface. Since there is not much reef here we can't back up against it for protection and the stuff on the bottom ain't big enough for cover.

He was making me nervous and I told him so.

"Good," he replied. "Sharks are like the devil. Getting too close can get you into trouble."

"Interesting analogy."

"If one does start gettin' frisky," he continued, "don't be afraid to whack it a good one on the nose with this." He produced a long, heavy flashlight which he tucked into my belt. "Then don't stick around, just swim smoothly back to the boat. I don't wanna scare ya, but if you do manage to find yourself in a shark's teeth, fight like mad to get out." He needn't have added that last bit.

After explaining how to use the breathing system, how to swim with my flippers, how to move sand to search for artifacts, and how to deal with currents, McSweeney handed me a metal detector, gave me a quick lesson in how to use it and we were ready to set off. Before I dumped myself into the sea, I muttered a muffled prayer for protection and safety.

The water closed around me in a splash and suddenly I was in a world of silence save for the sound of my own breathing, heartbeat, and the bubbles rising from my mouthpiece. Following McSweeney through the clear water, I descended and swam away from the boat at an angle. The sunlight sparkled through the shimmering aqua water and a few curious fish swam past. The low reef below us consisted of uneven corals and an assortment of plants waving in the slight current. In between clumps of coral, flat areas of white sand spread out. McSweeney motioned me forward and once I managed to get my flippers heading me in the right direction, I swam after him. Pointing downward, he indicated the spot where he had found the gold block then he slowly began to move his metal detector from side to side over the surface of the sand. I followed suit, keeping a sharp look-out for unwanted visitors. A little, fat fish dressed in black with white polka dots swam over for a look at us then darted away, and a ray cruised past with elegant wings rising and falling like poetry. Everything was so beautiful.

Together, we scoured the rocks and reefs, scanning the surface of the sandy bottom with our metal detectors. Brilliantly-coloured fish swam by to check out our activity before scuttling away into the corals. At one point we startled a moray eel hiding in a rock crevice but we backed away and so did the eel. After what seemed like more than an hour under water finding nothing, we had drifted so far from the boat that I could no longer see its bottom. I signalled to McSweeney my concern and he turned back toward the boat but then stopped. His metal detector had found something.

McSweeney motioned me over and began to wipe sand away in a circular pattern, flicking it out of the way to create an indentation. I watched then helped him dig. He brought his metal detector back to the area for another check then moved to the right about six inches before continuing to dig.

Suddenly a dark shape appeared. Nearly black and sticking up out of the soft sand bottom, it looked like an old button. McSweeney plucked it up and let it settle in the palm of his hand, swishing sand away from it and turning it over. I swam in for a closer inspection and saw that it was not a button at all, but an old coin, irregular in shape and dark with tarnish. Silver! We had found a Spanish coin, I felt sure of it.

Now I was really excited. I dropped my own metal detector to the sand in the same area, circling it around the hole and beyond, ready to find the treasure chest containing the gold of the Spanish main as well as the remaining gold, block-shaped beads. McSweeney bumped my leg to get my attention. I knew we should head back toward the boat, but I didn't want to. I wanted to find more treasure. I looked around to let him know that I wanted to stay longer and try to find more artifacts but he was nowhere to be seen. I spun the other way and saw that he had followed our hoses toward the boat but by now he was several yards away from me.

That's impossible, I thought. He only just nudged my leg a second before. I glanced around and a scream lodged in my throat as I found myself staring into the open jaws of a shark. I froze in horror as the shark's sleek body slid past me. I could have reached out and touched its grainy skin. I held my breath and watched as it swam away. Then I remembered McSweeney's instructions. *Don't panic, Jill,* I told myself, forcing myself to stop gulping air. As calmly as possible, I began following my breathing tube back toward the boat, swimming in an awkward sideways stroke to try and keep my eyes on the shark. My metal detector dangled from my arm as I used one hand to hold my breathing hose aloft and the other to propel myself forward.

I could see the shark now behind me and McSweeney ahead of me, each about twenty feet away. Following McSweeney's instructions, I tried to move calmly through the water but inside me there was nothing calm going on. With my attention on the shark, I didn't notice the loop on my metal detector catch on a branch of coral, wedging into a crack between two rigid protrusions. I tugged hard on it, but it wouldn't dislodge. From the corner of my eye I could see the shark, which had been swimming away, turn and begin to head back in my direction. Really frightened now, I dropped the metal detector to retrieve later. As it fell it came free from the coral and descended awkwardly to the sand, landing at a funny angle with the read-out unit toward me. The moment it came to rest on the bottom, I could see that it had found something.

Seeing that I was no longer beside him, McSweeney turned to swim back toward me. In a split second, I caught the alarm in his face as he looked past me. I glanced over my shoulder and saw the shark zigzagging toward me in humping frenzied jerks. The shark's mouth opened wide as it sped toward me like a silver streak. McSweeney was still too far away for us to present a united front. I was totally on my own against the sea's most feared predator.

Before I could hope to swim to safety, the shark bore down on me. I could see its cold, dead eyes glinting in the sunlight that shone through the shallow water. I had no hope of saving myself now, so I did the only thing I now knew to do. I called out to God for help. In seconds the shark was within two feet of my body with jaws unhinged for attack. I braced myself for the worst.

Then a strange thing happened.

A dazzling pop of light, like an impossibly white, stationary bolt of lightning, exploded in the space of water between my thigh and the gaping mouth of the shark. It crackled and sizzled for a half second, then it was gone. The light was so brilliant that it momentarily blinded me and I blinked, squinting into the turquoise water and reaching for my flashlight. The shark's teeth were about to rip into my leg. But nothing happened. I opened my eyes wider and looked around. The shark had disappeared. I spun in place, fearing that in my disorientation I would find it about to chomp my neck, but it was nowhere near me. When I focused farther out into the calm waters, I saw only a tail swimming speedily out to sea.

The next second McSweeney was by my side, grasping my arms and checking my leg. I clung to him for a moment. He signalled for me to follow him to the surface. Then I remembered my metal detector lying next to a clump of coral.

Tapping him on the arm, I indicated that I wanted to go back and pick it up. He nodded and followed. The detector lay half buried in soft sand, the small red light on the read-out blinking steadily. I picked it up and moved it around the area, listening for the audible beeps it emitted into my headphones by remote. As I edged it toward the area drawing the most attention, I thrust it into the sand, pushing sand up and away from the edge of the coral. When this movement revealed nothing, McSweeney reached down and brushed sand from the area, first to the right, then to the left and finally digging straight down at the base of the coral branch. He scooped up handfuls of sand, tossing them aside, and in one of these handfuls my eyes caught a tiny glint. I grabbed his arm. Using my fingertip, I gently brushed the sand away and there in his leathery palm, almost identical to its twin in the boat and an exact miniature golden replica of the stones, lay another tiny gold block.

CHAPTER 24

"What was that all about?" Quentin McSweeney demanded. Collapsed in deck chairs in the shade of a faded canopy on his boat, we had scuba gear scattered all around us. McSweeney's meaty fingers clutched a chicken salad sandwich like the thing wasn't dead yet.

I took a sip from a tall, cold glass of strawberry lemonade. "What do you mean?"

"Don't be cute, Moss. That shark had you. You were a goner."

"I know."

"So what happened?"

I lifted one shoulder and let it drop. "I'm not sure how to explain this," I began. "I guess you'd have to call it supernatural intervention."

"Go on," McSweeney growled as he chomped a hunk out of his sandwich.

"Mr. McSweeney," I said, "I don't know what your beliefs are, but I believe in divine protection. As a believer in Jesus, it is part of the whole salvation "package," if you will. I am aware that a lot of people, even earnest Christians, don't believe in supernatural intervention, but I'm not among them. What happened down there, I believe, was a direct result of the prayer I said before I got into the water plus believing in the protection that God has already provided for me. Your little speech about sharks put me on guard, so I asked for special security from God, should any of his less friendly creatures decide I would make an appetizing meal. I didn't expect something like that to happen, but I wanted to make sure I had extra protective covering if it should. In the same way that the host city hires extra security during the Olympic Games, I needed extra protection today. When that shark came after me, God intervened and scared it away. I don't know exactly what happened. It seemed like a bolt of lightning to me, only I didn't get zapped. If you find that answer unsatisfying, well, too bad. There it is."

McSweeney took a swig of his lemonade and dragged the back of his hand across his mouth. "Good," he said.

"Excuse me?"

"I was just checkin'." The barest hint of a grin played around the corner of his mouth.

It was after noon now and hot. I pulled the wet hair from the back of my neck and twisted it up into a knot, hoping it would stay there. "What are we doing out here, Mr. McSweeney? Besides looking for little gold blocks, I mean."

He stuffed the last bite of his sandwich into his mouth and chewed on it while looking out to sea. Finally, he swallowed and turned to me. "Do you know why you're on this mission?"

The question surprised me. "Yes," I answered. Then I said, "No, not really. I'm doing Neil a favour since I know he's in trouble."

"Yeah," he replied, "but not as much trouble as you think."

"What does that mean?"

McSweeney took another long gulp of his drink and set the empty glass down on the deck with a clunk. "We chose you to pick up the stones for a reason," he said.

"What do you mean, 'we'?"

"Neil and me," he answered. "Who else?"

I studied him for a moment. "Tell me what you know," I demanded.

"Here's the deal," he said. "And I'm tellin' you from the beginning so you won't fill in the blanks yourself. I want you to know the truth because you may run into others who'll tell you different. In fact, you may have already, I don't know." He got up suddenly, pushing his beach chair backward with his legs, which sparkled with pale, sun-bleached hairs. "I think we've got some tarts here somewhere. My wife, Angela, baked some yesterday and said she'd stick some on the boat for me." He tromped out of sight into the galley kitchen and I could hear him fumbling around in the cupboards. In a moment he re-appeared carrying a plastic container. Peeling back the lid he revealed an assortment of tiny, rich tarts with cherry, lemon, and pecan filling, and offered it to me. I chose a cherry one. McSweeney pulled his chair back under the shade of the canopy and sat down, popping a whole lemon tart into his mouth. He set the container down on the deck between us and said, "Help yourself, eh."

I took a pecan tart and waited for him to get to the point.

"Where was I? Oh, yeah. Here's what happened. Neil and I were together when he found the stones. And by the way, I have one here for you, so don't let me forget to give it to you before I drop you off. I kind of went along for the ride on that trip, just for kicks, and we were digging around in Mexico in some of those Mayan ruins he loves so much when we came across this set of stones. At first we didn't know what we'd come upon, but Neil recognized the languages even though he couldn't decipher them. The Mayan and the Olmec were easy to recognize, for him anyway, but the third one was weird. He figured it was some kind of Middle-Eastern thing so he took a picture and sent it over to another guy, who we'll meet later, and got him to take a look. To our surprise, this Dr. Silverman gets back to Neil right away telling us that these things are really special and not to let them fall into the wrong hands, or there could be dire consequences. Now, I like excitement as much as the next guy, or gal," he added, nodding toward me, "but I'm not too keen on 'dire.' So when ole Doc Silverman tells us that these things are really important we figured we'd get 'em to a museum vault somewhere quick where we could take a better look at 'em. Here, have another tart," he said, pushing the tray toward me with a bare toe.

I shook my head.

"Okay, so here we are, gettin' these blocks packed up and we were just about ready to head out of the jungle when who should show up but a couple of Mexicano banditos carrying sub-machine guns and telling us they'd be taking anything we had found. Somehow they got wind that we'd dug up something significant and figured it was like a treasure map and would lead them to a big cache of gold. Where they got that notion I'll never know, but my guess is that one of the local workers we hired let some stories leak out and they came to the wrong conclusions. So far as Neil and I know, there ain't no Mayan gold at the end of this rainbow."

The boat bobbed on its anchor and had turned so that the sun beat down on the back of my neck. I got up, pulled my chair into the shade again and sat back down.

"What happened then?" I asked.

"Well," he said, removing his cap and scratching his head, "it's kind of hard to say. A bunch of the workers showed up out of nowhere with machetes and pick-axes and sneaked up behind us. Before we knew it, we were surrounded and in too close a range even to get our guns up. We had a choice. Drop our weapons and run or get hacked to bits by the crew. We got out of that fix by the grace of God and let the Mexicanos sort themselves out. It made us realize just how consequential this bunch of stones was and that we had to have a plan for keeping them from falling into the wrong hands."

"How did I come into this picture?"

"Neil came up with the idea of sending them individually to different people he knows and trusts around the globe. We thought that would make it difficult for anyone trying to trace them, and it would keep their whereabouts secret for a while. Neil was already a target, so it was imperative for him to disappear, since we knew that those bad hombres probably had friends and weren't likely to give up easily. But we still had the problem of how to get the blocks back together so we could decipher their message. We knew that we had to find someone to pick them up for us because obviously Neil couldn't do it. It didn't make sense for me to go either, since I had been with him on the dig. So we put our heads together and came up with you."

"You came up with me? But you don't know anything about me."

"I didn't before, but I do now," he said, pulling his cap onto the back of his head and grinning. "It'd probably surprise you just how much I know about you."

"Like what?" I demanded, gaping at him.

"Relax," McSweeney said, waving a hand. "I don't know anythin' that you wouldn't want your own uncle to know."

I didn't think it was the same thing and told him so, but he snorted. "We chose you because Neil told me that you hear God better than anyone he knows. He said you've spent your life learning to have that kind of up close, cozy thing with God that most people only dream about. Being able to do that gives you an edge. It's like having a direct line to the biggest security outfit in the whole universe. When he told me that, I said, 'She's our girl.' Besides, you're not stuck in some office job that you wouldn't be able to get away from. We were hoping' that it'd only take a week or so for you to get all the stones, but it looks like it's gonna take a little longer now. Complications, I guess you could say."

"You think?" I retorted. "Yes, I've had the odd complication, like being chased all over Europe by heaven knows how many different gangs of thugs, shot at, and wounded, tricked, in danger all the time."

"Wait a minute," McSweeney broke in, "I didn't know you were shot. Where were you shot?"

"In Barcelona."

"No, I mean where on your body?"

"Oh," I answered, losing a little steam. "Here, on my side. It's only a flesh wound, but it still hurts like crazy sometimes."

"Why didn't you tell me you had an open wound?"

"Why should I have? I only met you a few hours ago. I had no idea you would need to know that. Is it a problem?"

"It can be. We'd better get that cleaned up if you don't want to have infection set in. Usually sea water isn't a problem, but there is bacteria you can get that will cause you more problems than you want."

I sighed. "Fine. I'll go get the first aid kit."

McSweeney sent me below to clean up my sore side and I heard him muttering as I descended the few steps. When I returned, clean, dry, and in my clothes, I flipped my wet swimsuit over a railing.

"I guess that puts the kibosh on any more diving today," he said. "Too bad, too, since we might have been able to find a few more of them pretty, little gold blocks."

"Never mind that," I said. "You haven't finished telling me what you know about the stones."

McSweeney took a deep breath and blew it out through his lips as he looked longingly into the water. After a moment, he seemed to resign himself to staying dry for the remainder of the day. "Yeah, okay. After we decided to get you to pick up the stones, we needed to figure out where to send them. Old Neil went through his list of contacts and picked out the folks he thought he could trust."

A seagull glided over the boat, cocking its head to the left and right, scouting for food. Until now we had been all alone with the sea and the sun, but now I could hear a motor far off in the distance. McSweeney said that he and Neil had set up the pickup points and made the first travel arrangements for me.

"But why did Neil send me his old Bible?" I asked, still puzzled about its connection to the stones.

"Well," said McSweeney, "that's another story." Then he stopped and turned his right ear toward the reverberation which now sounded closer. His head snapped around in the direction of the oncoming craft and he leapt up from his chair. "It looks like we're about to have company. We'd better get out of here," he said, racing up the ladder to the wheel.

I followed him. "What's the hurry?"

"Darlin', these here waters are crawling with weekend treasure hunters lookin' to find the mother lode. Most of them don't have a clue where to begin and they just go where someone else is already diving. I don't want anyone to lock onto this location or I might never find the rest of our little gold blocks. Besides, there might be a heck of a lot more gold and silver down there, and since we've already found a silver coin, chances are pretty good that there's more where that came from. So we're outta here." The twin motors roared and the bow of the boat bucked out of the water as we took off across the rippled surface.

Within seconds we had covered a lot of distance so I leaned back against a railing. In a few minutes, McSweeney would slow down and continue telling me his story. But the boat that we tried to lose was not getting lost. In fact, it seemed to be gaining on us. I tapped McSweeney on the arm and pointed over the stern. A look of genuine alarm splashed across is features. He gunned the engines. I hung on as the boat careened across the tops of the wavelets, sending a deep wake out behind.

Keeping my eyes on the other boat, I hollered, "I think they're chasing us."

"Take the wheel," McSweeney yelled, clapping my hand on the wooden ring. "I'll be right back."

"I don't know how to drive a boat," I screamed.

"If you know how to drive a car, you can drive a boat. Just keep going straight," he yelled over his shoulder as he leapt down the ladder and out of sight.

I gripped the steering wheel with both hands while trying to keep the approaching boat in sight. I edged the throttle forward like I had seen McSweeney do, but could soon tell that no matter how much gas I gave this boat, we were out-classed. By now I could see figures on the other boat, someone driving it, and a few others standing up front. I rammed the throttle as high as it could go, but it made no difference to the distance between the boats. The next second, McSweeney re-appeared carrying two machine guns.

"Here," he said, jamming one of them into my hand. "You might need this. Compliments of our Mexican friends."

My eyes widened. I might be able to hold the steering wheel of a boat, but I certainly didn't know how to use a sub-machine gun. As though reading my thoughts, McSweeney said, "Watch this," and gave me a thirty-second lesson on operating the weapon. "I really hope we don't have to use these, but just in case, be prepared."

By now the cruiser had drawn up almost beside us and I could clearly see the others on board. A swarthy man waved his arms indicating that we should slow down and allow them to come alongside. At that second, McSweeney cranked the wheel over hard and the Angela swung into a tight curve away from the other boat. "If we're lucky, we might be able to outmanoeuvre them," he shouted. "Now would be a good time to start prayin' again."

I couldn't agree more. Our boat turned in a circle and McSweeney headed in what seemed to me to be the direction from which we had come, except the sun was not at the same angle. The big cruiser roared on, executing a wide arc and swinging past us. With the throttle on full, we dodged inside their curve and jetted past them, heading toward land.

Within minutes they had completed their turn and again bore down on us. "Hang on," McSweeney shouted. "I'm gonna try that again. Maybe this time we can ditch 'em for good."

All this time I had been praying out loud, but the roar of the boat engines drowned out any sound but the rush of wind in my ears. Off to my right I could see a frilly, dark line of greenery embellishing the surface of the turquoise water along the horizon. I grabbed a railing as our boat lunged into another tight spin, sending the other boat zipping past us again. Just before we surged away from them, I spotted a guy on the deck, a gun to his shoulder, and then heard the clatter of bullets hit the side of the Angela. I screamed and ducked as we lurched away from our pursuer.

"I'm gonna try to make it to that island over there," McSweeney bellowed, jerking his thumb toward the narrow strip of land. "I've got a smaller boat, so we should be able to get away from them in the shallows. Hopefully," he growled, gripping the wheel knuckles white. I swung around to find the other boat and saw that it had turned again and crept closer to us with each passing second. Now I could see three men on the decks, all with guns pointed in our direction.

"Oh, God, oh, God!" I cried out. "We need your help here. Right now!"

"Get ready to shoot," bawled McSweeney. "We'll hit them before they can hit us."

Shooting this machine gun was the last thing I wanted to do, but I had no time to think up a different plan. I shouldered the gun and steadied it on a railing. Holding the steering wheel with one hand, McSweeney leaned over my shoulder. "Now," he shouted, as the other boat rushed up beside us. I held on tight, aiming for just below the men on the decks. I really didn't want to kill anybody; I just wanted to let them all know that they should stop bothering us. Now. Taking a deep breath, I squeezed the trigger. The machine gun bucked against my shoulder and shot wildly. I felt like a little kid holding a fire hose.

"Push up against this," McSweeney directed, shoving the barrel of the gun into the corner of the railing. "Hold it hard into that corner." With his right hip wedged against the boat's steering wheel, he leaned over my shoulder and his own gun now burst into a clatter of shots so close to my ear that it nearly knocked me off my feet. "Sorry," he said, patting my back. The men on the other vessel ducked. I aimed again, and compressed the trigger of my gun. One of the men on the other boat jerked sideways and clutched his arm, dropping his gun into the water below. His companion gave him a single glance then took aim again. By this time we had ventured into water that looked no more than a few feet deep and I saw the speed of the big boat drop off sharply as we raced away from it, heading directly toward a beach. McSweeney saw what I saw, and hauled back on the throttle. The Angela ground to a halt just before the bottom of the hull hit sand.

"Are you okay?" he asked, not waiting for my answer. He watched the cruiser turn away and head back the way it had come. "Give me that," he demanded. He peeled my fingers off the machine gun and set it down, along with his own. Then he reached out and folded me into a bear hug, thumping my back with his big mitt of a hand. "It's okay now. They've gone."

I stepped away from him and looked down at my hands.

"Man, you look like a ghost," he said.

My whole body shook and my hands felt as weak as leaves. "I shot someone," I whispered. Tears filled my eyes. "This is not fun anymore. I don't want to go around shooting people, or being shot at. I don't want to do this anymore. I want to go home."

McSweeney took me by the shoulders and urged me down the stairs and into the little galley below. "Sit down here," he commanded, pressing me into a corner of the bench surrounding the table. "I'm going to make you a cup of tea."

He pottered about, filling the kettle and putting it on the burner, getting out a round, brown teapot and stuffing a bag of Earl Grey tea through the opening in the top. I dried the tears from my eyes and blew my nose in a paper napkin I grabbed off the counter. He took the container of tarts out of the cupboard and tore the lid off. Placing them directly in front of me, he turned back to the stove, poured the boiling water over the tea bag, then took a couple of mugs from another cubbyhole and put them on the table. Picking up the teapot, he set it down between us as he squeezed between the table and the wall across from me.

"Here," he said as he poured tea into a mug into which he had already poured some milk and dumped a spoonful of sugar. "Drink this, and have a couple of them tarts. You'll feel better in a minute. Tea fixes all kinds of troubles."

I did as I was told, mainly because my mind felt so numb that I couldn't think of anything else. I sipped the tea, burning my mouth, and ate a lemon tart as he watched me.

"Feel better now?" McSweeney peered into my eyes.

"Yes," I nodded. "A little."

"Good. Now let's get something straight. They shot first, so we were simply defending ourselves by shooting back. The fact that you winged one of those turkeys is purely coincidental. You did the right thing. Got that?" I nodded again, not taking my eyes off his. "Besides, don't you think it is poetic justice shootin' those Mexicans with their own bullets?"

His attempt at levity didn't work. "Did you know that was going to happen?"

"No, but I'm not surprised. I think they've been watching me for a while."

"So that's why you had the guns on board."

"Yep."

"I see." *More than I want to*, I thought. I stood up, then sat down again. "You said that Neil isn't in as much trouble as I thought. Where is he?"

"There's only so much I can tell you right now, Jill," he said, using my given name for the first time. "I can tell you he is safe and he's with people who can protect him."

I slammed the palm of my hand down on the table top, making the mugs rattle and tea slosh out. "Why can't you tell me where he is? I'm already in this up to my ears, and I'm risking my neck more than the rest of you, yet all I ever get is bits and pieces of information. And where is Dennis? It has been days since I've heard anything. Is he hurt; is he even alive? Who kidnapped him and why? I haven't talked to my family for days, either. I'm afraid the calls will be traced and they will be put in danger, and that whoever is looking for me will know where I am."

"Whoa, whoa, Moss. Take a breath."

I didn't want to take a breath. I wanted to hit somebody, but McSweeney was almost twice my size.

"From the top," he said, tackling my list of grievances, "I don't know where Dennis is, or whether he's okay. We have a fix on who kidnapped him, and we received a communiqué yesterday demanding the artifact in exchange for his life. But by the wording, it sounds like the captors aren't real sure what the 'artifact' is, or they would've asked for it specifically. My guess is that they're working on hearsay, but they know that it's something of value and something that fits in with their cause."

"But who are they, and why did they go after Dennis?"

"They snatched Dennis because he was the closest link to Neil they could find. Because he lives in Mexico he was easy to track down and he speaks the language. What we've been able to find out is that the group that has him is a wing-nut fringe of some Middle-Eastern religious group. These creeps are not too principled and will do whatever it takes to get what they want. We believe it's one of these quasi-terrorist types of groups who have kidnapped Dennis. Obviously, their goal is to get the stones, and we think it's because there may be some kind of ancient technology connection." He shook his head. "That's all I can tell you."

"Poor Dennis," I said. I leaned my forehead into the palm of my hand and stared at a map on the wall without really seeing it. "What can we do to help him?" I asked, looking back up at McSweeney.

"You can't do anything except pray. There's a lot of people involved in this mission besides you and we're doing everything we can to free Dennis unharmed. Your job is to continue to pick up the pieces of the stone ring so we can get them all together and figure out what the message on them says. So don't worry about him; it will only distract you from what you are supposed to do."

I sighed. He was right. There wasn't anything I could do unless I abandoned picking up the stones. Then something else occurred to me. "You never finished telling me about Neil's Bible. Why did he send it to me and what do all those markings represent?"

McSweeney ran a hand over his bearded chin. "There's someone you need to meet," he told me, tipping his mug up for the last gulp of tea. "He can tell you about that a whole lot better than I ever could. So you'll just have to wait until we get there. I don't think you will be disappointed."

CHAPTER 25

Sugarloaf Key lies north of Key West, one of those former mangrove swamps turned high-end real estate by the addition of a lot of development money and a few dredged canals. The waters of the Caribbean were so shallow here it was hard to imagine skimming the surface with any craft larger than an inner tube floating a six-year-old. I felt a lot calmer now that the shooting had stopped, McSweeney had explained a few things to me, and I'd been able to catch a nap on the Angela.

Edging alongside a wooden dock, McSweeney cut the motor and leapt out to tie off the boat.

"Here," he offered, "let me grab that bag for you."

I handed him my suitcase and he reached for my hand as I stepped off the boat. Through a high, white-painted, wrought-iron fence at the end of the dock I could see a pink and white confection of a house. As we approached the gate, the lock buzzed and McSweeney pulled the iron entry door open and held it for me. Skirting the blue-tiled pool, I looked up to see a gigantic man running out of the house to greet us. A halo of white hair framed his balding head and he was dressed in a pair of baggy khaki shorts and a white shirt with the sleeves rolled up to the elbows. A wide grin brightened his deeply tanned face. He reached down and threw his great arms about McSweeney.

"How good to see you again, my friend," he cried.

McSweeney stepped away from the exuberant embrace and introduced me to Doctor Enoch Silverman, who took both of my hands in his, making mine appear the size of a toddler's. When he bent at the waist to kiss both of my cheeks, I realized that the top of my head came barely to the middle of his chest.

"I am enchanted to meet you, my dear," he said. The corners of his warm, brown eyes crinkled into a childlike smile. "Come, come. You must come in where it is cool."

By now, the sun had sunk toward the horizon like a neon tangerine about to be extinguished in the silver ocean. Dr. Silverman dipped his head as he led us through a pair of tall glass doors and into a spacious living room.

I looked around the room, which held an assortment of dark rattan sofas and chairs, holding lofty cushions with palm frond motifs. A broad-leafed tropical plant, reaching nearly to the ceiling, stood in one corner, and two tall lamps lit the room with a soft glow.

"Please feel free to look upstairs if you like," said Dr. Silverman. "I need a few moments to converse with our friend Quentin. If you need to use facilities, you'll find them at the top of the stairs on the right."

I recognized the hint and left the room, walking up the wide, winding staircase to find the bathroom. After using the toilet, I stood before the mirror and gazed at my reflection. My hair, flat and messy from a morning in salt water, now looked dull and dirty. Sunburn lit my face with a pink flush and beyond the fatigue I saw something in my eyes that I had not noticed before. A certain steely determination stared back at me from the glass. Where had that come from?

Out in the upper landing, I glanced around, then ventured into the large master bedroom, again, decorated island-style in bamboo and rattan. A huge four-poster bed draped in sheer netting stood against one side of the room and a wall of glass looked out onto a spacious balcony. Twilight had descended and, leaning against the arm of a tall-backed chair, I slid the blinds apart to survey the street below. It was empty except for one vehicle, a big, black SUV. I could just make out the shape of the driver still sitting behind the wheel. He was tall and wore a dark shirt. For a second he turned his head my way and my heart leapt. I thought I was looking at Marco. Then I shook my head. That was impossible. No one but McSweeney and Dr. Silverman knew I was here. Dropping the blind, I descended the stairs and found the two men seated in generous armchairs, deep in conversation.

"Ah, there you are, my dear," cried Dr. Silverman when he spied me. "We are just about to have a meal and now that you're here, we can begin."

"Your house is beautiful," I said.

"Thank-you," replied Doctor Silverman, "but it is not my house. I am merely renting it for a short time." He stood to his feet and stretched out his hand. "Come, let's eat."

He led me to the dining room table, then stepped to a long sideboard and took serving dishes from warming trays. "My cook has gone home," he explained, "so we have to feed ourselves."

My stomach growled as I took my seat and Doctor Silverman blessed our meal. "I have heard from Neil today," Silverman said as we began eating, "and everything is going according to plan, except for a little interference."

I swallowed hard and set my fork down. "Interference?" I said, glancing at McSweeney. "Is that what you'd call our encounter this afternoon? A little interference?" Both men stopped chewing and looked at me. "And what do you mean you heard from Neil? Where is he? Is he all right?"

McSweeney spoke first. "I brought you over here to see the Doc so he could explain a few things to you. He has his fingers on the pulse of the operation."

"What do you mean by 'operation'?"

Doctor Silverman placed his hands on the table and looked into my eyes. "I suppose now is as good a time as any," he said. His eyes darted to McSweeney who confirmed his statement with a nod.

"We have been reluctant to give you much information before now," he began, "for your own safety and for ours. The less you knew, the better. However, you are entitled to know the fate of your own family members. To begin with, your uncle, Neil Bryant, is safe. After the incident in Mexico with the men and their guns, we realized that his safety was of paramount importance. From the moment I saw the photos of the ring of stones, I knew that we must get them out of the country and make sure that they never fell into the wrong hands. With the criminal element in Mexico aware of their existence, it was also imperative that we move quickly."

At this point McSweeney picked up the story. "Neil and I high-tailed it out of that jungle over the worst roads I've ever seen in my life. We threw the gear into the back of the jeep and abandoned the site immediately, doing our best to camouflage it before we left, since we were pretty sure those guys would be back. We paid some of the workers to act as guards, but once we had fled the scene, there's no telling what they would do. Probably pack up and go home. We could only hope that the mob after the stones would not destroy the dig site looking for more, but there's no way to guarantee that."

"Where did you go?"

"Well, first we wound up in this little place called Izamal, where, believe it or not, the whole centre of town is painted yellow-gold and dominated by a huge convent and church. Not far from the town centre is another Mayan pyramid, right there in town. Amazing. Anyhow, we didn't stay there long enough to get comfortable. We went on to Merida, out there on the top end of the Yucatan, and hopped on a flight to Key West. We had a meeting with the good doctor here, and that's when we decided to split up the stones and get in touch with you."

"I see. What happened to Neil?"

"That's where I come in," Doctor Silverman interjected. "I recognized the writing on the outside of the stones as an ancient Middle-Eastern text. The fact that it was situated in a Mayan ruin in Mexico and that the other languages are clearly of Mayan and Olmec origin throws light on some extremely interesting possibilities."

"Such as?"

"To begin with, it is commonly believed that no one from the east side of the Atlantic ever set foot in the Americas until Columbus sailed, aside from perhaps a small settlement of Vikings into Atlantic Canada. This is untrue and we have proof. Unfortunately, most of the scientific establishment doesn't want to acknowledge it. No matter." He dismissed them with a wave of his hand and stabbed a piece of lemon-roasted chicken with his fork.

"The Doc here is the world's leading authority on ancient Middle-Eastern languages," McSweeney said. "There's nothin' he doesn't know."

"On the contrary," replied Silverman. "There is plenty that I don't know. However, I do know that the writing on the stones originates around the time just after the great deluge, or Noah's flood, as it is more commonly known. It is my belief, and I am not alone, that before the flood, as well as an abundance of sin and debauchery, there also existed an abundance of technological knowledge. Highly-developed civilizations existed with knowledge that we still have neither discovered nor developed. There is too much evidence of this fact to ignore it."

"So I am led to believe," I commented, finishing my meal and pushing my plate away. "How do the stones fit into this picture?"

Doctor Silverman continued. "It is my belief that the stones were created around the time just after the great flood. Once the waters had receded and Noah and his family left the ark, they set about recreating what had been lost. They still had all the knowledge that had existed before the deluge and in a short time this family had begun repopulating the earth."

I remembered the accounts that I had read in Neil's Bible about the genealogy of Noah's family following the flood and how it was clear that they all lived hundreds of years and had continued to reproduce throughout their lives. It made for a virtual population explosion.

"If you know your Bible history," Silverman said, "you'll remember that it didn't take long until these folks decided they would build a tower to heaven. That idea puzzles us today since we have some pretty impressive skyscrapers, yet the idea of one being tall enough to touch heaven is ludicrous. So either heaven was much nearer in those days, or the people were simply dreamers."

"Which do you think it was?" I inquired.

Silverman shrugged. "I don't have the answer to that question yet. A third possibility is that their technology allowed them to access spiritual realms in ways that we don't understand to this day. However, once the people began building that tower at Babel, God put a stop to it once and for all by destroying the tower and causing the people to speak different languages. Can you imagine what confusion that must have caused? But God's purpose was accomplished and the people groups began to disperse, drifting away from those with whom they could no longer communicate. But whatever technology they possessed went with them. We believe, for example, that they had water craft that could cross oceans. After all, Noah certainly had, and even today we know that it is possible to cross oceans in fairly small vessels and arrive safely."

"So you believe that this ring of stones originated sometime after the flood?"

"Definitely. Societies began a slow but steady decline after the flood so along the way a lot of high-level knowledge and technology gradually became lost. The burning of the libraries at Alexandria in Egypt and the ones in Greece also caused a lot of knowledge to be lost forever."

I remembered some of the facts that Profesor Alvarez and Gerhardt Mueller had shared with me. "But what about all the other mysteries, like the stones at Machu Picchu and that ruin near Cuzco in Peru? And that building in Lebanon with the massive stone foundations…how were those built?"

"No one knows for sure," Doctor Silverman replied, "but I suspect those cultures possessed technological know-how that is still lost to us today. For example, the ability to circumvent natural laws like gravity, using magnetic fields, is one possibility. The other factor we must take into account is the existence of giants in those times, working together, who would be able to achieve amazing physical feats."

"You mean, like Goliath?" Could the markings in Neil's Bible be the explanation for some of the world's ancient architectural marvels? Was it really possible that these mega-humans existed all over the world? I remembered the passage in Genesis chapter six about the sons of God and daughters of men marrying and producing giants. To be honest, I'd never given that idea much thought, but now it was beginning to make sense.

He nodded, smiling. "People in Noah's day were of much greater stature than people today, myself excluded, of course, just like people today are of larger body size and height than those of the Middle Ages. Visit some of those five-hundred-year old inns and pubs in Britain and you'll see what I mean. Even you would have to duck to get through the doorways, and the top of your head would brush the ceilings."

I glanced from Silverman to McSweeney. "Why are these stones so important?"

"Let me answer that," McSweeney said, rubbing a hand over his beard. "What we've been able to figure out is that each of the three languages is from the same era, yet one of them is from the other side of the world from the other two. The Olmecs and the Maya lived in Central America, but there is speculation that the Olmecs originated in Africa. If you have ever seen pictures of the giant stone heads they created, it is easy to come to that conclusion. All this evidence suggests that international travel was involved with people groups who everybody thinks never travelled out of the Middle East or

Africa. Neil can decipher the Mayan language pretty closely, but he can't read the Olmec. Doc Silverman, here, can read the Middle Eastern language but not the other two. So far we haven't been able to get the Olmec translated and we haven't had time to put the information all together, but we're working on that."

"Aren't the languages just a different translation of the same message?" I asked.

"No," said Silverman. "That's where the tricky part comes in. Not only are they not a translation, they are different parts of a puzzle. We have at least two problems. First we have to figure out how the stones fit together in order to read each message, then we have to learn what the messages mean. To do that, we have to get all the stones together in one place. We believe that these stones hold the key to a piece of ancient knowledge of some kind the finding of which may change the course of history."

"That's a big assumption."

"It is, but nothing else has come close to unlocking certain mysteries, since, well, since the Rosetta stone."

"Are you telling me that these stones have the same historical significance as the Rosetta stone?"

Both men nodded. "But unlike that stone," Doctor Silverman continued, "we believe that these stones will reveal much more. Think of the repercussions if we can access the technological knowledge of ancient civilizations. What if we can learn how to defy gravity, for instance? Imagine how this kind of knowledge would change the balance of power in the earth today. That's why it is so important that they do not fall into the wrong hands."

"Oh, my goodness!" I cried, searching their faces. "Then why on earth are you entrusting them to me?"

McSweeney was the first to speak and his Scots accent overtook the Texas drawl this time. "Why not you, Moss?" he demanded. "We're all just people here, doing our part. Your part is to pick up the stones for us. We need you to do that and keep doing that until they are all gathered. Once that happens, we can put them together and figure out what they are trying to tell us."

"That's right, my dear," said Doctor Silverman, softly. "We need you to carry on. Compared to us, you are almost invisible. You are a pretty, middle-aged lady on a little trip. No one suspects people like you of anything. You have an honest face. You are the ideal candidate for the job."

I stood up and turned my back on the table. Walking through the living room, I stopped by the window and stared out into the darkened street for a long time. I didn't care for the image they had of me as an invisible, middle-aged lady.

I could quit if I wanted to. I could give them the stones I carried in my bag and hand over the key to the safe deposit box in Switzerland and tell them to go collect the rest themselves if they wanted them. I could tell them to go find some other invisible, middle-aged lady to risk her life for them. I rubbed the back of my neck and sighed. Even with the obvious growing danger, I knew I had to carry on. I could not give up now, not with Dennis still missing and Neil counting on me. My only hope lay in trusting God to look after me until the stones had all been picked up.

A streetlight flickered on down the block and I noticed with alarm that the black SUV was still parked across the street. Edging closer to the window, I slid my finger between the semi-sheer drapery panels and peered out. I could see the shape of the driver slumped behind the wheel. Turning back toward the table I said, "Did you know that someone is watching this house? He has been there since we arrived this afternoon."

McSweeney leapt to his feet and strode across the room, peering out between the sections of fabric.

"Come on," he said, placing an arm around my shoulder, steering me back toward the dining room, and giving my back a little push. "You come away from there." Then he pulled the cords that closed the heavy drapes over the sheers, shutting out the pale light from the street.

"We'll need to be going soon," he said to Silverman.

"Where are we going now?" I asked.

Silverman and McSweeney exchanged glances. "One phone call and it's all arranged. Sit down for a few minutes, Moss," said McSweeney, "and we'll tell you what happens next."

Five minutes later, I had learned that I would be flying out of the little regional airstrip on Sugarloaf Key to Galveston Island as soon as I was ready. Once there I would be met by a woman named Miss Eleanora Buckingham, whom Silverman described as a lady of Jamaican parentage and impressive stature. I begged a shower before leaving and dashed upstairs to jump into the steaming spray. Half an hour later I was ready to go. With dried hair and clean jeans and shirt on, I felt almost brand new.

As I lugged my suitcase back down the stairs, Doctor Silverman called to me from another room. Following the sound of his voice, I found him in an elegantly paneled office holding a telephone in his hand.

"Someone wants to speak with you," he said, handing me the bulky telephone which had a heavy aerial jutting diagonally from the top.

With a puzzled look, I took it from his hand and said hello.

"Hello Jill," said Neil. "How is it going with my wild goose chase? I hope it hasn't been too hard on you."

I clutched the edge of the desk and sank into a nearby armchair. "Neil, where are you? Are you all right?"

"I'm fine, honey. Don't worry about me. I can't tell you where I am right now because it's better if you don't know."

"I understand."

"We only have a minute here, so I want you to know how much I appreciate what you are doing for us. You have no idea the magnitude of your contribution, but one day soon you will have a clearer picture."

"Okay, Neil, I'm expecting that."

"I'm sure you are getting an inkling of what's going on but none of us has a full understanding yet."

"Neil, what about Dennis?" I asked. "What has happened with him?"

For a moment there was silence on the other end of the telephone. "I don't know yet," he said, finally. "I just don't know. We have some people on it now."

"I have been praying for him and I'm sure the rest of the family has, too. I am confident of his safe return. You know that 'peace that passes understanding'? Well, I have it. God is coming through for Dennis and for the rest of us."

"You're right, of course," Neil replied. "It's just that he's my son and I wish he'd never been dragged into this."

McSweeney tapped my arm and put out his hand for the satellite phone. Reluctantly, I said goodbye and handed it over.

The street was empty and the SUV gone by the time we backed Doctor Silverman's car out of the garage. In my tote bag lay two more stones from the ring of sixteen, making the count now eleven. Only five stones more to go, then I could go home and paint, prune my roses, and have tea with my daughter again. At the tiny airstrip a sharp, cool wind blew stands of hair across my eyes. As I pushed them away with a fingertip, I saw a small, sleek aircraft waiting on the tarmac, twin engines whining.

Turning to McSweeney, I shouted, "You expect me to fly across the Caribbean in that?"

"Relax," he hollered back, grinning as he pulled my suitcase from the trunk of the car. "That baby will get you there without even trying. It has twin turbo-props and a range of almost eighteen hundred miles. Galveston Island is fewer than nine hundred miles from here. You'll have fuel to spare. Besides, any woman who can fight off sharks can handle a little thing like a night flight across the open sea."

A door toward the rear of the craft flew open and a man hopped to the ground and ran toward us. In the glow of our headlights, I could see a muscular guy with blonde hair, probably in his late thirties. He shook hands with the men, then reached for mine.

"Hi, I'm Casey Franklin," he shouted, grasping my hand. "You can sit up front with me. It'll just be the two of us tonight. Let's go."

I followed Casey Franklin to the plane where he threw my case in and jumped in behind it. I turned to McSweeney to say goodbye.

"I'll see you soon, Moss," he growled, giving my shoulder a thump. Doctor Silverman bent and kissed both my cheeks again. I climbed into the plane and sat down in the cockpit next to the pilot.

"Buckle up, ma'am," he said. "With this wind, it could be a rough flight tonight."

CHAPTER 26

The light from Galveston Island airport terminal glowed blue-white out of the darkness as the plane halted on the tarmac. Casey Franklin had gripped the plane's wheel with white-knuckled concentration through more than three hours of a rollercoaster nightmare. Winds over the Caribbean had thrown the little plane all over the sky and I spent the entire trip gripping the seat's arms to avoid bashing my head on some part of the cockpit. I staggered toward the building, clutching my suitcase handle with one hand and my stomach with the other.

At nearly six feet tall, Miss Eleanora Buckingham would have been easy to spot in any crowd but tonight, except for the old man cleaning floors, she stood alone in the terminal. Her walnut-brown skin stretched across a broad, open face now split by a wide smile. I lurched toward her and shook her hand.

"You just come home with me, Mrs. Moss," she said, after one look at my ashen face. An abundance of spiral curls bounced at her cheekbones as she nodded. "Mmm-hmm, I'll have you fixed up in no time." Within minutes she had deposited me in her tiny car and headed onto a broad avenue along the ocean. Seeing the waves crashing onto the wide white beach in the pale moonlight made my head spin and my stomach churn. I closed my eyes and rode in silence.

Miss Buckingham's house stood on a street in the old part of town, overhung with massive trees that whipped and swayed in the night wind. A plaque in front of the house claimed that it was listed on a state registry for historic buildings and had been built in 1884. In the winking light from a streetlight, the house looked like an ornate Victorian beauty struggling to retain its glorious youth. Miss Buckingham hustled me inside and pushed the door closed behind us.

"It's late," she stated. "No point in staying up unless you could do with a cup of herbal tea or something."

"That would be lovely," I answered, "if it's not too much trouble. My stomach is still a little upset."

"No trouble at all, honey," she said, patting my arm. "I'll just put the kettle on and then I'll show you to your room. It won't take a minute."

When she returned, she led me up the long, wooden staircase to the second level. My heels tapped on the hardwood floor of the hallway. Pushing open a tall paneled door, she introduced me to a spacious and pretty room. The epitome of Victorian splendour, it had an elaborately carved bed, windows that stretched nearly to the ten-foot ceiling, and a white marble fireplace. After that ghastly flight, it looked like a little piece of heaven.

Miss Buckingham went back downstairs to make the tea and I met her there ten minutes later. The unrest in my stomach had begun to subside, but a cup of hot tea sounded very soothing.

"It's chamomile," she said, handing me a china cup decorated with violets. "It'll help you sleep." She dropped into a high-backed chair, kicking off her shoes and sticking her long legs out onto the Persian rug that lay before another marble fireplace.

"I don't think I'll need any help tonight," I said, yawning into my hand. "I've had a really long day."

"I hate to say it," she observed, "but you look a little green."

We made small talk and after drinking my tea I went straight up to bed. Within moments of closing the door of my room, I crawled into the big soft bed, turned off the lamp and fell fast asleep.

Eight dreamless hours later, I woke to the sound of a saw scraping back and forth outside my window. I tilted the shutters and looked down into the back yard. Broken branches and twigs lay strewn about the lawn and leaves were piled up against the fences. Below me I could see someone at work with the saw, his elbow moving like a slow piston as he cut apart a thick, fallen branch.

I washed my face and dressed, packing all my belongings back into my suitcase in preparation for leaving again, not knowing when that might happen. Downstairs in the kitchen, I found my hostess making pancakes on an electric griddle while bacon sizzled in a frying pan on the stove.

"Well, good mornin'," she said as she flipped her handiwork. "Did you sleep well?"

"Unbelievably," I replied. "I don't think I moved all night. The sound of the saw woke me."

"Sorry about that," she said. "That's my little brother, Calvin, cleaning up the yard. A lot of branches came down last night in that wind."

I walked to the window and looked out to see Calvin heaving a hunk of tree branch the size of his arm onto a pile. Tall like his sister, but slim to the point of being skinny, he moved gracefully like a fly fisher casting a line. His hair stood out from his head in a mop of tightly twisted ropes.

"He is staying with me for the summer," Eleanora explained. "He's just turned nineteen. He needs to get himself sorted out."

The table had been set for breakfast and Eleanora opened the back door and called Calvin to come in. He dropped the saw and headed for the door, kicking his shoes off inside, and washing his hands in the kitchen sink.

"I'm pleased to meet you, ma'am," he said softly when introduced, dipping his head and holding out a limp hand.

"Calvin ran into a little trouble a while back," his sister explained as we sat down at the round table in the sunshine to eat pancakes sprinkled with cinnamon and sugar. "He took a trip to Haiti looking for adventure and got in with the wrong crowd." I glanced at Calvin who sat with his head bent. He was concentrating on his breakfast plate like it might get up and run away. "It seems he got involved with some voodoo practitioners there."

Calvin's head snapped sideways to glare at his sister. "It wasn't like that," he snarled, surprising me with the scorn in his voice. "I just wanted to see what they do."

"Like I said," she continued, unfazed, "voodoo was somehow involved. And I don't know what happened that night, but ever since he came back, he's had the most awful temper, haven't you, Cal?" She didn't wait for a reply as he fixed her with a look of smouldering fury. "He flies off the handle for no reason and it's like a volcano erupting, spewing everywhere, horrible language. It's just not like him. I think something happened down there on the island. Like someone put a hex on him or something."

Calvin slammed his fork down and hissed, "I don't have to listen to this."

"Calvin," I said, attempting to defuse the situation, "can you tell me more about the voodoo ceremony, please?"

"I just went to one of those all night services to check it out. They worship spirits and give sacrifices, stuff like that. It was kind of weird, but interesting." He calmed a bit as he spoke to me, but looking into his eyes, I could see something looking back at me that did not seem to belong, something glittering and vile. It made me shiver. At that moment I heard the Holy Spirit speak into my mind saying, *He has a demon*. I blinked and looked more closely into Calvin's eyes. He was telling me about the ceremony, something about dead chickens and candles and songs, but instead of listening to his voice, I tuned into the voice of the Lord. *I want you to cast out that demon*, God said. My first reaction was, *Oh no, I don't know how to do that.* Then the Spirit reminded me how Jesus had said that even the spirits, meaning those of the enemy, are subject to his believers. Though reluctant, I knew I had to obey. I had only just met this young man, but I could not allow him to continue to suffer from this evil.

"Calvin," I said, reaching across the table and taking his hand. "Would you like to be free of what is bothering you?"

Eleanora's eyes grew wide and she nodded her head up and down, coaching Calvin to agree.

"Yeah, I guess," he answered, slumping back in his chair. Then his eyes went wild again, and he cried out, "Leave me alone," trying to wrench his hand from mine. The evil spirit knew it was in trouble and was acting out.

Still holding tightly to Calvin's hand, I said in the calmest voice I could muster, "In the name of Jesus Christ, I command you evil spirit to come out of Calvin. I overcome you with the blood of the Lamb and the word of my testimony and command you right now to come out of him and leave. I take authority over you in Jesus' name." I kept my grip on Calvin's hand so he wouldn't leap up and take off. What happened next shocked me. He flung his head from side to side and he let out a grinding cry followed by a horrible retching sound, during which I thought he might vomit all over the table. Instead he clutched his middle, gave one huge belching cough, then sat still.

"And don't ever come back," I commanded, for good measure. "I now cover Calvin with the protection paid for with the blood of Jesus," I said. Calvin took a deep breath and exhaled slowly, blinking his eyes and sitting up straight.

"What just happened, ma'am?" he asked, staring at me.

"Calvin," I said, glancing at Eleanora, who gaped at me, her mouth open. "The Lord Jesus just delivered you from the clutches of a demon. I don't know exactly what happened in Haiti but I suspect that you allowed a demonic spirit to come into your life. It moved in and took over, forcing you to do things that you wouldn't ordinarily do. Does that sound accurate?"

"Yes, ma'am," he said. "There was this witch doctor priest guy there and he told me I had to say a bunch of words and to make a sacrifice to some spirit. I thought it was kind of a joke so I went along with it, but ever since then I haven't been the same. Now I feel so different. This is amazing."

"Calvin, do you believe in Jesus?" I asked. "Do you believe that he is the Son of God and that he died for you?"

"I'm not sure what you mean."

Eleanora regarded me with a bemused expression as though to say, *You go girl.* "Do you agree with me that none of us is perfect?" He nodded, glancing at his sister with a wry smile. "Here is what I believe," I continued. "God is perfect, and for us to be in his presence we have to be perfect, too. But we can't be. There is too much bad in the world and even a tiny bit of imperfection in us keeps us away from God's presence. Without perfection, we actually deserve to die. Even if we try with all our might, it is impossible for us to be perfect enough to have a relationship with God and to go to heaven and be with him when we die. But because he loved us so much, he devised a plan that would make us perfect enough to be with him. That plan was to send his one and only Son to take our place and die for us."

Calvin shifted in his chair and picked up his fork, twirling it between his fingers. "I remember something about that from Sunday School when I was little."

"When we choose to believe in Jesus and accept the sacrifice of his life that he gave for us, he comes into our lives and sweeps us clean. We become like brand new people. From that moment on, God sees us as perfect in his eyes. Evil spirits can no longer live in us because Jesus' own Spirit moves in and lives there. He fills our souls with light and love. Would you like that?"

For a moment he said nothing, turning his head to look out the window as he pondered. Then he nodded. "Yeah, I want that. I don't want any creepy spirit stuff in my life again."

"Then the next part is simple. Just ask Jesus to come into your life and make you new again. He will never force you; he is waiting for you to ask him, but when you invite him, he will come and live in your life."

"Okay," Calvin said, looking up at the ceiling. "Um, Jesus, how 'bout you come and do that, like this white lady said. I don't want no demons no more. You can come into my life and make me new, if you will. Okay? Um, good then." He took a deep breath and grinned. "I feel different now," he said, "like somebody just turned the lights on." He looked at Eleanora who had tears streaming down her cheeks. "I'm sorry El," he said. "I didn't know. Things will be different now."

She leaned over and pulled him into her arms. "Oh, Calvin, this is so wonderful. Now you know Jesus, too. I've been praying for you I don't know how long. Praise the Lord, you are born again!" She took him by the shoulders and held him away from her, looking into his face with love and affection. "This is just wonderful!" she said, hugging him again.

"It is, isn't it," I agreed. "It always is."

After breakfast, Calvin went back outside to finish clearing the yard, but this time he was whistling.

"Eleanora," I said, "I'm not sure what is supposed to happen today. Do you have instructions for me?"

"Oh my, yes," she cried. "I'm so thrilled about Calvin that I forgot all about why you are here." She went to a drawer and pulled out some slips of paper. "This here is your badge for the Antiques and Antiquities trade show going on down at the Convention Centre. I'm to take you down there to meet some other people. Then I'll take you over to the bank. I have something for you here that your uncle sent." She pulled the drawer out farther and handed me the little square package, addressed to me at her address.

"How do you know my uncle?" He seemed to have a vast circle of acquaintances.

"I'm an Assistant Professor of Marine Archaeology over at Texas A & M University, which is only about half a mile from here. We met a couple of years ago when Neil was doing some exploration in the Bahamas, looking at Bimini. Are you familiar with that area?" I shook my head. "Well, it's kind of a long story so I'll leave the details for another time, since you have got to get over to that show. Suffice it to say there are architectural ruins below the sea there that we've been studying for some time. I'm sure you would be fascinated. I know I am."

"I agree on both counts," I said. "That it sounds fascinating and that I don't have time to learn more about it now."

She handed me the badge which identified me as an exhibitor, a stretch if I ever heard one, but who knew if that wasn't what I'd be doing within the hour. The company was called Undersea Treasures.

I went upstairs, brushed my teeth, and carried my suitcase downstairs, setting it beside the front door. Eleanora had gone to fetch her purse so I walked through the house and went out the back door to say good-bye to Calvin. He was raking leaves away from the base of a tree.

"I'm leaving now, Calvin," I said.

He stood the rake against the tree and came over to me. "Mrs. Moss, ma'am, I don't know how to thank you for what you did for me. I don't think my life will ever be the same again."

"I'm sure it won't," I replied. "But there is something you need to do. Please get yourself a Bible and read some of it every day. Will you do that?"

He nodded, solemn and serious. "Yes, ma'am, I will."

"Good," I said, standing on tiptoe to kiss his cheek. If his skin had not been so dark, I'm sure I could have seen him blush.

"It shouldn't take you very long to do your pick-up," Eleanora said as we pulled up at the main entrance to the Convention Center. "I'm going to park in the lot across the street and you go in. I'll wait out there for you." The plan was for me to find the Undersea Treasures booth and collect the next stone from a couple named Glen and Barb Turnbull, then turn around and come right back out to where Eleanora would be waiting. From there we would go to the bank where the stones would be placed in a safe deposit box to be collected later. Carrying several stones at once put me in too much danger and increased the probability of a chunk of them being stolen should I be apprehended. I prayed that would never happen.

I flashed my badge at the security guard and entered the show floor, studying the guide to find the Turnbulls' booth. Booths filled with everything from antique furniture to bicycles to oil lamps crammed every available space and exhibitors hovered around their caches like mother hens in an electrical storm. Pressing through the crowds in the aisle, I passed a booth full of Civil War memorabilia next to one filled with Elvis prints and records. Farther on, a collection of Japanese glass floats sat in baskets next to ships' bells and boat tackle. I slowed down when I passed an array of artifacts that looked Mexican and glanced at replicas of Mayan calendars and Aztec masks. When the vendor came over looking hopeful, I moved on.

The Undersea Treasures booth was at the far corner of the show floor. As I approached, I could see a table laden with odds and ends of encrusted boat paraphernalia from various eras and another table of glass-lidded cases filled with dull, silver coins. A big-bellied man wearing a safari shirt leaned over the trays of coins while a red-haired woman browsed. Another man was polishing a brass pulley with a blackened cloth. I checked the booth number against the map and stepped into the cubicle.

The man put down the pulley and came over. "I'm looking for Glen Turnbull," I said.

"Well, you found him. What can I do for you?"

"I've been instructed to tell you that the apple doesn't fall far from the tree," I said, repeating the phrase that McSweeney had instructed me to use.

"Ah," he replied, "You'll want to come with me." He pulled apart the draperies at the rear of the booth and stepped into the space between the fabric and the wall. Once out of sight, he placed a finger to his lips for silence. I nodded. The space was cluttered with plastic tubs and bubble wrap. A hand cart stood against the wall. Glen Turnbull rummaged around in one of the tubs and drew out a little cardboard box. I was pleased to see that the tape and labels had not been disturbed. As I dropped it into my bag, Glen winked at me and whispered, "I'd sure love to see what's in that box." He raised his eyebrows and tilted his head toward my bag.

"Sorry," I mouthed. "Not today." He shrugged, then stepped out from behind the curtains into the booth. I followed him, stepping over the electrical cords and around the edge of a ship's wheel.

"Well, look who's here," Glen cried, rushing into the aisle and throwing his arms wide. The man at the coin table stepped backward, blocking my view. I edged past him, anxious to get out of there.

"There's someone you have to meet," I heard Glen say. I looked up, and directly into the face of Claire Jamieson. I froze.

"Mrs. Moss, allow me to introduce one of my dearest friends and a fellow lover of all things antique. This is Marie Cavendish." Glen's wife, the red-head, squealed with delight and threw her arms around Claire. My mouth was open but nothing came out of it. There was no mistaking this woman was the same one who had picked me up at my hotel in Paris only last week, had tried to get away with a stone in the hotel in

Tours, and whom Marco had smacked at the Gatwick airport. Why were these people calling her by a different name?

When Barb let go of her, Claire put out her hand to shake mine. "I'm pleased to meet you," Claire said, her voice as brittle as icicles. "It looks like we have something in common."

"Oh," I said. "And what might that be?"

"Why, a love of ancient artifacts, of course." I'm sure I detected a note of triumph.

"Excuse me," I said, moving around her, "but I have to go now."

"Oh, don't go yet," she said, placing a hand on my arm and blocking my path. "You have to meet a friend of mine. I'm sure you wouldn't want to miss this." A look of malicious anticipation lit her eyes as she turned and motioned with her hand. At first, all I could see were the crowds jamming the aisle.

Dimly, I realized that Barb was beside me babbling, gushing about Claire's or Marie's accomplishments. I wanted to swat her, to shut her up. When I glanced back to Claire, a tall, dark-haired man stood at her side, one hand placed at the back of her neck in a gesture of shared intimacy. Her arm reached around his back at the waist and drew him close to her body. He didn't resist.

Confused, I remembered the man I had seen her with in the restaurant in France, and at Gatwick. It had always been a sleazy-looking character with slicked back hair. I felt dizzy and shook my head. I felt like I had just been punched in the stomach.

The man's face that I now looked into was Marco's.

CHAPTER 27

The dress did not fit me well anywhere. It sagged from my shoulders and drooped under the arms, but fortunately, it came with a belt. Together with a few strategically-placed pins begged from the purser's desk, I managed to make it look a little less like a bad joke. Made of black, stretchy satin with beads stitched here and there, it was meant to be a tight-fitting, sexy little cocktail number but the effect was lost on me. I stuffed a sock into each cup of my bra to fill out the darts in the bodice and spent nearly fifteen minutes bunching, scrunching, pushing, and squeezing to smooth the lumps out. The shoes provided for me, a pair of glossy black four-inch heels, pinched my toes, but after walking back and forth in the cabin a few times, I decided they would have to do. Women on the run from just about everybody have to be adaptable.

I clipped on a necklace, the only one I had with me, added a pair of gold earrings and hoped that my look would be presentable and at the same time unremarkable. Giving the short auburn wig a shake, I pulled it over my own hair, stuffing the loose wisps up under the cap. I turned to examine my back view when I heard a knock on the door. Three quick raps then a pause, followed by two slow ones.

Bobby stood there wearing a tuxedo.

"Whoa!" I said. "You came prepared, didn't you?"

"I always try to be prepared for anything, ma'am. Are you ready to go?"

232

I picked up a tiny, beaded evening bag and slipped my cabin key card inside, threw a silvery shawl as delicate as a spider's web over my shoulders, and pulled the door closed behind me. Taking Bobby's arm like we were meant for each other, I minced down the corridor in my too-tight shoes, smiling as we passed others dressed up in evening garb.

Three hours later, I closed the door to my cabin, kicked those instruments of torture from my feet, tossed my wrap and bag on the bed, and pulled open the sliding glass door that led out to the balcony. Leaning on the chest-high railing, I gazed at the water far below, shining in the moonlight. The air was soft and warm, infused with a touch of salt and the faint scent of lime.

I could hardly believe only hours before everything had been so different.

Closing my eyes, I could once again see Marco's face; one side of his mouth quirked up in a half-grin, with Claire Jamieson pressing herself into his side like a cat on a visitor's leg. The shock of seeing him in Galveston sent a surge of electric-blue panic through every nerve in my body. I had left him only two days before when he had kissed me goodbye in Gatwick airport, calling me sweet names and holding me close. And now, here he was standing in front of me with a smug look on his face, playing lovey-dovey with the one person I hoped never to see again in my life. I had felt the overwhelming urge to grab that pulley thing that Glen had been polishing and smack her over the head with it. And after she went down, I would take aim at Marco's head.

But I didn't, satisfying though it may have been. Instead I had a split second thought about the treasure in my tote bag, all the blocks I had acquired since Switzerland, and how I could not risk losing them to this horrid woman and Marco, who obviously had something going on with her. Then the thought of Dennis flashed through my mind and I knew I could not jeopardize his chances of survival by acting out my fury and pain. Neil was still counting on me, as were McSweeney and Doc Silverman.

Then I acted. Giving Claire, or whatever her name was, a colossal shove, I unbalanced both of them and dove past, tearing down the corridor while dodging shoppers and leaping over little kids, my heavy tote flying behind me. I shot one quick glance over my shoulder and saw that Marco had charged after me. Zigzagging down different aisles, I made it to the main entrance and yelled, "Emergency, out of my way," as I parted the crowd and sprinted for the exterior doors. Bursting outside, I skidded to a halt in the glaring sunshine, shielding my eyes with my hand, and scanning the parking lot for Eleanora's little grey car. I couldn't see it anywhere. Dodging traffic, I raced across the street and pushed through some spiny bushes, emerging on the other side between a green mini-van and a motorcycle. "Where on earth are you, Eleanora?" I cried in a whispered scream.

Just then she pulled up in front of me and pushed open the passenger door. "Get in," she commanded, "and get down. No point in having you seen now." She swerved past a row of cars entering the lot and sped out the exit, squealing her tires on the hot pavement.

"I take it things didn't go so well in there," she commented drily, turning left without signalling, then swerving right. "You can get up now. There's no one following us."

I sat up from my bent position and took a deep breath, leaning my head against the back of the seat. "There was someone there I hoped never to see again," I said.

"Mmm-hmm."

"And someone else I thought I wanted to see again, but I've changed my mind." My voice wavered and Eleanora glanced my way.

"Mmm-hmm," she said again, this time in a tone that said, *I see and it's not good.* "Well, chances are you won't have to see either of them again. Just wait until you meet Bobby. He'll look after you."

"Who is Bobby?" I asked, plucking a tissue from the box on the console.

"You'll see," she replied. "We'll be there in a minute." True to her word, one minute later she pulled the car to a stop in the side parking lot of a small bank. "Come on," she commanded. "We don't have much time."

I followed her into the bank and through to an office at the back where she pushed open a door. "She's all yours," she said, giving my back a little shove before striding away. Lounging in a chair behind an empty desk sat an enormous, dark-skinned man wearing a suit, his biceps straining the fabric. A bulging duffel bag sat at his feet.

"Hi, I'm Bobby Buckingham," he said in a quiet voice, getting to his feet and extending his hand. "If you will just follow me, ma'am, we'll tuck those things you're carrying into a safe deposit box and get out of here." I shook his hand and followed him to the vault.

Seven minutes later the three of us climbed into Eleanora's car. I swear I heard the poor little thing groan when Bobby squeezed into the back seat. As soon as my door closed, Eleanora stomped on the gas pedal and sped away, drawing to a stop in front of the cruise ship terminal.

"When this is all over," Eleanora told me as we got out in front of the terminal, "I want you to promise that you'll come back and visit me, hear?" The steward had already taken my suitcase and Bobby's duffel away when Eleanora handed me a packet. I flipped it open to find tickets and documents allowing me to board the vessel sitting at anchor on the far side of the building.

"I promise," I said as we hugged good-bye.

"Nobody will think to look here for you," Bobby whispered as we edged through the line-up toward the counter. Once on board, I saw that Bobby's stateroom was directly across the corridor from mine. Bobby ducked into the doorway of my cabin, unzipped his duffel bag, and handed me a bag of clothes. "You'll need some of these. In fact, from now on you are a red-head named Janice Isaac. I'm still Bobby, and I'm your special friend. People can think what they want." Since he was at least ten years my junior, people were bound to think something, but so long as no one recognized me, I didn't much care.

Bobby turned to leave when I said, "Bobby, before you leave I want to ask you something." He shrugged. "Tell me who you are and what you are doing here with me."

"Sure, ma'am. I own an international security company and I've worked with your uncle on many of his projects. He trusts me and he pays me well. I'm here to make sure you get where you are supposed to go and all in one piece."

"I see. And where am I supposed to go?"

"Tomorrow morning we get off in Cozumel. We take our luggage with us and we don't board the ship when it sails on to Grand Cayman. There's someone you need to meet on the island. So please be ready after breakfast, ma'am."

"Why didn't we just fly there?"

"That was the original plan, but the airport is probably the first place someone would look to try to find you, don't you think? At the last minute, Eleanora called our cousin, June, who owns a travel agency, then, when we were in the bank, she ran down the street and picked up the documents. We thought this would be safer."

"What about the disguise?"

"Intuition and experience," he explained. "I guessed at the sizes and grabbed what we had in stock, ma'am."

"Thank-you, Bobby. There's one more thing."

"What's that, ma'am?"

"Could you please stop calling me ma'am?"

"Ma'am, I'm from the South. If we don't call ladies ma'am, our mommas slap our heads. When we're in public I will call you Janice, as pre-arranged. Otherwise, ma'am, I'll be calling you ma'am."

"Okay," I agreed, "but do you mind if I don't call you sir?"

Bobby grinned. "I'll call you ma'am and you call me Bobby, and we'll get along just fine."

"Okay."

Now, standing alone at the railing of my balcony suite watching the moonlight sprinkle the sea with a stream of silver glitter, I could not help thinking about Marco. I had never felt so betrayed in my life. He had treated me like a princess, like he really loved me, and I had fallen for it. I had fallen for him, the whole line and the whole package; the dark eyes, the long legs, the way his hair curled around my fingers. I remembered every kiss, every smile, and every touch. It had all seemed so genuine at the time, but now tasted like ashes in my mouth. I had even gone so far as to believe I was falling in love with him. How could I have been so duped? I felt like a fool and worse, I realized that letting my emotions get the upper hand may have jeopardized my whole mission.

Recognizing that by letting Marco become a part of my journey – the trip from Madrid to Barcelona to Thun – meant that he had learned a lot about what I was doing, probably far too much. He had to have been conspiring with Claire all along. How could I not have suspected? Surely there must have been clues that I missed, or perhaps he was just a consummate con-artist preying on gullible me.

And how had they found out about my connection in Galveston? Something was terribly wrong, but I could not think what link in the chain had broken. I felt quite sure Bobby wouldn't know anything since he had just come on the scene as my bodyguard. Did Neil know anything about Marco and his connection with Claire? Did McSweeney? I dropped my chin onto my arms and stared out to the open sea.

"Father God," I prayed, "please tell me what I need to know. I am missing something here and don't know how to find out what it is. I need you to help me." The sound of water slapping against the hull of the ship far below and the hum of the engines were the only sounds I could hear except now and then the voice or laughter of another passenger rang out from one of the decks. The other balconies in my area of the ship seemed to be deserted. Then I heard the voice of the Lord speak to me. He said, *"Go to bed, Jill."* I stood up straight and sighed, then did as I was told.

In the morning, I ordered a room service breakfast and ate it in the comfort of my bed while gazing out at the azure sea. I was slicking on lip gloss when I heard Bobby's knock on my door. I opened the door to find him leaning against the opposite wall of the corridor with his duffel at his feet.

"Ready to go?" he inquired.

"Give me one second and I'll be right there."

The sun had already hammered the pavement on the dock into a shimmering plain of heat and light when we disembarked on the island of Cozumel. I thought we looked conspicuous leaving the ship with our bags, but no one said anything so we just walked away. At the curb Bobby hailed a cab, a heap of metal held together by paint and someone's will. We crawled into the back seat after tossing our bags in the grubby trunk and Bobby gave the driver directions in Spanish.

Driving away from San Miguel, I watched as first hotels and stylish restaurants, then beach hangouts and surf bars, slid past my open window. The turquoise waves of the Gulf of Mexico rippled onto white sand beaches along the road. On the land side, low, scrubby vegetation punctuated by the occasional palm tree stretched toward the centre of the island. The smell of the sea rushed in the window on a wind that whipped my hair around. Bobby sat beside me taking up three-quarters of the seat, his knees almost in his armpits.

After about forty-five minutes, the driver pulled off the paved road onto a narrow sandy track leading past a marsh, dodging potholes and rocks. The brush grew thicker and taller here. Eventually, we turned off the dirt road onto an even smaller trail overshadowed by leafy trees and so rough we both clutched the door handles to keep from banging into each other. Dampness ringed the underarms of Bobby's shirt and he tugged his collar away from his wet neck.

"We're taking the long way," he said. "It shouldn't be far now."

Within a few minutes, the driver pulled his rust-bucket car into the bush under a canopy of fronds and leaves that slapped at the open windows. At the end of this jungle tunnel, I could see that the vegetation opened up to the sky. When we emerged from the forest's shade into a sun-filled clearing, I looked through the grimy windshield of the car and saw a house. It was not a large house, but verandas circled its perimeter, giving it the appearance of expansiveness. At the sound of the vehicle, a couple of skinny dogs careened around the corner of the house, barking like fools. Bobby unfolded himself from the back seat and stepped out, giving the driver instructions as he closed his door.

"What did you say to him?" I asked as we climbed the steps to the veranda.

"I suggested he take a nap and stay right there if he wanted to get paid."

The dogs gave us both a thorough sniffing out and went back to flop down in the shade of a broad-leafed tree. Bobby knocked on the wood-framed screen door, making it clatter against its frame. The inside door stood open and I could see straight through the house to another screen door at the back. A fly buzzed against the screen and somewhere inside the house I could hear an electric fan whirring. Bobby knocked again and I called out an exploratory "Hello."

From the back a voice called, "Hold onto your shirt. I'm coming."

Around the corner of the house came first a calico cat that took one disdainful look at me before curling her body around Bobby's leg, followed by a short, black-haired lady wearing a bright-flowered sundress.

"Ola, hello," she said, smiling. "You must be Jill. I've been expecting you." She took my hands in both of hers. "I'm Consuelo Hanna." Her black eyes sparkled.

"It's a pleasure to meet you," I said.

239

"And who might you be?" she inquired, gazing up at Bobby.

"Bobby Buckingham, ma'am," he answered, shaking her hand. Her head was even with his elbow.

"Well, you'd better come in," she said, then hesitated, glancing toward the taxi where the driver lounged with his hat over his face. "On second thought, let's just go around back and sit on the veranda. I'll get us a cold drink. You two go on ahead and I'll catch up."

Several rattan chairs and a couple of longer settees sat in the shade along the spacious veranda between potted fan palms. Fuchsia-coloured bougainvillea spilled over the railings and trailed onto the wood flooring. Bobby took a seat on one of the settees and I sat down with my back against the house and put my feet up on a small footstool. The jungle had been pushed back far enough to allow for a garden patch, where neat rows of vegetables sprouted from the sandy earth. After a few minutes, Consuelo Hanna appeared, pushing the screen door open with her elbow and carrying a tray of tall, icy glasses of fruit juice.

"I know you don't have much time," she said sitting down opposite me, "so we should probably get right down to it." Her eyes flicked to where Bobby sat, then back to me. "Is he supposed to hear this?"

Bobby sighed and heaved himself to his feet. "I won't be far away," he said, heading to the corner of the veranda and disappearing from sight. I could hear the legs of a chair scrape on the wood and the wicker creak as he sat down.

Consuelo pushed a stray lock of hair away from her eyes. "Before I forget, I had better give you what you came for." She went back into the house and returned with the small box. It had been opened.

"I couldn't resist taking a peek," she apologized, handing it to me. "But I checked with Neil before I opened it. I didn't want to risk the sky falling or anything." The corners of her eyes crinkled as she grinned.

I pulled the wrapping away from the stone and lifted it out of the box, turning it in my fingers. Like the others, it displayed cryptic messages in long-forgotten languages on three sides and though similar to the others, the inscriptions were not the same as any of them. I gently placed it back in the bubble-wrap and closed the box. "What do you have to tell me?"

She leaned back in her chair and lifted the glass to her lips. I watched as a drop of condensation rolled down its side and fell onto her dress. "I've known your Uncle Neil for many years," she said, setting the glass down. "In fact, we are now into decades. You will find, my dear, the archaeological world is rather small and it's hard to keep secrets. Amongst our particular branch, if you will, this find of Neil's is causing quite a stir."

"Really? Who else knows about it?"

"Very few at present but among those who know, Dr. Bernaud, Profesor Alvarez, and a few others, like Silverman and McSweeney, we know that when it gets out, it will turn a lot of the old-guard thinking on its ear. I'm sure you are aware that the combination of languages inscribed on the stones does not fit with the accepted timeline of European discovery of the Americas. Only some of us are spiritually aware and knowledgeable enough about early history from the Bible to have an idea what really happened in that time, like your uncle and the others who think differently from both the archaeological and the church establishment. Our specialty is what you might call spiritual archaeology, an understanding of both physical history and the spiritual world."

"That's an interesting term," I commented, "but it seems appropriate, especially in Neil's case."

She smiled. "Not only is it a sub-classification, it is also a sub-culture. We all know each other and regularly keep track of what each is up to, where the digs are, and what we have found."

"And where do you fit into this picture?"

"For the past thirty years my husband, Charles, and I were one of the leading teams studying Bible history and Central-American archaeology. Two years ago he died and I retired. I didn't want to carry on alone, though I have to admit, I miss the field work a lot."

"Why don't you go back to it?"

"I may. But you are not here to talk about me."

"Please tell me what I need to know."

"My people are the Maya," she said. "I have spent my life studying the past of my people. What I have found may surprise you; in fact, it may surprise a lot of people."

"How so?"

"For one thing, very little has been revealed yet. The few of us who have been working on certain projects have kept things quiet, even from the main archaeological community, since it will upset a pretty big apple cart. You see, there are lots of accepted ideas in the archaeological world, a lot of big names, and a lot of material printed. Most of it is the result of an incredible amount of research, field work, and lives spent looking for facts. But like most other pursuits, there is very little original thinking. Everything is built on what went before. It's not new, but it is a simple case of "All we, like sheep, have gone astray." All it takes is one person of note to get it wrong and everyone else follows along behind, even when plenty of evidence is found to the contrary of a conclusion. People prefer to twist the facts to fit their theory, rather than changing the theory to fit the facts. The scope of possible explanations for new information is narrowed, eliminating the possibility of discovering something original."

"You see it over and over again," I remarked.

"Many of the conclusions drawn regarding the history the Mayan peoples are, I believe, correct. However, based on my research and that of my late husband, I have drawn different conclusions taking into account the biblical perspective as well as archaeological findings."

"For instance?"

"The stone that I just handed you is a perfect example. Contemporary archaeology tells us that ancient civilizations did not venture far from their homelands, yet the world is full of evidence to the contrary."

I remembered the maps that Profesor Alvarez had shown me and the photos I had seen at Gerhard Mueller's tiny flat. "This is fascinating," I said, "but what is it specifically that I should know and why?"

Consuelo took a deep breath. "You've seen pictures of the many pyramids built by the Mayan people, haven't you?" I nodded. "It has been supposed that slave labour was used to push those massive stones into place and carve the inscriptions on all of those stone surfaces. The ancient Mayans had a reputation for brutality, so enslaving their enemies to do the work is certainly possible. However, there are two other possible explanations for the building of such colossal yet intricate structures like ones that exist all over the world from Egypt to Peru to China, India, North America, and Mexico."

I leaned forward, my chin on my hand. "What are they?"

"The first explanation is that giants existed not just in Goliath's day and in the Middle East, but all over the world."

I raised an eyebrow. "And the other?"

"The other is that the ancients had knowledge of magnetic and electrical fields that cover the surface of the earth, knowledge that modern man has yet to understand. The ancients knew how to use these magnetic and electrical grids to defy gravity and they used this knowledge to create the fantastic architectural structures, many of which still stand today. I believe that these stones you are collecting may hold the key to unlocking that ancient technology."

"The stones hold the key? Are you sure?"

"No, but I believe so. Now can you see why they are so important? Whoever can unlock these mysteries could rule the world."

CHAPTER 28

The tweet of a cell phone rippled through the late morning air, breaking my concentration. I heard Bobby say, "Yes, sir. Yes, sir. Got it, sir." Then he came around the corner of the veranda and said, "It's for you, ma'am."

Puzzled, I took the phone. "Hello?"

"Moss. McSweeney here. Only got a minute, so listen up. You have to get to Merida and go see Frederick Chin. He's a little Chinese guy who pastors a church there. It's in a big old mansion. You'll probably love it. Chin has the next instalment for you and will tell you where to go next. Bobby's gonna make sure you get there. I already talked to him. No planes. You go by land and sea. Got that?"

"Yes. How soon?"

"As soon as you can get there. Any other questions?" I took a breath. "Good," he barked and hung up before I could say anything. I handed the telephone back to Bobby.

"We should leave within the hour, ma'am," Bobby said, disappearing around the corner again.

"Let me tell you a few more things you should know before you have to hit the road," Consuelo said, her eyes bright with enthusiasm.

"Please."

"Have you ever wondered how the ancient peoples cut those huge stones that they used to build their cities, the ones that are cut at such odd angles, yet they fit so perfectly together that you can't even slip a piece of paper between them?" Without waiting for a response, she continued. "The theories put forth so far don't hold water, in my opinion. In Mexico alone there are up to eighty geometric stone cities, many with buildings as much as two hundred feet high. The stones of these buildings can weigh up to forty tons. How did these so-called primitive societies move such massive stones with nothing more than simple tools? What did they use to cut them with such precision? The pyramid of Quetzalcoatl was two-hundred and ten feet tall with a base that covers thirty square acres. I'm telling you ancient peoples were not a bunch of dim-witted, half-animals. They had extremely advanced civilizations and technology that even included electricity, a type of which we still do not understand. Oral legend among the Mayans and the Aztecs tell about cities where the lights never went out, day or night for centuries. And do you know that in the pyramids at Giza in Egypt cosmic radiation inside the pyramid is of a kind that contradicts any known source in science or electronics, and has an energy field that radiates from the apex of the great Cheops pyramid?"

"I was not aware of that. How is it I've never heard about it before?"

She shrugged. "Perhaps we are kept in the dark on purpose. I have never had this experience myself, but I have heard that at certain times when you stand at the top of the pyramid at Chichen Itza, your hair will literally stand on end. There is some kind of electrical or magnetic field associated with the pyramidal structure that is not clearly understood. There is more to the purpose of these ancient structures than religious or ceremonial significance. Here is another example. The largest heads carved by the Olmec peoples at San Lorenzo, Tenochtitlan and Potrero Nuevo in Veracruz weigh around twenty tons each. It is still considered a mystery how these stones were cut and moved around. As a side note, the faces do not resemble the features of any known indigenous peoples but rather look like South Pacific Islanders or Africans.

How could that be if international travel did not exist until Columbus sailed?"

"What's your theory?"

"I believe that after the great flood, the knowledge that existed prior to the deluge was still known by ancients and after the Tower of Babel spread people around the world, they took their knowledge with them. That knowledge included ocean-going vessels, microscopes, telescopes, and complicated calendars more accurate than those of today. Gradually, over the generations the knowledge declined, the old ways gradually became lost. Civilization is not always ascending; sometimes it goes into decline for reasons that we may never know. These reasons could include disease, drought and famine, bad weather conditions such as floods, storms, avalanches, the sort of things which force migration. Bad governments, new threats of conflict, war, moral decay, you name it. Any number of factors can cause a society to decline. It could be as simple as the kids wanting to move away from home and do something more adventurous or that the society or location can no longer sustain growth. With the decline goes the technology, particularly in times of great terror or trauma where survival is at stake."

"Can we get back to your theory about how the great structures were built?"

"It is evident from the size, the intricacy of the work, and the locations where many of these structures remain that the builders used material, tools, and machinery that does not exist today. There is nothing that we know today that could move the stones used to build Machu Picchu or Sacsayhuaman in Peru, even the cranes that are used to build our modern-day high-rise towers. And how did those people cut the stones with such exactitude?"

I shook my head. "Evidently, they knew something we don't know."

"Exactly. But we are still not sure what that is, which is why I believe that your stones are so important. From talking with Neil and some of the others, I am guessing that the message on the stones will lead us to the answers to the secrets of mastering the natural elements of the earth like gravity, magnetic fields, crystals, and light."

"It sounds like the stuff of movies."

"There is still a lot of mystery surrounding ancient civilizations in the Americas, particularly those where dense jungles and unfriendly locals prevent exploration. In the 1970s, a claim was made that a vast series of tunnels and underground chambers had been discovered in Ecuador, but because of politics and earthquakes, the entrances were sealed up."

"Do you believe they exist?"

"Yes. I also know that there are tunnels in the Yucatan connecting cities and ancient sites that have yet to be excavated. Knowing about these places and not being able to do anything about them is enormously frustrating."

"Why can you do nothing about them?"

"Look at me," she said. "I am no longer young."

"Mrs. Hanna," I said, "I have a great deal of respect for you, for the work you have done, and for the knowledge that you have. I also respect that you can stop working if you choose. But if you feel like your life work is not complete, or that you are not ready to lay down your tools, then you must carry on. Forgive me for being forthright, but I believe that the world still needs people like you."

I didn't notice that Bobby had come around the corner of the house again until he spoke.

"Mrs. Moss, ma'am," he said quietly, "I think it's time we be going."

I jumped, startled by his voice. "So soon?" I asked, glancing at my watch. It was nearly noon. "I would love to stay here all day talking with you, Mrs. Hanna. You have so much to tell me." I stood to my feet.

"My dear," said Consuelo, standing up also, "you have inspired me tremendously. After my husband died, I stopped doing most things and retired here to live quietly and enjoy my grandchildren. But you are correct. I must not stop doing the work I am meant to do."

Taking her hand I said, "I hope we meet again. I want to continue our conversation when we have more time."

She smiled. "I have a feeling we will."

The cab driver woke with a snort, pushing his cap back up on his head and turning the key in the ignition while Bobby and I crowded into the back seat. As we pulled away from the house, I turned to wave. Consuelo Hanna stood at the bottom of the stairs, the sun glinting off her blue-black hair, and a new fire in her eyes.

I could easily see what drove archaeologists like Consuelo Hanna and Neil. There is so much yet to be discovered and so much only hinted at, yet the answers remain lost in time. But as I was learning, the world seemed to be littered with clues, clues that have not all been correctly interpreted. Perhaps, all it would take to put them together would be knowledge and understanding coupled with spiritual insight and communication with God. No wonder Neil's passion for antiquity was unquenchable.

The taxi driver stopped and let us off at the same spot where we hired him. Before Bobby hauled himself out of the cramped car and got our luggage from the trunk I tugged the wig on my head and stuffed a few stray strands of my hair up under it. Then I stepped out onto the sidewalk and paid the driver.

"Come this way, ma'am," Bobby said. "The ferry to the mainland is right over here." We walked down the promenade along the street, the beach on one side and the town on the other. The noonday sun shimmered off the pavement. I slipped on my sunglasses and checked my hair with my hand as I walked, tugging my suitcase along behind me. I had worn knee-length walking shorts and a light cotton top when I got dressed and was now happy I had read the weather correctly.

The ferry, scheduled to leave in ten minutes, stood waiting at the pier. We bought tickets and stood in line, then boarded the boat and found seats. No sooner had we set our luggage down than I could hear someone calling Bobby's name.

"Bobby, hey, Bobby. Bobby Buckingham. Up here." Bobby leaned over the railing and looked up. "I'll be right down," the voice called. Within a minute, a rangy, long-haired man leapt down the steps from an upper deck and ran toward us. For a moment Bobby's expression registered nothing, then suddenly his face lit up.

"Hey, if it isn't Matt the Bull!" he shouted, throwing his arms open. The two men embraced, thumping each other and laughing. "What are you doing here, Bull?"

"I live in Playa," Matt replied. "Hey, who's this?" he said, spying me standing next to Bobby.

"Oh gosh, I'm sorry," Bobby said. "This is my friend, Janice." Turning to me he said levelly, "Jan, meet my old pal, Matt Bullard. We were in the Marines together." We shook hands and sat down as Matt and Bobby launched into reminiscing about old times. Matt was tall like Bobby but built lighter. He looked like he was about the same age as Bobby but had not aged as well. Nervous hands pushed straggly wisps of greying blonde hair away from a lined face that looked as though too much time had been spent with drugs and booze.

Matt told Bobby that he ran a little boat charter business out of Playa del Carmen but that the motor of his boat conked out and he'd come to San Miguel for parts. As they talked, Matt's eyes darted around the crowded boat.

Thirty-five minutes later, we docked in Playa Del Carmen.

"Let me give you a ride," Matt offered, hanging back as the rest of the passengers left the vessel. "Where are you headed?"

"Oh, we're fine," Bobby replied. "We can find our own way. It was great seeing you again, Bull." He held out his hand to shake Matt's.

"I insist," Matt said, ignoring the hand and slapping Bobby on the shoulder. I bit my lip. We needed to get on the road.

"Actually," Bobby said, "we kind of would like to be alone, so we'll just say good-bye and be on our way." He picked up his duffel and turned to go.

"No," Matt said, his voice flat. "You have to come with me." He lifted his shirttail just enough to reveal the barrel of a pistol pointed at Bobby's belly.

"What are you playing at, man?" Bobby demanded in a soft, controlled voice. "Put that thing away before someone gets hurt."

Matt shifted his feet. His jaw jerked from side to side like he was chewing on his tongue. "You guys gotta come with me," he said. "I don't want to have to shoot you. So, come on. My car is just over there." He tilted his chin toward the street as he dug his keys out of his pocket.

"Who put you up to this?" I said, glaring at him.

His eyes twitched away from mine and I followed his flickered glance. On the street people milled about and tourists wandered along enjoying the sunshine and poking in the shops. I glanced back at Matt's face, but he refused to look at me.

"I'm not going anywhere with you until you tell us what's going on, Matt," Bobby stated, his voice low and firm.

"Look, man," Matt whined. "I didn't want to do this, but they made me. I needed the money, so just come with me now and no one'll get hurt."

"I have a better idea," Bobby replied. "First, you tell us who 'they' are."

Matt squirmed like a beaten dog. "Man," he bleated, "I don't even know who these guys are. They just turned up this morning, asking about you. They showed me your picture and asked if I'd seen you. I said, yeah, I've seen you but not for a long time. Then this guy says he thinks you're in town and they need to talk to you about something. He said you knew about a big heist or something. They told me that if I brought you to them, they'd pay me."

"How much?" Bobby and I said in unison.

Matt glanced from my face back to Bobby's. "Aw, man. They said they'd pay me five hundred bucks just for bringing the two of you in. I figured they were government agents or something. Besides, like I said, I could use the money. It's nothin' personal, Bobby. You know that. I just need you to come with me. When I hand you over to Señor Menendez, I'll get my money and be on my way."

I gasped. Both men's heads snapped around to look at me.

"What is it?" Bobby said.

"I know that man, Menendez," I replied. "He doesn't work for the government."

"Where's your car, Bull?"

Matt pointed toward the street with a furtive twitch of his head. "It's that beat up green Mazda over there," he said. Without turning our heads, we could see the vehicle parked across from the beach.

"Okay," Bobby said, "here's what we're going to do. You're going to give me the keys to the car, nice and gently. Janice and I are going to borrow it for a few days, okay?" Matt's eyes were wide and unblinking but he nodded almost imperceptibly. Bobby stepped close and took them from his hand. "Now," Bobby continued, "I'm going to throw a punch at your jaw, overpower you, and toss you into the sea. Understand?"

"Uh-huh," Matt murmured.

"Then we're going to take the car and go where we need to go. When we have finished using your car, we'll let you know where you can find it, and you can come and get it. Inside you will find the five hundred dollars that you will have lost by not bringing us in plus reimbursement for any other costs we incur. Got that?"

A look of pure relief spread over Matt's face. "Don't hit me too hard," he said. "I don't want to have to use the money to get my teeth fixed. And be careful. Menendez and a couple of his pals are skulking around here somewhere, keeping an eye on me. So once you dump me in the drink, run like hell." He winked at me. "Nice meeting you, ma'am," he said. "I just wish it hadn't been quite like this." Then he looked back at Bobby and I saw the point of the gun drop. "Whenever you're ready, man, let me have it."

A second later, Matt's body hit the water with a satisfying splat and Bobby had slung his duffel over his shoulder, grabbed my bag in one hand and my wrist in the other and together we tore up the length of the dock, dodging sightseers and vacationers. To my left, I saw a tall, dark man in a black suit run toward us. I scanned the beach both ways and saw another man, this one shorter, heavier, and wearing tan pants and a white t-shirt, also break into a run in our direction. At the end of the dock, Bobby raced across the street, waving at the traffic. Tires squealed on the hot pavement. Someone shouted.

Reaching the green car, Bobby yanked open the back door and flung our bags inside. Slapping the keys into my hand he said, "Here, you drive, I'll navigate."

"Are you nuts?"

"You do drive, don't you?" I saw one of the men leap into the street.

"I drive," I said, jumping into the driver's seat. It was positioned too far back for me, but I knew there was no time to change it so I slid forward in the seat and twisted the key in the ignition as Bobby dropped into the passenger seat and slammed the door.

"Hit it, ma'am," he shouted. I jammed the gearshift into drive and jerked the wheel. Stomping on the gas pedal, I swerved into the traffic, drawing more honks and shouts. Pedestrians stopped walking and stared. I glanced over my shoulder for our pursuers but saw neither one. My eyes swivelled back to the street ahead.

"Oh-oh," Bobby said.

Directly in front and a few cars ahead, a man stepped from between the parked vehicles and levelled a gun at my head.

"Oh no, you don't," I shouted, jerking the steering wheel left and standing on the accelerator. A second later, a shower of glass sprayed us as a shot pierced the windshield, low and centre. I heard Bobby grunt. As I bore down on him, the gunman leapt out of the way and I tore past. Spinning the steering wheel in both hands, I forced the car to rocket around the nearest corner. Pedestrians scattered on both sides of the street. Not caring where we went, I drove like a mad-woman, turning first left, then right, and left again. Within minutes we were lost in the back streets of the city among rows of low, colourful houses and tiny grocery stores. Plastered walls covered with graffiti and scrubby bushes lined the roadsides where I sped across a major avenue and dove in amongst the pokey residential streets again. Checking the rear view mirror, I saw that we were alone. So far, no one had tried to follow us.

"Bobby, where are we? I don't know where to go next. You're supposed to be navigating," I said, still perched on the edge of the driver's seat. "Bobby?"

I took my foot off the gas and slowed down, glancing over at Bobby. My stomach convulsed. Bobby lay slumped against the car's filthy door clutching his left arm. Blood covered his hand, ran over his fingers, and soaked his shirt. Bobby had been shot.

CHAPTER 29

Even with the gas pedal pressed hard against the floor boards, the car would not go any faster. In the passenger seat, Bobby slouched against the door sound asleep, his mouth drooping open and tiny glistening beads of sweat dimpling his forehead and upper lip. Deepening twilight edged over the surrounding forest and fewer and fewer cars passed. Not happy to be out here driving, I pushed harder on the gas, even though I knew it would make no difference. A headache crept up the back of my neck from prolonged tension in my shoulders and my hands ached from gripping the steering wheel. If I'd had it my way, we would be in Merida by now.

Realizing that Bobby had been injured on the street in Playa del Carmen, I had turned the car into a narrow alley between a high wall and a construction site. At a bend in the lane, a dusty tree hid the car from view. Pulling into the shade under a smattering of drooping leaves, I turned off the key. Heat pulsed through the still air.

"Bobby," I said, my heart still pounding. "Can you hear me?" I didn't know where the bullet had entered nor how badly he was hurt, but his eyelids flickered open and I could see him struggling to focus on my face. "Bobby, you have to look at me and tell me where you're hurt." He lifted his head and blinked, then pulled his blood-covered hand away from his arm and stared at it.

"I don't feel so good," he said, a sloppy grimace twisting his features. "My arm's been hit. I think we had better do something about this before we go any further."

I nodded. "Will you let me see it?" By now, the entire sleeve of his shirt was drenched in blood. "I'm just going to cut away the sleeve so I can have a better look, okay?" His head dropped back against the side window. I reached into my tote and fished around until my fingers grasped a pocket knife I had thrown in before leaving the ship. Whipping out the tiny scissors, I snipped the cotton fabric above the elbow and held my breath as I revealed the bloody mess. When I had cut the sleeve away completely, I gently pulled it off over Bobby's hand then wadded it up and used the driest parts to mop the blood away from the wound as best I could without actually touching it. Having been through a gunshot-wound-dressing myself recently, I felt almost like an old hand at this.

"It's a good thing you have so much muscle," I said. "It doesn't look like it hit the bone. What do you think?"

"I think you're right about that."

"And it looks like the bullet went clean on through, but it sure made a mess on its way." I reached around to the back seat, unzipped my suitcase and pulled out a clean t-shirt. Stretching it taut, I wrapped it around Bobby's upper arm and pulled it tight, hoping to cut the bleeding, though it had already begun to coagulate.

"We have to get this attended to, Bobby. You need to get to a hospital."

"No."

"Yes."

"No. I'm not hurt that badly. We have to get out of town before we're discovered again. All I need is to get this cleaned and bandaged. A few painkillers wouldn't hurt either. If we can find a pharmacy, you can go in and buy what we need."

I bit my lip, torn between the urgency to get away from the danger here and the certainty that Bobby needed more care than I could offer. "Okay," I said, "we'll try it your way first and if you feel all right and your arm stops bleeding, then we'll figure out what to do next. If not, I'm taking you to the hospital and calling the police."

"No you're not," Bobby declared. "I'm going to be fine. Let's go."

"I just hope something is open this time of day," I muttered as I started the engine and put the car in gear. "It seems to me that people in this part of the world close up shop and go home for siesta about now." I pulled the car ahead and out of the alley, onto a dusty side road. The streets were empty and the sun beat white on the pale sand. I pushed my sunglasses onto my face with one hand and cranked the wheel with the other.

"There's a GPS in my bag," Bobby panted, barely above a whisper.

"There's a what?"

"A GPS. You know, a Global Positioning System unit." He stopped and took a long, slow breath. "It's in my bag. Dig around in that side pocket and you'll find it. I told you I'd navigate, didn't I?"

"Why didn't you say you had one sooner?" I demanded, pulling over to the side of the street to look for it.

"I was preoccupied."

I found the GPS and held it in my hands while Bobby instructed me how to turn it on and locate our whereabouts. Within five minutes, we had found a tiny pharmacy on a quiet street. Thankfully, it was still open. I parked the car around the corner from the shop and left Bobby there while I ran in. Once inside, I could see that resources for wound care were limited and I would have to make do with whatever I could find. A young boy, barely old enough to shave, watched as I grabbed some painkillers off a shelf and found a roll of tape, but I could find no gauze. Glancing around for a substitute I discovered several boxes of sanitary napkins. They were the kind with sticky tape on one side to make them cling to underwear, but nothing else in the store seemed like it would do as good a job of sopping up blood so I picked up a box of the super-heavy-duty ones, plus a couple of two-litre bottles of water and a bottle of rubbing alcohol and paid the pre-pubescent clerk.

Back at the car I pulled open the passenger door and helped Bobby turn in his seat so his bloody arm hung over the ground. The car wasn't much but I assumed that Matt the Bull would prefer not to get it back saturated in dried blood. Gingerly removing the t-shirt from Bobby's arm, I opened a bottle of water and trickled it over the injury while dabbing away the blood with a sanitary napkin. Once the blood had been washed away, I could see the extent of the damage. The bullet had blown clean through his flesh. Glancing past him, I could see the hole where it had pierced the back seat of the car. The muscle lay pulverized, like raw hamburger, with ragged ends of dark red flesh against his brown skin. I took a deep breath and stood up straight, looking away for a moment before exhaling and going back to work.

"Take a couple of these," I said dispensing some pain-killers into his good hand. He washed them down with a gulp from the other water bottle. "What happens next is probably going to hurt." Dropping to my knees I opened the bottle of alcohol and poured some onto a clean napkin then dabbed the wound as lightly as I could while still allowing the disinfectant to make contact with the tissue. Bobby gasped and clenched his teeth. A low moan escaped from somewhere in his chest.

"I'm sorry, Bobby. Really, I am, but we have to do this or I'm taking you to the hospital." Once again, my days of binding up my son's hockey injuries came in handy. I had never been particularly squeamish, but I did not enjoy inflicting pain and I could see that Bobby was holding it together only by sheer dint of will. The wound was not deep, though it had torn away much more flesh than the gunshot wound to my side had. "What do you think, Bobby? Does it need stitches?"

"Ma'am, I've seen worse than this on a playground. Just wrap it up with one of those pads and let's get out of here."

"All right," I agreed with reluctance. "It's your arm." I bound it tightly with pads and tape and put the water and painkillers within easy reach for Bobby's right hand. Using a pair of pantyhose that I had packed for no apparent reason, I rigged up a sling to keep the arm immobile. Unorthodox, but effective.

"Find me the airport on that GPS," I said, starting the car again.

"What for? McSweeney told us not to fly."

"McSweeney said no planes. He didn't say anything about helicopters. If we charter a helicopter we can be in Merida in no time. Then I can get you to a doctor and get your arm looked after properly." *Why spend agonizing hours on a highway*, I thought, *driving through the jungle in this heat, when we could skip it and have it over in a fraction of the time by flying in comfort?*

Bobby put the GPS in his shirt pocket. "I don't think that's the right decision."

"Have you got a better idea?" I snapped.

He studied me for a full minute before answering. "You know what you have to do already," he said. "Don't ask me."

I dropped my head back on the headrest and stared up at the car's tatty interior roof. I didn't want him to be right about this. I turned off the engine and got out of the car, slamming the door behind me and stalking down the street. Days of tension and strain had caught up with me. I was hot, tired, and stressed, had a gigantic, injured man in my care and a bunch of hoodlums with guns on my trail. I didn't want to drive across half of Mexico in a borrowed piece of junk that might not even make it. I was fed up with enduring the hardship, the danger, and the fear of it all.

"God," I said as I paced down the road. "I want to rent a helicopter and fly to Merida. What do you think of that?" I didn't really want an answer unless it agreed with what *I* wanted. I stalked on, hearing nothing. "I'm going to drive to the airport and find someone to fly us to Merida. That way I can get help for Bobby and get this whole escapade over with faster. You know that there are only two more stones to pick up. I can't think of a single reason to drag this out any longer, can you?" Dust puffed around my sandals and turned my feet chalky. I could feel the sun burning the back of my neck. "Unless you tell me something different right now, I'm going back to the car and we're going to go find a helicopter." I turned around and started back but before I had taken four steps I heard one word. *"Don't."*

I stopped. "Pardon me?"

He spoke again. *"Don't take a helicopter, Jill. Drive."*

"But why?" I tried, I really did, to keep the whine out of my voice. I rarely felt anything resembling petulance, but today was an exception. I stopped walking and looked skyward. "Why?" I asked again. No answer came. Sagging, I said, "Okay, Lord, we'll do it your way. I know that you must have some reason for me to do this even though it makes no sense to me whatever." I trudged back to the car and yanked open the door. What made the most sense to me didn't always turn out like I expected anyway, I had to admit.

"So?" Bobby asked when I slid behind the wheel.

"We're driving."

He grinned and I could see him biting the inside of his lower lip.

"Shut up," I said, cranking the key in the ignition and ramming the car into gear.

"Yes, ma'am," Bobby replied, looking straight ahead.

Using the GPS, we managed to avoid the main roads out of town. We headed south along the beach road, on one hand surmising that Menendez and his thugs might expect us to use the main highway north to Cancun, and on the other, because we had prayed about which way to go and both felt that this was the best route. While a few roads led west out of Playa del Carmen, the GPS told us that they all trailed off to nothing somewhere in the jungles. Our best option was to drive south toward Tulum and turn inland, staying on the smaller roads as much as possible. Even so, I felt uneasy once we turned onto the highway, not knowing what Menendez and his cohorts might be driving and realizing that at least two of them had seen our distinctively ugly, green car. It couldn't be helped though; we had to get to Merida, and I knew that my life and Bobby's were in God's hands.

As we neared the ruins and town of Tulum, a huge signboard indicated that to the left, in the direction of the sea, stood the Mayan ruins. The town was straight ahead and the road to Merida on the right.

"You can't imagine how much I would love to stop and tour the ruins," I murmured, not expecting Bobby to be listening.

"Another time," he replied, his quiet voice heavy with fatigue. His skin had taken on an ashen hue.

By now it was approaching two o'clock. "I'm a little hungry, Bobby. Are you? Maybe we should go into town and find something to eat," I suggested.

"I'm fine," he replied. "But if you like, why don't you stop somewhere and we can pick up something to go? I want to put as much distance as we can between us and Playa as quickly as we can."

I pulled into the parking area of the first roadside restaurant I saw and ordered a couple of burritos and drinks to go. Once out on the highway again, the road stretched ahead like a cut line through the surrounding forest and a few clouds floated overhead. The afternoon had become muggy and even hotter. The car had no air conditioning, but with the windows open, the fist-sized hole in the windshield made by the bullet provided a steady circulating breeze.

Even after having eaten, Bobby still looked wretched. A fine sheen of sweat covered his face and his eyelids remained closed except for the odd flutter when a semi-truck roared past on the other side of the road, rocking the car and sweeping my hair into a swirl. I had long since yanked the wig from my sweltering head and flung it over my shoulder into the back seat.

At Valladolid, we crept through the centre of the city and continued on a secondary highway toward a little place called Cuncunul. This highway would take us directly to Chichen Itza, one of the largest and most famous of the Mayan ruin sites. I thought of Neil and how he had spent years tramping around in trackless jungle just like the growth bordering this pothole-peppered asphalt. I also thought of Marco but whenever I did, a palpable pain hit me in the solar plexus. Again and again, I had to push the thought of him out of my mind.

As we neared Chichen Itza, the traffic slowed. Diesel tour buses lined the road and tourists traipsed back and forth between the parking area and the ruins. Creeping along, I glanced through the trees and caught a fleeting glimpse of the famous pyramid.

"Bobby," I said, reaching over and gently prodding his knee. He jerked awake and gazed around with glassy eyes.

"What is it?" he mumbled.

"We're at Chichen Itza. Look, there's the great pyramid." His head swivelled to follow where I pointed and I saw him wince as his arm moved. We could just barely catch sight of the grey stone structure as we passed by before the trees closed in again, obscuring the view of the ruins.

"Are you feeling okay?" I asked. "You don't look well."

"I think I'd better take another painkiller," he said, rummaging on the floor at his feet for the bottle of water. "And I'm cold," he added, after taking a sip of water to wash down a couple of tablets.

I reached over and placed the palm of my hand on his damp forehead in the same way I had with my children. "You're burning with fever," I gasped.

"That might be an exaggeration," he commented drily. "I'm sure I'll be fine."

"How far is it to the nearest town?"

Bobby consulted his GPS. "There's a little place right up the road, but if you're thinking of dumping me off at a hospital, I doubt that you'll find one there."

"I'm not thinking of 'dumping you off' anywhere. I'm thinking that you need to see a doctor and I intend to find one."

We drove up the road and in a few minutes entered the tiny town of Piste. The main road ran through the centre of the village and was lined with restaurants, small hotels, and shops selling souvenirs like masks, hammocks, and rugs. Tour buses on their way to the ruins rolled through town without stopping. Along the roadsides, market tables stood filled with colourful goods but few shoppers braved the afternoon heat to examine the sellers' wares. Being an artist, I longed to stop and talk with the artisans, even though I spoke almost no Spanish.

Bobby slouched in the seat next to me and stared dully out the window. I drove through the main part of town without seeing anything that resembled a clinic and then I turned the car into a back street in hopes of finding something there. Once off the paved road, the residential streets stood in sharp contrast to the view visitors would see from a bus window. Chickens picked through garbage along the sides of the dusty, unpaved streets and one-room homes stood in various states of disrepair. I wondered how it was that these people could not be benefitting financially from having one of the world's foremost tourist attractions right on their doorsteps. Mesmerized by the apparent poverty I saw, I couldn't tear my gaze away.

"I don't think we'll find any help here," Bobby said, pushing himself upright. "You might as well head back to the main road and go on to Merida. I'll be okay until then. It's not far now." We rounded another corner. Unlike the other streets we had seen, this one had modern-looking houses and, driving past one, I could see children playing in a swimming pool at its rear. Not a very fancy pool, but a pool all the same.

By now the gas gauge showed nearly empty. I would have to fill up here in Piste since I had no idea where I might find a filling station farther on. I had seen a station on the main road and I knew I should do as Bobby suggested and head for

Merida. But something compelled me to check one more street. There might be a clinic, or there might not, I thought, but I had to look.

"Where are you going?" Bobby asked. "The highway is the other way."

"I know. I just want to take a quick look down this street and then I'll go get some gas."

Scanning the street for some sign of a medical facility, I manoeuvred the car around bumps and potholes in the neglected lane and saw nothing. Bobby was right. There was no point trying to find help in this town. And, judging from his demeanour, the sooner I found a doctor the better.

I could see the sign for a gas station at the highway intersection ahead. I pressed the accelerator and the car lurched into a pothole. At the same moment, the sun, reflecting off a pickup truck window, flashed in my eyes. Had it not been for that blaze of light, I might have stopped in time. Squinting, I thought I saw a figure dash out from behind a run-down mechanic's shop. I shielded my eyes with one hand. Tattered and filthy, the man zigzagged, half bent over, across the narrow street toward the car. As he ran, his bare feet, caked with dirt and grime, left dark smudges on the gravel. I gasped and slammed on the brakes, spraying dust and gravel under the skidding tires. From the corner of my eye, I saw Bobby reach for the dash with his uninjured arm to keep from ramming his head through the fractured windshield.

The car scraped to a stop, but it was too late. I watched in horror as the man's body, like a bloody bag of rags, hit the grill and rolled toward us over the car hood. A pair of handcuffs clasped his wrists behind his back. For a fraction of a second, his face turned toward mine before he soared off the side of the hood and landed in a crumpled bundle on the gravel road.

Bobby flung open his door with his good arm while I leapt out of the car and ran to the injured man. He lay face down in the dirt. His bound arms stretched behind him at a hideous angle and his bare feet oozed fresh blood. Hunks of matted brown hair stuck to his head. Where the ragged shirt twisted up his body, I could see cuts and abrasions all over his back. Bobby gently reached under him and lifted his body with one arm, while I carefully brought the man's bound arms back into alignment. Then taking his head in my hands, I gingerly lifted it and turned his face toward me. From the battered face, the man's eyes fluttered open and he groaned.

A stifled cry escaped my lips.

"What?" Bobby said.

"Bobby," I whispered, "I know this man! He's my cousin, Dennis!"

CHAPTER 30

A fluorescent tube buzzed overhead and someone sneezed twice as a nurse walked past, her white shoes squeaking on the tile floor. Two women came in, one carrying a listless child of about three years old, the other leading a taller girl by the hand. They approached the desk and spoke with the admissions clerk. An announcement barked from a ceiling speaker but since it was in Spanish I couldn't understand it anyway so I didn't listen.

My head ached.

A thin man came through the doors into the emergency waiting lounge. With straight, black hair that stood right out from his head and narrow black eyes, he was obviously Chinese. He walked across the room toward me.

"Mrs. Jill Moss?"

"You must be Frederick Chin," I said, rising to shake his hand.

"Please, call me Fred. Come, let's sit for a moment. How are your friends?"

"Bobby needed stitches in his arm and they want to keep him overnight. He is dehydrated and may require antibiotics but they think he will be feeling much better by tomorrow. Dennis is in far worse shape. I don't know how long he will have to stay here. He has been through a lot in a week."

"I see. Perhaps you would like to come home with me for the night. My wife is expecting you and has prepared a meal and a room."

"That's very kind," I said, "but I don't think I should leave. There are people who would stop at nothing to interfere with the continuance of this... mission. Both Bobby and Dennis are still in danger."

Frederick Chin patted my hand. "Leave it to me." He pulled a cell phone from his pocket and punched in a number with a fine-boned finger. I leaned my head against the wall and waited as he spoke in Spanish. When he flipped the phone closed and dropped it back into his pocket, he said, "It is all arranged. One of the members of my church owns a security company. He is coming himself with three of his top men to guard your friends until it is no longer necessary."

Twenty minutes later, four men strode into the room. Fred introduced me to the owner, Carlos Suarez. Though shorter than I, he was built like a bulldog and wore a long handlebar moustache and a wide-brimmed hat. He reminded me so much of Yosemite Sam from cartoons I had watched as a kid, that I had to bite my lips to keep from giggling. He spoke passable English and introduced me to his men, who spoke only Spanish. They all wore crisply-starched black and yellow uniforms. We explained to the nurse at the admissions desk that these guards would be spending the night with two of the hospital's patients. After a brief conversation, of which I understood not a word, she shrugged and waved us away. The men took up their posts and I left the hospital with Pastor Chin.

After the accident in Piste, Bobby and I managed to get Dennis loaded into the car. I was thankful then that Dennis is not a big guy and that Bobby is, since he could lift more with only one arm than I could, heaving with both of mine. I was afraid that Dennis may have had internal injuries from the crash but Bobby's military training had taught him how to assess physical damage, and though Dennis was clearly in dire condition, he did not appear to have suffered any broken bones. The next few hours, however, would tell us how seriously he may have been harmed.

Before we had folded his body into the back seat of the car, Bobby fetched a set of lock picking tools from his bag and removed the handcuffs from Dennis' wrists, flinging them onto the floor of the car. We managed to get some water into Dennis as he slipped in and out of consciousness, but that was all. Once we were in the car and back on the road again, Bobby lapsed once more into a kind of hazy stupor. Like air from a leaky balloon, the energy that had propelled him from the car to help Dennis wheezed away just as quickly, leaving him dazed and hurting. In the back seat, Dennis lay in a state of exhaustion. The few times he woke, I tried to discover what had happened and why he was in Piste, but his slurred answers told me nothing so I gave up and just drove.

Taking the smaller highways meant we arrived at the outskirts to Merida as the sun dipped below the horizon. Sitting in traffic, I studied the GPS, looking for a hospital. Once I found one, I took my wounded passengers straight to the emergency entrance where the ambulances arrive and ran inside through the sliding doors, shouting for someone who spoke English. My tactic worked. Within minutes, eight medical personnel swarmed the car and had both Bobby and Dennis on gurneys.

Now both injured men slept under armed guard and I hoped I could relax, at least for a few hours. After examining Dennis, the English-speaking doctor on duty told me that he was severely dehydrated, had likely not eaten for several days, and had many cuts and abrasions, some of which had become infected in the sweltering heat. The doctor, a young Mexican woman with long, dark hair pulled into a ponytail, assured me that she had studied medicine in Texas. Dennis had immediately been placed on an intravenous drip and a couple of nurses began working him over. I was directed to wait in the visitors' lounge.

Half an hour later, the doctor reported that Dennis had no broken bones except for the little finger on his left hand, but because of the differing stages of healing of the extensive bruising all over his body, he appeared to have been beaten repeatedly with some kind of blunt instrument. Since the doctor had ordered a sedative to keep him quiet for the night, there was nothing more I could do. Bobby, too, was asleep when I looked in on him, so I that's when I called Frederick Chin.

The Chins lived on the second floor of an old colonial-style house which, as Delores Chin explained, was in a constant state of renovation. The church that the Chins pastored used the main floor of the building for services and congregational activities and, as we arrived, a group of young people tumbled out of the big, double wooden doors and onto the street.

Delores, who preferred to be called Lori, a petite Mexican woman with laughing eyes, had a pot of tortilla soup simmering on the stove when we arrived and the three of us sat down for a simple meal. The couple's two children, a fifteen year-old boy and a twelve year-old girl, were both staying with friends for the night.

"If you don't mind me saying so, Mrs. Moss," Fred said when we had finished eating, "you look very tired."

"Please call me Jill," I answered. "And yes, I am tired. I have had an extremely eventful day." I looked at them with a thin smile.

"Let me show you to your room," Lori offered. I followed her down the hall.

The light from a streetlamp outside the window streamed between the half-open drapes and fell in glassy pools on the blue-tiled floor. The small room featured a narrow bed against one wall and a washstand with a basin and pitcher of water next to the door. A wobbly, wooden chair of ancient origin stood between the two tall windows.

Though the ticking clock on the bedside table showed only half past eight, I changed for bed immediately and used the water and basin to wash, then pushed back a patterned curtain, its wooden rings rattling along a wrought iron bar high above, and gazed out onto the quiet street. The church's young people had all gone and Fred had already been downstairs to lock up the building for the night. Except for a few cars next to the curb down the block, the street was deserted. I dropped the curtain and turned away but a movement caught my eye. Peering through the crack in the draperies I saw a black Volkswagen pull up outside the church. The doors opened and two men got out. Since I was looking straight down on the tops of their heads, I could not see their faces but could tell that one man was tall with dark hair while the other short, big-bellied, and bald. The short man said something to the tall one who nodded and closed his car door. As this man was about to round the vehicle, he stopped and for a second looked directly up at my window. Then with three long strides, he disappeared under the awnings covering the sidewalk. My heart skipped a beat.

The man looked so much like Marco Jimenez that I could hardly breathe. *It's not possible that he's here in Merida*, I thought. It must be the fatigue and stress playing havoc with my vision. I rubbed my tired eyes and yanked the draperies closed. Downstairs I could hear the low rumble of men's voices.

But what if my eyes were not playing tricks on me? If the man downstairs was Marco, I had to know. But I could not let him see me. After my encounter with him in Galveston, I couldn't risk it.

My feet felt rooted to the floor as random thoughts jackknifed through my mind. Had he been following me? How was that possible? But if that was not the case, why was he here?

I had to find out.

I pulled a shirt from my suitcase, slipped it on over my nightgown and tiptoed to the door. My bare feet made no sound on the cool tiles as I stole out of the room. The hallway lay dark and quiet but I could see a light still on in the kitchen and hear the sound of Lori doing dishes. Earlier Fred had shown me around the building so I headed for the back stairs against the outside wall that led down to the church sanctuary. Gliding through the moonlight, I felt my way down the stairs and crept toward the back door.

Suddenly, a small shape darted out from behind a big, terra cotta planter containing a lemon tree and I froze, my heart pounding in my ears. Then I felt it brush against my leg and I let out my breath. The house cat, a fluffy orange creature, curled her body around my ankles and I could hear the soft rattle of purring. I pushed her away with my foot and took another couple of steps forward, reaching out and slowly turning the doorknob with my fingertips. It was locked.

Sidling over to the nearest window and flattening my body into the shadows I peered through the glass. The lights were off in the room next to me and a lacy curtain hung over the window, partially obscuring my view. In the room beyond I could just make out the figures of three men in the soft light. The tall one whom I had seen on the street now had his back to me. I gulped and moved to get a better look through the lace but it didn't help, so I slid along the wall to the next window. As I peered through that window, he turned slightly to speak to the man on his left and I caught a fleeting glimpse of his face in profile. If that man was not Marco, then he had a twin brother.

With my feet glued to the spot, I watched as they all shook hands, patted each others' backs and turned to leave. If I could get back up to my room by the time they went out the front door, I might be able to catch another look at him. I spun around and ran for the stairs, but before I could reach them my foot caught on a furry lump and I went down, my knees crashing into the rough terra cotta tiles on the terrace as I lunged for the stair railing to catch myself. The cat squalled and shot away into the dark courtyard. My fingertips brushed the stair railing but not before my ribs connected with the planter pot. The air went out of my lungs in a mighty gust then I lay flat on the paving tiles gasping for breath.

"Ow," I moaned, biting back the urge to howl in pain. My opportunity to identify Marco shrank with each passing second. Hauling my body up, I dragged myself to the staircase. The blow to my side had ripped at the site of the gunshot wound and pain throbbed through my entire body. In the pale light of the moon, I could see that both knees were bruised and bloody but I couldn't think about that now. Grabbing the railing, I heaved myself back up the stairs, gasping for every breath. When I made it to my room, I scurried in as quickly as I could manage, flinging the door closed behind me. I hobbled to the window and threw back the curtains just in time to see the car below drive away into the night. I watched until it disappeared from sight then limped to the narrow single bed, rolled onto the covers, turned my face into the pillow, and sobbed.

In the first grey streaks of dawn light, I awoke cold and sore. Rolling stiffly off the bed, I found the bathroom down the hall and turned on the light. With my nightgown pulled up, I inspected the bruises and cuts incurred during my espionage duty the night before. A vicious, purple bruise covered most of my side and I felt around tentatively with my fingertips for broken ribs.

Inhaling slowly, I checked for sharp pains and thankfully felt none, only dull ones. The bandage on my gunshot wound had been ripped away and the gash stood out against the surrounding skin as an angry, purple-red slash. I found a dark washcloth in a cabinet and dabbed the dried blood and dirt from the scrapes on my knees. After fixing the bandage on my side and washing my face, I went back to my room, bandaged my knees with bits of stuffing torn from a sanitary pad and tape left over from fixing Bobby's arm. Then I went back to bed and lay down, covering myself this time with a sheet and two thin blankets. Four hours later, I woke to the sound of tapping on my door.

"Good morning, Jill," Lori called out when I answered her knock. "I hope you slept well." She came in carrying a tray with a full American breakfast, enough for three people, and set it on my lap as I pulled myself up with my back against the pillows. "Fred asked me to let you know that he has time this morning to speak with you, whenever you're ready."

"I've been waiting for you," Fred said when I sat down in a chair in his office after filling myself with eggs, toast and fruit and hastily getting dressed. The room, no bigger than a walk-in closet, was tucked away in one corner of the main floor.

"Sorry to keep you," I replied. "I guess I needed the sleep."

He smiled. "That's not what I meant. I've been preparing for this appointment with you since Neil first contacted me." He pulled open a desk drawer and handed me a small box. It had been opened already so I pulled back the wrappings and drew out the stone, turning it over in my palm to see the different designs on each of its three inscribed sides.

"You opened it."

"Yes," Fred said. "It was addressed to me. I'm sure you are as curious as I am about the message on that little block."

I placed the stone on the edge of the desk. "Perhaps you can begin by telling me something about yourself," I said, "and how you came to be involved."

Fred Chin laughed. "You don't beat around the bush, do you?"

"Not usually."

"Fair's fair," he answered. "I've known Neil Bryant for probably twenty years. We met when I was in university and became friends because we had a mutual interest in archaeology, biblical history, and future prophecy. His specialty was digging stuff up. I like to have cleaner hands, so I studied theology and went into ministry. I believed that was God's direction for my life and I still believe it. I am from California originally but God led me here. This is where I met Lori. Neil and I have been in touch regularly over the years, keeping each other updated on new developments and discoveries. When he first found the ring of stones, he contacted me to help him with their collection and safe-keeping. As you already know, this is a significant find but I'm not sure you know how far-reaching the repercussions will be once the message or messages on them is revealed."

"Wait," I said, holding up my hand. "Before you go on, there's something I need to know."

He looked puzzled. "What is that, Jill?"

"Who were those two men who came here last night?"

Chin drew in a breath and pursed his lips. The question lay between us like a snowdrift. "Alright," he said finally. "Those two men are what you might call security personnel, though not really. They are more like collaborators. They are connected with Neil and McSweeney and with Doctor Silverman. There are a lot of people involved in this mission, my dear, some of whom you may never meet."

"Don't patronize me, Fred," I said. "I'm in this up to my neck."

"Please forgive me. I never meant to imply..."

"Tell me the names of those two men you met with last night."

"I can't."

"Why not?" I demanded.

"Put simply, it would jeopardize the mission." He paused before going on. "I am sorry. You will find out when the time is right, but for now it's best that you don't know."

I looked past his shoulder and out the window. Sunshine beat on the brick walls surrounding the courtyard garden and a black bird flew in and landed on a hibiscus tree. "All right," I conceded with a sigh. "Go on."

"Thank-you. As I'm sure you are aware, Neil left a series of cryptic markings in his Bible that I believe you have. Is that true?"

"Yes."

"Would you mind if I take a look at it with you? I believe I can help you decipher the intent of the markings as they apply to the stones, to history, and to future prophecy." I went back to my room and fetched my bag.

"Let's begin at Genesis, shall we?" he said when I handed the Bible to him. "We probably don't have much time to go over this, so forgive me for launching right into it."

I pulled my chair to the side of his desk so we could both see the book. "Here, for example," he said, locating a reference, "in chapter four, verse seventeen we find this statement, 'And Cain knew his wife; and she conceived, and bare Enoch: and he builded a city, and called the name of the city, after the name of his son, Enoch.' This is very early in history, yet Cain was building a city. So we know that civilization was not undeveloped at this time."

"Are you saying the Hebrew language has existed since long before the Maya or Olmec civilizations?"

"It explains why it is possible for those three languages to be on the stone blocks. The Phoenician culture, a civilization of great seafarers, most likely sailed the whole world, not just round their own little pond, the Mediterranean. If the Phoenicians did it, wouldn't other cultures of the time?"

"I can't think why not."

"All right," Fred continued. "We have established that antediluvian cultures, peoples who existed prior to the great flood travelled across oceans and had written languages. I am sure you have talked with others who agree. Let's take a look at another scripture." He turned the thin pages of the old Bible and stopped at Exodus chapter twenty-eight. Running his finger down the column of verses, he rested it on the red dot next to verse thirty. "Ah, here it is. 'And thou shalt put in the breastplate of judgment the Urim and the Thummim; and they shall be upon Aaron's heart, when he goeth in before the LORD'. What is this breastplate and what are the Urim and Thummim? Are you familiar with this?"

"Only vaguely."

"There is something in the Hebrew inscription on the stone I just gave you that makes me think there is a connection." He leaned back in his chair. "You wouldn't happen to have more stones, would you?"

I pulled the stone out of my bag that I had received from Consuelo Hanna the day before and handed it to Fred. He placed the two stones side by side, settling the indent on the side of one into the depression on the other. Holding the two up together, he studied them silently for several minutes then changed their positions. "I don't think these two go together," he said finally. "I don't understand the Mesoamerican languages but I do read Hebrew. And although it is not clear, it seems to indicate a reference to Urim and Thummim."

"Why is that important?"

"Urim and Thummim were used in ancient times to communicate with God. There is still some disagreement regarding what they meant and how they worked, but from what we can discern from scripture and other writings, they were two stones that the priest in Moses' time placed in a pocket behind a breastplate that he wore along with other priestly garments. Urim is the plural for the word 'light' and Thummim is plural for 'completeness,' or something similar. Though there is plenty of conjecture, there is no real explanation in scripture as to how they worked and evidently, there was only one set of Urim and Thummim. It was passed down through the generations until Nebuchadnezzer captured Jerusalem in 597 B.C. He burned the temple and carried all of the sacred objects and other spoils off to Babylon. From there the Urim and Thummim disappeared. However, take a look at this," he said, turning to the book of Daniel.

Here Neil had marked more passages. "Belshazzar, whiles he tasted the wine, commanded to bring the golden and silver vessels which his father Nebuchadnezzar had taken out of the temple which was in Jerusalem."

"It seems likely to me," Fred continued, "that the objects that ended up in the palace in Babylon probably included the Urim and Thummim.

"Perhaps they were destroyed," I ventured.

"Possibly, but in both the books of Ezra and of Nehemiah they are mentioned, so evidently the people believed that the Urim and Thummim still existed somewhere. Since the Babylonians would not allow the Israelites to take their stuff with them when they came out of captivity, it stands to reason that the artifacts remained in Babylon."

"Do you believe that they remain there today?"

Fred shrugged. "Maybe, maybe not. Cyrus the Great from Persia conquered Babylon in 539 B.C. so there is no telling what happened to the temple objects after that."

"But how does this all fit with the age of these stones? If they originated not long after the flood, around 3000 B.C., why would there be information pertaining to the Urim and Thummim if those artifacts had not even been stolen from the temple in Jerusalem until about 600 B.C.?"

"Good question. Perhaps the messages on the stones are not telling us about the location of the Urim and Thummim at all. Perhaps they reveal how they worked. It's clear by the markings on these stones that people from the Middle East visited Central America a few thousand years before Christ." He leaned forward. "What if these stones hold the secret to technologies employed by ancient peoples that allowed them to communicate directly with God?"

I shook my head. "Why would that be such a big deal? I do that every day."

"So do I, but we're able to do that because of our new covenant in Jesus Christ. Now think of the millions of people on earth who do not share our faith. People are hungry for a spiritual connection to something divine. Many have rejected Christianity but are searching for connection with God. Think about people who would view this kind of supernatural knowledge as a way to gain power, wealth, or control. Can you see what would happen to whoever was able to make them work? Or, they could just claim that they alone have direct access to God. Who knows what might happen?"

I stood up and walked to the window. A sun-sparkled fountain stood in the middle of the courtyard and the sky shimmered overhead like a swath of pale organza. "No wonder everyone wants them."

"Precisely."

The telephone rang and Fred picked up. A minute later he put the receiver down and said, "Bobby's being released from hospital and Dennis has come around. Want to drop over there and see them?"

I nodded and picked up my bag, tossing the stones and the Bible into its depths and said, "Let's go."

CHAPTER 31

I found Bobby waiting in the hospital lounge and together the three of us went upstairs to see Dennis. When we arrived, the blinds were open and Dennis was sitting up in bed. His head lay against a stack of pillows and he turned to look at me when I pushed open the door.

"Hey, cuz," said Dennis in a dry voice. "Who'd have thought we'd run into each other like this?"

I walked to the side of the bed and took his hand in both of mine. "If you would quit throwing yourself at my car, I wouldn't have to run into you like that."

"And a thoroughly ugly car it is, too," he said with a weak smile. "Where did you come by that monstrosity?"

"It's a long story," I replied. "Can I give you a hug or would that hurt too much?"

"Come here," he said lifting his arm. "Just don't squeeze too hard."

I introduced Bobby and Fred. "Bobby lifted you into the car yesterday," I said, "almost single-handedly and with one shot-up arm." Fred shook hands with Dennis as I explained that I had spent the previous night at Fred's house then he and Bobby went off to find the hospital cafeteria so Dennis and I could be alone.

"Okay, tell me what happened," I said, sitting on the edge of the bed.

One hour later, Dennis lay on his pillows looking like a deflated balloon, pale and spent. He had told me that when he had come home from roaming the hills he found the two men waiting for him.

"I was immediately on alert," Dennis said, "though there was no clear reason to be. You know how the Holy Spirit warns you sometimes? I had been out for days and had started for home around four in the morning so I could travel before it got hot. My old truck has no air conditioning so I generally drive late at night or early in the day. When I pulled into the yard this big, black car was parked facing the road, which right away I thought was odd, but I parked my truck and got out. Two men in suits got out of the car. Where I live, nobody even owns a suit. They wore sunglasses and one guy had a hand in his pocket. They walked right up to me and asked me if my name was Dennis Bryant. I hardly had time to say yes before they jumped me, threw me into their car and peeled out of the yard. I caught a glimpse of Emily through the kitchen window of the house with a look of horror on her face."

"We have to get in touch with the family right away," I said. "I haven't talked to anyone for days because I've been afraid to put them in jeopardy or give away my location. I will find a way to let everyone know you are free now." I squeezed his hand. "What happened next?"

"We didn't go far before they stopped the car, hauled me out and blind-folded me, tied me up and tossed me into the back seat again. It seemed like we were on the road a long time after that. I fell asleep for a while since I'd been up long before dawn. At one point they stopped and gave me a drink and something to eat. They took me out of the car in the middle of nowhere, took off the blindfold and tied my leg to a tree. I had no idea where we were since we were in pretty dense brush and I couldn't see over the treetops."

"But isn't it arid where you live, as in, no trees?"

"Mostly that's true, but as you get farther south, the vegetation changes and anywhere even a trickle of water flows, you'll find trees. They always seemed to be able to find some out-of-the-way place to stop. We travelled on decent highways but I didn't hear a lot of traffic noise. I couldn't tell where they were taking me until we ended up on the Yucatan. It's flat here and the brush is different. Every day we would stop and eat then they tossed me back into the car and drove on. I know that we went through some urban areas because they would pull into a roadside food place and pick something up then wait until we were out of town before stopping. When we stopped at night, we camped out or stayed in shacks in the middle of nowhere. I was bound, gagged, blindfolded and tied to something solid every time. Breaking away was out of the question. I think they took turns guarding me too, though I slept whenever I got the chance."

"Do you have any idea who these people are?"

"They never took their sunglasses off until we got to the house, but I'm pretty observant so I memorized everything about them that I could detect."

"Like what?"

"Well, first of all, they were Israelis. I never let on that I could understand their language. I'm a bit rusty, but I studied it in university years ago so I was able to follow their conversations. They both spoke English with me but Hebrew between themselves."

"Israelis?" I squeaked. "What on earth do Israelis want with you?"

"Well, of course, they were trying to get to Dad and get their hands on the stones."

"But why? And how do they know about them?"

"Good questions. They kidnapped me to use as leverage to get to Dad, but it didn't work very well. They were going on the assumption that I knew where Dad was hiding or where the stones were, or both, but of course, I knew neither. All I knew was that you were somewhere in France last I heard and that Dad had gone into hiding. I stopped worrying about him years ago. He knows what he's doing and I trust the Lord to look after him."

"Go on."

"They finally took me to a house deep in the jungle. There was nothing else nearby, as I found out. It wasn't much of a house from the outside, pretty run down and dilapidated, but inside was another story. I only saw the outside of the buildings after I escaped. Inside, they had every piece of electronic equipment you could imagine including computers, generators, and satellite dishes, plus a bunch of other devices that I didn't recognize. The place was fairly spacious and only one level. They locked me in a little room off the main area where the equipment had all been set up. The room where they kept me had a single cot and one window with bars on it and only let me out to eat and use the bathroom. They took off my blindfold but left the handcuffs on. When it came time to eat, they re-cuffed me with my hands in the front so I could get food to my mouth. I guess they didn't care if I saw what they were doing since they probably planned to kill me after they got what they wanted anyway."

"You were in pretty rough shape yesterday, even before the collision. The doctor said you had been beaten," I said, grimacing.

"They weren't great big guys, not like Bobby, but they were bigger than I am and there were two of them. Once we arrived at the house, they started demanding that I tell them where Dad was hiding and when I said that I didn't know they started banging me around. Then they'd throw me back into the room and lock the door. After a while they'd start up again. I kept telling them I didn't know where Dad was hiding and I think they finally got it through their heads that I was telling them the truth. From my room I could sometimes hear them talking together or talking to someone on the phone or through their computers."

I poured a glass of water and handed it to Dennis. He leaned forward and took a long drink then fell back on the pillows. I could see that talking was taxing his strength.

"What did you overhear them saying?" I asked, settling back on the foot of the bed.

"Jill," Dennis began again, "these guys are bad dudes, seriously dangerous, and not just to our personal safety."

"What do you mean?"

"These two are part of a big organization; that much I could tell. They were monitoring a lot of things all the time. The phone rang constantly. There is something big going on but I'm not sure what. I heard cars drive in and doors slam a couple of times, but my room faced the back of the clearing so I couldn't see who came and went. I woke in the night once and heard maybe a half-dozen people in the big room, including at least one woman. They were arguing about something and getting kind of loud; then someone remembered that I was in the closet next door and shushed everyone up.

"What were they arguing about?"

"I'm not sure, but it sounded like they were planning something involving certain high-level government people. They never mentioned names. In fact, they had code names like pelican, parrot, and falcon. Come to think of it the names were all names of bird species. Weird, eh?" He stopped talking and closed his eyes. For a moment I thought he might be losing consciousness but he opened his eyes again and said, "They said that the falcon was gathering the pigeons and getting ready to strike."

"I wonder what that means."

"I began to put these bits of information together. After all, I had lots of time to think. Here's what I came up with. These two guys and their friends are part of some kind of paramilitary organization; maybe they are terrorists, but I don't think so. Their agenda seems more covert since they were dealing in information more than arms, but who knows? It's definitely political. Several times I caught them making reference to the stones you've been gathering and that there is some connection to ancient technologies that have some kind of power that they want to get their hands on. When they couldn't get any information out of me about my Dad's whereabouts, they started demanding I tell them where the stones are. I couldn't tell them anything about that either. I let on that I had never even heard of the artifacts they were talking about. It took them a while but they eventually caught on that beating harder was not going to help." He lifted his hand and let it drop on the yellow cotton blanket. "And don't tell me anything about the stones now either. I don't want to know."

"Do they know about me?"

Dennis shook his head. "I don't think so. They seemed to be grasping at straws. They must have had an informant who told them about the stones in the first place and they were scrambling to get their hands on them by using me. They never mentioned you, so hopefully they don't know your connection or whereabouts."

"I hope you're right," I said. "Can you tell me what these two looked like?"

"Sure. One guy looked stereotypically Jewish – dark, curly hair, long nose. He was average height and build and a bit taller than I am. The other guy was bigger, more muscular and looked like a bar bouncer from Edmonton whose hockey career got cut short by too many fights. He had a scar across his top lip and little piggy-looking eyes. I tried to keep out of his way as much as possible." He shuddered and went on. "They were both in their mid- to late thirties I'd guess."

I plucked at a tuft in the yellow blanket and saw Dennis' eyelids droop. I tried to think of a connection between these Israelis and any of the other people with whom I had come into contact in the past week and a half. Was it possible that Menendez was connected to an Israeli plot? I remembered the man who had followed me in Switzerland when I was shopping along the Hauptgasse and that Gerhard Mueller's flat had been ransacked. Had these same people been involved? Then there was Claire and her travelling companion. Where did they fit in this picture?

Dennis opened his eyes again. "I just thought of something else you should know."

"What's that?"

"One day I heard the two of them talking, muttering about something that I couldn't work out. They were talking too quickly and too quietly for me to follow, but then one guy got up and walked across the room. He called back to the other guy that when they had the power and Israel was under their control things would be different. He said something about all the pieces falling into place including the financial backers coming on stream and that once they had the technology there'd be no stopping them."

I felt the blood drain from my face. "You know what this means, don't you?" I said, shaken.

Dennis looked back at me with a steady, solemn gaze. Finally, he said, "I think so. Things are setting up for the final days."

"Were you able to find out who is backing them? Who is behind this?"

Dennis shook his head. "The only names I heard were names of birds. I gather that Falcon is some kind of leader. The pigeons could be loyal followers or intended victims."

"What about the other birds? The pelican, was it? And the parrot?"

"Your guess is as good as mine, but given what we know about end-times prophecy, I suspect those names refer to current high-level people, either political leaders or shadow figures in their organization."

I got up and walked to the window. Parting the lateral blinds with my fingers, I gazed out on the parking lot below.

After several minutes of silence, Dennis said, "Jill, don't worry. No matter what happens, it has to play out according to prophecy."

I turned back to face him. "I'm not worried. I have one more stone to collect and then I'll see what Neil wants me to do with them." I walked back to the bedside. "I've been trying to remember a passage from the book of Daniel that I read a couple of days ago. It said something about how in the end time evil men will be at their worst state and a ruler who is able to understand mysterious sayings will rise up. He'll have great power but his power won't come from himself because it is spiritual. He will cause a lot of destruction and kill a lot of good and holy people in the name of peace. Only Christ will be able to conquer him."

"I know the one you're talking about. It's in Daniel chapter eight. Do you think that these Israelis have something to do with this?"

"I honestly don't know. I'm sure there are people who have no interest in God but want to see Israel become a world power and will stop at nothing to accomplish their ends. Their agenda is evil and their ultimate plan is world domination. It doesn't take a genius to see Satan's hand at work. Contrast these people with true Jewish peoples and messianic Jews who love God and want to see the establishment of the nation of Israel according to God's plans alone. World events are setting up for a big cataclysm. I'd be lying if I said I don't find it scary."

Dennis reached over and awkwardly took my hand in his. The splint on his little finger stuck straight out. I could see that it caused him pain to grasp my fingers in his, so I gently pulled my hand away and placed it on his arm. "Whatever happens," he said, "we will get through it by the grace of God."

"I know," I replied, patting his arm. "I know. Now, tell me how you got away from those gangsters."

He laughed. "Okay. First, I prayed that the Lord would get me free. Since they kept a close watch on me and had me locked up most of the time, I had a lot of time to pray but not much opportunity to run. A couple of nights ago, I was lying in bed. Everything was quiet so I assumed my captors had gone to sleep. As I lay on my cot wide awake, the moon broke through some cloud cover and I saw something shining in the dust along the base of the wall. Getting up to investigate I found that it was a twenty centavo coin. I crouched down with my back against the wall and picked it up. Then I asked the Lord to tell me what to do next. My attention was drawn to the set of bars on the window, which was held in place with screws. It took me most of the night working with my hands behind my back to get that thing off. I left it hanging by one screw so it wouldn't come clanging to the floor and wake them up, and I moved it aside just far enough to squeeze through the hole. The window was easy to open. Anyway, before dawn I lit out. I got off the trail that led to the house as soon as I could so I couldn't be followed."

"Why didn't you just take their car?"

"The keys had to be in the house somewhere and I had no idea where to look for them. Also, I assumed that the car doors would be locked. I didn't want to take the chance of getting caught since they might just decide I was too much trouble and dump me into the nearest crocodile-infested swamp. I might be good with first aid and plumbing, but I don't know how to hot-wire a car. I didn't want the car alarm going off in the night either and besides, it's hard to drive with your hands behind your back so I took off on foot. Unfortunately, they had taken my shoes away."

"Hence the bloody feet."

"Yes. I ran until the sun came up then stopped for a rest and slept for maybe an hour. Then I got up and ran and walked and ran some more. I was extremely thirsty and really hot but about then I came across a cenote, one of those sinkholes that dot the Yucatan. It was not very deep and had one side that dropped off at a gentle slope so I slid into it out of the sun and heat. The water comes from some underground source in those things and is clear as air. I stayed there resting in the shade out of sight until the sun started to go down, then took off again running through the jungle. I kept going until I couldn't see anything. There was moonlight, but it wasn't very bright. At one point, I found an old road through the jungle and walked along that for a couple hours in the dark but once daybreak came along, I figured I had better get out of sight."

"There's something I'm puzzled about," I said. "Why did these guys bring you all this way to the Yucatan when they could have beaten the tar out of you five miles from home?"

"I wondered that too, but I think part of their original plan was to make me help them find the ruins where Dad discovered the stones, which is somewhere in the Yucatan. I think once they realized that I didn't know anything, there was no point trying to get me to find the ruins."

"How did you end up in Piste?"

It was the first town I came to when I emerged from the jungle. When I saw your car I ran out because I thought it was more likely to be a local than anyone connected with my abductors. I didn't actually intend to get run into, but wanted to make sure you stopped."

"You made sure, all right," I said.

"It was a miracle that it turned out to be you."

"I wanted to charter a helicopter and fly to Merida from Playa del Carmen," I said, sheepishly, "but the Lord told me to drive. Now I know why."

Bobby pushed open the door to Dennis' private room and came in followed by Fred Chin. "I've had a phone call," said Fred. "We'll have to leave Dennis here to recuperate on his own."

"Why? What's happened?"

"Bobby is going home," Fred replied, "and you have been instructed to go somewhere else. I will give you the details in the car on the way back to the house then I'm taking you both to the airport. We have to hurry."

I gave Dennis a good-bye hug, "Fred will keep an eye on you until you can leave here and make arrangements for whatever you need. Right, Fred?"

He nodded. "I'll drop by later this afternoon and see what the Doc has to say. In the meantime, the security guards are posted right outside the door so you can rest peacefully. I will also get in touch with your family and let them know you are alright."

Back at Fred's house, I gathered my belongings, then the three of us went straight to the airport, but rather than dropping us at the main entrance, Fred took us to a different terminal, explaining that two planes had been chartered, one to take Bobby home to Galveston and the other to take me to San Francisco.

Standing on the tarmac before boarding Bobby said, "I've taken care of the car, so don't you worry about it."

I laughed. "Do you really think Matt will want it back?"

"He'll want the five hundred bucks, I know that," he replied with a grin.

"Thank-you for everything, Bobby," I said, giving him a quick hug. "I'm going to miss you."

"I'm just sorry I can't carry on to San Fran with you. I feel like I'm letting you down."

"You just go home and take care of that arm. I'll see you again, I am sure." He turned and climbed the metal stairs to the plane door then waved and disappeared from sight.

I shook Fred's hand. "Thanks for all your help."

"My pleasure," he replied. "You have that note with your instructions, so be careful now. I will be praying for your safety and the outcome of this mission. Please keep in touch."

"I will." When the view of the city of Merida had disappeared behind me, I reached into my tote bag and drew out the slip of paper that Fred had passed me and unfolded it. I looked at it for a long time then refolded it and put it back.

CHAPTER 32

The sleek private jet taxied onto the runway, not in San Francisco as I had expected, but north of the city at the Napa County Airport. As the terminal drew near, I pulled the note from my pocket and read it again. It said that I would be met by someone I knew and to wait in the terminal until he appeared. *Would this mystery person not be there when I arrived?* I wondered. As usual, I had little choice but to follow instructions.

The terminal was deserted except for a few rental car counter attendants. I walked the length of the building, which didn't take long, then found a place to sit where I could have a good view of an entry door. Afternoon sunshine streamed through the windows and it wasn't long before my eyelids got heavy.

A growl penetrated my dreams. "Moss, wake up." I blinked as a hand shook my shoulder. "Come on. We gotta get out of here."

My eyes flew open. "What are you doing here, McSweeney?"

"Never mind that," he replied. "Just come with me." He grabbed my suitcase and headed for the door. I picked up my tote and ran after him. Outside it had clouded over and looked like it might rain. McSweeney had a rental car waiting nearby. He popped the trunk with the automatic key, tossed my bag inside and slammed it shut. Clicking the doors open, he barked, "Get in," and slid behind the steering wheel.

"What are you doing here, McSweeney?" I asked again, snapping my seatbelt into the buckle.

"Our other guy couldn't make it."

"Who is 'our other guy'?"

He glanced over at me for a second then said, "You'll find out when you need to know."

It seemed pointless to press the matter. "Where are we going?"

"You'll see." I clung to the door handle as McSweeney raced through the traffic, dodging the slowpokes and honking at anyone in his way. He didn't appear to be in the mood for conversation, so I held on and kept quiet. Twenty-five minutes later we pulled up in front of a cute little yellow cottage with a white picket fence. A porch swing on the veranda swayed gently in a soft breeze. McSweeney pushed open the gate and strode up the walk to the front door. Banging on the screen door with the side of his fist, he turned to watch me as I followed in his footsteps.

"Who are we meeting here?" I asked, joining him.

"The foremost authority on the Olmec civilization in the world," he said, pulling open the screen door and knocking on the inside door. From somewhere in the interior of the house, a small dog began yapping and in a moment we could hear its claws scratching the other side of the door.

"Just a minute, I'm coming," a voice called out. The door opened just far enough for a face to poke out. "Ah, you must be Mr. McSweeney," said the woman, opening the door wider and pushing a wild strand of pale brown hair away from her freckled face. Tall, she had green eyes, a long nose and thin lips. "I've been expecting you. Please come in."

Barbara Dumont introduced herself. I guessed her age at around fifty-five. She wore a pair of rolled up jeans and a bright lime tunic top and had a pair of rubber thong sandals on her feet. She invited us into the kitchen. After we had seated ourselves at the table in a bay window alcove, McSweeney said, "Jill is here to collect the package that Neil Bryant sent you and see if you can help with a bit of information."

"Call me Barb," our hostess said as she shook my hand and offered us herbal tea. I accepted. McSweeney declined.

A Yorkshire terrier bounded over to me and placed her tiny front paws on my leg.

"Josie, get away from there," Barbara scolded.

"It's all right, come here," I said, picking the dog up and cuddling her on my lap. "I like little dogs."

Barbara took the small package out of a kitchen drawer and handed it to me. "I haven't opened it," she said. "Since it was addressed to you in care of me I thought that would be snooping, but I have to tell you I am curious. Everything Neil comes up with is so exciting." She looked at me expectantly. I glanced at McSweeney, who barely lifted one shoulder and let it drop. Tearing the packing tape away, I opened the box and pulled the sixteenth stone out of the wrapping. Finally, I had the last one of the ring of stones in my possession.

"May I?" said Barb, holding out her hand and slipping a pair of reading glasses on her nose. I placed the stone in her palm. "Wow," she breathed in wonder. "This is incredible." She set the stone on the table in front of her and began to trace the markings with the tip of her finger. Then she turned it over to study the inscriptions on the other two sides. "Well, this side is definitely Olmec in origin though there is something different about it," she said, surveying the inscription on the top of the block. "You wouldn't have any more of these that I could see, would you?"

I reached into my tote and drew out the two I had with me and placed them on the table next to the other one. Barbara sucked in a long breath and held it. Then she let it out with a gust and cried, "These are amazing! I've been hoping to find something like this all my life. Leave it to Neil, the old fox!" She grinned and studied the stones. McSweeney leaned back in his chair and gazed out the window at the garden. Following his line of vision for a moment, I could see that scattered raindrops splotched the paving stones that wound between plantings of Shasta daisies and hollyhocks. Barbara turned the stones in her hands, holding each lovingly.

"They are so different, but the likeness is unmistakable."

"What do you mean?" I said.

"A few years back there was a significant discovery of Olmec writing on a tablet. To date it has been the only known artifact that indicates that the Olmecs had a written language. There are some skeptics of course, there always are," she laughed, "but I'm convinced it's the real thing. But these," she caressed the surfaces of the stones, "these are unique. They are similar to the Cascajal block, yet more sophisticated. Any idea how old these stones are?"

"Not really. I'm no archaeologist but Neil seems to believe that this find is highly significant. Other experts have suggested that they might be as old as 3000 B.C."

"Yes, my guess would be that they are older than the Cascajal block because of the style of the writing. You would think that the quality and skill of the writers would improve over time but it doesn't always happen that way. I believe that in that era the opposite is actually true. There was a high point around 3000 to 2500 B.C.then many of the world's civilizations began a decline. Once a culture has begun to wane, their written language also deteriorates, particularly if there are times of prolonged hardship. The people simply have more important things on their minds than sitting around carving rocks."

This theory echoed what the others had said regarding the progress, or lack thereof, of civilizations. I wondered if Barbara Dumont knew of Doc Silverman, or Profesor Alvarez, or Docteur Bernaud. Since they practiced in similar fields, it seemed likely.

McSweeney looked at Barbara. "Do you have any idea what they say?"

"I have an idea," she replied, "but until I see others in the group I can't be sure. There are others, aren't there?"

I nodded. "There are sixteen in all."

She gasped. "Oh, I would love to see them all. When can I take a look at them?"

McSweeney reached across the table and picked up the three stones with one hand and jabbed them at me. "Put these away," he muttered. "We need to hit the road."

Surprised by his abruptness, I took the stones from him and placed each back in its box then tucked them into my tote. Then I took a sip of the herbal tea that Barbara had set before me.

"I'm sorry our visit has to be so short," I apologized, getting to my feet. "I wish I could tell you more about the other stones, but..." I trailed off as McSweeney headed for the door. Reluctantly, I followed him. As I passed back through the living room something caught my eye. It was a prism or cut stone hanging from a transparent thread in front of the window and it caught the light coming in from outside. Though the day was rainy, this bauble twirled in the air casting subtle flashes of colour around the walls.

"What is that?" I asked as Barbara came up behind me. Before she could answer, McSweeney leaned around me, gave her hand a perfunctory shake, and strode out the door, letting the screen door slam behind him. "I'm sorry," I said again. "I don't know what he is in such a hurry for, but if you don't mind, I am interested in that prism."

She walked over to where it hung and took it in the palm of her hand. "I found this on a dig in Guatemala," she explained. "I don't think it is particularly ancient and neither did the others on the dig, but I found it intriguing so I brought it home with me. I believe it has special powers."

"What sort of powers?"

"Healing powers, the power to alleviate pain, promote mental clarity, and release negative energy. The vibration within the crystal elevates your own vibration and refracts disharmonious energies while attracting positive energy. It's a connection to the divine."

Naturally, I had heard about people who believed that crystals had powers but had never actually spoken with someone who subscribed to such beliefs. I decided McSweeney could wait another minute or two. Dr. Dumont's knowledge would be valuable in deciphering the messages on the stones, but I was curious about her spiritual beliefs. "Can you explain how that works? I don't understand the science behind it, or is there any? Is it just spiritual?"

"Well, it's both," she said, caressing the stone in her hand. "Quartz crystal healing therapy can be used to increase your own well-being through vibrational energy. A professional crystal healer might work with the energies of multiple crystals by placing them in a grid work system. This could be used for a major illness, for example."

"Really? They can do that?"

"Oh yes," she breathed. "It's truly amazing. You see, quartz crystals are composed of silicon dioxide and scientists have found that silicon crystals have special energy transduction properties, particularly when fused with other elements. They can conduct electrical and thermal energy because their atoms are arranged in a lattice and the crystalline structure makes them the most orderly substances in nature. They respond to different forms of energy like light, heat, sound, even gamma rays."

"Just a second," I said. "What's transduction?"

"It is just a way of describing how energy moves from one electron to another and in the process it changes."

"Oh."

"It's very exciting, Jill. The understanding of how crystals work is ancient technology that we are just beginning to understand. There is much more to it than meets the eye. Crystals represent perfection. For example, I use this crystal when I put my wishes out to the universe."

"You do what?" I tried not to sound skeptical.

"You know, the law of attraction? Like attracts like. The universe is kind and when you put what you want out there, you can manifest whatever you want."

"Well," I replied, "I have heard of the law of attraction, but I was under the impression that opposites attract, positive, negative, that sort of thing." I didn't believe in the so-called law of attraction because I felt that it simply diverted people's attention from real truth, a common tactic of the enemy, but I was curious about what this lady believed.

"Oh, but there is!" she cried. "I totally manifested the stone that Neil sent here."

"How did you do that?"

"Well," she replied, earnestly, "I wanted to see more artifacts with Olmec writing so I put my intention out to the universe and here you are."

"Perhaps it was just a coincidence," I suggested. "After all, if you are the foremost authority on Olmec writing, it stands to reason that Neil would choose you to consult on the find since he recognized the languages on the blocks."

"Jill," she said, placing her hand on my arm, "there are no coincidences. It was meant to be."

"I see," I said, noncommittally. I glanced around the pretty room, decorated in fresh pastels, and noticed a small bowl of stones on a side table. A painting of a glowing pink and blue angel hung over the sofa and a small statue of another angel stood on the floor near the entrance to the dining room. "Do you believe in angels?"

"Definitely. Don't you?"

"As a matter of fact, yes, I do." Somehow I doubted that I believed in the same way Barbara did. Suddenly, a sweet aroma invaded the room. I sniffed and turned to locate the source but nothing had changed.

"What's that smell?" I asked. It smelled like peaches that had been left out on the counter too long and had begun to rot, attracting a swarm of fruit flies.

Barbara eyed me with a puzzled expression. "I don't smell anything," she said slowly.

I sniffed again. The scent had grown stronger and more sickly than sweet. I sensed something in the room and it was not pleasant. I felt sure it was demonic. In a flash of recognition, I understood that a spirit of new age religion lived here. I glanced out the window to where McSweeney sat waiting in the car.

"I'd better be going," I said. "Mr. McSweeney is impatient to be off." I said good-bye to Barb and shook her hand. When I looked into her eyes, I felt a wave of love wash over me in her direction, as though the Lord wanted me to know how much he loved her and how it hurt him to see her deceived. "I'm sure we will meet again," I said, not sure why.

McSweeney turned the key in the ignition as I got in the rental car. "What happened in there?" he asked as he pulled away from the curb.

"She was showing me a quartz crystal that she found in Guatemala," I explained. "Why did you want to leave so quickly?"

"I couldn't stand the smell. I thought I was going to puke."

"What smell?" I asked, surprised to hear him mention it. I hadn't smelled anything until only a few moments before.

"Couldn't you smell the stink in that house? It smelled like rotten fruit."

"Yes. I smelled it," I said. "But it wasn't rotten fruit. It was the smell that sometimes accompanies the spirit of new age religion."

McSweeney took his foot off the gas pedal and stared at me. "No kidding. How do you know that?"

"How do you think? The Holy Spirit revealed it to me when Barb and I were talking."

McSweeney pulled to the side of the street and stopped the car, thrusting the gear shift into park. "So, what, the Holy Spirit walked in the room, walked right up to you, and said,

'Oh, by the way, that smell here that you think is rotten fruit is really the stink of weird religion'?"

I turned my body and looked at him, then I drew in a patient breath and said, "First of all, you have no right to speak to me like that. No, the Holy Spirit didn't 'walk into the room' and walk up to me. He came into the house with me. *In* me." I paused. "And he spoke *in* me. I hear his voice in my spirit. That's where he spoke to me. You smelled the stink in the house before I did, but there was no rotten fruit lying around, was there? He was trying to tell you that there was a rotten spirit in the house, but you didn't understand, so he told me, too."

McSweeney stared at me. "Oh," he said. "Look, Moss. I'm sorry. I was out of line."

"Thank-you," I replied. "And yes, you were. You have to trust me sometimes. I'm not stupid. You told me yourself that you and Neil chose me for this mission because I've learned how to hear the voice of God."

"Yeah, you're right." He stared out the window for a moment then turned the key in the ignition. Before he could shift gears, a big, pearl-white SUV rolled past his window and a man turned and looked straight at us. Through the tinted windows of the other vehicle I could just make out a face. It was Menendez.

"Looks like we've got company," McSweeney snarled. Slamming the gearshift into drive, he stood on the gas pedal. In a smoking screech of tires, we spun around in the middle of the quiet street and shot away, the car fish-tailing down the pavement. At the first corner, he cranked left and put his foot to the floor, zigzagging through sleepy neighbourhoods and careening around quiet corners in the afternoon sunshine. I checked my rear view mirror and twisted in my seat. Twice I caught a glimpse of the SUV following us. We managed to lose it both times but only briefly. We flew out onto the main highway at a speed that made the trip from the airport seem like a summer stroll.

"I hope the cops are all having coffee right now," said McSweeney as the car went into a sideways drift around a curve, narrowly missing a cube van in the oncoming lane.

"Where are we going?" I said, grabbing the dashboard to brace myself.

"We have to get to the water front. I've got a boat waiting for us there."

"Isn't that kind of far from here?"

"Of course. Why do you think I'm driving so fast?"

I rolled my eyes. "Then what?"

"Can't you see I'm trying to drive here, Moss?" McSweeney bellowed.

"Can't you see that I'm trying to find out if I'm going to live through this?" I shouted back.

"Of course you're going to live through this. Now, would you shut up and let me get you to the boat?"

I opened my mouth then shut it again, my teeth clenched. I clamped my arms across my chest, braced my feet against the floor and stared straight ahead.

Within minutes we screeched into the parking lot of a marina and McSweeney slammed on the brakes and skidded to a halt. "Let's go," he snapped. "Those guys are still on our tail." He leapt out of the car and headed down the dock.

"What about my suitcase?" I yelled after him as I kicked my door closed.

"Oh, for crying out loud!" he hollered, running back to the car while clicking on the key device in his hand. He grabbed my suitcase and took off again, shouting over his shoulder as he ran, "If you don't want to get shot, get a move on!"

I broke into a gallop at the same moment the SUV tore into the parking area. Slinging my bag over my shoulder, I charged after McSweeney. Up ahead I could see him throw my suitcase onto a boat and vault aboard. Throwing a glance behind me, I saw Menendez and his companion running full out after me down the length of the dock. I shrieked and ran faster. I was within a few feet of the boat when a hand grabbed me from behind and spun me around.

McSweeney leapt off the boat like a mad bull and ploughed into Menendez's cohort, ramming a fist into his mid-section. The man grunted and doubled over.

At the same time, Menendez seized my arm in a vice-like grip with one hand and with the other grabbed for the strap of my tote bag. "Give me the gold," he snarled into my face.

"What gold?" I spat back. "There is no gold, you idiot!" From the corner of my eye, I saw McSweeney thump his opponent again, sending the man plunging into the water between a pair of sailboats. At that moment, a marina security car pulled up at the end of the dock. "Police," I screamed. "It's the police!" It was just enough to break Menendez's concentration for the split second it took for me to wrench my arm from his grasp. With all my strength, I punched him square in the nose and simultaneously thrust my knee up into his groin. He howled and swung around to hit me, blood spurting from his face, but McSweeney was too fast for him. With one powerful slug, McSweeney snapped Menendez's head back on his neck. He let go of my purse strap as he staggered backward, flinging his arms in the air he reeled. But he took one step too many. Plummeting into the water, he banged the back of his head on the gunwale of a dingy floating alongside a tethered sailboat.

"Ooh," I said. "That had to hurt."

McSweeney grabbed me and threw me onto his boat then dashed to the controls. I heard the engines roar beneath me as I tripped over my suitcase and reached for something to hang onto, but before I could grab anything, he gunned the engines. A spume of spray shot out from behind the boat as he swung the wheel. His shoulders hunched over the controls and the boat sloshed from side to side as he swerved between the sailboats lilting in the swells. From somewhere onshore, I heard a shout and glanced back toward land to see two uniformed security guards running toward us. There was no sign of Menendez or his man. Just then McSweeney rammed the engines into full throttle. I lunged for the stainless steel tubing that ran the length of the gunwale but missed, spun, and fell sideways, arms thrashing. I came down hard against the side of the boat. A searing pain shot through my temple and erupted into my sinuses over one eye.

Then everything went black.

CHAPTER 33

Cold. My body felt so cold. The black became grey then I could hear sounds, something throbbing beneath me. I tried to open my eyes but only one would open. What was wrong with my other eye?

Then I saw McSweeney's face swim into view, hanging over me.

"Wake up, Moss," he said, sounding far away. Throbbing pain pulsed through my skull, pounding in my temples with a steady beat. I put my hand up to my face and felt something cold and wet. Panic seized me by the throat.

"I can't see, I can't see," I cried, straining to sit up.

"Settle down, Moss," McSweeney said in a surprisingly gentle voice. "You have an ice pack on your eye. Let me take it away and see what the damage is." He lifted the bag of ice off my face and I blinked a couple of times to clear my vision.

"I can see now," I said, reaching for his arm to pull myself up. McSweeney leaned in, studying my face. He frowned.

"What?"

"You look terrible," he said.

"Thanks," I said, looking around. "Where are we?" I could see nothing but water in every direction. The rain had stopped and the clouds parted to reveal a steamy sun sliding toward a watery horizon.

"We're off the coast of California."

"We must be pretty far off the coast if I can't see land," I said, standing up with McSweeney's help.

"Not really," he replied. "A bank of fog rolled in along the coastline. We're only a couple of miles out. Why don't you go down and clean yourself up?"

"What happened?"

"You fell and hit your head on…there." He pointed to a spot on the boat's body then whipped a red handkerchief out of his back pocket and scrubbed my blood from the gleaming white surface.

"Ooh," I said, suddenly feeling woozy. I grabbed for McSweeney's arm again and he guided me toward the stairs into the hold, clamping one of my hands onto a railing. "Go wash up and then sit down for a while. You'll feel better. We have to get moving, so you just go take care of yourself and I'll get started."

"All right," I agreed, clutching the railing. "Where are we going?"

"To an airport at Half Moon Bay."

"Okay," I said. I staggered into the tiny bathroom facility on the boat and turned on a light. For a second I didn't recognize my reflection. A deep-purple bruise spread across the left side of my face from a gash just above my temple down toward my eyebrow, where it turned an ugly indigo blue. A smear of blood ran down past my eye from the cut on my forehead and the skin around the outer corner of my eye had turned a nasty, mottled red-violet like the flesh of a blood orange. Splashing warm water on my face stung like crazy so I dabbed the blood off the side of my face with the corner of a towel and patted it dry without touching my skin. It was going to be one prize-winning shiner.

McSweeney turned to take a look at me when I joined him on deck. "Well," he said, "that looks better." I sensed false enthusiasm. "You'd better hang on now. I'm putting this thing in high gear and I don't want you flippin' off the stern." I sat down in the nearest seat and gripped the armrests.

Before long the beach cliffs hove into view and we veered wide around the point where breakers crashed against the rocky headland. At the dock in the marina, McSweeney edged the boat in alongside a sleek, two-masted sailboat. As our hull nudged the bumpers, I stepped out onto the dock, steadying myself with one hand on the gunwale.

"Wow! What happened to you?" called a voice from the sailboat. Shielding my eyes against the sun, I looked up to find a sixty-something woman in pink Bermuda shorts and a tank top gazing down at me.

"I had an unfortunate encounter with the side of this boat," I replied, "and am seriously considering never setting foot on another boat again as long as I live."

"I don't blame you," she laughed as McSweeney hopped out of the boat beside me. "You have to take better care of your wife," the woman instructed him, shaking a finger in his direction.

McSweeney glared up at her then gave me a sidelong glance. Yanking the handle of my suitcase up, he rested his other arm around my shoulders and said, "Come on, honey. Let's go find a clinic and get that cut looked after."

Once we got in the taxi, McSweeney looked me over and pronounced me well enough to travel. There would be no stop at a clinic. A small jet stood waiting on the tarmac when we stepped out of the taxi and we walked straight out to it and climbed on board. McSweeney seemed to know the pilot. Within minutes of boarding, the two of them fell into deep discussion. I settled into my seat and clipped on my seatbelt. All I wanted to do was go to sleep.

"Where are we going this time?" I asked once McSweeney sat down opposite me.

"Galveston," he replied, "to pick up the stones."

"Then what?"

"We go get the rest of them."

"In Switzerland?"

"That's where they are, isn't it?"

"Of course."

"What if I want to go home now?"

"You can't," he said. "You're not done yet."

"I've picked up all the stones. They are all secure, including the three that I have in my bag right now. Surely someone else can take over from here. Haven't I done enough?"

"You're the only one who can take them out of the banks."

"Wasn't that a little short-sighted? What if something had happened to me?"

McSweeney rubbed a hand over his beard. "We made sure that nothing did is all."

"What do you mean?"

"Moss, your uncle will tell you everything when you see him. Now, would you please take a break and let me get some sleep? I've been up since three o'clock this morning." With that he dropped his seat back, stuck his feet out in front of him, and closed his eyes.

"Hold on a minute," I said. "When will I see Neil? Where is he?"

The only answer I received was a rumbling snore from deep in McSweeney's throat.

I woke with a start when the plane's wheels hit the runway in Galveston. I had been dreaming. Closing my eyes again, I slid back into the dream and saw a red convertible, a dark road; I felt the soft night air, and there was Marco. For a moment I allowed my mind to skim the surface of the memory of that night drive from Barcelona to Switzerland. I remembered the way his hand touched mine and the how easily I could get lost in his dark eyes.

I shook my head, sat up, and rubbed my eyes, yelping when I touched the bruised side of my face. Reality came back in a rush of pain. Pulling a small mirror from my tote, I examined my face, turning this way and that to check the damage. *A face like this could scare small children,* I thought. A little concealer makeup applied ever so gently around my eye and up toward my temple and forehead modified the frightening appearance, but not by much. Half of my face was black and blue.

And by now, so was the sky. Peering out the tiny plane window, I could see the first evening stars appearing in the inky heavens. The lights of the airport glided into view and in a few minutes it was time to disembark. McSweeney threw his well-worn backpack over one shoulder. When my feet hit solid ground, I saw Bobby standing across the dark expanse between the plane and the terminal and broke into a run. It seemed like years since I had seen him yet it had been only hours.

"Hey, Bobby," I said giving him a quick hug.

"Howdy, ma'am," he said with a grin. "If you don't mind me saying so, you look worse than you did last time I saw you."

I stood back and looked up into his face. "It's temporary. But how are you? Is the arm going to be all right?"

"Oh, heck, yeah," he said. "I had it looked at again as soon as I got in to Galveston. It's going to be fine. You did a pretty good job of patching me up with those pad things."

"Bobby," McSweeney said, reaching to pump the other man's hand. "Good to see you again."

"And you, Mr. McSweeney, sir."

"Cut the 'sir' garbage," McSweeney said.

"Yes, sir," Bobby said, grinning. "Whatever you say, sir."

"It's no use," I told McSweeney. "You won't talk him out of the sir and ma'am stuff so there's no point in trying."

We followed Bobby out to a waiting car. "You'd better drive," he said handing the keys to McSweeney. "Mrs. Moss can't see straight and I can't drive straight. You're the only one here who's in one piece."

We drove directly to the bank where I had deposited the stones only a few days before. In spite of the late hour, we were met at the door by the bank manager, a well-dressed lady with streaked blonde hair and a face that spoke of too many years with a cigarette in her mouth. Bobby introduced us all.

As we were about to enter the bank building, an armoured vehicle arrived. Fifteen minutes later the stones from the deposit box had been removed from the safe deposit box and, together with the stones from my bag, had all been packed into a steel case and placed in the armoured car.

"You won't have to worry about carrying those things around anymore, ma'am," Bobby assured me. "We'll take it from here."

"You don't know how much that means to me," I told him. "Those things are heavy. I think my back has a permanent twist in it from lugging a bag of rocks all over the world."

We spent the night at Eleanora's house again with Bobby and one of his men standing guard. Except for when I rolled onto the painful side of my head, I never woke from the time my head hit the pillow until the sunlight streamed through the bedroom windows. After showering and dressing, I met McSweeney and Bobby at the bottom of the stairs.

"What's the plan?" I asked, looking from one to the other.

"We're flying out of Houston to Zurich this evening, ma'am," Bobby said, "so we have a little time to kill before we have to head up there. How would y'all like to go out for breakfast?"

Eleanora appeared from the kitchen. "I would love that," she cried, "as long as you're paying, Bobby."

The restaurant Bobby chose was in a heritage building on the old downtown street called the Strand. I took a seat next to the window as we ordered coffee all around. The day had dawned bright and clear and from the open window beside me, I could hear the cry of gulls over the water just a couple of streets away. A few early tourists wandered in and out of the shops that lined the tranquil street, peering into windows and carrying take-out coffees. Across the street, a man sat reading a newspaper on a sidewalk bench.

"Moss, are you listening?" McSweeney said.

"Sorry?" I answered, yanked out of my reverie. "What did you say?"

"Bobby's coming with us to Switzerland. It wasn't the original plan but we both think we need the added security."

"Oh," I replied. "Are you sure you're okay to travel with that arm?"

"Yes, ma'am," Bobby said. "It'll hardly slow me down a bit."

"I doubt that, but if you two think it's the right thing to do, all right."

"I think he should stay home and take care of it," Eleanora said, placing her elbows on the table and pointing at Bobby with her fork. "You know you're still in pain and you should go straight home to bed." The two of them argued back and forth and I took a bite of my eggs and turned to watch the life go by on the street. A woman in a pink coat walked past the window with a mincing toy poodle in a matching pink coat and leash. Across the street, a man sat down on the bench next to the man reading the newspaper. The light glinted off his sunglasses. I spread some grape jelly on my whole wheat toast and took a bite, then looked out the window again. The man who had sat down in the bench had taken off his sunglasses. There was something about him. I studied his face for a minute then gasped, choking on my toast and coughing. My eyes watered.

"What's the matter?" asked McSweeney, seated beside me.

Wiping my eyes with my napkin, I pointed out the window. "I've seen that man before," I squeaked between coughs. "He was tailing me in Switzerland! The others turned to look where I pointed and at the same moment the other man lowered his newspaper ever so slightly and turned to speak with the Swiss tail.

"That's Marco," I whispered, grabbing McSweeney by the sleeve. "We have to get out of here without being seen."

"Relax a minute, will ya'?" McSweeney said, looking over my head. "You say you know those guys?"

"Yes, I met Marco Jimenez in Spain. He drove me to Switzerland. I thought he was a decent guy until he turned up at that antiquities show here a few days ago. He was with a woman named Claire Jamieson who has been after me since I first landed in Paris. She was introduced to me at the antiquities show, only she was using a different name. I can't remember what it was. Remember, Eleanora?" I turned to her and saw her nod. "What are we going to do?"

"Right now we're going to finish our breakfasts. They must already know you're here so until they make a move, there is no point in doing anything," McSweeney reasoned. "Do you agree, Bobby?"

Bobby nodded. "I'll take care of it," he said, directing his comment at McSweeney.

"And just what are you planning to do?" Eleanora asked, looking at Bobby's arm and raising her eyebrows. "Do the one-armed bandit routine and gun them down?"

"I said I'll take care of it," he replied evenly, "so you never mind."

We finished eating in wary silence as we all watched the two men across the street. They sat and talked for a few minutes, then the Swiss tail got up and left. I reached across the table and gripped Bobby's wrist, pointing out the window. Bobby nodded.

"Okay, McSweeney," he said in his usual soft voice. "You take Jill and Elly out once I cross the street." He seemed much too calm to me but then he made his living by remaining calm in crisis. McSweeney nodded and pushed his chair away from the table.

I stepped out onto the sidewalk into a wave of heat. Humid and close, the bright morning promised another sizzling day. From the corner of my eye, I saw a look ricochet between Bobby and McSweeney.

"Don't you worry, ma'am," Bobby said, patting my arm. "Everything's going to be all right." Then he stepped out onto the street and headed toward the man on the bench.

McSweeney placed a hand under my elbow. "Come on, Moss. Let's get out of here." I turned to accompany him, but my eyes followed Bobby. There was something I had to do. I had to know if that man sitting there behind the newspaper was really Marco. Jerking my elbow from McSweeney's hand, I sprinted after Bobby, but before I could reach him, a little blue sports car sped around the corner, tires squealing on the hot pavement. It came straight at me. I lunged to get out of the way but my toe caught on the tram track that ran down the centre of the street. I tried to catch myself but was too slow and landed hard on my knee before spinning onto the asphalt. The sound of the approaching car's engine filled my head and I scrambled to get to my feet but knew that I wouldn't make it. The car would hit me full on the side of my body. I saw its bumper bearing down on me and in a freakish moment even read the license number on the plate before it struck me.

Only it didn't. In less time than it took to draw a breath, I was lifted from the pavement by a pair of strong arms and hurled, along with my rescuer, to the side of the street unscathed. The car sped off down the street as though nothing had happened. When I gained my footing and stood back to see who had so gallantly saved my life, I looked up into the face of Marco.

"*Ola, mi amor*," he said. "I see you are still trying to get yourself killed."

CHAPTER 34

"Get away from me!" I shouted, flinging Marco's hands from my body. "Don't touch me." As I glared at him, I felt the start of tears sting my eyes. The dazzling smile slid from Marco's face as he stared back at me.

My right knee hurt like crazy. I took a limping step backward and fell against McSweeney's chest. At the same time, Bobby came up behind Marco and jumped him, wrapping his huge arm, the injured one, around Marco's neck and snapping his head back. With his good arm, Bobby yanked Marco's wrist high up his back.

"You're coming with me, pal," Bobby growled in Marco's ear, dragging him off his feet. Even with Bobby injured, Marco was no match for his strength.

McSweeney slid an arm around my waist, folding me against his side, and nearly lifted me off my feet as he turned and steered me away. Eleanora, who had followed when I ran across the street, took my other side, clucking and muttering about silliness, and men, and blood on my clothes. I glanced down to see that my pants had a jagged tear across the knee and the mangled flesh beneath oozed blood and gravel down my leg.

"We're getting you back home right now," she declared. "I don't know what you think you're doing, running out in the street like that, nearly getting yourself run over. Who was that man anyway?"

"I met him in Spain," I explained, wincing with every step.

"Oooh," she replied. "He's the one you saw at the show. No wonder you had a problem."

"Mm-hmm," I said, hopping up on the curb with McSweeney's help. In a quick glance over my shoulder, I saw Bobby drag Marco around the corner of a brick building and out of sight. Marco didn't seem to be struggling at all. Good thing, I thought, because Bobby could cream him in a second.

Once back at Eleanora's house, she cleaned and bandaged my knee and I changed from my torn and bloody summer-weight pants into a clean pair of jeans even though I knew it was too hot for them. Frankly, I was running out of clothing choices since everything I had packed was now dirty, bloodstained, torn, or had bullet holes in it. I couldn't imagine that I would have any time to shop in the near future either, but as it turned out, once we had checked in for our flight to Zurich, Bobby and McSweeney went for coffee and I was free to browse the shops in the airport. I found a pair of white Capri pants, some black walking shorts, and a fuchsia tunic top to wear with either, plus a printed skirt with a top and jacket to match, and a simple sundress. Since I had not yet been briefed on our destination once we picked up the stones in Thun, I hoped that these items would be versatile enough for anything. Well, almost anything. I would be happy to have no more bloodstains or bullet holes.

I met up with McSweeney and Bobby in the boarding area. McSweeney pulled a rolled-up newspaper from under his arm and buried himself behind it. Bobby pretended to read a magazine but I knew that there was nothing that he didn't notice.

Sitting down next to McSweeney, I withdrew Neil's Bible from my tote bag, opened it, and slowly turned the pages. Perhaps I could find more clues that would reveal the meaning of the stones. The message hidden in the inscriptions on the sides of them was one thing, but I knew Neil intended for me to find something in the scriptures too, perhaps something that connected with the stones' messages or their purpose. Why else would he have marked so many passages? But if so, what was this connection? So far it had eluded me.

I turned to McSweeney. Over the black frames of his reading glasses furrows grooved his forehead as he scrutinized an article in his paper. Across from me, a harried young mother sat down with a little girl of about three years and a fussing baby in a stroller heaped with bags and bottles. I glanced around at the others waiting to board the plane. A grey-haired businessman in a grey suit and pink tie clicked away on his laptop off to my right. A pair of scruffy backpackers, wearing baggy pants and Tibetan ponchos, sat on the floor sharing snacks. Others straggled in as the take-off time drew closer.

Looking at them, I recognized that any one of these people could be an enemy of some kind. I hoped that we had finally shaken Menendez and his cronies, but how could any of us be sure? I felt equally wary of encountering members of the political group that had kidnapped Dennis. According to Dennis, the group was well-organized and determined. Since they knew about Neil's find and about Dennis' whereabouts, it could be only a matter of time until they realized my part in this drama and fixed their sights on me. Knowing that, I felt thankful that we were leaving the country again, if only to stay one step ahead of them. In spite of all that, I still felt calm, trusting in God's promise of help in every circumstance. It still stood, regardless of the danger.

The child in the seat across from me whined for a drink of juice and the baby began to wail. My heart went out to the young mother, travelling alone with such tiny children. I was about to offer to help when I heard the Holy Spirit say, "*I want to talk with you.*" I left my seat and walked down the concourse to an empty boarding area. Still close enough to hear announcements regarding my own flight and watch the boarding progress, I sat in a quiet seat next to the window and resumed my interior conversation.

Opening the Bible again, I heard the Spirit say, *"Go to Second Kings, chapter twenty-four."* I began to read at verse one, but felt impelled to skip through the chapter until I stopped at verse eleven. There I read, "And Nebuchadnezzar king of Babylon came against the city, and his servants did besiege it." I skimmed down the page. "And he carried out thence all the treasures of the house of the LORD, and the treasures of the king's house, and cut in pieces all the vessels of gold which Solomon king of Israel had made in the temple of the LORD, as the LORD had said. And he carried away all Jerusalem, and all the princes, and all the mighty men of valour, even ten thousand captives, and all the craftsmen and smiths: none remained, save the poorest sort of people of the land." I pulled my journal from my bag and noted the passages that God had shown me. Even in King James English, it was not hard to tell that the temple was full of riches. The next passage described how, except for a few inconsequential folks everyone was carted off or killed.

As I reviewed the notes I had jotted down and looked again at the verses, it came as no surprise that they had all been marked by Neil's red pen. Again I silently asked, "What is it that you want me to see?"

Then a verse in Second Chronicles came to mind. It read, "And all the vessels of the house of God, great and small, and the treasures of the house of the LORD, and the treasures of the king, and of his princes; all these he brought to Babylon."

I asked what I was supposed to see. *"Do you notice that the treasures were stolen from the temple and taken to Babylon?"* the Holy Spirit asked.

"Yes," I answered. "I notice that."

"They have never been found nor returned."

"Are you telling me that the stones have some connection to the whereabouts of the temple artifacts?" I could feel the thrill beginning to ignite somewhere in my gut. A large hand clamped my shoulder and I leapt so violently that I dropped Neil's Bible on the floor.

"Moss," McSweeney said, "It's time to board. Haven't you heard the announcements?"

I threw my journal, pen, and Neil's Bible back into my bag. "Sorry," I said. "I was occupied."

"What were you doing over here?" McSweeney asked, walking with me to the boarding line-up.

"Just talking with God," I answered. "You won't believe what he showed me," I said, taking a couple of little dance steps along beside him as excitement bubbled to the surface.

McSweeney eyed me from under lowered brows. "Well, you can tell me all about it later," he said. "Come on, we've got priority boarding this time."

I had no idea who sprang for the upgrade but as we slid into our wide seats in first class, I thanked God for them. McSweeney lowered himself into the seat and said, "Okay, tell me what you've got."

Shoving my bag under the seat in front of me, I paraphrased in a hurried whisper everything that the Lord had just shown me. Even though I had already been through so much in the quest for the stones, I realized that I was only now beginning to grasp the import of Neil's find. The stones had something to do with the artifacts from Solomon's temple, I felt sure. The question was what?

"How do you do that?" McSweeney asked, once we had buckled our seatbelts and the plane lifted off.

"Do what?"

McSweeney studied me, his brows drawn down over his eyes so that two deep lines scored the space between them. "You know. That talking to God thing you do?"

I gave him a sidelong look. "It's not that much different than talking to anyone," I replied, opening the newspaper on my lap. "I talk, he listens. He talks, I listen. People try to complicate it too much. Religiosity gets involved and people get hung up on form and forget that God is a person. Well, like a person, only more so. You know what I mean."

"So you're telling me that God just talks to you and you hear him?"

"Of course. But I don't have a premium on it or anything. Most people don't hear God because they don't expect to, so they don't listen. I suspect what happens to lots of people is that they go to God, praying about whatever is on their minds, which is usually something they need or want. They cry out to God and beg for answers, but about the time God starts to answer they quit listening, get up, and go do something else. Or they just keep moaning about their problems because they don't really expect him to answer. God is not as silent as most people think."

"Do you hear him speak out loud?"

"Hardly ever. I hear him speak into my mind, or technically, my spirit." The flight attendant backed his cart up to where we sat and offered us drinks. I accepted a glass of orange juice and flipped my tray table down. "I know what you're going to ask," I continued when the attendant had moved on. "How do I know it is God's voice and not just my own thoughts? Am I right?"

McSweeney nodded. "Yep, pretty much."

"It takes practice and trust. To start with, you have to believe that God wants to talk to you and that you will be able to hear him when he does. But Jesus said that if we believe in him, we would be able to hear him so it seems to me that if we can't, it's because of something we're doing, or not doing. Usually I can tell that it's God speaking and not just me because he tells me things I haven't thought of myself, even after I've worked on something for a while. He also tends to have better ideas than I come up with on my own. After a while, of course, I just grew to recognize his voice without thinking about it. Kind of like when your wife phones you. You recognize her voice without her having to identify herself, right?"

"Sure. I recognize my wife's voice. But do you ever miss it? I mean, make mistakes or hear wrong?"

"Unfortunately, yes. I'm human. Sometimes I am so emotionally involved that my own feelings get in the way. But when that happens, I try to get alone and quiet for a while to calm my mind down. I haven't had many opportunities to do that on this trip though."

"What got you going on this, this talking with God stuff?" McSweeney asked, pushing the back of his seat back and stretching his legs out under the seat in front. I did the same, vowing never to fly economy again.

"When my husband died, I had a lot of unanswered questions," I began, not sure how much I wanted to reveal. "I had heard of other people being able to hear the voice of God in their lives and I know that God doesn't play favourites, so I figured that if other people could do it, why couldn't I? I just started talking to God like I'm talking to you, asking for answers. I had decided that I would not give up until I got them. It didn't take long once I had determined that's what I would do."

"And did you get your answers?"

"Yes."

"What were they?"

"They are kind of personal." I handed my empty glass to the flight attendant.

"Sorry," McSweeney said. "I didn't mean to pry."

"I have a question for you," I countered, changing the subject. "You know those gold items we found in the water?" McSweeney nodded and I leaned close to whisper. "Did you find the rest?"

He held up six fingers.

"Where are they?" I mouthed.

"Doc Silverman has them," he replied.

"What's going to happen to them?"

"He's bringing them with him. We'll be meeting him tomorrow."

My eyebrows shot up. "We will? Is he coming to Switzerland, too?"

McSweeney shook his head.

"All right," I whispered. "It's time you tell me where we're going."

He hesitated for a moment and glanced at the passengers around us. Across the aisle from McSweeney, Bobby snoozed, almost horizontal in his seat, his head lolling sideways. All of the other passengers nearby seemed to be sleeping, reading, or watching movies. McSweeney crooked his finger for me to lean closer then whispered in my ear, "Don't react when I tell you this." I frowned at him, but his expression was deadly serious so I nodded and leaned toward him. "We're meeting Neil in Israel."

I kept my eyes lowered. Never once had it crossed my mind that Israel would be where Neil was hiding. For some reason I assumed that we would meet at a university or a museum somewhere where the other experts in the ancient languages would have congregated in keen anticipation of deciphering the stones. Of course, this now seemed ludicrous to me. Given the danger involved, any kind of public venue would provide far too many opportunities for sabotage. A hundred questions raced through my mind and I opened my mouth to start asking them, but McSweeney put a finger to his lips, shaking his head ever so slightly.

"We'll talk later," he whispered. Then he leaned his head back and closed his eyes.

Outside, the sky had begun to darken. In a few hours we would be landing in Frankfurt and from there taking a private flight right into Bern. At Bern airport, a car and driver would take the three of us directly to the bank in Thun. After that, the stones retrieved from the bank's vault would be transported on to their destination without me in the same manner that the stones from Galveston had.

I didn't think McSweeney was asleep and when I looked over at Bobby I saw that he had awakened and was flipping through the in-flight magazine. I opened the newspaper on my lap and read the headlines, then turned the pages looking for an interesting story to occupy myself until I felt sleepy enough to drift off. Three pages into it, I saw a heading that woke me up completely.

"Look at this," I said to McSweeney, jabbing him with my elbow and shoving the newspaper under his nose. He opened one eye and glared at me. "Come on," I said, "I think this is important." He sighed and reached into his chest pocket, pulled out his glasses, and pushed them onto his face.

"Okay, Moss," he said, taking the paper from my hand. "What have you got?"

The story, released that day, told of Iran's development of nuclear weapons and Israel's concern, given Iran's connections with Hezbollah in Lebanon and Hamas in the Gaza strip. Though Iran claimed that its nuclear research and development was purely for civilian purposes, its harsh rhetoric against Israel and its president's denial of the holocaust reminded me of the threat that faced Jews in Europe before the Second World War.

"That's not exactly new," McSweeney said, handing the paper back to me and taking off his glasses.

"Did you read it all?"

"Yeah, pretty much."

"Look at this," I said, pushing the folded paper back before his eyes. "Read the last sentence."

He sighed and took the paper from my hand again, jamming his glasses back on his nose. I watched as his eyes slid over the words, left to right, left to right, then they stopped and backed up, reading the same words again. A frown creased his brow and he glanced over at me.

"Kind of puts a little more urgency in our mission, doesn't it?" he said, handing the newspaper back.

"You could say that," I replied carefully. I glanced down at the short paragraph that ended the article and re-read the words. "Iran's leaders also alluded to their country's acquisition of certain ancient artifacts which employ technologies they claim will enable them to wipe their enemies from the face of the earth."

CHAPTER 35

A chilly wind whipped through the streets of Thun in the late afternoon when we pulled up in front of the bank. Our driver, a silent character in his sixties, drove the car around to the lot behind the bank, where Marco and I had parked not many days before.

Gerhard Mueller stood just inside the glass doors of the bank and opened them for us when we appeared. He kissed my cheeks, once, twice, three times, signifying our friendship. With the others, he offered a hand to shake then led us all to his office. While McSweeney and Bobby waited there, I followed Gerhard to the vault and retrieved the stones that lay in the locked compartment.

"Where will you be taking the stones?" he asked when we were alone.

"I've collected all sixteen," I said, "and the rest have been sent on ahead to their destination. I'm sorry I can't tell you where that is, but I'm sure Neil will share the information with you when he's ready." Actually, the more I learned about Neil's situation, the more I doubted whether he would share information with anyone but a very select group of people. It was possible that Gerhard would be included in that group, but I didn't know.

We packed the artifacts in a special container and handed them over to the armoured car company that Bobby had arranged to transport them on to Israel. We said good-bye to

Gerhard, which included three more cheek kisses for me, and got back in the car. Winding through the traffic out of town, we headed directly to the small municipal airport where a helicopter waited to take us to Geneva. The sun angled toward the horizon and turned the snow-capped peaks of the Alps to liquid gold, casting long shadows up their dark forested slopes.

At the airport in Geneva, the three of us were shuttled to a waiting jet, which McSweeney identified as a Gulfstream Five. By now I didn't care what kind of machine it was so long as it flew and I could get some sleep. My body didn't know what time zone to adapt to and my mind was too numb to do the math and figure it out, so I quit trying and trudged up the steps to the plane's door.

The pilot and co-pilot greeted us as we entered the aircraft and found our comfortable seats. Before we had even taken off into the night sky, both Bobby and McSweeney fell asleep as the lights of Geneva disappeared from view.

I woke once during the night flight. Sitting up, I lifted the window shade and gazed down at the earth below. It seemed to me that we weren't flying at a very high altitude since I could see the moonlight reflected on the sea. I crept out of my seat so as not to disturb McSweeney or Bobby and found the lavatory near the rear of the plane. The light came on when the door closed, momentarily blinding me, and I covered my eyes with my hand for a moment while I gradually got used to it.

Squinting at my reflection in the little mirror, I noticed that the bruising around my eye had already begun to turn from purple to green on the edges and the swelling had subsided enough that I could now at least open my eye fully. I lifted my shirt to take a look at my side. The bruises from my encounter with the planter pot in Merida had now begun to fade to a sickly yellow-green and the scrapes had scabbed over. When I dropped my pants, I tentatively plucked away the bandage on my knee to check the healing process of the scrapes from both the planter pot incident in Merida and the stumble in Galveston. Thankful that the damage had not been extensive and that the abrasions had already begun to heal, I taped the dressing back in place then checked the gunshot wound on my side. It had started to itch in the last day or so and I found myself having to resist scratching. Though the itching indicated healing, sometimes it nearly drove me crazy. One more day and I would be able to discard the bandages from that one too, I hoped as I stuck it back in place.

I looked at my watch which I had set to Swiss time before we took off, and since there was only an hour difference in time zones, the calculation to our destination was easy. Regardless of the time zone, it was still the middle of the night here. My body, however, thought it was daytime. I closed the lavatory door softly and padded back to my seat in my stocking feet, then lay down and closed my eyes. Thoughts raced around my mind like circus monkeys bouncing off the walls, flipping, turning, muddling, and fixating on the craziest things for the next hour until, for some unknown reason, they all got tired and I dropped back to sleep. Then I dreamed of Marco again.

Dawn had not yet broken when I awoke to hear McSweeney and Bobby muttering together, leaning toward each other across the aisle of the jet. With my eyes closed, I lay still, enjoying the comfort of having nothing to do, and strained to hear what they were saying. It was no use. The noise of the plane's engines drowned out their words. I opened my eyes and said, "What are you two talking about?"

They both jumped as if stung. "We're just catching up, ma'am," Bobby answered, a little too quickly. McSweeney sat up and turned toward me.

"You decided to stop snoring, eh?" he said, smirking.

"I won't dignify that remark with an answer," I said, pulling my chair back up straight and pushing the window shade up. Below, I could see the purple-shadowed countryside sliding beneath the plane and, farther out, the surface of Mediterranean shimmered like a tray of black pearls in the pre-dawn glow.

"How long until we land?" I asked.

"We figure about ten-fifteen minutes," Bobby replied. "Have you got your seatbelt on?"

Fifteen minutes later, the plane taxied to a stop at a secondary hangar at Ben Gurion airport. Immediately, five uniformed men with machine guns surrounded the plane and as the door opened, two of them rushed on board, guns ready. While one man guarded the three of us, the other communicated with the flight crew. In a few minutes they relaxed and suggested we follow them from the plane. Inside the hangar, we met with customs officials and filled out the requisite forms while the guys with the guns stood around us, unsmiling. Finally, a tall man in a crisp, white linen suit appeared, introduced himself as Guy Bernstein, and asked that we follow him to a waiting car. He had dark, wavy hair and wore a pair of sunglasses.

"Hold on," I said as the others turned to follow him. "How do we know who you are and who sent you?"

"Please don't take my word for it," Guy said, smiling. "Though I have already been in touch with Mr. McSweeney, I am happy to provide credentials for you. It's important that you trust the right people." He took a cellular phone from his pocket and moved his thumb over the number pad. "Please," he said, handing me the phone.

Taking it from his hand I placed the telephone next to my ear and said hello. Immediately, Neil's cheery voice crackled through the device. "Jill, is that you? You have finally arrived."

Walking away from the others so they couldn't hear me speak, I asked Neil if we should go with this person named Guy Bernstein. Neil laughed and assured me that he was completely trustworthy.

"Are you sure no one is holding a gun to your head and making you say that?" I wanted to know.

"I'm quite sure," he said. "Now get along. I can't wait to see you again." He was still laughing when I closed the phone and handed it back to Guy Bernstein.

"Okay," I said, "you check out. Let's go."

The car turned out to be a large armoured vehicle with walls of solid steel and window glass two inches thick. As we pulled away from the airport, past the checkpoint security, and out onto the freeway, the morning sun edged over the horizon, casting long fingers of light onto the surrounding terrain. In no time we had put all traces of the city behind us as we set out over undulating hills covered with forest. This was my first time in the Holy Land and I strained to see everything I could from my limited view in the van.

Before long, Guy turned the vehicle off the highway onto a smaller road and then to a narrow track. The pine forest grew close on both sides and as we ventured deeper into the mountains, the forest floor vegetation grew sparse and the ground lay covered in dry needles. Occasionally, the trees parted to reveal small, open meadows covered in yellow grasses and skinny saplings that waved in the morning breeze. Soon the trail became nothing more than a couple of barely-visible tracks through the brush. The van lurched over hummocks and dips and finally stopped at the vertical face of a cliff.

I glanced at Bobby and saw that he was chewing the inside of his bottom lip, his jaw tight. McSweeney had sunglasses over his eyes so I could not read his expression, but he leaned forward, elbows on his knees, and shoulder muscles bunched. I felt the prickle of sweat break on my palms.

"What happens now?" I said. My voice came out high and wavering.

Guy turned to me and said, "We wait. It shouldn't be long."

So we waited. Ten interminable minutes dragged by. Bobby drummed his fingers on the side of the car in tune to a beat in his head. McSweeney slouched back in his seat and leaned his head against the head rest and might have looked relaxed had it not been for his grip on the armrests.

"Can we get out and get some fresh air?" I asked finally, pushing my hair away from my neck.

"Best not to," Guy answered. "Don't worry, it won't be long."

I couldn't stand it. "What won't be long?"

Guy grinned at me. "Have patience, Mrs. Moss," he said. "You'll see."

I sighed and stared out the front window at the wall of rock before. Suddenly, it moved. I blinked. A sheet of solid rock the size of an oversized garage door lifted away from the cliff, shifted upwards and slid into the top of the opening, revealing a cavern lit with a line of glowing overhead lamps.

"Here we go," Guy said, thrusting the van's gearshift into drive and pulling the vehicle through the opening. Once inside, he turned the engine off and opened the side doors. "Please follow me," he said, setting off down the tunnel. Behind us, the rock door slid back into place over the tunnel opening.

About one hundred meters into the belly of the mountain, we came to a set of double doors. Guy slid a pass card through a reader on the door frame then punched some keys on a number pad. As I followed him through the doorway, my jaw dropped. I glanced at Bobby and saw his wide eyes. McSweeney stood with hands on hips, smirking and shaking his head.

"That old dog," he muttered. "That crafty, old dog."

We stood in a huge room filled with tables covered with equipment. Overhead, steel tracks ran the length of the room, hung with lights and gear. On the tables and counters the usual laboratory apparatus alternated with complicated devices and machines covered with meters, digital readouts, and dials. Two dozen or more people were busy operating equipment or using the many computers. Near the opposite wall, I could see a couple of men crouched on the floor, both holding some kind of device, and objects moving just above the floor. These resembled remote control toy cars, only they had no wheels. Around the perimeter of the room, the walls were punctuated by closed doors with translucent glass that made it impossible to see in or out.

"What is this place?" I asked Guy.

"This is the research lab," he replied. "Neil is around here somewhere. I think he will want to see you right away."

A timer buzzed somewhere and a young woman wearing jeans and a striped t-shirt checked some meters and made notes on her computer. At another counter, a little man with a fringe of grey hair sat on a high stool and bent over a microscope. "Let me see if I can locate him for you," Guy said. He pulled out a cell phone and pressed a number, but just then Neil emerged from one of the side rooms with another man and looked our way. Waving his arms, he ran toward where we stood.

I had not seen Neil in a long time but he seemed to look even younger than I remembered him. Almost six feet tall and always slim and fit, his hair had only a few grey hairs streaking its natural dark brown. His laughing eyes still sparkled with the same blue as always. I dropped my tote bag on the floor and threw myself into his arms. He lifted me off my feet and spun me around.

When he set me down and stepped back, his happy smile turned to a look of horror. "What on earth happened to your face?" he gasped, examining my bruises.

"I met with a little boating accident," I replied, glancing at McSweeney. "It's just bruised. I'm sure it will be back to normal in a few days."

"Quentin," Neil said, reaching for McSweeney's hand. The two men embraced, thumping each other on the back, then Neil reached for Bobby's hand.

"I can't tell you how good it is to see you all," he said, leading us to a large office with a broad, dark wooden desk and leather furniture. There were no windows but the room felt like a cozy family room.

Neil sat down on one of the sofas and invited us to take seats. "While I've been squirreled away here, I could hardly stand knowing that you were out there somewhere, Jill, tearing around the world. I don't think I will ever be able to thank you enough. But now we have all the stones. They arrived a little while ago and we're going to start work on them right away." Neil offered us drinks and Guy went and fetched them. I had just taken a long drink of mineral water when I heard the door behind me open.

"Hey," Neil cried, "look who's here." I swivelled to see Doctor Silverman stride into the room. When he saw McSweeney and me, his face lit up and he ran the few steps between the door and my chair and swept me up in his arms in a bone-crushing hug, lifting me up off the floor and squeezing my battered sides.

"Ow," I said, wincing.

"Oh, my goodness," Doc Silverman gasped, setting me gingerly back on my feet. "I completely forgot you had an injury to your body, and oh, my goodness again," he cried, placing his enormous hands gently at the sides of my head. "Look at your face! What has happened to you?" Doc looked around the room. McSweeney raised his hand.

"My fault," he said. "Bad driving."

"Bad boating," I corrected. "That guy is a madman on the water. And on land, for that matter!"

"What happens now, Neil?" McSweeney asked when Doc had drawn up a chair next to me.

"Dr. Dumont will be arriving in a couple of hours. Guy is heading back to the airport to pick her up in a few minutes. She has not seen all the stones yet, only the one that you showed her. Once she gets here the three of us, Barbara, Elijah and I, will convene in the office complex upstairs and begin deciphering the messages. I have already done the Mayan ciphers since I took photos before I sent them away. I believe that Elijah," he nodded at Silverman, "has done the same."

Doctor Silverman answered, "I want to get my hands on the real thing since we also have to determine the order of the stones and we can't do that until Dr. Dumont interprets the

Olmec side. I just hope that she's ready to get to work on it right away."

Neil nodded toward McSweeney, Bobby and me. "The three of you can take a break and rest for a while. I will show you around briefly and get you settled in your rooms. We have a café on the premises so you can get some breakfast. I'm assuming that you're hungry."

McSweeney answered first. "Like a bear," he said, "and Bobby here looks downright faint."

Bobby grinned and said, "I could use something to eat. It has been a long night, or two, or three. I can't remember."

"There is one thing I need you all to know before we go," Neil said, his face serious. "Barbara Dumont does not have any idea what goes on here. While the rest of you are, for all intents and purposes, in the 'inner circle,' Barbara is not and we're going to keep it that way. I hesitated bringing her in on this project because I know she has some peculiar beliefs, but she's the leading authority on the Olmec so we need her expertise. As you will see once I've shown you the rest of the complex, there is a distinct divide between the above ground people and those who work down here. Everything below ground it under highest security and top secret. Above ground is our front for the company. I have the utmost trust in all of you, but you need to know how sensitive this situation is. I'm not exaggerating when I say the future of this country is at stake. Indeed, we are part of the great drama called the end times, and what happens here will have a direct effect on the outcome of major events in the world in the near future."

We got to our feet as Neil led us to the door.

"One more thing," Neil said. "Guy will provide you with your security clearance individually once he returns from the airport. In the meantime, there's nothing that you will need to do that I won't be involved in so take this opportunity to relax. It won't last long." We followed Neil out of the office and through another door, which he unlocked with a keyed card and a code punched into a panel on the wall. At the end of a long corridor, an elevator door stood open. We stepped out of the lift into a small anteroom, then passed through another door into a janitorial room lined with shelves and cleaning supplies. The anteroom door was hidden behind another door in a notch in the wall. This was behind a row of shelving with a solid back so that its existence from inside the room was nearly impossible to detect.

"This is a secret elevator," Neil explained, pushing the shelving out of the way on a hinge. "Only authorized personnel know it exists. When you get your security clearance, you will be able to use it. I don't think I need to tell you that the utmost discretion is advised under all circumstances. Your security clearance must be shared with no one, for any reason." He led the way out of the room, which opened into another hallway, then through another door using his key pass and code. Turning left, we followed Neil out into a large open area which resembled the lobby of a resort. Soaring pillars of polished wood rose up two storeys and floor-to-ceiling windows opened onto a breathtaking view of the forest and valley below. A long, curving reception desk stood near the back wall. Two women worked behind the counter. Neil led us across the imposing lobby and up a wide, curved flight of stairs to a mezzanine, then down a wide hallway.

"You'll be staying here for the next couple of days. Once we get the stones deciphered and see what they have to say, you should all be able to go home."

"I'm looking forward to that," I breathed. Neil shot me a sympathetic look and patted my arm.

"It won't be long," he promised. "We just have to know what secrets the stones hold. We may find that it's nothing more than a laundry list created by a bunch of housewives in an ancient craft class." I raised an eyebrow and looked at him. "But I don't think so," he said. "No. I don't think so."

CHAPTER 36

The ringing of the telephone jolted me out of a deep sleep. I reached for it, knocking it off the bedside table with a clang. Dragging the receiver by the cord up to my ear, I said hello.

It was Neil. "Sorry to disturb you but Barb Dumont is arriving shortly and we'll be examining the stones together. Before she gets here I would like to have a meeting with you. Is it all right if I come up to your room right now?"

Ten minutes later, after washing my face and taming my wild hair, I opened the door at Neil's knock. Neil sprawled across the love-seat next to the window and I sank into the chair facing him. "I wanted to debrief you on a few things before others get involved. I know you didn't come into this project altogether willingly."

"I'm not going to say it was all fun," I replied, "but it certainly has been interesting."

"I'm sure it has. I will take you on a tour of the lab later, but first let me bring you up to speed on what's going on here."

"Thanks," I replied. "It will be nice not to be in the dark anymore."

"We had to do that for your safety and for the security of the artifacts." Neil explained, leaning forward, elbows on his knees. "I'm sure you're wondering what the lab has to do with the stones."

I nodded.

"Our scientists are the top in the world. We've recruited the peak contributors in the fields of mathematics, physics, biology, archaeology, and materials sciences from universities and companies all over the world. We also have some of the world's most creative and imaginative thinkers," he said, "actually, people a lot like you. Our work here is highly classified so our choices have been extremely strategic. We are pushing the boundaries of science and technology on several fronts. I won't go into details at the moment but what I can tell you is that we have the most powerful computers available today in our labs and our scientists have created programs that do the kinds of calculations in minutes that until recently took many people months to accomplish. We are using these machines and others that we've developed to study elements of technology that would shock most people, even those in technological circles. Information that has been sought throughout the modern ages and has stumped even geniuses, we now have the technology to access. We can now or are close to answering those age-old questions for which archaeologists and physicists have searched for millennia."

"Can you answer the kinds of questions I have discussed with the people like Profesor Alvarez and Dr. Bernaud, for example?

"Yes, that and more."

"So are you saying that you know how the Incas cut and moved those massive blocks? What about that place in Lebanon, Baalbek is it?"

"Yes, we think so."

"That's exciting, Neil! Can you show me your experiments?"

He laughed. "Certainly, at least some of them. I will put that on the list of things to do before you fly out of here. Right now there are few other details that we need to talk about. I understand that you have been followed by a man named Menendez."

"Unceasingly. It seemed like every time I turned around there he was. I saw him a couple of days ago near San Francisco. McSweeney decked Menendez and his sidekick and sent them both flying off the boat dock. Last I saw of them they were going under. Who is Menendez anyway?"

"He is a member of a particularly nasty crime syndicate in Mexico. I don't know how they got wind of my find, but they concluded that there was gold at the end of the rainbow and they wanted to get their hands on it. Menendez is their star tracker and he's as tenacious as a bulldog with a steak in his chops."

"I can't imagine how he kept up to me since I didn't stay in one place for more than a minute. But he did mention getting "the gold" just before I punched him and kneed him in the, um, you-know-what. I told him there was no gold, so maybe he'll lay off now."

"You did that?" He seemed surprised and delighted at the same time.

I nodded. "I didn't have much choice. It was him or me going into the water."

"He will lay off, but not only because you took the boots to him. I have just been informed that a couple of our field operatives have dealt with him. He won't be bothering you anymore."

I frowned. "What do you mean by 'dealt with'?"

"You don't really want to know," Neil said.

"You're right. As long as he's not going to show up at my door, I'm fine with him being dealt with. Did he have anything to do with kidnapping Dennis?"

Neil shook his head. "Those guys are a different kettle of fish."

"Who are they, or do you even know?"

"Oh, we know, all right," he said. "Those two are part of a larger, sub-military faction whose political aim is first to take control of Israel, then ultimately set up a one-world government. They have a clear agenda and are backed by some heavy-hitting financial players, names you would recognize if I mentioned them, but their ultimate plan is world domination. Sound familiar?"

"Scary familiar," I said. "Prophecy is being fulfilled before our very eyes, isn't it?"

"Faster than we know," he agreed. "Our operation has been set up to thwart the enemy's attempts at destroying Israel. What has been prophesied will come to pass, but we can't be sitting ducks waiting for the inevitable. Too much is at stake. The front part of this business is a real high-tech corporation with contracts all over the world. The below-ground operation is involved in high-level experimentation and weapons development working with governments here and in the west. The technology that we are producing here will revolutionize the way a lot of things are done, including flight."

"How?"

"With the study of electromagnetic fields and electrogravitics, among other things."

"This is big stuff, isn't it?" I reflected. "What will come, will come, eh?"

"It will, but it's important that none of us be deceived by what's going on because, as you know, the enemy's main weapon against us is deception. In the last days many will be deceived, the Bible says, and many will fall away. Even the elect will be deceived by some of the events that transpire and by the words of leaders who rise to power. 'Watch and pray,' Jesus said, with good reason."

I looked at Neil. "Heaven help us," I said, leaning back in my chair. When I tucked my feet up beside me it twisted the wound on my side. I winced.

"What is it?" Neil asked.

"It's nearly healed," I answered, straightening to relieve the tug on the bandage. "I was shot in Barcelona by someone whom I assume was connected with Menendez."

"Ah, yes, I heard that you'd been injured."

"You did? How did you hear?"

"I was notified by one of our security people."

"That must have been Father Francisco."

"No."

I frowned. "Then who..?" A knock sounded on the door.

Neil jumped to his feet and strode to the door. Guy stood in the hallway.

"Dr. Dumont is here," he said. "We're ready whenever you are."

"Let's go," he said, reaching a hand toward me.

The meeting room, situated on the main floor of the company complex, also had a wall of windows, now covered in heavy draperies. When we arrived, I saw that Bobby stood next to a big mahogany table in the centre of the room talking with Doc Silverman who towered over him. Barbara Dumont stood by the window chatting with McSweeney, who periodically tugged at his collar while watching the door. Neil asked us all to take a seat around the table as Guy walked in carrying a large tray-shaped box. He set it on the table and removed the lid. Inside, on a bed of soft cloth, lay all sixteen stones arrayed in a complete circle.

Barbara gasped and stood to her feet, leaning over the box. Enoch Silverman also stooped for a better look.

"Ladies and gentlemen," Neil said, standing at the head of the table. "Our quest to re-unite these stones has finally come to an end, thanks to Jill and many others, some of whom are here now." He glanced from face to face. I thought of Father Francisco and Mrs. Mac; Bobby's sister, Eleanora; Rebecca on her skates, and Consuelo Hanna. Fred Chin had played such an important part in caring for Bobby and Dennis and me. Even Marcel and the owner of the café who helped me escape from Claire Jamieson played a role. They had all given something of themselves to the quest, making this moment possible.

"I suspect it will take the three of us," he said, indicating Enoch, Barbara and himself, "some time to decipher the message on these stones. We are happy to have you stay and contribute from your own knowledge where applicable but please don't feel compelled. You are free to walk around this building. There is a library just down the hall and a swimming pool out back. It is a nice sunny day, so feel free to enjoy the sunshine and the pool. We have high security in place everywhere so you are completely safe here."

With that the team set to work, selecting the blocks and studying each one. All the sides had been previously scanned and now were projected up on a screen for all to see in detail. Each piece reflected the genius of the artisans who had created these works of art. Slide by slide, stone by stone, the meanings began to be revealed.

Barbara pored over the each stone, making notes and diagrams in cryptic shapes, studying the Olmec writing on each stone thoroughly. Her fingers traced the shapes and curves of the figures as her lips moved silently. When she finished with a stone, she handed it over to Neil or Doc Silverman for perusal and went on to the next.

"I think," said Neil to Barbara, "that we'll let you work on the order of the stones first. You set them up how you think they should be arranged then Enoch and I will see how they correspond in the other languages." She agreed and went back to work.

"It's a story," Barbara said finally, "an account of how the pale-skinned visitors came from over the sea. It's vague, because the Olmecs did not have a highly developed written language but it appears to date from much earlier than anything else that has been previously found."

"How can you tell?" Neil asked.

"By the shape of the characters mostly, though they definitely bear a resemblance to later works. In my studies I have worked backwards from more recent texts looking for similarities in the various glyphs. These appear to pre-date anything I have seen to date."

Bobby spoke up. "What is the story?"

"I'm afraid it's incomplete from what I can work out, but it says that these people had visitors from across the sea who looked strange and spoke another language. The Olmec people assumed that they were gods but evidently they managed to clear up the misconception because it says that they stayed in the city for some time mingling with the people." She picked up another stone and studied it under a magnifying glass. "It seems that someone from the Mayan peoples also appeared in the area at that time. What do you think, Neil?"

"Absolutely," he replied. "From what I'm seeing, there is an overlap in eras or territories. The Olmec civilization was dying out about the time that the Maya were rising to power and building their great cities and pyramids. Perhaps the Olmec people were conquered or assimilated into the Mayan civilization. I suspect that these stones were created by a small group of these mixed peoples living off in the jungles away from the main groups."

"I would concur with that," Barbara said. "Here," she pointed to the inscription on one of the stones, "it indicates that these people lived in a remote area near the sea, but not accessible from it."

"Which makes one wonder," interjected Doc Silverman, "how the Hebrew people even found them."

"That I can answer," Barbara said. "They said their god or gods led them there. It's not clear how long these people spent together but perhaps the other two languages will tell the rest of the story. They were guided by a power not of this world. Can you imagine what that could mean?" she breathed. "Perhaps they were guided by extra-terrestrials or aliens from another planet."

"Well, that's one possible explanation," Neil said gently. "But they were Hebrews so it is more likely that they are making reference to God leading them, don't you think?"

Dr. Dumont shrugged. "We don't know that there is a God," she said. "There is a school of thought that believes the earth was populated by aliens and that they still visit this planet. There is lots of evidence to support that philosophy." I detected a note of defensiveness in her voice.

"There is a great deal that we still do not know," said Doc Silverman. "Perhaps once we have the rest of the message decoded we will have more answers. Let's wait before we draw any conclusions, shall we?"

I glanced at my watch. We had all been so focused on interpreting the stones that three hours had flown by like leaves in a whirlwind. "I'm getting a little hungry," I said. "Do you think we could take a supper break, Neil?"

"Oh," Neil said, looking around. "What a good idea. Just let me make a quick call and we can head down to the restaurant." The call produced three armed security personnel who stood waiting outside the door as we filed out. Neil had concealed the stones from view under an open newspaper and as the last person left the room he made sure it was locked and double coded for re-entry.

I had just stirred my after-dinner coffee and laid my spoon down when Neil leaned toward me. The others at the table were in a heated discussion about Olympic team sports. "I need to talk with you," he whispered. "Let's take a walk." We rose and walked out through the sliding glass doors onto the patio. A small swimming pool shimmered blue and gold in the lowering sun and a cool breeze had come up, lifting the heavy heat of the late afternoon. I could smell the scent of pine wafting off the mountain slope outside the high stone wall that enclosed the gardens and pool.

"We have to get rid of Barbara now that she has finished decoding the Olmec," he said. "Any ideas?"

"We could drown her in the pool," I suggested.

Neil shot me a horrified glance then laughed. "That is a bit more drastic than I had in mind."

"What about just telling her that her part is done and sending her on her way?"

"She won't go for that. She thinks that we are about to discover life on other planets or something and will not easily give up her front row seat."

"I'll tell you what," I said. "You go back to work and I will stay out here and pray about it. Let's put it in the Lord's hands. If she isn't supposed to be here, he will see that she is removed."

Neil reached out a squeezed my hand. "Did anyone ever tell you that you're a smart cookie?" he asked, kissing my cheek.

"Yes," I replied. "Happens all the time." He chuckled and turned back toward the dining room, waving one hand at me as he walked. "Let me know what the two of you come up with."

I found a stone bench under an umbrella palm and sat down facing the pool, the setting sun warm on my face. "Lord," I said, "you know what our situation is here and that we feel that Barbara Dumont should be excluded when we figure out the final message on the stones. If we're correct and you agree, could you please show us a way to remove her from these proceedings, or can you remove her in your own way? I'm just going to sit here and listen now." I folded my hands in my lap and closed my eyes, leaning my head back against the stone wall behind me.

Forty-five minutes later, I got up and walked back to the meeting room. I knew that God had a plan and neither Neil nor I need be concerned with the details. As I walked across the lobby, one of the desk attendants flagged me, and asked me to deliver a message to Dr. Dumont. I hurried to the meeting room and knocked on the door. Neil opened it and as I stepped inside I heard Barbara say, "That's about all I can tell you. It looks like my part is finished. I can hardly wait to find out how it ties in with the other languages because I'm sure there is more to the story." She looked expectantly from Neil's face to Enoch's when I interrupted.

"There is a call for you at the front desk," I told her. "They said it's urgent."

Barbara ran from the room and returned a few minutes later. "I'm so sorry," she cried, wringing a tissue between her hands. "There has been an accident and I have to leave." A collective gasp rippled around the room. "I'm sure everything will be all right," she said, seeing the concern in everyone's face. "It's just that my mother, who is ninety-two years old, has fallen and broken her ankle and her wrist. She still lives alone and her next door neighbour called the ambulance to take her to the hospital, but she has no one but me to look after her when she gets out." She gazed longingly at the stones. "Now I won't be able to find out the rest of the story on the stones."

Neil put an arm around her shoulders. "Don't you worry about a thing," he said. "Guy will take you to the airport and help you get a flight. I'm sure your mother will be very happy to know that you are coming to help her." His voice was soft and soothing and he drew her into a warm hug, but over his shoulder he winked at me.

Barbara left immediately.

"What did you do?" McSweeney said, eyeing me from under his brows. "You knew we had to eliminate her from the investigation now. How did you pull that one off?" I bit my bottom lip and shrugged.

"This woman is dangerous," he said to the others gathered around the table.

"I have friends in high places," I replied. "Very high places."

"Now," Neil said when the laughter had died down, "we can get on with the real work of decipherment." He surveyed the ring of stones before him and with a few deft movements flipped them all over. "There is a sequence here that must be followed for re-arranging the pieces. Doc and I have already deciphered our parts and with these here," he switched the position of two of the stones, then three more, "and these here," he moved two different stones into a position that only he and Doc Silverman seemed able to comprehend. "Voila! It all makes sense."

"What does it say?" the rest of us asked in unison.

"It's a set of directions to the location of an extremely important relic," Doc Silverman said. "It's one that the Jewish people have sought for centuries. We only needed the Olmec translation to get the whole picture. The messages have been created on two levels. One is simply a chronicle of happenings, like Dr. Dumont said, but the other tells a deeper story, one that you will only recognize if you are familiar with God's Word. I'm not exactly sure what we will discover but I suggest that we all get some rest because tomorrow we will go and find out where these instructions lead us. The location is up in the hills about two hours from here. It's too late to start out tonight. Besides, there is someone else we need on the expedition and he won't arrive until tomorrow morning."

"Who's that?" I asked.

"His name is Elijah Ben Shalev. He is, shall we say, the CEO of this operation."

CHAPTER 37

The burning sand shimmered with heat haze that quivered like watery sheets across the road ahead. As we drove south from the compound, the green hills and forests gradually gave way to rocky desert and striated mountain ranges, sienna sands, and a sky like a hot tin pan. Skirting Jerusalem, we went east toward Jericho. We turned south again after Jericho and the landscape rolled away in monochromatic ripples, hills upon hills, disappearing into the white horizon.

Guy drove and Elijah Ben Shalev sat up front with him while I occupied the centre seat, squeezed between Bobby and Neil. At every checkpoint, the soldiers took one look at Ben Shalev and waved us through. McSweeney and Doc Silverman sat in the rear of the vehicle muttering to each other in low growls. Like me, Bobby stared out the windows, his head swivelling from side to side, eager not to miss a thing. Once away from the towns, we saw a train of camels trailing over a hillside followed by a boy on a donkey and passed fields of date palms and fig trees. Soon the Dead Sea appeared on our left and we passed signs indicating the village of Qumran nearby.

"Isn't it near here that the Dead Sea Scrolls were found?" I asked Neil.

"It is," he answered. "Unfortunately, we won't have time to explore the area today but it is well worth a visit to see the ruins of the Essenes settlement. The Essenes were a strict Jewish sect who evidently created the scrolls, hiding them in the caves surrounding their monastery."

Twenty minutes farther on, Guy wheeled the van off the main road toward the mountains rising up from the Dead Sea. Guy dodged potholes and swung the steering wheel to miss jutting rocks until the barely-discernible track we were on simply vanished. We rounded a sharp curve in the ravine and Guy stopped the vehicle under a lone date palm. Below us a trickle of water meandered down a rocky stream bed edged in dusty shrubs and stunted palms and above us a high shoulder of rock hid the vehicle from view.

"This is where the hiking begins," Guy explained, walking to the rear of the vehicle and pulling out ropes and climbing gear. "I've brought along some hats because the sun is going to be brutal in a few hours." He glanced at Ben Shalev's bald crown and handed him a hat first. I took a broad straw sun hat from his hand, plopped it on my head then pulled a bottle of sunscreen out of my bag, offering it around to the others.

"Is there anything you don't have in that bag, Moss?" McSweeney asked, grinning. "I'll bet if I wanted a bath you could produce a tub out of that thing."

"Probably," I said. "You strip off and I'll get it out for you." Everyone burst out laughing, which helped to break the tension that fizzed between us. We were all aware of the danger.

"Okay, kids," Neil said, "no fighting." Then serious, he added, "Here's the plan. We're going to follow this stream up into the mountains there." He pointed past where I stood to the craggy shoulders of rock hunching in close to the gorge and rising high into the sky beyond. "I have the coordinates for the location we're trying to find, but I have no idea what we're looking for yet. I'm glad to see that you've all worn good walking shoes, as I requested, because this trek could be quite rough. I hope you won't find it too taxing, Elijah," he said, clamping a hand on Ben Shalev's shoulder.

Neil had told me that Elijah Ben Shalev was nearing seventy but, in spite of his bald head, he seemed like a much younger man. He had the piercing gaze of an eagle and more than once I had caught him eyeing me with a look that seemed to discern much more than I might want to reveal. Heavy black eyebrows shaded a pair of deep-brown eyes that seemed to smoulder with hidden fire. Hands like a dairy farmer's emerged from the sleeves of his white shirt, palms wide and fingers perpetually curved. He wore a wide, blue, cotton scarf twisted around his neck, loose tan trousers, and sandals on his feet. Later, I discovered that when the climbing got rough, he simply removed his sandals and leapt over the rocks in leathery bare feet as though he'd spent a lifetime climbing these mountains.

Guy distributed bottles of water and slung a backpack over his shoulders, explaining that he carried the first aid equipment and some lunch and snacks. He also tucked a gun into his belt and handed another to Neil and one to Doc Silverman. Bobby was already armed and Ben Shalev produced another weapon from a leather satchel that hung next to his hip.

"That's the one thing I don't have in my bag," I said, nodding toward McSweeney's gun.

Guy reached into the back of the van and pulled out a pistol. "Here," he said, holding it out for me to take, "you do now."

Reluctantly, I watched as he gave me a quick lesson on how to use the thing, then with two fingers I took it from him and dropped it into my tote.

"Are we expecting to have to use these?" I asked, throwing Neil a beseeching look.

"We hope not, Jill," he replied. "But we need to be prepared."

In a few minutes we set off up the ravine, stepping over rocks and sloshing back and forth through the creek. Neil and Guy led the way, periodically consulting a GPS and a topographical map. The rest of us followed along where sometimes a faint trail was visible, but often having to push shrubs and branches out of the way to find a path. Bobby took up the rear and more than once I glanced back to find him surveying the mountain sides and the valley below with a pair of binoculars.

As I walked, I removed the straw hat from my head and tied my hair back in a ponytail, pulling the loose strands away from my neck. In the dry air, moisture evaporated almost before I felt damp, but the incline had tilted sharply upward so that now sweat trickled down my back and dampened my forehead under the hat band. We climbed steadily for about thirty minutes then Neil suggested a short drink break. We found a spot under a scraggly tree that gave just enough dappled shade for us to sit down and rest.

Bobby pulled his t-shirt off over his head and mopped his brow with it, then flung it up in the branches of the tree to dry in the hot breeze while Doc Silverman fanned himself with his cloth hat. McSweeney stretched out on his back with his feet sticking out into the sunshine and closed his eyes, pulling his own hat down over his face. He was instantly asleep, snoring softly, and when we rose to carry on after ten minutes, he leapt up, fully rested. How I wished I could have done the same. When it was time to go, I dropped my water bottle back in my bag, stuck my hat on my head again and stood up. Suddenly, the landscape spun around me and I reached out a hand and grabbed the tree trunk to steady myself.

"Are you all right?" Bobby asked as he put out a hand to steady me, then pulled his t-shirt from a branch overhead. I closed my eyes for a moment and when I opened them everything had righted itself again.

"I think so."

"Take another drink of water," he suggested. "You might be a bit dehydrated."

"Good idea," I answered, removing the cap from my water bottle and taking a long drink. The others had started off already so, feeling better, I followed. With no trail at all now, we skidded across the top of a shale slope and clambered through a narrow gap that led away from the main gorge. Turning to look back the way we had come I could see the Dead Sea far below, blue and sparkling, and farther on, the shores of Jordan. The climbing was arduous and Guy and Neil slowed down, picking out a route between boulders and crags. Deep grooves cut through the eroded sandstone and once or twice I saw what I thought might be a cave but had no chance to find out for sure. I remembered reading that a copper scroll that told of other hidden riches had been discovered in one of the Qumran caves and visions of making such a momentous discovery danced in my sweltering brain.

"Look," Neil called back to Bobby and me from somewhere above us. "It's an ibex." I followed where he pointed and saw the animal, poised on a pinnacle of rock, its impossibly top-heavy antlers curving over a tan back. It regarded us silently for a moment then sprang away over the rocks and disappeared.

Neil led us on through a narrow crevice with rock so close and steep that I had to use both hands to pull myself up through the opening. At the top, the rocks opened out just enough for all of us to stop and catch our breath. Even Guy and Bobby, the youngest and fittest among us, gasped and leaned against the surrounding boulders, fanning themselves with their hats.

"How far do we have yet to go?" I asked.

Neil answered. "According to the coordinates and the GPS, it's not far at all now, but when you look at the topographical map, unfortunately, it's nearly straight up."

"I'm hoping we find an animal trail to follow," Guy interjected, "or we'll have to start using ropes."

Guy led us through a cleft in the rocks at the side of the clearing. Immediately, the terrain rose sharply. Pulling ourselves up from boulder to boulder with fingertip holds in the cracks, our fingers burned from the heat. Elijah Ben Shalev removed his sandals and scampered up the gap, his agile feet adapting to the curves of stone. Finally, we reached a plateau that led to a rocky ledge which grew narrower the farther we crept along, single-file, gripping the wall of rock at our backs. At our feet, the mountain fell straight down into the gorge and I could barely make out a trail of dusty green where shrubs lined the tiny creek, flowing from some undiscovered spring. Peering over the edge, my feet slid on the loose stones and I clutched for the rock wall behind me. Bobby's hand reached out and gripped my arm, pinning it against the wall.

"Careful," he said. "We don't want to lose you."

I stood still for a moment, catching my breath. "Thanks," I said. "I'm all right now."

The others had edged forward around a jut of rock and when I peered around it I saw a flat area the size of a small room. The near side of it was open to the valley below. Along one side, a sheer rock wall rose three or four meters almost straight up, but toward the back of the open area the top of the wall rounded so that it would be possible, with the right equipment, to scale the slope. On my right craggy, vertical slices of rock jutted into the clearing.

"Is this the end of the line?" McSweeney demanded when we had all assembled. Crouched on the sandy ground, Guy studied the GPS and topographical map, while Neil and Doc Silverman consulted their notes gleaned from the messages on the ring of stones.

"There's got to be something here somewhere. Everything indicated that this is the place," said Neil, brow furrowed.

While the others studied their coordinates, I ran my hand over the surface of the rough rock on the jagged wall, searching for anything out of the ordinary. Scoured by wind and weather, the colours ranged from deep chili red to palest cream with sunlight-reflecting glints. Fascinated by the variations in shades, I reached out and pulled a stone from a crease between two wedges of rock for a closer look when suddenly the whole crevice disintegrated in a minor avalanche. I leapt back as the jagged stones tumbled over each other and clattered to a pile at my feet. In the resulting gap, a narrow, dark opening appeared between the vertical rocks. I leaned forward as far as possible, holding onto the upright wedge of rock and peered into the opening.

"I think there is a cave in here," I said, my heartbeat accelerating. "This must be it!"

The men circled around me and began flinging the fallen stones away from the opening in the rock. Within seconds, the entrance stood clear. I pulled a flashlight from my bag and flicked it on. "Do you want to go first, Neil?" I said.

He grinned, "Ladies first, since you found it" he said, "but we'll be right behind you."

I turned sideways and squeezed through the small opening. "It's going to be tight for some of you," I warned.

Once inside, I paused, allowing my eyes to adjust to the darkness. Moving my flashlight beam around, I saw that a narrow set of perhaps a dozen steps led down into the gloom through a rounded tunnel about two meters high. Making sure the footing would hold, I slowly descended the ancient staircase. Near the bottom, the cavern widened out into a rounded cave perhaps three meters in height and four meters square. In the centre of the room I could see evidence of a fire pit, but there was no opening for smoke to escape overhead. Rocks and rubble lay around and at first I saw nothing else. Then Neil stepped to my side. Shining his flashlight beam around the cavern, he caught the edge of a smooth shape in a small cleft of rock near the back of the cave.

"What's this?" he said, striding across the rough floor toward the niche of rock. By this time, the others had gained entrance to the cave through the narrow opening and also flashed their lights in our direction. Neil pulled a small trowel and a fat paintbrush from his pack and began to remove the dust and debris from around the lip of what looked to be a large pottery jar. Using his fingertips he picked pebbles away and brushed loose dust off the top and sides of the jar. Step by careful step, the surface of the jar appeared under Neil's meticulous hands. With the paintbrush, he flicked away soil, raising a cloud of dust that made me cough and cover my mouth and nose.

"Sorry," he said. "I'll try to be less vigorous here."

Brush stroke by brush stroke, the jar emerged from the debris and stood alone in the niche in the rock. Almost knee-high, its dark surface glowed dully in the light. The top of the jar held a clay stopper. Neil grasped it and gently lifted. Nothing happened.

"A little sticky, this," he muttered, taking a small knife from his pocket. He wiggled the blade along the edge of the lid and it came away suddenly with a grinding sound of clay on clay. Neil grasped the round handle in the centre and pulled the top off, setting it on the ground beside his knee. Peering inside with his flashlight next to his right eye, I heard him gasp.

"Well? What is it?" McSweeney demanded.

Neil stuck his arm into the jar and slowly drew out the contents. A leather pouch stiff with age and wrapped in leather thongs emerged into the beams of seven flashlights. Neil blew on the package and dust puffed into the still air. Sitting down on a nearby flat rock, he laid the artifact on his lap and looked up at the rest of us.

"Well," McSweeney barked, "get on with it. Open the thing up and let's see what we've got there."

Neil nodded and began to remove the laces wrapped around the package, holding each piece with his fingertips and rolling the pouch over on his lap like a newborn baby. When the last circle of leather cord dropped away, the pouch loosened and Neil gently ran his hand over the surface of the ancient skin. The fragile old leather cracked as Neil folded back the flaps. I caught a glimpse of something shiny inside. When the last flap had been lifted from the artifact and smoothed down against Neil's leg, we gasped in unison.

"God be praised," cried Doctor Silverman. "God be praised."

I saw Elijah Ben Shalev glance at him and mutter something in Hebrew. Guy nodded. I looked back at Neil. An object of heavy cloth about nine inches square lay before us, and though the fine linen fabric was little more than powder filaments, the colours remained startlingly brilliant. Strands of sapphire blue mingled with the purple, gold, and scarlet threads on the body of the piece. It appeared to be a container of some kind like a flat pocket or pouch because it had an opening along one edge. On the front a series of twelve stones had been attached in three rows of four each down the surface of the pocket and, in spite of the ravages of time and dust, their various colours glowed in the semi-dark. Gold rings hung from each corner of the pouch.

"Do you recognize this?" Neil asked, looking from Doc Silverman to Elijah Ben Shalev. They both nodded solemnly.

"What is it?" McSweeney said, glancing from Neil's face to the other two.

"I believe what we have here is the breastplate that the priests in the temple wore in ancient times. The book of Exodus gives a detailed description of all the garments and accoutrements that Moses' brother Aaron and the priests who came after him had to wear when entering the temple. The rings you see here on the corners were used to attach it to another garment called an ephod. And the stones, see how they are all different," he said polishing each with a dampened fingertip, "represent the twelve tribes of Israel."

Doc Silverman spoke up. "There should be a sardius, a topaz, and a carbuncle in the top row. The second row," he said, bending at the waist, "contains an emerald, a sapphire, and a diamond. The third row down should be jacinth, an agate, and an amethyst, while the bottom row should be beryl, onyx, and jasper. And yes, you can see that they have all been set in gold filigree exactly like the biblical account. Look," he cried, pointing to the edges of the filigree settings, "these are the names of the twelve tribes of Israel."

I heard his voice quaver and glanced up to see tears streaming down his cheeks. Elijah Ben Shalev reached into the back pocket of his baggy pants and pulled out a folded handkerchief. He mopped his eyes and sank to his knees. I sensed this was a holy moment for these Jewish men as Guy, too, now kneeled and stared at the stones.

"There should be more to it…" Neil said, his voice trailing off as his fingertips flitted over the surface of the pouch. I could tell that the fabric was extremely fragile but as Neil gently lifted the stone-encrusted top layer the fabric held together and revealed the inner pocket. "Jill," he said, "your hands are smaller than mine. Slip your hand inside here and see if you can feel anything."

I crouched down and carefully placed my fingers between the layers of dry cloth. Moving my fingertips ever so slightly to separate the two layers, I pushed my hand deeper into the bag.

"I've found something," I said when my index finger made contact with a flat, hard object. "Wait just a second while I see if I can get it out with two fingers." Keeping my hand flat, I manoeuvred the round-edged object in between my index and middle fingers and withdrew it from the pouch, then dropped it into the palm of my other hand. A pale, off-white, translucent stone about three centimetres in diameter lay there glowing softly in the dim light. A faint inscription marred its polished surface. Doc Silverman reached over my shoulder and took it from my palm.

"There should be one more," he said.

"Okay," I said, sliding my hand in the bag again. Sure enough, my fingers touched its mate and when I withdrew it from the sack, I saw that it was nearly black, yet also translucent. Flecks of light reflected in its depth.

"You know what we have here, don't you?" Neil said in awe. "I have never even dreamed I would see something like this in my entire life."

"What?" McSweeney said.

"This has to be the Urim and Thummim. In the Old Testament, the priests and prophets used them to communicate with God and verify his directions for the people. No one is entirely sure how they worked, but the Bible says that they were used to discern the will of God, particularly when going to war."

"How on earth did something like this come to be up here?" Bobby wondered out loud.

"Good question," Neil answered, as though snapping out of a trance. "Wait a minute." He leaned over and shone his flashlight beam into the open jar. "There is something else in here." He stuck his arm into the jar and drew out a cylindrical object encased in a leather sack. "Perhaps you'll do the honours, Doc," he said, handing it over.

Doc Silverman held out his hands and Neil placed the roll onto his palms. Silverman removed the wrappings and revealed a tightly-wound scroll made from thin animal skin. While McSweeney and Bobby shone their lights on it, he slowly unfurled the ancient document. Completely open and flat, it was covered with cramped dark lettering. A look of pure rapture glowed from Doc Silverman's face as his fingers traced the message from right to left and he muttered breathlessly as he read.

When I could no longer stand the suspense, I said, "Tell us what it says."

"It is the story of how these temple artifacts came to be here," he began. "When the Babylonians raided the temple and carried off all the treasures and captured my people, they left those whom they considered worthless, the menial workers and what we might today call the "low-lifes" of society. One of those people was this man, who tells us that his position was at the bottom rung of the ladder, so to speak. He worked as a sweeper on the temple grounds." Silverman stopped talking and read some more. "When the Babylonians invaded, this man, whose name was Nadab, was at the temple. In the chaos and pandemonium of battle, he managed to sneak into the temple before it was completely destroyed and grab this breastplate complete with the Urim and Thummim inside. Because he was considered invisible to most of society, due to his low position, he was able to hide the breastplate inside his robes and escape with it. He was one of the few left behind when the Babylonians carted the people off to captivity."

"That's incredible," I breathed. "How did it come to be here?"

Silverman ran a finger over the rest of the text. "It says here that Nadab's people originated near here, so when the dust had settled after the conquest, he sneaked back to his homeland to live among the remnant of this own tribe. He found this cave and hid the artifact here with the plan to return it to the temple when his people returned. Unfortunately, the Jews remained in captivity in Babylon for many years, so the whereabouts of this treasure was never revealed."

"That's amazing!" I cried. "But how was this location foretold on the ring of stones when the stones were created hundreds of years before the temple was destroyed?"

I followed Neil's glance as it met Enoch Silverman's then Elijah Ben Shalev's. "We didn't want to say anything while Dr. Dumont was around," Neil said, "but the message on the stones had to be a prophecy recorded around the time just after the flood."

Outside, the cry of a bird startled all of us. "It's time we got out of here," Neil said, holding out his hand to Silverman for the two stones then placing them back into the cloth breastplate. He folded the flaps of the leather covering back over the breastplate then reached into his backpack and pulled out two large zip-closure plastic bags. Sliding the artifact into one of the bags, he handed the other to Silverman to enclose the scroll. Then he placed them back into the jar and put the lid on it, wrapped his arms around it, and stood up.

One by one we squeezed back through the cave's opening into the blinding sunshine. Neil came last and handed the jar and its contents through the opening and into my arms.

"I'll take that now," said a woman's voice behind me.

Startled, I spun around, the large clay jar clutched against my chest. Behind the woman stood three men with pistols pointed at us. McSweeney, Bobby, Silverman and Ben Shalev stood nearby, all with their hands in the air and guns in the dirt.

Once through the cave opening, Neil turned, took in the scene before him and without registering the faintest surprise, said, "Hello, Claire. How nice to see you again after all this time."

CHAPTER 38

"Here," I said to Neil, handing him the jar. Deliberately, I brushed the dust from it off my clothes with my hands. Claire stood before me, pistol levelled. Her minions, whoever they were, backed her up. My glance flicked over their faces and I recognized the man I had seen with her in France. The other two were strangers.

Ignoring her, I lifted both my hands and looked up to the sky then said in a loud voice, "Lord, your word says that you are an ever present help in times of trouble. Well, I would say that this is one of those times, so right now I thank you for your help and..."

"I said, hand it over," Claire shrieked, her voice like a taut violin string.

"Shut up," I said. "Can't you see I'm praying? Have some respect."

Undeterred, I continued. "Father God, you can see what our situation is here and you know that we are about your business, so again I thank you for sending the help we need right now, in Jesus' name." I put my hands down. A gust of hot desert wind licked up a puff of dust and sent it flying over the precipice and out into the gorge below. Across the valley somewhere, I heard a hawk cry. Claire glared at me, eyes smouldering with hatred. For a long minute, no one moved or said a word.

Then a strange thing happened. A tiny pebble, dislodged from the ridge above, began to roll down the slope of the rounded rock off to my right. I could hear its descent as it ticked against the shoulder of sizzling stone and trickled slowly down rolling, rolling. I turned to watch it and for a second it looked like it might catch in a tiny crack but it rolled on, picking up speed, and finally landed with a soft plop on the floor of the clearing. In the stillness, all eyes turned toward where it had fallen.

Before anyone could react, the air erupted and the stillness cracked wide open with cries of battle as five masked men, like dark angels, swooped off the rocks above, leaping away from the vertical sides of the mountain and landing on the backs of our attackers. Someone's gun went off and the sound ricocheted across the canyon and clattered away down the valley toward the sea. In seconds, these masked avengers, dressed in SWAT team army gear, wrestled the weapons from our attackers' hands and flung the three men to the ground, disarmed and subdued. It had happened so fast that none of our group had even moved.

Then Claire screamed and wrenched herself free from the grasp of her captor. With eyes blazing, she lunged for the jar in Neil's hands, her arms flailing to knock me out of her path. The side of her hand smacked the edge of my jaw and I blinked in pain, stumbling backward. But I caught myself just as Claire charged past me, and I stuck out my foot, catching her at the ankle. She stumbled and went down on one knee, skinning the palms of her hands in the sharp gravel. From the corner of my eye, I saw Neil step backward into the cave opening, taking the jar and its contents with him and disappearing into the gloom. This seemed to enrage Claire even more, and letting out a blood-curdling scream, she turned the fullness of her wrath on me, whirling in my direction, her fingers curved like the claws of a tigress.

I acted on pure instinct, using the same weapon I had protected myself with before. Pulling my tote bag off my shoulder I swung it in a wide arc. It struck Claire squarely on the side of her head and sent her reeling, teetering toward the precipice's edge.

"No," I cried, lunging after her as her feet skidded on the pebbly soil and she staggered toward the brink. I caught the back of her shirt with one hand and twisted the fabric in my fist, hauling back with all my might, but her weight was too much for me and I watched in horror as her feet slid over the edge. Skidding along the crumbling rim and clutching at air, I slid after her.

Claire twisted her body and scrabbled for a hold in the soft sand and my hand became hopelessly tangled in her shirt. In a second, we would both fall to our deaths. Then, just as my own feet slid over the rim, a pair of arms, like bands of steel, gripped me around the waist, dragging me backwards from the brink. At the same time, someone reached out and grasped Claire's wrist, arresting her descent like a stop-action film. My rescuer pulled me back into the clearing and set me on my feet, steadying me with his arms wrapped around me and I saw Bobby pull Claire back onto solid ground, where she stood quivering, tears streaming down her fear-contorted face. Then one of the masked men wrenched her arms behind her back, locking her into submission.

It was then that my legs buckled beneath me, but the arms around me held me closer and turned me around, wrapping me in a muscular embrace. "It's over," said the voice close to my ear. I gripped the sides of the man's shirt and stood there until my legs stopped quaking. From the corner of my eye, I saw the commandos herding their victims, bound and gagged, to their feet and onto the ledge and the canyon trail down. Just before Claire stepped out of sight, she turned and looked back at me. All the fury had drained out of her face, leaving her drawn and shaken. She stared at me for a long moment then lowered her gaze and followed the others.

Once the prisoners had gone with four of the captors, Neil emerged from the cave with the ancient clay jar.

I stepped away from my rescuer. "Thank-you," I said, dusting myself off and straightening my clothes.

"That was a close one, wasn't it?" he said, laughing. I froze. I knew that voice; that laugh. I looked into his eyes. I knew them, too. My heart flipped over and I took a step backward.

"Hey," he said, reaching for me, "I saved you once already today. Don't make me have to do it again." Then he reached up and removed the mask hiding his face.

"Jill," Neil said, "I believe you already know Marco Jimenez."

I stared, first at Marco, then at Neil. Like a movie on fast forward, my mind flicked through the frames of all my encounters with Marco, from the moment we met in his mother's house in Madrid, to the picnic in the mountains of Spain. The scene from the church in Barcelona where I had been shot flashed across the screen followed by Marco taking me to his friend's apartment to bandage the gunshot wound. The night drive to Switzerland streaked through, then the incident of accidently meeting him in London. That could not have been a coincidence. I turned my head away as I remembered him with Claire in Galveston. He'd saved me from being run over on the street there, too.

I looked at Neil. "What's he doing here?"

"He's the chief of security for our whole operation." Neil set the heavy jar on the ground and slapped Marco on the back. "Thanks for getting here just in time," he said.

Marco reached out and gave Neil's hand a vigorous shake. "No problem, Neil," he replied. "I was in the neighbourhood." They laughed and I glanced at Bobby and McSweeney, then turned around and looked at Doc Silverman's smiling face.

"You knew," I cried. "All of you knew!" Bobby shrugged and grinned. McSweeney held up both hands in a gesture of helplessness, and Silverman just nodded. I looked over at Elijah Ben Shalev. "I suppose you knew, too."

"Of course," he answered. "He's our top man."

I glared at Neil. "Why didn't you tell me he was on our side?" I howled. "Do you have any idea what you put me through?"

He stepped toward me and pulled me into a hug. "I'm sorry, honey," he said, "but we couldn't risk it. We did everything we could to keep you safe and part of that plan was to give you only as much information as you needed to complete the mission." He stood back and held me at arm's length, his hands on my shoulders. "Please forgive me," he entreated. "I never meant to hurt you."

"Listen," Marco said, "I've got to go with the others and deal with these characters. But I will see you again, *mi amor*," he said, leaning toward me to kiss my cheek. I stepped away.

"Okay. Have it your way," he said, shrugging. Then he turned and disappeared around the jutting rocks. I felt like my pilot light had just been blown out.

After Marco had gone, Neil apologized once more.

"Oh, Neil," I said. "Never mind. This will all be over soon and I'll go home. Then I can forget all about Marco Jimenez."

"That's my girl," said Neil, kissing my forehead. "Now, let's grab something to eat and get our treasure down the hill and into our lab before we run into any more trouble."

Two hours later, we pulled into the compound through the door in the mountain. By now, the day had begun to cool and a light breeze rustled the needles on the pines in the surrounding forest. Once inside the tunnel, I lifted my bag to my shoulder and dragged myself from the vehicle. The revelation that Marco had, all this time, been working for Neil had come as more than a shock. I felt betrayed and disappointed that I had been kept in the dark. Had Neil not trusted me enough to share the truth with me? Had they all really deemed me incapable of handling the truth? Worst of all, once I went home, I would probably never see Marco again so would never know if there had been anything real between us. Sighing heavily, I trudged off toward my room while the others prepared to take the clay jar with its precious contents to the lab.

"Don't you want to see what happens next, Jill?" Neil asked as I walked away from the group. "It might take us a while but I thought you'd be interested in the connection between the stones and today's finding." His eyes sparkled with excitement but I couldn't share it.

"Yes," I said, "I want to know. But right now I think I'd just like to be alone for a while. I'm a little tired and may lie down and take a nap. Let me know what you come up with."

An hour later the telephone rang. It was still light out, but just barely. I lifted my head from the pillow and grabbed the phone. "Jill, you've got to get down here," Neil said. "You're not going to believe what we've found!" I sat up on the edge of the bed. "Jill, are you there? Did you hear me?"

"Yes, I heard you," I answered. "I'll be right there."

"Hurry up, then. This is incredible." Neil hung up and I slowly placed the telephone back on its cradle. Then I got up and went to the bathroom and washed my face, staring at my reflection in the mirror. My hair, flattened into a ring around my head by the sun hat, looked dusty and lifeless and so did my skin. Taking a quick look at the clock, I hopped in the shower. Five minutes later I felt clean and fresh again.

When I opened the door to the lab, I saw that most of the staff had gone and Neil and the others from our expedition were clustered around a table in the centre of the room. As I approached, Neil swung around.

"You're not going to believe this," he exclaimed, eyes shining. Doc Silverman hunched over a keyboard and stared intently at a series of symbols and characters flashing on a computer monitor. Next to the monitor stood another device which resembled a large microwave oven. The ring of stones lay on the table on Silverman's left and as I watched, he turned them, rearranged their order, and typed furiously on the keyboard. I could see faint flashes of coloured lights coming from behind the smoky glass of the other machine.

"What have you discovered?" I asked, looking from face to face. Then I saw two other people whom I had not noticed before. A tall, young man, so thin that he looked like a skeleton with skin, smiled at me and stuck out his hand.

"Jason Elliott," he said in a British accent. Neil introduced Dr. Joan Karasova, a lady in her mid-sixties with plain, short grey hair.

"Dr. Elliott is our computer whiz," Neil explained, "and Dr. Karasova is in charge of electromagnetic research." His head swivelled back toward the screen.

"I think I have it," Doc Silverman said, sitting up straight. "Watch this." He picked up a small instrument that looked like an oversized steel pen, pointed it at one of the stones and slowly raised the tip of the device. We all watched in silence as the stone floated off the surface of the table and hovered in mid-air. Then he slowly moved the tip of the pen device to the right. The stone followed. He repeated the movement to the left and again and the stone followed suit. Lowering the tip of the steel stylus, he placed the stone back into the ring in exactly the position from which it had come.

"How did you do that?" I whispered.

Neil answered. "The breastplate and the Urim and Thummim held the answers."

"What do you mean?" I looked around the circle of faces.

Doc Silverman answered. "I'm sure you remember reading about how the ancient Hebrews used the breastplate and the Urim and Thummim to discern God's will. But the Bible does not go into details about how they worked. Some texts indicate that the stones lit up to indicate God's leading, but the information is not clear. However, we have always known that there was more to these texts than met the eye; we just were not sure what they were. I believe that it's time for the knowledge of great technologies that existed a long time ago to be understood again." He paused, turning a stone block over in his hands.

Elijah Ben Shalev took up the explanation. "The ancients used the Urim and Thummim because they could not talk to God directly, or because they could not understand him speaking. The priests or the prophets acted as intermediaries. God gave specific instructions to Moses for how the breastplate was to be designed for his brother Aaron to wear. Many people believe that God just makes up rules to control us, but nothing could be further from the truth. All of the intricate plans and patterns that God has laid down have a reason and a purpose. It is up to us to determine what those purposes are and we can do that by means that he has provided. One way is through direct communication, which is possible now because of Jesus' sacrifice and the presence of the Holy Spirit. But another means that God provides is through scientific knowledge. Many people are unaware that faith works through knowledge, through understanding God's laws and the science behind them. Nothing is accidental in God's universe. Everything has a place, is part of a plan, or has a distinct purpose."

"But what do the breastplate and the black and white stones have to do with this?" I waved my hand over the area where the Mayan stone had floated only moments before.

"This is where it gets exciting, Jill," Neil said, sounding like a kid on Christmas morning. "Until recently, our scientific knowledge was so behind that of ancient civilizations that we had no hope of figuring out how they made things work. It was all a puzzle to modern man because we only knew what we knew and the rest got relegated to the unexplainable. But in only the past few years, huge new discoveries have been made in the study of quantum mechanics, quantum physics and other things like zero-point energy fields. Don't ask me to explain what all that is. I'm sure Dr. Karasova could go into details but she would be the only one who would know what she was talking about. Suffice to say that our lab has the most advanced scientific equipment and the most powerful computers in existence today. We have been able, with the use of this little machine here," he patted the cabinet, "to pass a beam through the stones on the breastplate. When asked a question, they do flash, just as the Bible says, yet they flash at such a high speed that it's nearly impossible to see the frequencies. We think that's why in biblical times they could only get 'yes' or 'no' from them. They couldn't keep up because they had lost the ability to decipher the messages more precisely. However, this machine picks it all up, and with the help of the computer programs that Jason and his team have developed, we are now able to understand them. The flashes of light throughout the different stones form a code based on the frequencies of the flashes. They interact with the other two stones, the Urim and Thummim, and with the computer we have been able to pick up the code and translate it into language."

Everything he said was fascinating, but well beyond my understanding of physics. Doctor Silverman spoke again. "If you look on the screen here you can see the equations that make up a mathematical calculation. This represents the culmination of centuries of searching. Newton tried to figure this out, as did Leonardo Da Vinci, but they did not have enough information. Now with the computer program, we can read the code that explains how to overcome gravitational pull. At an atomic level, we can see how the electromagnetic fields can be manipulated to reverse gravity. Do you have any idea what this means?"

"I can only guess," I answered.

"There is something you need to know about our operation here," Elijah Ben Shalev said. "Yes, we are a technology company, exactly as we have told you. But we have only one mandate and that is to develop technologies faster and at a higher level than anyone else in the world. And we only have one client."

"Who is that?" I asked.

"The Government of Israel."

"It's a matter of survival," McSweeney spoke for the first time since I had arrived. "We all know that this tiny nation is surrounded on all sides by enemies who are intent on its destruction. But destruction of this nation isn't part of God's plan for his people. Our reason for all this," he waved his arm to indicate the rest of the lab, "is to find ways to support the continuation of the nation of Israel and we do it under God's leadership. Israel needs this kind of technology now to stand against her enemies. The world's political climate is changin', and according to the scriptures, Israel is gonna one day soon stand all alone against the world. Then you're gonna see God show himself strong on her behalf."

"I see."

"Remember that newspaper article that you read on the plane to Frankfurt; the one about Iran's plans for wipin' Israel off the face of the earth?"

I nodded.

Ben Shalev broke in. "This new finding allows us to move light years ahead of anything that they might have developed. This finding alone may make the difference between survival and annihilation."

"But what do the Mayan stones have to do with the breastplate and the Urim and Thummim?"

"That's what is so amazing about this," Neil cried. "The stones that we found in Mexico have parts of the code encrypted into the messages. When combined with the code from the breastplate and with the flashing from the black and whites stones, the code is complete. It is all we needed to understand how the electromagnetism works to defy gravity. With this knowledge, we can now move objects without making a sound and without any mechanical means or effort."

Dr. Karasova reached out and touched Doc Silverman on the arm. "I would like to try this on something bigger," she said, holding her hand out for the stylus. She stepped to the computer keyboard and typed something onto the monitor then got up and walked to the far side of the room. The rest of us followed like a troop of school children. Next to the wall sat a large piece of rock.

"We brought this in here for experiments just such as this," she explained, "but until now we have not been able to make use of it." She levelled the stylus at the stone and moved her wrist. Without hesitation, the rock lifted off the floor and floated to the right. Then she lifted the stylus higher and the massive rock flew up in the air and sat there. "I could send it through the window over there," she said, "but then we would have to replace the window."

"I get it now," I gasped. "This is how the Incas moved the stones for Machu Picchu and Sacsayhuaman. They knew the secrets to anti-gravity."

Neil laughed. "That's right. Around the time of the flood, people knew how to harness electromagnetic forces but over time the knowledge became lost. Now we have it back again."

"How do you see this applying to Israel's defence?"

Doc Silverman stepped forward and picked up a stapler from a nearby counter. "Here," he said, handing it to me. "Take this over to that wall over there." I followed his instructions. "Now," he called out to me, "throw it over here with all your might."

"Okay," I replied, pitching the stapler in a wide overhand throw. It hurtled through the air, but before it could land, Dr. Karasova pointed the handheld device directly at it. The thing stopped abruptly as though it had hit an invisible shield. It hung in mid-air for a few seconds as we all watched in silence then, with a flick of her wrist, she sent it flying back at me. I leapt out of its path and it clattered to the floor behind me. Stunned, I picked the stapler up and rejoined the others.

"How large of an object will this work on?" I said, placing the stapler back on the counter.

Silverman and Ben Shalev exchanged glances then Doc answered. "Buildings, planes, missiles," he said. "The applications and ramifications are endless."

Turning to Dr. Karasova, I said, "What about people? For example, can you move me?"

She smiled. "I think so. There should be no harm." Then she pointed the stylus at me and suddenly my feet left the ground and I flew into the air.

"Aaaaaaa," I cried. "This is too crazy. Move me over there." I pointed to the far side of the room and instantly I was there. She set me back on my feet and I bounded back to join the others. "That is so amazing! Here one minute and somewhere else the next. And all without making a sound." I jumped up and down, brimming over with excitement. "I have to get one of those things," I said, laughing. "Can you imagine how much I'll save on gas?"

CHAPTER 39

A single shaft of sunlight stole between the drapes and settled like a silken ribbon across my sleeping face. I opened my eyes and looked at the clock then rolled onto my back and stretched. I had slept twelve straight hours. It felt like pure luxury to be in my own bed again. Then I remembered that I had dreamed of Marco for the third night in a row. After our meeting on the mountain top in Israel, he had simply disappeared. Neil explained that he was involved in political security work, dealing with Claire and her gang, but I thought the least he could have done was call. I tried to put him out of my mind, but he kept popping back in. I couldn't seem to stop thinking about him in my life. I kept telling myself to cut it out and get on with it, but it wasn't working.

I had arrived home two days before, after spending a couple of days in Israel as a tourist. I visited Jerusalem and walked the ancient city streets where Jesus walked. I went to Bethlehem and saw what is purported to be the site of Christ's birth, and I journeyed back to Qumran and explored the caves of the Dead Sea Scrolls, floated on my back in the salt water of the Dead Sea and climbed the hiking trail along the waterfalls of Wadi David near Ein Gedi. I startled rotund hyraxes, the local ground-dwelling rodents, as often as they startled me. I saw more ibexes teetering on mountain ridges, and fell in love with Israel, complete with its complex problems. The gospels came alive to me as I explored ancient ruins and walked along the shores of the Sea of Galilee. Then I said good-bye to Neil and got on a plane.

Bobby Buckingham and Quentin McSweeney left the day after we de-coded the messages from the Mayan stones, the ancient priest's breastplate, and the Urim and Thummim. Doc Silverman stayed on to work with Neil and Elijah Ben Shalev to see what more could be discovered from these amazing artifacts.

Before I left, I called home, talking with my daughter Julia who shrieked when she heard my voice. "Where have you been?" she cried. "I've been frantic and Grandma and Grandpa are too. It's like you disappeared from the face of the earth." Once I had calmed her fears of my disappearance, she added, "Besides, I'm sick of looking after your bird. Pianissimo makes so much mess. I have to sweep the floor under his cage every day."

When I called my mother, she revealed that she and Dad had not been nearly as worried as Julia made them out to be. "We knew you were safe," Mom said. "The Lord told us. Besides, Dennis called a few days ago and said everything was fine and that you'd be home soon so we just continued to pray for you and left it at that."

Dennis answered the telephone on the first ring. "I'm fine, Jill," he said. "The doctor released me from the hospital the day after you left and I've been home ever since. I've got a few bruises yet to show for my experience, but otherwise it is business as usual here now and Em and the kids are fine." I breathed a huge sigh of relief.

Now I rolled out of bed and stuck my feet into a pair of flip flops and sauntered into my kitchen. At the sound of my entry, Pianissimo chirped, so I removed the cover from his cage and said good morning. In response, he burst into a high-pitched melodic trill to tell me he was happy to be home. Tamping freshly-ground beans into my coffee maker, I pushed the button for a cappuccino then pulled back the curtains from my kitchen windows. The roses were in full bloom and my yard needed mowing. After breakfast, I took a shower, got dressed in a knee-length skirt and a pretty blouse and walked to the Post Office for my mail. My box was so stuffed after having been away so many days that I had to yank on the letters to get everything out. Then I popped in to say hello to Phyllis.

"Where on earth have you been?" she cried, coming around from behind the counter to throw her arms around me. "If you had told me you were going away, I could have gathered your mail for you. Where did you go?"

"A few different places," I answered, "but mostly Europe." I didn't see much point in mentioning Florida, Texas, Mexico, California, and Israel as well.

"Well, my goodness! Did you have a wonderful time?"

"Absolutely incomparable," I replied.

After sorting through my mail on the kitchen table and tossing the junk, opening the bills, and discovering a cheque from a client, I grabbed my purse and sunglasses and headed to the grocery store. I was putting away the last of the provisions when my front doorbell rang. Tossing a bag of apples into the crisper, I ran to answer it.

When I pulled the door open, my heart stood still. There on the veranda stood Marco, leaning against a post by the steps, his arms wrapped around a huge bouquet of flowers.

"Hello, Jill," he said.

"Marco," I gasped. "What are you doing here?"

"Well," he replied, "I might be wrong but I am pretty sure that I'm here to see you. You do live here, don't you?" One corner of his mouth turned up in a grin. I put my hand out and touched the door frame to steady myself and nodded.

"Good," he said. "These are for you." He handed me the flowers. "I hope you like them."

"They're beautiful," I answered, taking the bouquet from him and inhaling the heady fragrance of freesias and roses.

"Aren't you going to invite me in?" he asked. "I've come a long way to deliver flowers."

"Okay," I said. I held the door open for him then went to the kitchen to find a vase. He followed me and stood in the kitchen doorway watching me arrange the blooms.

"How did you know that these are my favourite flowers?" I asked.

"I can't give away my secrets," he said, smiling so that a dimple showed in his left cheek. I leaned against the table. "Actually, I asked the florist down the street and she told me exactly what you like."

"Oh."

"I think I need to make an apology," he said, stepping closer to me, yet still staying just out of arms reach.

"Oh?"

"I thought you would know that I was on your side," he said, his brow furrowing. "But I guess I was wrong."

"I would say so," I replied. "How did you think I would infer that you worked for Neil when you never told me?"

"What does "infer" mean?" he asked. "I don't know this word."

I sighed impatiently. "It means to suppose, deduce, conclude, assume. What did you think would give away that you weren't after the stones when you kept turning up like you were following me around?"

"I was following you around. Those were my orders."

"You mean, everywhere I went, you went, too?"

He nodded. "Almost."

"When did you start following me?"

"The day that you received the package from Scott Marchand."

I gaped. "Where were you?"

He shrugged one shoulder and rested a hip against the kitchen counter. "Do you remember the courier who delivered the mailbox key?"

Stunned, I gasped, "That was you?"

"*Si.*"

"But we met for the first time in Madrid at your mother's house."

"*Si*," he replied, looking flustered. "But I was watching over you from the time you left home."

"Were you in Paris, too? At Dr. Bernaud's"

"Yes."

"Was that you down on the street with Francois Trouville?"

He nodded. "The only time I lost you was when you left that restaurant in France, when you were travelling in the truck with that young guy, what was his name…?"

"Marcel."

"*Si*, Marcel. But once you contacted Dennis, I was able to track you down again. I travelled with you on the train from the French frontier to Madrid."

"But I never saw you on that train," I said.

"Of course not," he replied. "I made sure that you never knew I was there."

"Then why did you come out in the open when I needed to get to Barcelona?"

"Because we had gotten word that Claire had teamed up with that renegade Israeli faction and they knew where you were."

"Wait a minute," I said, shaking my head. "You mean when Claire picked me up in Paris, she was working alone?"

"We're not sure when, exactly, she connected with the faction, just that she had dreams of glory and wanted more than anything to get her hands on the stones. When someone approached her offering help in her mission, she jumped at the chance. As I'm sure she has discovered, she didn't know how much trouble she was getting herself into."

"So the man who met her at that truckers' café where we stopped for breakfast was one of the same crowd who kidnapped Dennis?"

"That's right."

My mind raced over the images of scenes from the trip. "What about the man in Switzerland who tailed me on the street?" I stabbed a finger at him. "He was with you in Galveston when we were having breakfast."

Marco nodded. "He is one of ours. His name is Clive Morgan. I felt that backup would be a good idea, especially when Gerhard Mueller's flat got broken into."

"I see. And Bobby knew this when he hauled you away?"

He laughed. "Yes," he replied. "Did we look convincing?"

I scowled at him. "Why didn't you tell me what was going on?"

"We all thought it would be better if you didn't know. That way, if you got caught or kidnapped, you would not be able to identify me. If you assumed I was the enemy, it would work better."

"I hadn't thought of it that way," I said then remembered something else. "Why were you with Claire in Galveston?"

"Because we knew that she was catching up with you and I had to intercept her. Bobby had already been contacted to take over for me and get you into Mexico so I could help Dennis, but we had to waylay Claire so she couldn't follow you."

"And just how, pray tell, did you pull that off?"

He glanced out the window and looked sheepish. "I guess you could say I turned on my Spanish charm."

"This I've got to hear about," I said, folding my arms.

"Come on, Jill," he replied, sighing. "First I caused a little accident that I, of course, had to atone for with her then I fell all over myself telling her how beautiful she was."

"Not unlike how you were with me."

"No," he replied. "Not the same at all. With Claire it was just an act, a job. With you, I meant every word." He reached out his hand to touch my cheek and I swatted it away.

"Not so fast," I said. "Were you at Fred Chin's place in Merida?"

"Yes. Bobby had been shot so he couldn't carry on. I had to get there to make alternate arrangements."

"You caused me no end of trouble," I said. "While I was trying to see if it was you downstairs in the church with Fred, I tripped over the stupid cat and bashed my ribs. I'm still black and blue."

He laughed. "I'm sorry about that, but you can hardly say it was my fault. I didn't hire the cat to trip you."

"What did you tell Claire to get away from her?"

"What does it matter? I had managed to keep her off your tail until you could get out of Galveston, so I ditched her and got to Merida as fast as I could."

I stood looking at him for a full minute. "Why didn't you go to California with me if you were supposed to follow me everywhere?" I remembered my surprise when McSweeney had shown up at the airport.

"Because Dennis had been found and we needed to deal with his captors as soon as possible before they could get out of Mexico."

"And did you? Did you find them?"

"Yes. With Dennis' help we caught up with them before they could clear out of their jungle hideaway. They are awaiting trial right now for kidnapping and a long list of other offenses."

"How did Menendez and his band of merry men come into this?"

"His what?"

"Never mind. I understand that he is associated with Mexican mafioso types, but how did he find out about the stones in the first place?"

"Oh. Neil thinks that someone working on the dig tipped them off and they jumped to the wrong conclusion, that there would be a major gold find somewhere. They put Menendez on the job of finding the stones."

"So what happened to him?"

He hesitated. "I'm not going to tell you, since you don't need to know. But rest assured that he won't be bothering you anymore."

"That's good to know. He was becoming a real nuisance." I stopped and looked out the window. A light breeze rippled the leaves of the weeping willow in my neighbour's yard, making them sway like strands of hair in a stream. "When we were in Spain," I said, "you told me that you worked for a restaurant supply company. Was that a lie?"

He looked shocked. "Not at all! Of course, I work in the company, but actually I own it. My managers run it."

"Then how did you come to be mixed up with Neil?"

"My grandfather is a Spanish Jew," he said, "so when I was younger I decided to join the Israeli military. I trained in their Special Forces, dealing with espionage, security, and anti-terrorism. I left after a few years and moved back to Spain where I started my business, got married, got divorced, and now live. I met Neil through my father who, as you know, was also an archaeologist and worked with Neil on several projects. Neil used to come to our house in Madrid and meet with my father and with Profesor Alvarez from the museum. We have known each other for a long time. A couple of years ago, he got in touch with me when he started working with Elijah Ben Shalev and Doctor Silverman. They wanted someone to be on call if they should ever need expert security advice or help. I thought it would be interesting so I agreed. I still run my company, but when Neil called, I took the job of looking after you." He paused. "I think it's the best decision I ever made."

"Oh, Marco. I'm so sorry. I wish I had known all of this from the start."

"Neil knew that the mission would be dangerous and we knew that you took a big risk by agreeing to collect the stones. But we also knew that there was no one else better suited to the task. I want you to know that we all think you did a fantastic job, even McSweeney says so."

I laughed. "You're kidding. Even McSweeney?"

Marco nodded.

"So what happens now?"

"That depends," he replied.

"On what?"

"Well, it depends on whether or not you'll marry me."

"Marry you? I hardly know you."

"I know that. And I hardly know you. But I think that we're meant to be together, don't you?" I looked into his eyes and knew what he said was true.

"I don't know…" I said.

"Yes, you do," he replied. "You're the one who hears from God so well. What is he telling you now?"

I grinned at him. "I think I'm supposed to kiss you," I said. "Come here."

After a while, I leaned back and looked up into his face. "Promise me one thing," I said.

"What's that?"

"No more sneaking around behind my back."

He shook his head. "From now on, *mi amor*, there is only one place I want to be and that is right by your side."

"Good," I said, "now kiss me again."

EPILOGUE

The evening sun had just begun to drift toward the horizon when I sat down on my new patio swing. Marco and I had spent the afternoon assembling it and after a quick take-out dinner we could now enjoy the summer evening while the air still held the warmth of the day.

No sooner had he sat down beside me than Marco said, "I'm going to go buy a newspaper. Is there anything I can get for you?"

"If you're coming right back, I'd love a frappuccino."

"I'll be back before you know I'm gone," he answered, leaning over to kiss me on the forehead.

Two months had passed since I had returned from Israel and Marco had shown up on my doorstep. During that time we got to know each other, mostly by email, cell-phone texting, and online telephone calls. He had spent three whole days with me, considerately sleeping at the inn down the road, before Neil called him back to Israel. After that he'd returned to Spain to check on his business, which kept him there for a few weeks. Then he had returned to see me for almost a week before taking off again. Over the weeks we had decided that, yes, we were meant to be together. I had introduced him to my daughter, who pronounced him, "So hot – way to go, Mom," and we had decided that once married we would divide our time between my house in Western Canada and his in Madrid. The wedding was planned for two weeks hence.

As promised, within minutes Marco returned. In one hand he carried two disposable cups with plastic straws, dripping condensation in the humid air, and in the other a folded newspaper which he was reading as he walked. Sitting down beside me on the swing, he handed me my drink, took a slurp of his own and said, "Listen to this." He set his drink on a small table nearby and opened the paper, reading the headline out loud. "Israel makes missiles stand still."

"Let me see," I said, leaning closer to read along with Marco. I scanned the article and my heart began to race. It said that Israel had employed a new form of technology which the Israeli government had recently procured that had been developed by an unnamed private company. This technology allowed the Defence Forces to intercept incoming missiles, arresting their forward movement in mid-flight. Sources from within the Israeli military claimed that they also have the ability to reverse the direction of incoming missiles essentially marking them, "Return to Sender."

I looked at Marco. "Did you know they had already gone this far?"

"I had an idea they might have," he answered. "Ben Shalev and Silverman took over expediting operations because the military wanted to fast track the program. It looks like they got their wish."

I scanned the remainder of the article. "Look at this," I said, pointing to a short paragraph at the bottom of the page and reading aloud. "As Israel moves into a new position as a world power, western nations rush to ally themselves with the tiny country."

Marco laid the paper down on the table.

"Things are changing fast," I commented, taking another sip of my drink. "How will this affect you?"

"I don't know yet, *mi amor.* I could totally opt out, since I my involvement with the mission for the stones was like yours, a one-shot deal. I guess we'll have to wait and see. In the meantime, I intend to marry you in two weeks then carry you off to a sugar sand beach for three weeks of honeymoon bliss. How does that sound?"

"Heavenly," I answered and was about to kiss him when the telephone rang.

"Let it ring," he said.

"I would, but it might be my son, Tim. He said he was trying to get a flight home this week." I went in the house and picked up the call. Three minutes later, I returned the receiver to its cradle and walked outside again, stopping in the doorway.

"Is he coming home now?" Marco asked. "I can't wait to meet him."

I shook my head. "It was Neil."

"Oh? What does he want this time?" Marco asked, laughing.

"He wants us to go to Peru with him next month. He has found something and he wants us to 'help him out.' He says he needs an illustrator to catalogue artifacts and he'll need security personnel. Oh, and a camp cook. I'm not sure which one of us he has in mind for that position."

"What did you tell him?"

I closed the gap between us and sat down next to Marco on the swing. "I told him that we'd love to come," I replied. "Was I right?"

He looked into my eyes and smiled. "Anything you want, *mi amor*," he said, pulling me close. "Anything you want."

THE END